...rsity, so getting to ~~~~ is ~~~ ~~ dream true! Born in Abu Dhabi, Sophie grew up in Wales and now lives in a little Hertfordshire market town with her scientist husband, her incredibly imaginative and creative daughter and her adventurous, adorable little boy. In Sophie's world, happy *is* for ever after, everything stops for tea, and there's always time for one more page...

Christine Rimmer came to her profession the long way around. She tried everything from acting to teaching to telephone sales. Now she's finally found work that suits her perfectly. She insists she never had a problem keeping a job—she was merely gaining "life experience" for her future as a novelist. Christine lives with her family in Oregon. Visit her at christinerimmer.com.

Also by Christine Rimmer

Discover more at millsandboon.co.uk

AWAKENING HIS SHY CINDERELLA

SOPHIE PEMBROKE

A TEMPORARY CHRISTMAS ARRANGEMENT

CHRISTINE RIMMER

MILLS & BOON

First Published in Great Britain 2020
by Mills & Boon, an imprint of HarperCollinsPublishers,
1 London Bridge Street, London, SE1 9GF

Awakening His Shy Cinderella © 2020 Sophie Pembroke
A Temporary Christmas Arrangement © 2020 Christine Rimmer

ISBN: 978-0-263-27907-8

1220

MIX
Paper from
responsible sources

FSC www.fsc.org   **FSC™ C007454**

AWAKENING HIS
SHY CINDERELLA

SOPHIE PEMBROKE

For London, my favourite city in the world—especially at Christmastime.

CHAPTER ONE

RACHEL CHARLES HELD the skimpy piece of sequinned fabric against her body, sighing at her reflection in the changing-room mirror. If it even stretched across her curves, she imagined she'd look alarmingly like a disco ball, in both shape and blinding capability. Not exactly the look she wanted to project at the Hartbury & Sons department store Christmas party—especially not as the stepdaughter of the last remaining Hartbury in the business.

There were no '& Sons' any more—just Rachel's stepmother, Hannah, and her two stepsisters, Gretchen and Maisie. And Rachel's father, of course, since he'd married Hannah and become an enthusiastic part of the Hartbury family.

Unlike her.

She tossed the disco-ball dress in the direction of the pile building up on the chair in the corner of the large changing area. The store was closing, so she didn't need to worry about any customers coming in.

That didn't mean she was without an audience, though.

'What was wrong with that one?' Maisie asked, from her relaxed position draped across the chaise longue beside the full-length mirror. 'I thought it was perfectly festive.'

This was the problem with sisters—something Rachel hadn't experienced until she was in her early teens and her father remarried. For some reason, they seemed invested in Rachel's wardrobe—although in this case she suspected it was so Maisie could borrow the dress once Rachel inevitably chickened out of wearing it to the party after she'd bought it.

'I think that one's maybe more your style, Maisie,' she said dryly, reaching for the next contender in the pile. 'You'd look fantastic in it.'

How had her stepsisters even got involved in this shopping expedition anyway? Rachel had casually mentioned, when asked by her stepmother if she'd decided what she was wearing to the party, that she'd probably just wear the same black dress as last year. And then, the minute she finished her shift on the till that evening, Gretchen and Maisie had been there waiting, their arms full of half the stock from the womenswear floor, their smiles beaming enthusiasm at her.

She wanted to believe that it was a sweet, sisterly gesture. Maybe before last summer she'd have even been able to convince herself of that. But not now.

Now, she knew as fact, rather than just suspicion, what her stepsisters really thought of her—thanks to Tobias. At least she had something to thank her sort-of ex for, she supposed.

Just a few more weeks, Rachel reminded herself, as she drew the curtain on the changing room. As soon as her father's next set of test results came in, and he had his meeting with the consultant, she'd be ready to act. To move on and move out, at last, from the Hartbury family home.

It had made sense after university to move back home for a while. After all, Hartbury House was a four-storey town house in central London. It had plenty of room for the five of them and was far better positioned than anything she could have afforded on her own—even when she finally managed to get a job.

That had been the next issue, of course—finding employment. Her Oxford degree went a long way on application forms, but her lack of confidence made interviews a nightmare. Many Oxford grads she knew had come out of university with a determination to embrace opportunity, believing they could do anything.

Somehow, she'd emerged with the opposite world view. And apparently it showed in job interviews.

So when Hannah had suggested she work at the family business for a while, just until she found her feet, it had seemed like a logical next step. She'd found her own niche there, beyond just working on the shop floor, and had started to feel as if she might even be making a difference. Seven years later, it was hard to imagine working anywhere else.

She shook her head to stop her wool-gathering, and wriggled into the next dress on the pile. One thing at a time, that was how she had to do this.

First, she needed to know that her father was really okay after that terrifying rush into hospital earlier in the year, him clutching at his chest, and her trying to remember all the details of his blood-pressure medication to tell the doctors. She wouldn't get that assurance until nearer Christmas, maybe even the new year. That was the time to think about using her hoarded savings to find her own place to live. Then, once she was settled, she could think about maybe changing jobs.

One step at a time. Starting with finding a dress for the Christmas party.

The next dress was plain, a green velvet thing that stretched from her chin to her ankles, stopping at her wrists on the way. She supposed it was a little bit better than the disco ball—until Gretchen handed her a pom-pom-laden wrap to wear over it. 'To, you know, hide your lumpy bits.'

Rachel winced at her reflection. *I look like a Christ-*

mas tree. But she'd promised to try to keep the peace with her stepsisters, for her father's sake. He'd been so upset by their row last summer, after everything went down with Tobias, and Hannah believed that stress must have added to his heart problems. Maybe even caused the heart attack that followed not so long after.

Rachel was less convinced, but she wasn't going to risk it. However much Gretchen and Maisie provoked her.

Two months at the most, and I'll be out of here. I hope.

'It's very…festive,' she said.

Gretchen beamed. 'Exactly! And I knew you wouldn't want to feel uncomfortable and on display,' she added, shooting a look at the disco-ball dress, which had somehow made its way into Maisie's grasp.

She's trying to be kind. She knows I'm self-conscious about my curves. Maybe if she repeated the words enough inside her head it would be easier to believe them.

This was the *other* problem with sisters—well, with having two gorgeous, willowy stepsisters with legs that went on for ever and which often featured in the celebrity gossip pages, demurely climbing out of cars arriving at the latest hot spot or party. Gretchen and Maisie were heiresses in their own right, courtesy of their late, great father, the famed tycoon Howard Jacobs. Their money, combined with their looks, made them It Girls, the ones to be seen with around London.

Rachel was none of those things. Not tall or willowy, not rich or beautiful. She was short, curvy, and while she liked to think her face wasn't actively offensive, it was really quite normal, under her cloud of curly brown hair.

Gretchen and Maisie obviously found her a sartorial puzzle to solve. Maisie tried to put her in the sort of things she would wear, and Gretchen tried to disguise all her disagreeable parts.

Rachel sighed and thought wistfully of her old black dress at home.

Out of the entire pile of dresses her stepsisters had shown up with, there had only been one she'd liked—and that, Gretchen admitted, she'd only picked up by mistake. It was cranberry red with navy stags, owls and a woodland print across it, knee length, with a wrap front top and, best of all, pockets. Gretchen had whipped it away as soon as she'd selected it, though, declaring that it would draw far too much attention to her curves. Even Maisie had nodded, adding that it didn't even have any sparkle to distract the eye.

Because apparently she was so disgusting to look at that people's eyes needed to be distracted.

She studied the Christmas tree outfit again. Maybe if she took off the pom-pom wrap…

'Well, that's a look.'

Rachel froze. She knew that voice. That low, warm voice with humour lurking behind it. There was no cruelty in it, but that didn't stop her insides curling up and dying from embarrassment.

Damon Hunter. Her best friend's younger brother, the most attractive man she'd ever met in real life and, incidentally, the last person on the planet she wanted to see her dressed up like a Christmas tree.

Well, this was just *ideal*.

Forcing herself to take a deep breath, she looked up from studying the pom-poms on the wrap, and met his gaze in the mirror. 'Hello, Damon. What are you doing here?'

Her voice was even, friendly, and she was proud of herself for managing that much. She might look like a Christmas tree, but that didn't mean she had to throw all dignity to the winds.

She'd been hiding her crush on Celeste's little brother for the best part of a decade. It was second nature at this point.

'Celeste sent me to pick you up. For some reason she

seemed to think you'd try and wriggle out of attending this thing tonight.'

That was because Celeste knew her too well. From the moment they'd been put together in the halls of residence at university, along with three boys whose only interests were rugby, beer and pulling unsuspecting girls in freshers' week, Rachel and Celeste had been best mates. Rachel had always suspected that, if it hadn't been for those circumstances, the two of them would probably never even have met, let alone become friends. Neither of them was exactly the outgoing, friend-making type. In fact, she suspected she might be Celeste's *only* friend, the only person she'd ever looked up from her studies long enough to get to know.

It might have been sheer convenience, but Rachel still felt a little special, knowing that.

'You're going out tonight?' Gretchen asked, sounding faintly astonished. Rachel didn't take it personally; she was pretty surprised too.

'Where are you going?' Maisie had straightened a little on the chaise longue, her endless legs folded in the way that showed them off best, angled towards Damon, of course. 'Can we come? Unless it's a hot date, of course…' She and Gretchen couldn't help but giggle at that idea, apparently. Again, Rachel couldn't bring herself to blame them for it. The idea of gorgeous, outgoing, charming and successful Damon Hunter going on a date with a shy and dumpy shop girl *was* pretty hilarious.

Sighing, Rachel turned at last and faced Damon's amused gaze in reality, rather than just reflection. 'Damon, these are my stepsisters, Gretchen and Maisie. And this is Damon, Celeste's brother.' The girls looked blank at the mention of Celeste. 'My best friend, Celeste,' Rachel clarified.

'Oh, right!' Gretchen clapped her hands together as she placed the name, then turned to Damon with a conspiratorial smile. 'To be honest, we kind of thought Rachel had invented Celeste for the longest time. It's not like we ever see her.'

'Although if we'd known she had a brother that looked like you—' Maisie muttered, until Gretchen shot her a warning look.

'My sister isn't the most sociable of people,' Damon said, with an easy smile.

'Understatement,' Rachel mumbled. Damon obviously heard it though, as he shot her an amused look. Turning her head to hide her blush, she ducked into the changing cubicle again, drawing the curtain tight closed as she changed back into normal, non-Christmas-tree clothes. The curtain, and the rustle of velvet, did nothing to cover the sound of her stepsisters flirting with Damon, though.

She forced herself to think positively about it. Gretchen and Maisie were *exactly* the sort of women Damon dated—usually for about a fortnight, before moving on. Maybe if one or both of them were distracted by Damon for a while, they'd stop their latest humiliation tactic of dressing her up in Christmas ornaments. That was a bonus, right?

And really, she'd spent nearly ten years watching Damon date other women—starting with the fresher girl he pulled in that nightclub when he came to stay with her and Celeste in their second year of university. It wasn't as if he was ever going to date *her*, so what difference did it make *who* he dated?

It did, of course. But she swallowed the thought and pulled her black and grey jumper dress over her head instead.

'My sister is taking part in some weirdly academic quiz show about Christmas tonight,' Damon was saying when she emerged from the thick woollen cocoon. 'She wants Rachel and me in the audience to cheer her on.'

Gretchen and Maisie's enthusiasm about joining them

for the evening obviously waned when they heard their plans. But as Rachel emerged from the changing room, Maisie was listing places in London Damon should try for the nightlife—*and maybe he would see her there.*

'Ready?' Damon asked, the minute Rachel emerged.

Rachel nodded, but before she could grab her bag her stepmother, Hannah, appeared looking flustered.

'*There* you are!' She reached out to grab Rachel's arm. 'There's been an absolute disaster with one of the window displays. Some brat climbed in to try and get one of those silly mice you've put in every one of them and knocked half of it over. I need it fixed before you go home.'

Rachel nodded along as her stepmother dragged her towards the stairs. 'Of course. Five minutes?' she said, twisting her neck to look over her shoulder at Damon.

'Take your time.' That easy smile was back. Of course he didn't mind, Rachel realised, as she made her way down the stairs to the ground floor. He got more flirting time with Gretchen and Maisie.

She wondered which one of them would win him over by the time she'd fixed the display.

Damon watched Rachel go, her knitted dress pulled tight across the curve of her backside, and wondered what on earth had possessed her to swap it for the hideous green velvet thing she'd been wearing when he arrived. Then he looked back at the predatory smiles on her stepsisters' faces and twigged.

'So you guys were helping Rachel choose a new dress?' he asked lightly as he headed over to a stack of discarded outfits on the chair by the door.

The one in the leather miniskirt—Maisie, maybe?— nodded. 'For the company Christmas party,' she explained. 'Mum throws a huge one every year, and invites all the staff. It's so generous of her, really.'

'She told us that Rachel was planning on wearing the same old boring black dress she wears *every* year,' the other one—Gretchen, his mind filled in—went on. 'So *of course* we had to offer to help her find something better. It was our, well, *sisterly* duty.'

The girls exchanged a look that Damon pretended not to see. One that made his blood warm to a simmering boil on Rachel's behalf.

They weren't helping her, whatever they said. They were trying to humiliate her.

He knew how that felt—to be surrounded by people who thought they were smarter than him and thought he wouldn't notice when they used it against him. In his case, his family genuinely were cleverer; he didn't think the same of Rachel's stepsisters. All the same, he couldn't imagine Rachel liked it any more than he did.

Damon leafed through the pile of fabric. There were skimpy, showy outfits that he knew instinctively that Rachel would hate; oversized draping dresses in vile patterns and fabrics, that would cover every inch of Rachel's admirable curves; something that looked like a child's bridesmaid's dress in pink taffeta, complete with bow…all of them designed to make Rachel look ridiculous, he assumed.

She'd never been the show-off type, he remembered. Even next to his sister, who was always more likely to be found in the library than a nightclub, and prized the ability to quote Homer—the Ancient Greek writer, not the yellow cartoon figure, unfortunately, or else the siblings might have had more in common—high above the ability to put together a stylish outfit on a student budget. Rachel had been the one in the corner, tugging the sleeves of her cardigan over her hands, while Celeste got into an argument with someone about, well, pretty much anything. Rachel had been shy, quiet, mousy even, for all that he knew there was a dry sense of humour and a quick smile hiding behind those cardigans. And, as he'd discovered when crashing into her outside the bathroom one weekend when he was staying with them at university, when she was clad in nothing but a towel, some incredible curves.

He'd discovered more about her, one night—about her mind, her heart, her self. One night when it had been just the two of them, talking and dreaming aloud while they looked for Celeste together. One night, when he'd felt more of a connection to another person than he'd felt before or since.

But he tried not to think too often about that night. Not nine years ago, and definitely not now.

Because connection wasn't something Damon Hunter looked for in life.

The point was, the Rachel he'd known then, the Rachel he knew now, wouldn't wear any of these dresses willingly.

At the bottom of the pile, though, was something else. A quirky dress with woodland animals printed on it, in a great shade of dark red that would suit Rachel's colouring. 'Which one of you chose this one for her?' He pulled it out of the stack to get a better look. The neckline dipped into a low V-shape, it was tight through the bodice, then the skirt flared out to fall to, he imagined, around knee length. He smiled at the sight of the owls, stags and mice peeping out behind tree prints and fallen leaves.

It was, he had to admit, very Rachel. Maybe one of her stepsisters didn't have it in for her after all.

But when he looked up, Gretchen rolled her eyes. 'Oh, *that*. I picked that one up by accident—I was supposed to be putting it to one side for a client. I do personal shopping, you know. Helping people who have no idea of style to find things to make them look, well, less awful.'

'It's a nice dress,' Damon said, wondering how she could make shopping sound like a vocation *and* a way to humiliate people, all at the same time.

'Oh, but it would be *terrible* for Rachel—it would only draw attention to her, well, you know…' her voice dropped to a whisper '*…size.*'

Damon rather thought it would draw attention to her generous curves, which, in his opinion, could only be a good thing.

'I should put it away.' Gretchen reached out to take the dress from him, but Damon held it out of her reach as he checked the label. The size was the same as the other dresses in the stack, so it should fit her. And he'd bet money Celeste hadn't even thought about a Christmas present for her best friend yet. If he bought it, she could give it to Rachel as an early Christmas present, so she could wear it to the party. He'd have done a good deed, and he'd be in his sister's good books—hopefully good enough that she'd let him off Christmas shopping for their parents this year, since he never had any idea what to buy them anyway. Everybody won.

That was all. Nothing to do with that lingering connection he wasn't thinking about.

He flashed Gretchen and Maisie his most winning smile. They returned it, only for their faces to fall as he said, 'I think I'll buy it for her. Are there any tills still open?'

There weren't, but it only took a little fast talk and a few smiles to find an employee willing to put the sale through for him anyway—with their staff discount, to boot, not that he needed it. Then, leaving the stepsisters behind with their hideous dress choices, Damon took his Hartbury & Sons designer paper bag and ambled towards the ground floor window displays to find Rachel.

It took him longer than he'd expected. The storefront stretched around the corner to front onto two streets, giving it six huge windows to look out over the pavement. With the main lighting switched off for the night, and only a few spotlights left on to illuminate things for the cleaning staff, he had to check each window individually to locate Rachel, and even then he missed her. Only when he'd peered into all six windows without spotting her did he head back to the centre and call out.

'Rach?'

A torchlight beam swung around from the far window and caught him in the eyes. Blinking, he covered them with his hand, just as he saw Rachel clambering out from behind the window display in the first window he'd checked. God only knew where she'd managed to hide, but between the decorations and some sort of backboard, it was hard to get a good look in there.

'Sorry, sorry. Are we late?' she asked, switching off the torch.

'Not if you're ready to go now.' And if he drove just a tiny bit faster than was strictly advisable on winter city streets.

'I am, I am.' Grabbing her bag from the floor by the window, she rushed towards the door, half colliding with him on her way, which only served to make her more flustered. 'Sorry!'

With a smile, Damon calmly took Rachel's elbow and led her in the direction of the exit.

She'd always been like this, he reflected. The day he'd met her she'd managed to dump half the cup of tea she'd just made over herself, the floor, and the biscuit tin as he'd walked into the kitchen and Celeste had introduced them. Rachel was Rachel—a little shy, a lot clumsy. She still wore the same, oversized knits she'd worn at university too, and her hair still curled around her face the same way. She was a constant; he'd almost call her part of the family if that wasn't actually an insult, given his family. He *had* to put up with them. What made Rachel put up with Celeste he'd never been entirely sure.

He had a pretty good idea what Celeste got from being

friends with Rachel, though. On his bad days, it made him a little jealous.

'So, what happened to the window display that couldn't wait until morning?' he asked.

Rachel pulled a face, still looking frazzled. He supposed her evening so far couldn't have been the most fun: playing dress up with her stepsisters, then having to fix the window. He hadn't stopped to look at the Christmas displays on the way in, but these things were all much of a muchness, right? Bit of tinsel, a fake tree, a mannequin wearing a Christmas jumper and some boxes covered in wrapping paper. Much like the vignettes littering the inside of the shop—and Damon was pretty sure he wouldn't have noticed them at all if it weren't for the latest project he'd taken on, occupying his brain.

'Hannah was right, it was all my fault. It was the mice, you see. Too tempting, I suppose.'

'Mice?' Where did they fit into the Christmas theme? Or were these the same mice he saw scuttling about on the London Underground, on the rare occasions he travelled on it?

'Come on. I'll show you.' As they left via the side door, she dragged him around to the furthest window. 'Can you see the mouse?'

Damon blinked as he took in the display. Not a string of tinsel to be seen, although there were plenty of fairy lights, illuminating the scene for passers-by.

There were no mannequins in Christmas jumpers either, or fake presents. Instead, the window opened up onto another world filled with what looked like a whole village made of gingerbread—iced houses and shops with tiny Christmas cakes and cookies for sale behind their windows. There was a Christmas tree, of course—two, in fact. One was made from a giant stack of gingerbread stars, with iced decorations and pinprick fairy lights. The other was actually a tower of perfect white iced Christmas cakes, stacked from biggest to smallest, with a golden iced, star-shaped cake on top.

In between the trees, in front of the buildings and surrounded by icing-sugar snow, was a mirror lake with an ice-skating hedgehog, rabbit and even a deer with tiny skates on all four hooves. But no mouse.

'I don't see it,' he admitted, peering harder.

Rachel grinned. 'Then I've done it right. Try getting down to child level.'

Giving her a sceptical look, Damon squatted down closer to the pavement—and suddenly the scene took on a whole new dimension.

He'd assumed that the shop windows, with their tiny fake treats, were all there was to the buildings. He'd been wrong. From this level—the level at which the shop's younger visitors would be viewing it—he could see far more. Behind the windows there were whole new worlds: decorated living rooms, shops with tiny animal customers, and there, curled up on an armchair by a Christmas tree, a small mouse. 'I see him!'

Even Damon could hear the delight in his voice, and it made Rachel's smile widen further. 'There's a mouse in every window,' she explained. 'Hidden, as a sort of treasure hunt for the kids.'

'Are they all like this?' He looked back at the astonishing display. 'Because this is amazing. Did you do this?' Of course she had. It was total Rachel—nice to look at on the surface, but with so much more to offer underneath.

Stop thinking about it. He mentally pulled away from thinking about Rachel, even as she was standing beside him. It was easy enough. He'd had years of practice.

Unaware of his roving thoughts, Rachel ducked her chin modestly. 'Yeah. I do them every year. It's kind of my thing. But they're not all exactly like this; this one is for our food and drink gifting range. There's one for womenswear, one for homewares, one for kids' gifts…' She shrugged. 'Basically, I split the six windows to cover all the big areas of the store.'

'Can I see them?' In the back of his mind an idea was forming. One that had nothing to do with spending more time with Rachel, and everything to do with business. Just as it should be.

If all her window displays were as cool as this one, Rachel could be just what he needed to get his latest project working at last.

'Have we got time? Won't Celeste be waiting?' Rachel's teeth pressed against her plump lower lip, a line of concern forming between her brows.

Damon flashed her his best 'Trust Me' smile. 'Celeste can wait. I want to see your work.'

Spots of pink appeared in her cheeks, and he knew the smile had worked its usual magic. 'Okay. Come this way.'

CHAPTER TWO

IT WAS ANOTHER twenty minutes before Rachel eased herself into the passenger seat of Damon's flashy sports car. She had no idea of the make—cars weren't exactly her thing—but, knowing Damon as she did, it would be the most expensive, and the fastest.

He'd seemed oddly charmed by her window displays, she mused as he started the engine. She hadn't exactly imagined that Damon Hunter, entrepreneur and all-round playboy, would find much to admire in her tiny scenes of festive fun. But he had.

It had been a long time since she'd seen beneath the charming, suave exterior of the perfect businessman that Damon projected to the world—not since they were both teenagers. And even then, there'd only been one night where she thought she'd glimpsed the real boy behind the facade.

The fact that just that one night had been enough to fuel an almost decade-long crush was beside the point. Rachel had been fairly sure that, as he'd grown up, that boy had faded away. But his delight at her whimsical window displays made her wonder if he'd really disappeared after all.

'So you do those windows every year?' he asked now, as he eased the car out of its dubiously legal parking spot and into the central London traffic.

'Yep. It's kind of my thing.' Something to look forward to in between the monotony of shifts on the tills or on the floor of the department store.

Working at Hartbury & Sons hadn't exactly been her dream career when she'd been studying English at university in Oxford with Celeste. But then, if she'd actually had any idea what her dream career was, maybe she'd have made more effort to go after it.

And as her dad pointed out, there weren't many family businesses on the scale of Hartbury's still going these days. It was good that they were part of the tradition—even if it wasn't technically her family tradition at all.

'And do you do them for other stores too, or just your stepmother's?'

Rachel blinked in surprise. 'Uh…just for Hartbury's. I mean, it's part of my job. Working there.'

'I thought Celeste said you were doing marketing and social media these days? You know, freelancing, like me.'

She couldn't help the snort of laughter that burst out of her; for all she knew it was probably one of the least attractive sounds in the universe. 'Celeste exaggerated.'

'So what do you do, exactly?'

Why did he even care? Rachel couldn't imagine, but she shrugged and answered all the same. 'I work on the shop floor, on the tills, putting out stock, that sort of thing. Everyone has to put in time there when we're busy, especially at Christmas. But I'm also in charge of the window displays and I run the social media and keep the website updated—not the online shop, but the blog and stuff.'

It sounded almost impressive when she listed it out. The Hartbury & Sons social media accounts had exploded since she took them over, especially since she started posting photos of the window displays, and the blog got a decent number of hits too. She'd managed to talk her stepmother into coughing up for some online training for her, and the shop was seeing the benefits of her newfound expertise.

But it didn't *feel* impressive. Not when she was still living at home, suffering the petty meanness of her stepsisters, and the way her father never seemed able to see it. Not compared to Celeste's high-flying academic career and TV appearances. Not compared to Damon's business success. She didn't even pretend to understand exactly what it was his company did, beyond what Celeste had told her.

'Companies that are doing badly get him in, and suddenly they're in profit again. He's like a business wizard, I think.'

But whatever it was, he was clearly very successful at it. Even Celeste sounded proud of him—not that Rachel imagined her best friend would ever tell him so.

It didn't even feel particularly impressive compared to her own vague hopes and dreams for her career. She'd never found a way to articulate what it was she really wanted from her employment, but in the back of her mind she'd always known how it would feel.

She'd be in charge of her own work; she'd have control over her schedule. Probably working from home, doing something creative that fulfilled her. Maybe even being her own boss. The one who decided what she did and when.

Working at Hartbury's definitely didn't give her that.

One step at a time, she reminded herself. *Dad gets the all-clear from the docs, then I move out. Then I can think about my potential career.*

It was how she'd got through everything else in life— her mother's death, her father's unexpected remarriage, being a member of a new blended family she never really felt part of, being an outsider again at Oxford, and everything since. One step at a time.

Damon, she suspected, would hop, skip and jump all

over the place as the whim took him. He'd never had the patience to plod along like her.

'What's your favourite part of the job?' Damon asked, and there was genuine curiosity in his voice. It warmed her a little to think he cared enough to ask.

Nobody else did, it seemed. Even her father just told her he was glad she was doing so well working for the family business without ever asking her if it was what she wanted, or giving her a chance to tell him it wasn't, before he went on about his day.

He's got a lot on his mind, she told herself sternly. Ever since his suspected heart attack he'd been preoccupied, obviously worrying. Just like her.

But even before then he just assumed you liked working at Hartbury's, a nagging, alternative voice reminded her.

She shook it away. Her father had his faults, but she loved him anyway. He was her only real family since her mother died when she was twelve. And if he'd rushed into another marriage, another family, just a couple of years later, she knew well enough why he'd done it.

For me. He wanted to give me a family again.

She'd never had the heart to tell him that, as the years had passed, she'd felt less a part of a family with Hannah and the girls than she'd felt when it was just the two of them. How could she when he was trying so hard? And then, by the time she'd accepted that she would never be a real part of Hannah's family, she'd recognised that her dad already was. She'd lost her mother, and she couldn't risk losing him too by walking away from that new family.

Damon was still waiting for a response, she realised. What did he want to know? Her favourite part of the job…

'I like doing the windows,' she said slowly, thinking. Never having been asked before, she'd not really thought about the answer. 'They're fun and creative and I like seeing the kids' faces when they spot them.'

'But they're not your favourites?' A traffic light turned green and Damon instantly pressed the accelerator and sped forward over a brief patch of empty road, changing lanes at speed.

'I… I think I like the social media side of it more, actually. I didn't think I would—I mean, communicating with people has never exactly been my strong point.' She shot him a wry smile, and his gaze darted from the road to meet hers for a moment. He didn't contradict her, which she appreciated. Too often her family spoke over her, telling the story of her life as they saw it—or as they wanted to see it—rather than the one she was actually living. Being allowed to narrate her own life story was strangely liberating.

Or maybe he was remembering that one night where they'd talked almost until morning. *Stop thinking about it, Rachel.* That was a long time ago, and it wasn't as if it had led anywhere anyway.

'What do you love about it?' Damon swung the car around a corner into a darkened street between two much taller buildings. Rachel couldn't help but wonder how he knew his way around the city so well by car. She was reasonable enough at finding her way via the Tube, or on foot, at least in areas she knew. But she'd never even *tried* to drive in the city. It didn't seem to faze Damon, though.

But then, nothing really did. Even when he was a newly turned eighteen-year-old hanging out in their university flat, mostly to avoid being at home with his parents as far as Rachel could tell. Even then he'd had more confidence, more charm, than Rachel had ever dreamt of.

It was the kind of confidence she saw in some of her fellow students—usually the ones who had money, or whose family name and title went back generations. The sort of confidence you had to inherit.

Heaven only knew where Damon had got it, coming from the same family as Celeste. The Doctors Hunter, she knew from one awkward holiday visit, were academics, not aristocracy. They were well off enough, for sure, with a London town house many would envy. But while they, and Celeste, were always confident in their academic knowledge and their ability to be right, none of them had any talent for small talk or winning people over by force of personality rather than facts.

Apparently Damon had got all the charm in the family. And boy did he know how to use it. He'd brought enough university students back to their flat for her to be sure of that.

'So?' He swung the car into a tiny parking space between two SUVs without even setting off the parking sensors. 'What is it you love about social media?'

'Um...' Rachel tried to find the words to explain it, but before she could talk her phone started ringing loudly in her bag. Fumbling, she pulled it out. 'Celeste,' she explained, showing him his sister's name on the screen.

'Where are you?' Celeste asked, as soon as she answered. 'We're starting filming any minute!'

'We're here, we're here.' Rachel opened the car door, trying not to crash into the neighbouring car as she tumbled out. 'We'll be there any second now, I promise.'

'Okay. Hurry!'

'You can tell me later.' Damon nonchalantly clicked the button to lock the car, and strolled towards the entrance as if there were no rush at all. Rachel couldn't help but watch him go.

Wow, but he'd grown up well. He'd been gorgeous at eighteen, but these days he was something else. Broad at the shoulder, narrow at the waist and strong, muscular legs, she could tell, even through his suit trousers. The lamplight flickered on his dark hair. He looked like the final scene of a movie, walking away like that.

'Come on,' he called back over his shoulder, and Rachel hurried to catch up.

She wasn't wasting time on that daydream any longer. She had her own plodding plans to follow.

One step at a time.

Well, this was hideous.

Damon loved his sister, really he did, but that didn't make him blind to her many, many flaws. Most obviously right now, an inability to back down from an argument when she was convinced she was right.

The fact that she was always, always right hadn't made this trait any easier to bear during his childhood years and, right now, it didn't look as if it was making the situation easier for media darling Theo Montgomery, who had the bad luck to be hosting the Christmas Cracker Cranium Quiz.

'All I'm saying is that the answer you have on that card is incomplete and gives the audience an incorrect view about Christmas traditions,' Celeste said, her arms folded across the sparkly Christmas jumper Damon was certain had been foisted on her by the wardrobe department. He'd definitely never seen his big sister wear anything so…seasonal before. Or anything that wasn't black or white, for that matter. Celeste lived in monochrome. Colour, it seemed, was too distracting from her aims of being right, being clever, and climbing the academic ladder at the London university where she, and both their parents, worked.

Beside him in the audience, Rachel was visibly cringing, as if she were trying to disappear into her knitted dress. He couldn't blame her. This was excruciating.

He'd known it was going to go badly from the moment they'd arrived. Celeste had been waiting for them, just inside the building, wearing that incongruous sweater over her black jeans and tapping her foot impatiently.

'What took you so long?' she'd asked, grabbing Rachel's arm and pulling her into step with her. 'Let me guess, Damon was flirting with your stepsisters?'

He couldn't see Rachel's face to gauge her reaction to that, but he imagined she was smiling. After all, that was what he did, wasn't it? Flirt with pretty women in an irresponsible manner that resulted in him being late. If she were asked, he reckoned Celeste would say that was a reasonable assassination of his character.

But to his surprise, Rachel had defended him. 'Actually, it was my fault. I had to fix a window display before we left.'

She didn't mention that he'd then insisted on looking at all of them, and that that was what had actually made them late. He'd wondered why, but had put it down to Rachel just being nice like that.

Now, watching Celeste and Theo go at it again over the correct pronunciation of the answer to what was only question five of a half-hour show, he figured she just hadn't wanted to rile Celeste up any more than necessary. Not that it seemed to have helped.

'Isn't this supposed to be a "light-hearted, intellectual festive quiz"?' Rachel asked, leaning close to whisper in his ear. Her hair smelled like something Christmassy although he couldn't quite put his finger on exactly what. Something spicy, though. He liked it.

'That's what she told Mum and Dad at Sunday lunch the other week,' he murmured back. 'Of course, that didn't make them any more enamoured with the idea of her doing it.' They'd never really approved of any of Celeste's TV, radio or podcast appearances, not even the classics-for-the-masses documentary ones. Not academic enough for them, apparently. Much like Damon himself.

Maybe he and Celeste could have bonded over it, if she hadn't still been a thousand times closer to being their perfect child than he could ever hope to be.

Not that he wanted to be any more.

'This does not feel light-hearted.' Even in her whispered tone, he could hear how heartfelt that was. Rachel, he remembered, didn't like conflict. Presumably that was why she let her stepsisters walk all over her the way they seemed to. He couldn't imagine why else she wouldn't take a stand against their petty meanness.

Up on set, Theo made a joke that made the other contestants laugh nervously. Celeste just glowered at him some more.

He'd known that Theo and his sister were going to clash from the moment they'd entered the studio. Celeste might have fancy make-up on and her hair done in artful curls in a way she'd never bother to do herself, but underneath she was still the girl he'd grown up with. The big sister who could never let anything lie, could never move on from a fight without him admitting that she'd been right all along. The one who wrote long, persuasive essays then read them out to their parents to convince them to do things her way.

So when Theo had swept over to introduce himself, TV-star smile in place, all easy friendliness and 'let's all just get along and have some fun' vibes, Damon had *known* that he and Celeste were going to hate each other. True to form, from the moment he'd shaken Theo's hand, Celeste had been glaring at the presenter.

He could almost hear her thoughts: *Too suave, too smooth, only here because of his face and his name*—because who didn't know that Theo Montgomery was one of *those* Montgomerys?—*and doesn't know anything about the subjects we'll be answering questions on.*

If there was anything Celeste hated more than people thinking she was wrong, it was people who thought they were right when actually they just didn't understand the argument. Sometimes, they didn't even know they were arguing in the first place, but, in the Hunter family, every-thing was either a competition or an argument. Often both.

He suspected Theo had foreseen the potential clash too because he'd turned the charm up another couple of notches. A bad move because, as Damon could have pre-dicted, it only made his sister bristle more. Celeste hated people who were all style and no substance.

Damon assumed his sister tolerated him because he was family. Or maybe because Rachel had told her she had to. Sometimes he thought Celeste's friendship with Rachel was the only thing that had stopped his sister turning into their parents years ago.

The bristling between Theo and Celeste had now appar-ently turned into televised warfare. Damon had no idea how anybody was going to edit this to make it a 'light-hearted festive quiz' to air in the weeks before Christmas. He was just very glad it wasn't his job.

The director called for a break after the latest set of questions, and the whole studio audience gave a sigh of relief. Damon suspected that someone would be talking to his sister right now about appropriate quiz-show be-haviour.

He'd have done it himself, but at that moment he spot-ted a young woman with a clipboard making her way along the rows of the audience, talking to people as she went—and those audience members getting up and walking out of the studio.

Hmm. Was that because of Celeste or something else?

'Hang on,' he said to Rachel, and vaulted over the empty front-row seats to accost the girl with the clipboard. If there was something else more interesting going on somewhere, he wanted in.

Or, more specifically, out of this passive-aggressive rerun of all his worst childhood dinners.

And if he was getting out, he was taking Rachel with him.

* * *

Damon returned, smiling broadly, accompanied by a be-sotted-looking production assistant with a clipboard. The poor girl had spent barely three minutes in his company and she already looked half in love.

It was somewhat reassuring to know he had that effect on everybody, not just Rachel.

Right now, however, she was starting to worry he'd lost his mind.

'They want us to…what?' Rachel frowned, running his words through her mind again. They still didn't make any sense.

'Bring in the new year with a bang!' Damon said, beaming.

'Now?'

'Yep.'

'On the…' she checked the date dial on her watch to make sure she wasn't imagining things '…first of December?'

'Apparently so!' Damon was still grinning at the idea, so Rachel turned to the girl with the clipboard for some sort of explanation.

'We're filming our New Year's Eve countdown and party show a few doors down,' the assistant said. 'But there's some sort of problem on the Tube, and half our booked par-tygoers haven't shown up, so we're recruiting volunteers from other studio audiences right now.'

Rachel blinked. 'Wait. Is this the countdown show that goes out live on New Year's Eve? You know, the one that, well, counts down to midnight?'

The girl's pupils slid sideways as she broke eye contact. 'We never actually *say* it's live.'

'Come on, Rach, you didn't really think all those celeb-rities they have on had nothing better to do on New Year's Eve than hang out in a TV studio with the ordinary people, did you?' Damon asked.

It could have sounded cruel, mocking, and maybe from someone else it would. But Damon, standing just about far enough behind the production assistant that she couldn't see his face, followed up his words by widening his eyes, shrugging, and mouthing, *'Me neither.'*

Rachel stifled a laugh. 'Well, obviously not. So what would we have to do, exactly?'

The production assistant—the access card on the lanyard around her neck said her name was Amy—shrugged. 'Just, well, you know. Party. Dance. Have fun.' She looked Rachel up and down, and she could feel her taking in her oversized knit dress, her mostly make-up-free face, and her curls with a clear headband shoved in them to keep them out of her face. 'Do you think you can manage that?'

No.

Partying wasn't exactly her sort of thing. Even at university she and Celeste had been more the 'cups of tea and watching a movie on a Friday night' sort of students. In fact, the only parties she remembered them going to were ones Damon had somehow got them invited to during his regular visits.

Like the one where we lost Celeste and spent all night together looking for her... Not thinking about it.

The point was, she wanted to party. Even at university she'd *wanted* to get out there and meet new people. She just hadn't had—still didn't have—the confidence to try, and staying in with Celeste had been more comfortable and less stressful all round.

She should stay and support Celeste now in this show, however excruciating it was to watch her battling with the host. Somewhere in the back of her mind, though, a long-silenced voice was screaming at her to go. To have fun. To dance and party with Damon, just as she'd wanted to at eighteen.

Rachel ignored the voice, as usual. It wasn't in the plan.

Damon, however, had other ideas.

'Of course she can!' he said, gleefully. Grabbing her hand, he tugged her around the row of seats he'd vaulted over, then wrapped an arm around her shoulder to hold her close against him. 'You should have seen this one party at university! Trust me, she's an animal!'

Amy the production assistant looked understandably dubious. Damon gave Rachel's shoulder a little shake, and she forced a smile. 'I'd love to help with the New Year countdown show,' she said.

It felt as if the words were coming from another person's mouth. Or as if she were a puppet, controlled by Damon, saying something she'd never imagined saying in real life. If she'd ever let Damon drag her along to such a thing she'd have always made it clear it wasn't her idea so if it went horribly wrong she could duck out of any responsibility, or anyone thinking she'd believed for a moment she could do it in the first place.

But no, something had made her actually say what she wanted to do, and take responsibility for it.

She had a suspicion it was the way Damon was pressed up against her side, the fresh scent of his aftershave filling her every breath, and her whole body tingling with awareness of his closeness. Clearly his proximity had messed with her neural network, the part that made thoughts into words. It was the only explanation.

'Well, great,' Amy said, marking down another tally on her clipboard to add to the others from the audience. Then she paused, and looked up at Rachel again. 'Um… I don't suppose you have something more…partyish you could wear, do you? I mean, I can see if anyone's free in hair and make-up to help with that, but I'm not sure whether wardrobe will have anything…*appropriate*.'

She meant in the right size, Rachel realised. Most of the

shows filmed here seemed to feature those perfect size-six women, and Rachel was happy to admit she wasn't that.

She was short, curvy and healthy. Normally, that was enough for her. But here and now…she looked around the rest of the audience, queuing to take part in the New Year party—probably as an escape from the festive quiz show from hell. They all seemed to have dressed up rather more for the occasion than she'd thought to. Her usual policy was to wear clothes that enabled her to fade into the background. After all, if no one was going to notice her, it didn't much matter what she wore.

But if she was going to be on TV—actually on TV, not just sitting in the audience next to Damon, who would draw everyone's attention anyway—then suddenly her comfy old jumper dress and leggings didn't feel entirely appropriate. Especially not for what was supposed to be the party of the year.

She was about to back out again, to claim that she really had to stay and support Celeste after all, when Damon said, 'Don't worry, I've got that covered. Just need to grab it from the car. Hang on.'

Rachel watched as he eased his way through the queue with grace and charm, smiling and chatting as he went, and out through the door back to the car park. When he was gone, she turned back to Amy, who was still looking puzzled by this whole turn of events.

'I don't have any idea what he has planned, but I suspect I'm going to need to take you up on that offer of hair and make-up.'

Amy beamed. 'Follow me.'

CHAPTER THREE

WHEN DAMON RETURNED from his trip to the car, he found Amy waiting for him—and Rachel nowhere to be seen.

'Is that her outfit?' Amy grabbed the bag from him without waiting for much of an answer. 'Great. I'll give it to her. You head through there and help yourself to a drink; they're almost ready to start.'

Ambling into the studio, Damon took a glass of something sparkling from a waiter circulating with a tray, and surveyed the crowd. It was easy enough to see who had planned to be here and who had been drafted in at the last minute. The original female partygoers all wore the kind of sparkly sequinned dresses and heels he'd expect at a swanky New Year's Eve party, while the men were in dinner jackets or smart suits. The last-minute additions were more casually dressed, although most had at least dressed up for their visit to the studios anyway, so there weren't many jeans or trainers to be seen.

His work suit stood up well enough, he decided, and the dress he'd bought for Rachel would be fine too—even if it meant Celeste would now have to find her own Christmas present for her best friend.

The studio itself was party ready too. On the main stage area was a giant digital clock, ticking inexorably down towards fictional midnight. Right now, it seemed to think it was around ten-thirty at night, rather than, as his watch told him, not quite eight o'clock. There was a Christmas tree in the corner, decked out with tasteful decorations and lights—although no kind of display at all compared to Rachel's windows. Cocktail-bar-style high tables had been set up around the perimeter, allowing people to gather in small groups and chat. He spotted a couple of assistants with the same clipboard-and-microphone-headset ensemble as Amy darting around encouraging people to mingle. It seemed they wanted this place to look like an actual party—right down to the dance floor in front of the stage.

A band was setting up on the stage itself—a big band, the kind that played classic swing music—and every now and then a few bars of one of the Rat Pack's greatest hits would boom out across the party. The host—a well-known TV personality—was chatting with the director off to one side of the stage. Damon was surprised that Theo Montgomery, the host of the quiz show Celeste was appearing on, hadn't been tagged for the role, until he remembered that of course Theo would be doing the *actual* live broadcast on New Year's Eve. It would ruin the illusion to have him in two places at once.

Still, if Damon knew his sister—and he did—he'd bet that Theo would rather be here with a glass of warm sparkling wine than asking Celeste questions and having to deal with her dissatisfaction with the answers.

One of the assistants clapped his hands, obviously trying to get everyone's attention before filming. But Damon wasn't really listening. Because, at that moment, the door to the studio opened again and Rachel walked in.

I was right about the dress, was his first thought. It clung perfectly to those glorious curves she usually hid away, dipping to a slight vee at the front to give shape without being revealing enough to make her self-conscious, he hoped. The skirt swirled around her legs to her knees, above the same

ankle boots she'd been wearing earlier. The woodland animals in the pattern almost seemed to dance around under
the studio lights, peeping around the tree print on the fabric. It reminded him of the magical window displays she'd
created, he realised.

Maybe that was why he couldn't stop looking at her.
Sure, the hair and make-up team had done stuff to her
hair and face but, to be honest, he'd always thought Rachel
looked lovely without all that. And even her fabulous figure
wasn't a surprise; he'd always known it was there. He just
hadn't spent much time thinking about it lately.

Now, watching her cross the room towards him, he
couldn't think about anything else.

'You look fantastic,' he said, the words a little hoarse as
they made their way out of his suddenly dry throat.

'I can't believe you bought this dress—how lucky was
that? Who was it for?' Rachel glanced down at the dress,
her fingers holding out the skirt a little as she studied the
pattern. 'It's so cute.'

'It was for you,' he said, honestly. Rachel looked up
sharply, that frown line back between her eyebrows. 'I saw
it in the pile of dresses you'd been trying on and, well, it
was the only one that actually looked like *you*. So I bought
it. I figured Celeste might like to give it to you for Christmas, or something.'

It had seemed like a perfectly normal impulse when he'd
done it, but now he had to explain his reasoning he wasn't
so sure. Neither was Rachel, by the look of things.

'That was…kind of you.' Kind was better than weird,
right? He'd take it.

'It looks a bit like your windows,' he said.

Rachel beamed. 'That's what I thought when I saw it!
But Gretchen said it would draw too much attention to my,
well…size.'

'Trust me,' Damon said, with feeling, 'it's drawing exactly the right amount of attention to your figure. You look incredible.' And he really had to stop looking at his big sister's best friend that way. Not least because she'd never given him even the slightest hint that she wanted him to.

There was that one night, his brain reminded him. *That one night when you could have kissed her, if you'd wanted to.*

But he hadn't. Because she was Celeste's best friend. Because she wasn't the sort of girl you messed around with, and he hadn't known how to do anything else.

Because she'd seen deeper than he liked, and it had scared him.

Her smile turned shy and she went back to studying the creatures on her dress, thankfully oblivious to his thoughts. 'It *is* like my windows, isn't it?'

Somewhere someone clapped their hands again, and bellowed for them to take their places.

'Come on. We're starting.' Damon took her arm and led her towards the bar. He needed another drink, and she hadn't even had one yet. 'Let's grab a glass of something bubbly, and you can tell me more about your windows and your work until it's time to shout out the countdown, or whatever we need to do.'

'You really want to know more about the windows?' She sounded astonished at the prospect.

'As it happens, I really, really do.' And not just because of the way she lit up when she spoke about the things that mattered to her. Or because it would give him a chance to listen to her melodious voice. Those things weren't important to him. Or shouldn't be anyway.

No, he wanted to know more because he had the inklings of an idea that could help *both* of them get what they needed in life. If he could persuade her to take a chance on him.

It was just business. That was all.

He needed to keep reminding himself of that.

* * *

'And it's ten minutes to midnight!' the host bellowed as the band finished its latest song and the crowd whooped loudly. The free sparkling wine had been flowing merrily, and the last-minute partygoers had definitely been taking advantage of it.

'Funny,' Damon murmured. 'It only feels like quarter past nine.'

Rachel hid a grin behind her hand as one of the cameramen swooped past. 'Yeah, this is weird.'

Except somehow it really wasn't. Oh, the whole 'pretend it's actually December the thirty-first' thing was wacky as anything, but being with Damon for the night? That wasn't nearly as weird as she'd expected it to be when Celeste had told her he'd be there tonight too, and that was when she'd thought they'd just be sitting next to each other in the audience for the quiz show.

She felt a pang of guilt about abandoning her best friend, but pushed it aside. There was no way she'd have been able to sit through an hour or more of Celeste and Theo Montgomery verbally sparring anyway. If Amy the production assistant hadn't asked them to join the party filming when she did, Rachel had already been planning an emergency escape to the loos, and maybe getting lost on the way back. Conflict really wasn't her thing.

Hanging out with Damon at the fake party was a lot more fun than pretending to lose her way in the TV studio's corridors.

He'd meant it when he said he wanted to talk more about her windows. And not just the window displays; he'd asked more questions about her job, her career ambitions, her hopes and dreams, than anybody else had, ever. Not her family, not even Celeste—although, in fairness, that was mostly because Rachel had been shutting down conversations about what she wanted from life for so long now that

Celeste had stopped even asking. She knew her best friend meant well, but it was hard to talk about maybe possibly taking on some freelance clients who she could run social media accounts for as an actual career path, when Celeste's academic ladder was so well scaled already.

But with Damon…somehow, the fact that he was rich and successful didn't intimidate her the way his sister's success did. Perhaps because he was so casual about it compared to Celeste's laser focus. As if he was just doing what was fun, and what he was good at, and it all worked out rather well—although she suspected there had to be more to it than that, no matter how relaxed he was talking about his own business.

It had been fascinating spending this evening with him, seeing the man he'd grown into rather than the boy she remembered. They hadn't spent much time together in the years since she'd left university, and definitely not alone. In fact, in almost ten years of acquaintance, there was only one night where it had been just the two of them.

One night that was seared into her memory, even though nothing had happened.

Suddenly she needed to know if Damon remembered it too.

'Do you remember that night at university where we went to that party in our college and lost Celeste?'

It was just a casual question, a reminiscence of sorts. There was no reason for Damon to freeze up as suddenly as he did at her words.

Or maybe she imagined it, because a moment later he was smiling, his shoulders loose and relaxed again.

'She showed up in the library, didn't she?' he said.

Rachel nodded. 'She'd had an idea about her essay and the library was still just about open, so she'd snuck over to check her sources or something.'

'And got locked in,' Damon added. 'While we scoured the college—and the city—looking for her.'

'Yeah.' She met his gaze, and just for a second she could believe that he remembered that night the same way she did. As an unforgettable interlude in an otherwise boring life.

Except, of course, Damon's life was anything but boring. He probably stayed up all night and talked about his innermost dreams and feelings with people all the time. Back then, she'd hoped him opening up to her that way, listening to her talk about her own life, meant she was special. Now she realised, with the hindsight of age, he was probably that way with everyone. He had friends all over the world, and a whole list of women desperate to spend the night with him—and do a lot more than talk.

While she had Celeste, and her family. And tonight.

Which wasn't nothing.

'Do you think we're supposed to be going somewhere?' Rachel asked, suddenly uncomfortably aware that all the other partygoers seemed to be congregating on the dance floor.

'Apparently so.' Damon got to his feet and held a hand out to her just as the band struck up another tune—a fast, fun, reeling jig of a tune that had even Rachel's reluctant toes tapping.

She didn't dance. She *couldn't* dance. She'd been thrown out of junior ballet for her total inability, and hadn't ever danced since. She'd avoided it at every nightclub, every party, every wedding she'd ever attended.

Now she was expected to dance on not-even-a-little-bit-live TV. With Damon Hunter.

And the absolute weirdest part of all was that she *wanted* to. Because it was Damon. She'd never have sought out this opportunity, never even hoped for it, but now it was here… even though every bit of her emotional muscle memory was screaming at her to turn it down, to fall back on her usual *'Actually, I'm happier just watching'* line, she didn't.

Her stomach clenching with nerves, Rachel took his hand and followed him onto the dance floor, ignoring all the bits of her brain that were telling her what a terrible idea this was.

'It's ages since I've had a night out dancing,' Damon said, pulling her into his arms. Rachel tried desperately to remember where her hands were supposed to go—no, definitely not *there*, she reminded herself as she recalled how good his backside looked in his suit trousers—and was relieved when he took one of hers in his larger hand, entwining his fingers with hers, and rested the other at her waist.

The music had changed. When had the music changed? Probably while she was agonising over whether she could even remember how to dance, and the fact that most of her dance experience was actually just watching *Dirty Dancing* too many times as an impressionable teen. Either way, the lively, jive-like music had faded into something more sultry. Not slow, exactly, but definitely sexy. Definitely intended to get the audience up close and personal before the fake midnight gongs.

As the music instructed, Damon tugged her a little closer, one big hand at the small of her back, the other still holding hers. They must look ridiculous; she was more than a head and a half shorter than him, even in her low-heeled boots. If she wanted to see his face she'd have to crane her neck right back. As it was, she was mostly staring at his nicely muscled chest in his white shirt, trying not to imagine undoing the buttons.

'Okay?' Damon murmured, somewhere around the top of her head, and she felt the word vibrating through that very fine chest.

'Mmm-hmm.' She didn't trust herself to speak actual words at the moment. When would this song be over? She'd *known* dancing was a bad idea. She had no idea what her feet were doing, her hips were probably swaying far too much but she couldn't seem to stop them, and her face ached from smiling stiffly in case the cameras caught them.

'Only, you're gripping a little tight there, you know,' Damon said, casually.

Rachel's eyes widened as she looked down and saw his suit jacket fisted in her fingers. That suit was probably worth more than her entire wardrobe, and here she was scrunching it up. The only reason her other hand wasn't doing the same was probably because it was in his, and she was scrupulously trying to avoid touching him any more than necessary.

An endeavour that was promptly ruined by Damon himself. Taking his hand from the small of her back, he peeled her fingers away from his suit jacket, all while still moving in time to the music. Then, he placed her hand under his suit jacket, resting just above his hip, so she could feel the warmth of his skin through his thin shirt.

Oh, this was such a bad idea…

She glanced up. He was smirking. 'Better?'

'For your suit, I suppose,' she said, amazed she could find any words at all.

He chuckled, replacing his palm against her spine and sending a shiver all the way up it.

She'd never been this close to him before. And now, all she could think was that she might never be this close again.

Last time they'd been alone together for a night, they'd just talked. This time… Rachel couldn't help but imagine so much more.

All those repressed impulses she'd spent so many years ignoring bubbled up inside her, as if loosening up enough to dance had given them all the same hope of a way out. The possibility that she'd suddenly start taking chances she'd always swerved away from before.

She wouldn't, of course. But that knowledge wasn't enough to stop her thinking about them. Wondering what would happen if she just…gave in, and asked for what she wanted for a change.

One dance and she was thinking about breaking a lifetime of caution, reticence and wallflowerness. Heaven help her if Damon ever actually showed any interest in her.

Don't think about it. Especially not now, when you're in the man's arms, for heaven's sake.

But she *was* thinking about it. In fact, as the song finished, and the host grabbed the microphone again to start the ten-second countdown to fake midnight, it was all she *could* think about.

They'd stopped moving with the music, naturally, but they hadn't moved apart at all. Rachel tilted her chin up to look into his bright blue eyes.

'Five,' he whispered, and a buzzy feeling started somewhere in her chest.

'Four,' she said, her hoarse voice almost lost amongst the shouting. All around them, people were preparing for midnight, acting up for the cameras, and Rachel knew they should be too. But she couldn't look away from Damon's blue, blue eyes…

'Three. Two. One!' The crowd cheered, the confetti came down, Big Ben chimed midnight—presumably recorded—and it was officially a new year, a fresh start, a chance to do things differently…even if it was all pretend.

If it was all pretend, none of this would count tomorrow, right? It could all be forgotten. A dream, a fairy tale. Something that happened to another girl in another world.

That was what Rachel was telling herself anyway, as the band broke into the introduction to 'Auld Lang Syne', and she stretched up on her tiptoes, her mouth tantalisingly close to Damon's as he dipped his head towards her.

'Happy New Year,' she murmured. Every muscle in her

body was tensed, waiting for what happened next. What *had* to happen next. It had gone past being a choice, or something she asked for. Now it just felt inevitable, as if she couldn't pull away even if she wanted to.

And she *really* didn't want to.

'Happy New Year, Rachel,' Damon whispered back, and ducked his head just a little lower…

His lips against hers felt like heat and sex and they set New Year fireworks off behind her eyes—as though the sensation of kissing Damon Hunter after all these years might actually stun and blind her.

She could have kissed him for ever. Might have, if a production assistant in a sparkly dress hadn't elbowed her sharply and hissed, 'You're supposed to be singing!'

Sure enough, as she pulled back, Rachel realised that the rest of the guests were linking arms and bellowing out 'Auld Lang Syne', with varying levels of fidelity to the lyrics.

Damon rubbed the back of his neck with the hand that had, just moments ago, been holding her tightly against him. 'We should probably…'

'Right. Yes. Come on.' She darted back into the ring of people, linking arms with strangers who were suddenly far less scary than the one man she knew in the room, and hoping Damon took the hint to find some other people to sing with.

And then, when she was sure he wasn't looking, she ducked out of the circle, and headed for the door before anyone could stop her.

It wasn't midnight. It wasn't a new year or a fresh start, and she was still the same old Rachel Charles. Even if, just for a moment, she'd felt like someone else entirely.

CHAPTER FOUR

WHERE HAD SHE GONE? Damon scanned the room, taking in all the tipsy partygoers still hugging and dancing now the midnight celebrations were over. The band was playing again—something upbeat, a tune that wouldn't have allowed him to hold Rachel so tantalisingly close against him.

If he could find her.

He vaguely remembered from the briefing before they started filming that there would be another few songs, then the host would wrap it up for the night, and welcome everyone into a brand-new year. Would Rachel come back for that last planned shot of them all clapping as the camera swooped up and away? He suspected not.

He'd kissed her. After spending the whole evening reminding himself that Rachel Charles, his sister's best friend, was categorically one of the few women of his acquaintance who had never given him any hint of romantic interest, he'd kissed her anyway. Which made him, officially, the worst sort of person.

Except…the way she'd clenched her fist around his jacket. Had that been nerves or something more? The way she'd fitted into his arms, the way she'd curled against him as they'd danced, her cheek against his chest…had he really been the only one whose heart had beat double fast at the sensation?

And *she* had stretched up towards him as the clock chimes rang out midnight, hadn't she? Had he really imagined all of that?

He sighed. Probably, yes.

It was because she'd been talking about That Night. That one night in his life when he'd felt understood. Open. Close enough to another person for them to see who he really was inside. For her he imagined it was a funny anecdote—the tale of them searching Oxford for Celeste only to find her asleep in the library the following morning, her phone on silent as always.

But for him, it had been a crossroads. Oh, he hadn't realised it at the time, of course; he'd been eighteen, drunk and scared for his sister. He hadn't realised anything much at the time. But afterwards—the next day, the next visit, whenever he saw Rachel again—he'd started to understand.

He'd pulled away from the closeness and the connection between them that night because it had scared him. He'd known himself well enough to realise that he didn't want the kind of expectation that came with a connection like that. Rachel wasn't like the usual girls he spent time with; she saw deeper than they did, and that meant something. He wouldn't be able to sleep with her then leave her behind.

So he'd put her firmly back in the box labelled 'Celeste's best friend' and kept her there. Until she mentioned that night and…

And trying to justify his actions to himself didn't make things any better. He'd kissed her, and she'd run away from him. That was all the information he needed.

She'd probably been planning on a quick peck on the cheek or something, just for the cameras. And, in truth, he'd not exactly been planning anything more than that himself. But as she'd swayed closer, something inside him had changed. Her scent in his lungs, his hand at her back, her breasts pressed against him…all he'd been able to think about was kissing her.

Celeste would tell him that this was where all his problems always started: with the inability to pass up an opportunity to charm and seduce.

He sank onto a bar stool at one of the high cocktail tables, and watched the party continue without him, and without Rachel. Everyone else seemed to be enjoying themselves, at least.

He should go and find Celeste. She *had* to have finished filming by now, right? It was—he glanced at the large clock, remembered its fakeness, and checked his watch instead—gone nine-thirty. They'd been at it for hours for a thirty-minute show, and they'd already lost half their audience.

As the band finished up their final song, Damon let himself silently out of the side door and hoped no one spotted him leaving.

He found Celeste stomping out of the green room, back in her usual black clothes but still with her hair and makeup TV-perfect. The scowl on her face wasn't, though.

'Where on earth did you go? And where's Rachel?'

'We got dragged in to film some New Year party show. They didn't have enough partygoers because of some issue on the Tube, and your filming had already gone longer than it was supposed to anyway.' The poor warm-up guy, the comedian who had to entertain the audience while they were waiting or between takes, must have more than earned his money that night.

Celeste rolled her eyes as she pushed past him to continue stomping down the corridor. 'Only because *that man* kept getting things wrong.'

Damon hid a smile. 'In fairness, Theo Montgomery was only reading out the answers on the cards.'

'Because he's not bright enough to actually know anything himself,' Celeste shot back over her shoulder. Then she winced, which was not an expression Damon was used to seeing from her. Neither was the slight tinge of pink that coloured her cheeks.

Eyebrows raised, he turned around to see what had caught her attention and found Theo Montgomery emerging from a room behind him into the corridor. From his raised eyebrows, he'd clearly heard everything Celeste had said.

Damon stepped towards him, hand out for Theo to shake, which he did.

'Mr Montgomery. I'm Damon Hunter, Celeste's brother—we met earlier? I just wanted to take this opportunity to apologise for my sister.'

'No need,' Theo said. 'Trust me, I've heard worse. You stayed for the whole filming?' He sounded amazed at the prospect.

Damon shook his head. 'No, I just follow my sister around to make the necessary apologies. And now that's done, I'm heading home.'

'Where's Rachel?' Celeste asked again, obviously ignoring Theo. 'I said we'd give her a lift home.'

'She, uh…she left early,' Damon said. It was the truth, after all, but apparently he couldn't avoid sounding guilty as he said it.

Celeste's eyes narrowed. 'What did you do?'

'What makes you think I did anything?' He turned to Theo. 'Does it make you feel any better that she treats *everyone* this way?'

'A little,' Theo admitted.

'You always do something,' Celeste replied. 'Let me guess, you were flirting with some other woman at the bar and leaving her all on her own?'

'I can promise you that absolutely was not the case. I was attentive, friendly, we even danced together.' *And then I kissed her and she ran away.* Which made him feel sleazy and awful—not least because he was still reliving that kiss in his head. The way she had felt against him, how sweet her lips had been…

'Rachel *danced*?' Celeste asked, astonishment in her voice. 'I have never once, in ten full years, seen my best friend dance. There is something else going on here, and you are going to tell me all about it on the way home. Come on, let's get to the car.' Then, belatedly, she turned to Theo. 'Thank you for having me on your show, Mr Montgomery. I'm very sorry that the question team screwed up so many of your answer cards.'

Then she spun around and stalked down the corridor, obviously expecting Damon to chase after her. He sighed, and turned back to Theo.

'Once again, apologies for my sister's attempt at an apology.'

But Theo, surprisingly, was smiling. 'No need. She certainly livened up the experience—and I'm pretty sure our researchers will be stepping up their game if we ever have her on again.'

'I think *if* is the important word in that sentence.'

Theo laughed. 'You might be right. Goodnight.'

''Night.' Damon turned and headed after Celeste, steeling himself for the grilling he was about to get in the car. Maybe he should have just lied and told her he'd been flirting with another woman. He had a feeling that would have gone down much better with Celeste than the truth.

He practised telling her what had happened in his head. *I kissed your best friend.*

Yeah, no. That wasn't going to go down any better with Celeste than it had with Rachel.

He sighed. Nothing about this evening had turned out how he'd expected. And yet, as he remembered dancing with Rachel…he couldn't honestly say he wanted to change any of it.

* * *

Rachel could hear the Christmas carols playing on the shop floor, along with the chaos of a department store at the beginning of December as customers fought to find the best presents, most flattering party outfits and, of course, the best seasonal deals. In her tiny office—okay, fine, converted cupboard—at the far end of the homewares floor, she was mostly protected from the fuss and bother outside. She didn't have a shift on the tills until tomorrow, the window displays were all perfect, and that meant she could get on with designing, writing and scheduling Hartbury & Sons' seasonal messages.

When she'd brainstormed her seasonal campaigns back in August, she'd been excited to get started. But, as so often happened, the everyday requirements of her job and her family had taken over, and now here she was at the start of December and she still had most of her Christmas posts still to write.

Hannah and the store's board of directors were an old-fashioned bunch when it came to marketing. When it came to most things, actually. A couple of half-page adverts in relevant newspapers once a season and they thought they were done. After all, as Hannah always said, Hartbury's was an institution. They didn't *need* to advertise.

Except, as Rachel had tried to explain to them so many times before, the world was changing. Yes, people might have *heard* of Hartbury's, but unless they gave them a reason to visit, unless they showed them why they were still relevant to a new generation of shoppers, getting new people through the doors was only going to get harder. She'd eventually talked them into hiring a company to set up and manage the online store, but only because they could see that would give them actual sales from people living in corners of the world too far away to just pop down to Hartbury's—first she'd had to remind them that such places, outside London, actually existed but she'd got there.

Hiring an online marketing team, or even a social media manager, though, that was a step too far. Which meant it fell to Rachel to bring the store into the twenty-first century, whether she liked it or not.

She looked at the new images she'd created for her social media campaign, and wondered if they were just a little…blah. She'd gone for classic festive images, the sort that Hartbury's always used in their adverts, or around the store, but now she was thinking that maybe she could do something a little more…personal. Maybe she'd go and take some new photos of her finished window displays, and use those. Hannah tolerated the window displays because they delighted the kids, which meant the parents were happier while shopping, but Rachel knew she'd personally prefer something more traditionally Christmas. She'd probably hate the idea that Rachel's displays were representing the store online, but since Hannah didn't use social media, she might never notice.

And her window displays were good. Even Damon said so—

'Dammit!' Rachel picked up her notebook and made another tally mark, then checked her watch. Five minutes that time. She'd gone a whole five minutes without thinking about Damon Hunter, and That Kiss. That might be an actual record, the longest she'd managed since she ran out of the studio on Tuesday night.

Now it was Thursday, and she was still spending more time thinking about him than anything else. Not a great sign.

Celeste had called the next day to apologise for whatever her brother had done to offend or annoy her, but Rachel had told her it was nothing. In fact, she'd lied and said she'd just had a headache.

She could tell from the sceptical silence on the other end of the line that Celeste hadn't believed her, but it was clear that Damon hadn't told her what had happened either, and Rachel was determined she wasn't going to spill.

She'd been the besotted girl before, the one who thought a guy truly liked her only to find out it was all a joke— or at least, that she wasn't important enough to be serious about. In fact, she'd been that girl *twice*. Once in high school, when she figured it was normal to be that naive. But the second time had been only last summer, with Tobias, and that time Rachel really should have known better.

This time, she *did* know better. Damon had been in her life for a decade and at no point had he given her even a *hint* that he saw her as anything other than his big sister's best friend. He wasn't cruel enough to pretend to like her for a bet, or to laugh off any relationship between them as a joke as Gretchen's friend Tobias ultimately had, but she also wasn't going to let herself believe it was anything more than a spur-of-the-moment impulse. A New Year's Eve kiss in the moment and then forgotten about.

By him anyway.

Forcing herself to refocus, Rachel turned back to her social media work—until a knock on the door broke her concentration again.

'Rach?' Her dad stuck his head around the door. She looked up and scanned his expression, his complexion, looking for signs of how he was feeling, whether the medicine was working. As ever, there were no firm answers. 'Ah good, I've found you. Um…can I come in?'

'You can try.' Rachel looked around at her tiny cupboard office, and wondered exactly where her dad thought he was going to stand. By the time the desk, chair and precariously balanced bookshelf were accounted for, there wasn't really any floor space left.

He settled for hovering in the open doorway, giving Rachel a view past him of the shop floor and all the Christmas shoppers she was trying to avoid.

'Am I needed on the shop floor?' she asked, when her father stayed silent.

He shook his head. 'No, no. Just…your stepmother thought you'd been a little bit down the last couple of days. She thought you might be worrying about what to wear for the Christmas party.'

'I'm not—' Rachel started, but her father kept talking over her, desperate as ever to make everything all right again without ever understanding what the real problem was.

'So we bought you this!' He pulled a pine green and red tartan monstrosity out of the bag in his hands and held it up for her to appreciate.

She didn't know how they'd managed it, but her dad and Hannah had found a dress she hated even more than any of the ones her stepsisters had made her try on the other day. This one would cover her from neck to mid-calf, with the green and red tartan pattern swamping her completely. The fabric looked stiff and uncomfortable. And the whole thing was capped off with a bright red satin bow, as a five-year-old might wear.

'Isn't it lovely?' Her father looked down at the dress lovingly. She imagined he was seeing her as a little girl again, wearing it. Or maybe the heart medication he was on had affected his sartorial taste somehow. 'Hannah has such exquisite taste, and I know you'll be grateful she was thinking of you.'

There was just the edge of desperate hope in his words, the same tone she'd been hearing ever since her father re-married two years after her mother died. The subtle reminder that he was doing all this for her, really. That he wanted her to be happy. That he needed them all to be a family.

Her father was genuinely fond of Hannah, loved her even. But Rachel had often wondered if he'd have remarried so quickly if it hadn't been for her. He'd been falling apart after his wife's death, and all anyone seemed to say was that a teenage girl needed a mother, a family.

So he'd found Hannah, and Rachel had spent the last fourteen years not fitting in with the family he'd chosen for them. To start with, because she hadn't been ready to leave the memory of her mother behind. She'd been awkward, difficult—really, she'd been fourteen, that was all. Gretchen and Maisie were both younger, and their parents had been divorced for years. Rachel and her dad had moved into their family home, but otherwise nothing had really changed for them.

But for Rachel, *everything* had changed. And most days, she still lived with the fallout.

Wait for Dad's test results. If they're clear, I'll talk to him about finding my own place to live. One step at a time.

Rachel swallowed her true feelings about the tartan monstrosity, and tried not to think about the cranberry-red wrap dress with the forest animal pattern she'd worn to the party the other night. The dress Damon had bought her, because it made him think of her.

Her family looked at her and thought, *Cover her up with tartan*, or *Hide her away in the corner*, or even *Embarrass the hell out of her.*

Damon looked at her and thought she deserved a dress she loved, one that felt like the way she saw *herself.*

Surely that had to mean something, didn't it?

Her father was still waiting for her verdict on the dress. And she'd promised herself—and Hannah—that she'd try to keep the peace, try not to be difficult, while his health was so delicate.

'It's very festive,' she said, carefully picking her way

around the truth. 'It was so kind of Hannah to think of me like that.'

Her dad's face relaxed into a smile. 'I knew you'd like it! I'll take it home for you and hang it in your room. Save it getting creased in here.' He glanced around her office again with a frown. 'And you know, now you mention it, it is very busy on the shop floor today. I'm sure Hannah would appreciate it if you lent a hand.'

'I'll be right there,' Rachel promised, trying hard not to sigh. Apparently her social media campaign would have to wait. Again.

Closing down her laptop, she added another tally to her chart—thinking about the dress definitely counted as thinking about Damon—and prepared to head out to work. But as she grabbed her phone, she saw she had a new message.

From Damon.

What are you doing this afternoon?

He'd tried to forget that kiss, really he had. Tried to push aside whatever impulse had led him to kiss his sister's best friend. Tried to forget how spending time with her again had sent him back to that other night they'd spent talking, and how the connection between them had scared eighteen-year-old him so much he'd run in the opposite direction. To remind himself, hourly if necessary, that she was an old family friend who had never given him a *hint* of interest—and had actually run away from him when he'd showed some.

He'd tried.

He'd failed.

As he stood in the middle of his latest business project, Damon tried to convince himself that his interest in Rachel Charles was actually totally professional—the same way he'd convinced himself, nine years ago, that their connection was simply shared concern for the missing Celeste.

Fake midnight kiss aside, what they'd mostly talked about was her work—most especially, her window displays. He was genuinely interested in the tableaus she put together, and he had a legitimate reason to contact her about them. Nothing to do with the kiss.

The question was, if he called her about work would she answer?

There was only one way to find out, he supposed. His phone in his hand, his fingers hovered over the keyboard for a moment, then he dashed out a text and put his phone back in his pocket.

What are you doing this afternoon?

Neutral, giving her an easy out, definitely more of a friendly tone than anything else, right? So why was his heart pounding waiting for her answer?

This was about work. He had to remember that.

As if the universe figured he might need some help doing so, the gate at the far end of the Cressingham Arcade creaked open and his client, Lady Cressingham herself, strode in.

Lady Cressingham was, Damon had learned over the last week or two, quite simply a force of nature. Today, she was dressed in a rich plum-coloured wool coat with a fake fur collar, matching leather gloves and shiny black boots. Her hair was perfectly set despite the winter wind, and large diamonds glittered at her throat and earlobes.

Her eyes narrowed as she approached him, the heels of her boots clacking against the tiled floor of the arcade. 'So? Any progress to report?' she asked, her clipped upper-class tones as cold as the icy weather.

Damon raised an eyebrow, and glanced surreptitiously

over his shoulder. Ah, that explained it. Old Mr Jenkins was watching them from his shop window, polishing cloth in his hands as he set out his jewellery display for the day. He was the biggest hold out to their whole plan, so Lady Cressingham always took care to be sharper, more professional, when he was watching.

In truth, their whole acquaintance had started at a party held in a top London art gallery, hosted by a mutual friend. Damon always made a point of talking to new people at events like that; just chatting with the same old crowd rarely threw up any new and interesting opportunities. When he'd spotted Lady Cressingham in her scarlet evening gown and silver wrap he'd just known she would have an interesting story—and he'd been right.

He'd never asked her age, and Wikipedia had been strangely coy on the subject, but he guessed she had to be in her sixties, if not her seventies. She'd been married to Lord Cressingham for as long as anyone could remember; the rumours were that he'd been cheating on her since their wedding day. Not just rumours, actually. Lady Cressingham had been quite open on the subject the night they'd met.

'We have an arrangement of sorts, I suppose,' she'd told Damon. 'I ignore the fact that he's a philandering son of a you-know-what who can't keep his trousers fastened, and he lets me spend his family fortune on causes that appeal to me, and to speculate on projects that have the potential to make me a lot of money, while also helping others.'

She was a jack of all trades when it came to businesses, just like himself, it turned out. Maybe that was what had drawn them together in the first place. All he knew was that a month after that party, she'd called him up out of the blue with a proposition.

'Come and run my latest project for me. I need someone with an entrepreneurial eye.'

Damon had been between projects and he'd been intrigued. And so he'd said yes.

Which was how he came to be standing in the middle of the shabby, slightly crumbling Cressingham Arcade, being glared at by an antisocial jeweller, imagining what magic Rachel could work with the window displays in this place.

Lady Cressingham was still waiting for a project update, though.

'I do have some new progress, and some new ideas to talk through with you.' His phone buzzed in his pocket. 'Excuse me one second.'

Pulling it out, he checked the screen and saw the one-word answer from Rachel.

Yes.

'In fact,' he went on, stashing his phone away again, 'if you have time for afternoon tea today, there's someone I'd like you to meet. Someone who might be the key to turning this place into everything you've been dreaming of.'

Lady Cressingham raised a sceptical eyebrow, but nodded all the same. 'Book us a table at the Ritz at three. If nothing else, I want to make the aquaintance of the woman whose text message just put that smile on your face.'

CHAPTER FIVE

RACHEL HAD LIVED in London her whole life and never been for afternoon tea at the Ritz. She supposed most people hadn't, really. It wasn't exactly an everyday occurrence. Unless you were Lady Cressingham, apparently, who seemed to know all the waiters by their first names.

She'd assumed, when Damon had told her to meet him at Piccadilly Circus, that it would just be the two of them. And she definitely hadn't imagined he'd be taking her to the Ritz. If she had, she might have worn something slightly more suitable for the occasion. Or not, because actually, now she thought about it, she wasn't sure she even owned anything suitable for taking afternoon tea with a member of the aristocracy at one of London's most famous hotels.

Maybe the dress Damon had bought her. Except she wasn't allowing herself to think about that dress, or what had happened last time she wore it.

Because this wasn't a date, or even a friendly catch-up. Or, as she'd sort of assumed, Damon's attempt to let her down gently. Last time she'd thought she was close to Damon, even without a kiss to mark the occasion, he'd made it obvious—in a kind way—that it was just a one-off. The next time he'd visited, she'd been very clearly relegated back to 'Celeste's friend,' rather than a friend of his in her own right. And she'd stayed that way until he'd kissed her two days ago.

Of course he'd want to set the record straight again. The thought had occurred to her as soon as she'd seen his text. Damon, despite his playboy reputation, was always scrupulously honest with his flings—she knew that from Celeste. He never led them on, and always made it clear up front how much—or how little—he was willing to give.

As Celeste put it, *'I understand him not wanting to get into a romantic tangle. They can be so* messy *if you aren't both straight upfront about what you're entering into, or if one of you has higher expectations than the other.'*

She made it sound more like a business arrangement than a love affair, Rachel thought, though she hadn't said that.

'But Damon doesn't even have those discussions with his girlfriends. He just tells them straight not to expect anything past one night. Anything extra is just a bonus.'

But he hadn't had a chance to tell Rachel that, so she figured he was worrying she was reading more into that midnight kiss than was really there. All the way to Piccadilly on the Tube she'd been planning the most casual way to let him know that she had absolutely no expectations of him; she knew better than that.

Except it seemed that wasn't why he'd invited her at all.

'How are you finding the cucumber sandwiches, dear?' Lady Cressingham asked her, across the table. Between them, sitting at the end of the loaded table, Damon sat devouring a scone slathered in jam and cream, apparently oblivious to the many, many questions Rachel had about this whole gathering.

'They're delicious.' She put her half-nibbled sandwich down on her plate. 'In fact, this whole spread is incredible. I'm just…wondering, well… I mean, I just wasn't sure…'

'Why Damon invited you to tea?' Lady Cressingham

finished for her, shaking her head. 'Damon, dear, I was led to understand that you were much smoother with the ladies than this.'

Rachel's eyes widened and she sat bolt upright, ready to correct the obvious mistaken assumption. 'Oh, no, Damon and I...we're old friends, that's all, really.'

Lady Cressingham looked unconvinced, but waved away Rachel's protests all the same. 'I'm not sure our Damon *has* old friends, only new ones. But in this case, I believe he's brought you here for a business proposal, rather than a personal one.' She shot an unreadable look along the table at Damon. 'At least, that's what he seems to believe.'

Confused, Rachel turned to Damon too. 'A business proposal?' How could she possibly be of use to him with one of those? She didn't even really know what his business *was*.

'Lady Cressingham has hired me to manage her latest project for her,' Damon explained. But before he could say any more, Lady Cressingham took over.

'The Cressingham Arcade,' she explained. 'It's not exactly in the most fashionable area of the city, but it's respectable enough, and it's been languishing in my husband's property portfolio for far too long. I decided it was time to make proper use of it for a change.'

'A shopping arcade?' Rachel asked, still baffled as to what her part was going to be in this.

'A small one. Set back from a reasonably busy shopping street, but currently woefully ignored by passing shoppers.' Lady Cressingham shook her head at her bite-sized lemon cake. 'Such a waste. And of course my husband has completely forgotten that he even owned it.'

How rich did a person have to be to forget that they owned a shopping arcade? Rachel could hardly imagine. She gazed around at the opulent surroundings of the Ritz restaurant and its patrons. Perhaps for a person who judged tea there as an everyday occurrence, property ownership became just as ordinary.

'It has eight shops,' Damon went on, ticking them off on his fingers as he went. 'At present, three are unoccupied, two are recently let and three have long-standing occupants. So right now there's a jeweller's, a florist's, a stationer's, a chocolate shop and a wedding dress boutique.'

'It sounds…lovely?' Rachel said, still confused as to her part in this.

'It could be,' Lady Cressingham said, dryly. 'It needs a lot of TLC, but Damon has the decorators and builders coming in for that. It needs some more tenants too, but I've got my feelers out. I only want a certain sort of business in my arcade.'

Rachel nodded. Clearly the aristocracy had standards about who they rented to. She shouldn't be surprised about that.

But Damon shot a fond smile at the older lady. 'You're giving Rachel the idea you're elitist, you know.'

Lady Cressingham drew herself up to her full seated height. Which, since her posture had been impeccable since they'd sat down, was quite an achievement. 'Well, I do have very strict criteria.'

Damon rolled his eyes. 'What she means is that she will only rent the unoccupied shops to people, usually women, looking for a fresh start in life.'

That…wasn't what Rachel had expected at all. She gave the aristocrat across the table a surprised look, which Lady Cressingham politely pretended not to see as she poured herself another cup of Assam tea.

'People need a little help sometimes, when they're starting over,' she said, stirring her cup. 'And I'm in a position to give them that. That's all.'

But she didn't have to, Rachel knew. Plenty of people had all the money in the world and only used it to make more.

And while she was sure that Lady Cressingham intended for the arcade to become a profitable business, that didn't change the fact that she wanted to do some good with it too.

Rachel still couldn't see exactly where she fitted into all this. But suddenly, she desperately wanted to know.

This could be the first step she'd been looking for, without even knowing it. She'd been so focussed on following her plodding plan—get the test results, make sure Dad was okay, move out, start thinking about new jobs—and Damon, in his usual chaotic style, had come in and ripped up the whole strategy.

But he was giving her an opportunity she hadn't even envisioned. The chance to do something that might matter to people, just a bit. That was what she needed, and she hadn't even realised it until now.

Plus, working on a new project might distract her from thinking about that kiss. That was just an added bonus.

Placing her forearms on the table, she leant forward. 'Okay. How can I help?'

Damon saw the moment when Rachel went from wanting to run away from this strange tea party to actively wanting to help. He smiled to himself as Lady Cressingham pushed the plate of scones towards her. She approved of Rachel, he could tell. He wasn't sure why that was important to him, but apparently it was.

More crucially, Rachel approved of the Cressingham Arcade project. And that really did matter to him.

He wanted to talk to her about the other night—*about that kiss*, his brain supplied, unhelpfully—but there hadn't been time between meeting her off the Tube, and meeting Lady Cressingham at the Ritz. And since he still wasn't entirely sure what he wanted to say about it, beyond apologising if he'd got the wrong message, he hadn't exactly pushed the point. Also, that uneasy feeling of being with someone who saw too deep inside him, the way she had years ago, seemed to be back and he didn't like it any more now than he had then. He needed to re-establish some boundaries, and talking about kissing definitely wasn't going to achieve that.

The personal could wait. They had business to discuss first.

'Like Lady Cressingham said, the whole place is having a bit of a do-over. We're putting in new tiles for the floors, touching up all the paintwork, having new signs painted, the works. But all that means we're not going to be able to open properly to the public until later in the month—'

'Right before Christmas,' Rachel said, grasping the problem immediately. She worried her lower lip between her teeth, in a way Damon tried to convince himself he didn't find adorable. The line between her eyebrows when she was concentrating was pretty cute too.

Focus, Damon.

'Exactly,' he said. 'Which means we're missing a lot of the prime Christmas shopping time.' Hell, it was already the third of December. They'd missed a lot of it already, but that couldn't be helped. And it wasn't as if the arcade was doing a roaring trade before they started, however much Mr Jenkins might be complaining now about the disruption.

'You need to get people talking about the arcade before it even opens,' Rachel said, thinking aloud. 'You want a buzz about the place, so people are excited to visit that first day, maybe even hold off on some of their shopping until you open.' Her eyes widened as she seemed to realise that she was telling Lady Cressingham what to do. 'I mean, that's what I'd suggest. Or what I'd do. But I'm sure you both know better than I do about these things.'

Lady Cressingham selected a miniature Victoria sponge from the cake stand. 'Actually, dear, I don't think we do. That's why Damon brought you in. So, tell me: what else would you do to make my arcade the only place anyone wants to shop this Christmas?'

Rachel hesitated. Watching her closely—not least because she was nibbling her bottom lip again and he just couldn't look away—he tried to figure out what was stopping her. She knew this stuff; he'd checked out the social media accounts for Hartbury's, and as far as he could see they were head and shoulders above what most stores were doing. People really engaged with her posts about the window displays, more than anything. Her stepmother must be thrilled at all the extra attention she was bringing in…

Her stepmother. Hartbury's. Of course.

'The arcade would be a completely different sort of business to Hartbury's,' he said, quickly. 'Different clientele too. I mean, the stores there sell personalised, one-off sort of items most of the time. Lots of handmade things too. Nothing like your stepmother's store.'

Lady Cressingham caught onto the problem promptly. 'Absolutely! We'd never ask you to undermine your family business, of course not. And Hartbury's has a very fine reputation. But I do not believe that the products sold would truly be commensurate with those sold in the Cressingham Arcade.'

Rachel gave a slow nod. 'You're right, I suppose.'

'And you did tell me the other night that you'd like to go freelance one day, doing social media and marketing for other companies,' Daman added, persuasively, he hoped. 'This could be your first step. Help you start building your portfolio.'

'Of course, we'd pay you fairly as well,' Lady Cressingham put it. 'I'm aware that we're asking a lot here, but from what Damon has told me—and showed me, online— I think you're the perfect person for this job.'

Damon hid a smile. Even Lady Cressingham had been

beyond charmed by the photos of Rachel's window displays. She'd seen instantly what he was suggesting.

'We need to bring the whole arcade together,' Damon explained, remembering that reaction. 'At the moment, they're more of a mishmash of enterprises. We need to somehow make it feel cohesive, like they belong together.'

'Like each shop is part of the bigger whole…' Rachel mused. 'You're thinking about the window displays?' she guessed.

Damon grinned. 'Of course! Between your incredible displays *and* your social media skills, plus my more traditional and modest abilities, I think we can have half of London begging to visit the Cressingham Arcade by the time we open.'

'Only half?' Lady Cressingham asked, over the rim of her teacup. 'Dear boy, I don't think you're aiming high enough.'

By the time crumbs and tealeaves were all that was left of their afternoon tea, Rachel had worked her way through fear, doubt, uncertainty and at least some of her imposter-syndrome issues, and arrived at excitement. Despite all the courses she'd taken, all the work she'd put in at Hartbury's, a part of her, deep down, had never really believed she'd be able to do this sort of thing for a real job, outside the family business.

Today, Damon had shown her that she could.

She was excited by this project, by the chance to put into practice all the ideas she'd been dreaming up that she knew her stepmother would never let her use. Excited to work towards Lady Cressingham's dream of a shopping arcade that could be beautiful, a shopping destination, a helping hand for people changing their lives *and* a viable business, all at the same time.

Excited, although she refused to admit it, even to herself, to work with Damon too.

They'd hashed out a plan between them of all the work there was to do. Quite when she was going to fit it all in, between her shifts at the department store, work on Hartbury's social media and her own Christmas preparations, Rachel wasn't entirely sure. But she *would*. Because this mattered to her.

She couldn't remember the last time something other than her father had really, really mattered to her like this.

Maybe this was what had been missing for so long. Maybe *this* was the push she needed to change her life.

'So,' Damon said as Lady Cressingham paid the bill. 'Do you want to come and see the arcade now?'

His smile was wicked, as if he were inviting her up to see his etchings. Maybe he was, in a way. This project, this opportunity, was the perfect way into her heart—or at least into her pants. Making her feel competent, talented even, and wanted. It didn't take much, did it?

'Yes. Definitely.'

But Damon hadn't even mentioned the kiss. Probably because he hadn't thought of it since it happened—while it had consumed her every waking moment.

She wasn't the kind of girl that guys like Damon wanted. Her experience with Tobias should have taught her that.

Rachel shook away her thoughts as she reached for her bag and coat. This was about more than a kiss, or an attraction anyway. This was a professional opportunity she wanted to take full advantage of.

The chance to figure out her own path in life, not just the one her family expected her to walk.

This was work. Not pleasure.

But as she moved to put her coat on, Damon took it from her and held it out for her, like a proper, old-fashioned gentleman. Swallowing, she smiled her thanks and turned to ease her arms into the sleeves. Damon assisted, lifting the coat over her shoulders and smoothing it down over her arms.

Rachel froze at the close contact. She could almost imagine he was about to wrap her up in his embrace. To hold her as close as he had when they'd danced.

For a long moment, he remained near enough that she could catch hints of his cologne, could almost feel his breath against her cheek. For that long moment, hope blossomed in her chest...

And then he stepped away.

'Come on, you two,' Lady Cressingham said, either impatience or amusement colouring her voice, Rachel wasn't entirely sure which. Maybe it was both. She didn't seem like the sort of woman to waste precious minutes only having one emotion at a time. 'I've had the car brought round.'

The Cressingham Arcade was everything Rachel had hoped it would be.

From the elegantly curving iron gates to the vintage tiled floor between the shop fronts—which Damon assured her they'd be restoring rather than replacing—it screamed refined elegance, much like Lady Cressingham herself. The shop names were a mishmash of different styles, but Damon showed her the prototype for the new ones. Each shop face would have a matching wooden sign painted in the colours taken from the floor tiles—dark forest greens, creams, duck-egg blues and hints of blush pink—with the name of the shop in a scrolling vintage font.

Between each shop rose sleek columns, tiled to match the floor, until they reached the ceiling and met as carved stone overhead, almost like a cathedral. Rachel tilted her head as far back as it would go, and imagined fairy lights illuminating every shadow up there.

And then there were the windows. The beautiful, deep

bay windows that jutted out from every storefront into the passageway that formed the arcade, each with a wooden display area inside just *begging* to be decorated. Standing there, Rachel felt a million ideas start to swirl inside her brain, and knew she'd never be short of ways to decorate or promote this magical place.

'What do you think?' Damon asked, his voice suddenly very close as he rested his chin on her shoulder to stare into the window with her.

'It's magical,' she whispered, and felt him smile.

'This is what your windows reminded me of. This place. And I just knew I had to get you involved over here, to make the arcade everything it can be.'

Warmth flooded through her at his words. Damon Hunter thought *she* was a match for this wonderful, secret place. And suddenly, she could almost believe it too.

Damon stepped away. 'Come on. I want to introduce you to some of the shopkeepers here.'

The next half an hour was a whirl of new people, more than Rachel thought she'd met in one go since university. Lady Cressingham was deep in conversation with an older gentleman at the end of the arcade so Damon started the introductions at the nearest occupied shop—a florist called Belinda, with incredible wreaths of ivy, holly, berries and such sitting on tables out front.

'Technically we're still open,' Belinda explained. 'Although you wouldn't know it from all the cones and boards out front. But I had a wreath-making class booked for today and I wasn't going to cancel it just because this one wants to spruce the place up a bit.' She jerked her head towards Damon as she said 'this one', and he rolled his eyes in response. But they were both smiling, so Rachel assumed everyone was okay with what he had planned for the place, despite the disruption.

'The wreaths are beautiful,' she said to Belinda, who

beamed proudly. 'They'd be wonderful in a window display…' She could envisage it already: a forest scene, with a wreath on every tree, lights throughout, Christmas tubs and pot plants at the base of the trees…

'Belinda always keeps the window clear,' the florist's assistant, Ursula, said as she tidied away the wreath-making supplies. 'She likes to be able to see out.'

'Oh. Right.' Rachel shot a quick glance at Damon who shrugged, as if to say, *This is what I'm dealing with. Why do you think I need you?*

Deciding to try a different tack, Rachel asked, 'It looks like the wreath-making workshop was a great success. Did you promote it on social media?'

'Oh, these are just the wreaths I made to show people what's possible,' Belinda explained. 'The four people we had in took their wreaths home with them, of course.'

'I did put the dates up on our new Facebook page,' Ursula added. 'But I don't think many people saw it. You know how it is.' She shrugged, and went back to clearing up.

Rachel quickly learned that it was the same story throughout the arcade. People were focussed on their shops, on keeping their heads above water. They didn't have time to learn the ins and outs of social media algorithms or how to build their fan base online.

That was what they needed her for.

As Damon led her out of the florist's, they discovered that most of the other shopkeepers had come out to meet her too. Rachel smiled politely, and tried hard to affix names to faces and shops in her brain, knowing that the odds of her remembering them all were slim. She'd have to get Damon to write them all down for her later. He was the people person, after all, not her.

And that had never been more evident than here. With every new arrival Damon was able to introduce them without hesitation, and tell her the basics of their work there. But more than that, he interacted with each person on a level that showed he knew their circumstances, their opinions, and remembered everything they'd ever said to him.

Rachel could barely remember her own computer password most days. Or the names of some of her seasonal co-workers. She didn't *do* people, not the way Damon did.

And with every introduction, he managed to lead the conversation around to exactly where she needed it.

'Jasmine's bridal boutique is one of the newest shops in the arcade, isn't it, Jasmine?' he said, motioning over a petite blonde woman in a pastel-pink jumper. 'She's keen to convince London's brides that she's got the perfect dress for them—which means getting the message out to the world that *her* boutique has the unique dresses that others just don't.'

'We only stock smaller designers,' Jasmine explained. 'And I design bespoke gowns for brides too.'

'So this is where to come if you want a wedding dress that doesn't look like everyone else's?'

'Exactly!' Jasmine said, beaming.

Rachel filed that information away in the part of her brain that was already planning everything she could do for the shopping arcade. Information, she could remember. It was people she struggled with.

But the people were what was going to make Cressingham Arcade special, she could feel it.

CHAPTER SIX

BY THE TIME Damon had finished introducing Rachel to all the occupants of the Cressingham Arcade—right down to the ornery Mr Jenkins, who grumbled through the whole meeting about not agreeing with all this modern stuff—the sun had long gone down. The shops were all shut up and the shopkeepers departed for home. Even Lady Cressingham had left. Apart from a few sad-looking fairy lights outside the florist's shop, the arcade was almost in darkness, the glow of the moon and the streetlights outside only just penetrating the gloom.

'I should probably get going,' Rachel said, glancing at the backlit screen of her phone and checking the time. 'It's getting late.'

He should let her go, Damon knew. She was right, it *was* late. And it wasn't as if he didn't have more work to do. And yet...

'Wait here a moment.' Dashing back into the small office at the far end of the arcade, Damon pulled out two torches from the well-stocked emergency drawer, then shut and locked the office behind him.

'We couldn't just turn some lights on?' Rachel asked as he handed her the torch.

He grinned. 'It's more fun this way.'

The arcade looked so different at night, something he'd

discovered over late nights working in the office, planning out the renovations and scheduling the work. Without the modern lighting, and with the streets outside quietening, it was almost as if they'd travelled back in time—back two hundred years or more, to when the arcade was first built.

'So where are we going?' Rachel asked, turning on her torch and shining it around the tiled floors.

'We're staying right here,' Damon explained. 'I want to show you the other side of the arcade. Not the every-day shopping one that everyone sees. The magical, after-hours one.'

'I'd like to see that.' Even in the pale torchlight, her smile was unmissable. It warmed Damon's heart, despite the chill of the winter air. There was mischief in that smile, and a love of life that he had rarely ever seen from Rachel before.

Apart from when I kissed her.

He pushed down the memory. 'Come on, then.' Grabbing her hand, he led her to the far end of the arcade, to start his after-hours tour.

'Down here, we have one of my favourite details of the whole arcade,' he announced grandly. Then he shone his torchlight on the spot in question, a bit of wall just above the floor.

Rachel crouched down to get a closer look, jumped back a little, then laughed—just as Damon had hoped she would.

'Someone painted a mouse and a mouse hole on the wall?' She stood up again, and he moved his light so he could see her face. She looked utterly charmed by the detail.

He nodded. 'Nobody knows when—could have been decades ago, to be honest, or possibly even when the place was built, although I suspect the paint would need to have been touched up from time to time.'

'But why would they do it?' she asked. 'I mean, is it vandalism or whimsy?'

'I figured it was like the mice in your window, actually,'

Damon replied. 'A little surprise for those who look deeper. That's not the only one, either.'

'There are more?' Rachel's eyes were wide in the torch-light. 'Can we see them all?'

How could he refuse her when she looked so delighted at the prospect? 'Of course. Come this way, milady.'

They found four more mice at ground level and Rachel was so thrilled he probably could have stopped there. But he wanted to keep that smile on her face, that wonder in her eyes. She was falling for this arcade the same way he had. Well, maybe not quite the same way—he'd been more enamoured by the business potential first, then the people, then the whimsical discoveries he'd made as he'd explored the place. He could tell that Rachel had seen the potential this afternoon, talking with the shopkeepers, seen how much of a difference she could make here. This creature treasure hunt was only cementing that.

'Is that all of them?' she asked as he led her back to where they'd started.

'Not quite.' He was holding her hand again, Damon realised. When had that happened? Or had he never let it go? No, he must have done, because she'd moved away to trace the outlines of the mice they'd found right by the front gate. Which meant he'd reached out and taken her hand again— or she'd taken his.

It made sense, in the darkness. It was practical, that was all. But still, now he was aware of it, he couldn't ignore the tingling sensation her fingers, intertwined in his, gave him. Or how natural it felt.

He wasn't a hand-holding kind of guy, never had been. The women he tended to take out might hold onto his arm, more for balance or support in their uncomfortable shoes than anything else, he suspected. But they never held hands. That was too…intimate. Somehow more so than taking a woman home to bed.

But Rachel was holding his hand as if it was the most natural thing in the world. And weirdly, it felt as if it was.

'Where are we going?' she asked as he opened a door that was hidden between two tiled pillars, and painted to look like an extension of the walls.

'Up,' he replied, cryptically.

The curving metal staircase clanked under their feet, the sound echoing off the walls of the silent arcade. At the top, Damon fiddled with the latch on a second hidden door, pushed it open, then stepped back to let Rachel through first.

He could sense her nerves, her uncertainty of walking into the unknown, but he knew it would be worth it for her. Squeezing her hand, he let go, and she stepped out onto the small wrought-iron balcony. Shining the torch out beyond her, to the ceiling of the arcade, he waited.

'Oh!' Rachel gasped, and turned back to face him, her hand over her mouth and delight in her eyes. 'Look at them!' She grasped the metal rail of the balcony and leant out, just a little, her chin tilted upwards as she stared at the ceiling. 'How did I not see them from the ground?'

'They're hidden in the pattern.' Damon stepped closer behind her, looking upwards to take in the painted butterflies scattered around the ceiling. 'From the floor, it just looks like an attractively painted ceiling. But from here...'

'It comes to life,' she breathed, finishing his sentence for him. Above them, intricately decorated butterflies almost seemed to flutter around the archways and shadows of the arcade. 'It's like the houses in my window.'

'Exactly.' It was what had made him think of Rachel, of bringing her in. The moment he'd seen the tiny mice living their secret lives in her window displays, out of sight of the adults hurrying past, he'd known that she was meant to be here at the Cressingham Arcade, with the mice and the butterflies. And him.

She spun around suddenly, catching him by surprise, and he wrapped an arm around her waist instinctively, in case she lost her balance on the narrow balcony. She didn't, of course, but now she was pressed almost against him, so close he could feel the warmth of her breath against his neck as she looked up at him. Her eyes were luminous in the faint light from the torch he now held at the small of her back, and her lips were slightly parted. They looked soft and inviting and… He was thinking about kissing her. Again.

'Thank you for bringing me here,' Rachel whispered, and hearing the hoarseness in her voice he wondered if she was thinking about it too. If maybe he wasn't the only one remembering how it had felt that night on the dance floor, her mouth under his… 'For showing me this, I mean. It's very special.'

So are you, he thought, but didn't say it.

She was his sister's best friend. Celeste would never forgive him if he seduced Rachel, not even if she wanted to be seduced. Not when he had nothing to offer her beyond a few nights in bed together.

Rachel deserved more than that. He'd known that much since he'd first met her, and only had it cemented when he'd spent a whole night talking with her. Rachel was special. Anyone who could put up with Celeste as a best friend deserved a medal, at the very least. But more than that, she deserved love.

And Damon couldn't give her that. So…

'I thought you'd like it.' He stepped back, letting go of her waist. It seemed harder, this time, than it had when he was eighteen.

That night, he'd known that if he'd kissed her, she'd have fallen into his arms. But he'd also known that one night with her wouldn't have been enough—for either of them. And he didn't do more than one night. So he'd pulled away, just like now.

If she was disappointed, she didn't show it. Instead, she nodded vigorously. 'I do. Not just the hidden animals...the whole arcade. I can already see how magical it could be—*will* be, I hope.'

'So you'll help Lady Cressingham and me with the project?'

She met his gaze with her own excited one and something caught in his chest again as she answered. Something somewhere in the vicinity of his heart.

'I will.'

Rachel covered a yawn with her hand as she waited for the staff meeting to begin. There was still an hour before the department store opened, which meant it was far too early to be dealing with the crowds of staff pouring in, especially without coffee.

And especially given the late night she'd had the night before.

Her hand hid her smile too, for which she was grateful when she looked up and realised her stepsister Gretchen was watching her, eyes narrowed with curiosity...or mistrust. Probably still smarting after watching Rachel disappear with Damon earlier in the week for the TV studio. And Gretchen had definitely been suspicious when she'd skipped out early on the end of her shift the day before. Rachel had merely said she needed to meet someone—not that she was having afternoon tea at the Ritz, of all places—but even that was unusual enough to raise Gretchen's curiosity.

Her family weren't used to Rachel going places or seeing people. To be honest, Rachel wasn't used to it either. But it looked as if they might all have to grow accustomed to it.

She yawned again and saw Gretchen turn to whisper something to Maisie. Neither of the girls really worked on the shop floor, exactly, but both offered their skills as personal shoppers, and were especially popular at this time of year, when everyone was looking for Christmas party outfits. Rachel knew they were only at the meeting because Hannah insisted on it. She liked to emphasise the family nature of the business as much as possible—and loved it when Rachel showcased the girls in her social media posts for just that reason.

It was also why she took at least one of the staff meetings each week herself, to remind her employees—long term or seasonal—that they were all one big happy family. A family that was expected to work overtime without extra pay, but still family.

At the front of the room, Hannah clapped her hands together and called the meeting to order. The last of the errant staff members edged into the room, letting the door bang closed behind them as she began to speak.

'Good morning, everyone, and thank you for another week's hard work!' She threw a meaningful look at her daughters and the two of them started applauding, the rest of the staff following suit after a few moments. 'Now, the rota for next week's shifts is already up on the system, and I have a printout on the wall over there.' She waved a hand at a spot of wall just behind Rachel.

Gosh, she must have been tired not to notice it there. Usually Rachel relied on the electronic schedule to tell her when she needed to be on the shop floor since she was usually in the building most days anyway, doing the other parts of her job. But after the late night with Damon she'd forgotten to check it since the new rota went up. Now she craned her neck backwards to find her name—and almost let her chair tip over backwards.

What had happened? Normally she only put in occasional shifts on the shop floor, but this week she'd been put down to work there every day. How on earth was she supposed to work at the Cressingham Arcade, do all her social media work for Hartbury's *and* put in so much time behind a till? It simply wasn't going to work.

She had to make a choice.

Did she continue life as normal, here at Hartbury's, and give up on the arcade? Or did she speak out and ask for something different?

When was the last time she had asked her family for something, rather than the other way round? She couldn't remember. And wasn't that kind of sad, now she thought about it?

She'd always tried to keep the peace. Even when it became clear that the Big Family Experiment her father had signed them up for wasn't the happy families scenario he'd hoped for. He tried so hard to keep all of them on the same page, all getting along, that she'd always felt she had to do the same too. For him.

For her mum, who'd made them promise to look after each other, as she lay dying. Leaving them.

For the dad she remembered from before, when she was little and life was magical.

For herself, even, because it was easier to keep her head down and fade into the background than stretch her head above the parapet and get it chopped off. Metaphorically speaking.

Keeping the peace had become the default—even more so since Dad's health problems had started. The mild heart attack he'd experienced had been the culmination of years of him 'just not feeling right'. The same way her mum had felt 'off' for months before the diagnosis that had changed their lives and stolen her away.

Rachel had been so focussed on making sure her dad was okay that she'd forgotten to even think about what she needed. She'd put off all her own plans—moving out, changing careers—out of fear that he might go downhill as rapidly as her mum had.

But he hadn't. She'd started to think about moving on—until last summer's heart attack had sent her spiralling back again. So now, years after she started worrying about his health, she was still in the same holding pattern, waiting for the next set of test results before she made a move.

Sitting there in another staff meeting, just like all the others, Rachel admitted the truth to herself: there'd be another round of tests after this one. Another reason to be worried about leaving her dad. Another excuse to put off spreading her wings and chasing her own dreams—if she could even decide what they were.

There would *always* be an excuse.

But there might not be another opportunity like the one Damon was offering her. If she wanted it, she had to change things to take it. She had to risk disturbing the hard-earned family peace for once.

She wasn't even asking for much. Just to have a life, and a career, away from the family business. That wasn't unreasonable, was it? Given all the unpaid extra time she put in at Hartbury's anyway, surely she'd earned some time off this festive season.

She just had to gather her courage and ask for it.

The worst they can say is no, right?

'As ever, if you have any questions or issues with the rota—' Hannah started, and Rachel suddenly made her decision, thrusting her hand up into the air before she could change her mind. 'Rachel?'

'I, uh…' And now she was remembering all the other worse things than them saying no. The pitying looks her stepsisters were giving her, the assumption that she was about to make a fool of herself somehow in front of everybody. How, she had no idea, and probably they didn't either. But it was the same look they'd given her every time she'd ventured an opinion or tried to change something about her little life, ever since she was a teenager.

The same look she'd seen in everyone's eyes last summer when Gretchen's friend Tobias had laughed and told their group that he'd only ever shown interest in her as a joke, or out of pity. Even though she'd known the truth—and also known that he'd never admit it.

'Yes?' Hannah said, impatiently. 'Is this important, or can we discuss it later?'

'I'm down for a shift every day next week, but I'm afraid I have other commitments.' The words came out all in a rush, and Rachel could feel the heat in her cheeks. Which was ridiculous. She was merely asking for a change to the rota, not an invitation to a royal ball.

It was interesting how similar Hannah, Gretchen and Maisie all looked when they each raised their eyebrows in that same look of disbelief.

'"Other commitments"?' Hannah repeated. 'Darling, I'm sure whatever else you have planned can't be more important than our team effort here to make this the best Christmas season Hartbury's has ever seen.' There was a desultory sort of cheer from the staff at that, mostly led by Maisie, as far as Rachel could tell. 'Now, moving on—'

'I was just wondering if there was anyone who would like to switch shifts with me,' Rachel interrupted, her voice wavering a little. 'Someone who might need them more than me.' That made it sound more like a team effort, right?

'Actually…' Across the room, another hand went up. 'I did ask if I could pick up some extra shifts between now and Christmas, but I've only got two shifts next week.'

Rachel spun around to beam at the woman, a seasonal worker, she thought, who had spoken. 'Perfect, then! We can swap!'

At the front of the room, Hannah was glowering at them both. But she couldn't very well object without making a scene, Rachel knew.

'If we've all quite finished messing around with my rota?' she said, her voice sharp. 'Let's get on.'

Smiling to herself, Rachel settled back down in her chair. She'd asked for what she wanted, and she'd got it.

She just hoped her family didn't show too much interest in exactly what her other commitments were.

Damon looked up the few steps to the familiar door of the London town house and sighed.

'Once a month,' he muttered to himself. 'It's only once a month. How bad can it be?'

The black door opened and his sister stuck her head out. 'Are you coming in? Or are you abandoning me to suffer the disappointment and disapproval of our parents alone this month?'

She sounded cheerful enough despite her words so Damon could only assume that the drinks trolley was out at least.

'I'm coming.' Reluctantly, he climbed the steps and shut the door behind him. Shrugging off his coat, he hung it in the small cupboard at the bottom of the stairs, the action firing his memories of doing the same thing a thousand times before—stretching up to try and reach the hooks as a small child, Celeste laughing at him as she reached them easily.

The house was full of memories. A whole childhood's full.

And how he hated reliving any of them.

'Damon. You're late.' His mother pressed a distracted kiss to his cheek as he entered the kitchen.

Handing over the two bottles of wine he'd brought, one white and one red, Damon apologised. 'Sorry. What delights await us at the table today?'

Diana Hunter rolled her eyes. 'Your father is in charge of the main course this month, so he's banished me from the kitchen for most of the day. I've only just been allowed in to check on my dessert. I had to make it yesterday, and of course your sister has brought her starter from home. She's made some sort of salmon terrine, I believe. And I've been experimenting with a walnut and stilton cheesecake—a sort of amalgam of pudding and cheese course in one.'

It sounded foul, although Damon didn't share the thought. And Celeste *knew* he hated salmon. Which made him wonder why she'd picked it; normally it was the two of them against the older generation at these events. If she'd taken against him he was doomed.

He had a horrible suspicion that she must have been talking to Rachel.

'None of them will hold a candle to my pièce de résistance!' Jacob Hunter, broad-chested and booming, emerged from the dining room looking triumphant. 'I am most certain to take the crown, not just this month, but for the whole year, with my main course.'

Because naturally, the monthly family Sunday lunch was a competition, just like everything else in their lives. A chance to prove that they were brighter, better, than each other. At the university, his parents competed academically, Celeste striving to keep up, to surpass them, to show them that she was as clever, as accomplished, as they were. His sister had never realised, in her twenty-eight years, that their parents were simply too busy focussing on their own achievements to ever really appreciate those of their children.

Damon, on the other hand, had realised young that he'd never be the academic genius they expected, or even the sort of person who could focus his talent into a lifelong goal or project. So he'd stopped trying to compete altogether.

He followed his own path instead, one that twisted and

splintered as he followed every passing interest, using his entrepreneurial brain to take on varied projects that kept his interest and his bank balance high.

And every month he brought the wine to family dinner, rather than succumbing to the ongoing contest to produce the most interesting dish of the month. Never even the tastiest, just the most interesting.

Salmon terrine was as boring as it got. He was definitely in trouble with Celeste.

His sister reappeared from the dining room also, giving him a knowing look as he passed her. The table, decorated by Celeste as the person in charge of starters this month, was festooned with candles and golden platters, while what sounded like harp music played through the speaker in the corner.

Damon frowned, trying to put his finger on the theme.

'I was going for Tudor,' Celeste said, eyeing her handiwork. 'But I got distracted at the last minute by a call from Rachel and didn't have time to pick up all the trimmings I wanted.'

A call from Rachel. Well, that wasn't going to be good.

Fortunately, Celeste didn't have time to press the point because at that moment their parents arrived, both in period costume—different periods, but still—and their dad rang the gong to begin dinner.

Damon pushed his salmon terrine around his plate, shredding it into smaller and smaller pieces to hide under the toast crumbs and token salad Celeste had provided, while the rest of the family talked about research papers they'd read, who was in line for the head of faculty position at the university, which professors had already lined up students for their summer archaeological digs, who had got the coveted funding for their latest research... Damon tuned it all out. It was another world to him, one he'd never wanted to belong to.

In the Hunter family, like any family, love was supposed to be unconditional. If asked if they loved their children equally, Damon was pretty sure his parents would look surprised at the very question, and say that of course they did. And maybe, in the abstract, that was true. But in practice…

Love wasn't an abstract emotion, that was what his childhood had taught him. It wasn't something a person said they felt and that was enough to make it true. Love was what a person did, every day. It was attention given, it was focus. Love was when a person cared more about another person than whatever had previously been important in their own life.

He'd seen it with friends, acquaintances. The moment they had a child, or met the love of their life, their previous existence just fell away. Especially when it came to kids. What they'd wanted before suddenly wasn't as important as what their child needed.

Somehow, Diana and Jacob Hunter must have missed that memo.

They'd ticked 'getting married' and 'having children' off their to-do lists early, then gone back to focussing on what they really cared about: their research and their academic careers. And when Celeste had followed in their footsteps they'd been thrilled, totting the child genius around archaeological sites, or to lectures at the British Museum. They'd guided her career and, as long as her path matched the one they thought she should be taking, all had been well.

Damon, meanwhile, had always known he couldn't match up. So he hadn't even tried.

Starters over, they all marked their meal scorecard with their score—Damon gave it a two, because at least the toast had been nice—then sat back to wait for Jacob to return with the main course.

'I saw some of that festive TV show you were associated with, Celeste,' Diana said, her frown disapproving over the fluttering of what he assumed was an authentic replica of a regency fan, to match her dress.

'Uh…really? Where did you see that?' Because of course their parents didn't have anything as pedestrian as a television in their house. Celeste reached across the table for the wine bottle and refilled her mother's glass, as well as her own. Clearly stalling for time. Damon stretched out his legs under the table, crossed his arms over his chest, and waited to see how his sister would talk her way out of this one.

'A colleague sent me a web link to a clip from it.' Diana's fan fluttered a little faster, even as Damon's smile grew. Finding out that Celeste was taking part in a low-brow, populist TV quiz was one thing. Finding out from a colleague was far worse, because that meant that Other People Knew. People who mattered to his parents.

No matter that the colleague probably thought it was a bit of festive fun. The Professors Hunter didn't *do* fun—at least, not when it came to things that mattered, like history or archaeology, their respective specialist subjects.

'Um, which part?' Celeste asked, desperately.

'You, arguing with some gameshow host about how Christmas trees came to be a British tradition.'

Damon couldn't hold in his laughter any more. The argument had been awkward to watch in filming, but through some genius editing the show that had aired two nights before had made it far more entertaining. The whole half-hour quiz show had basically dissolved into Theo and Celeste bickering about festive traditions, and it seemed that social media had lapped it up—in the usual, hyper-critical way.

'That link is everywhere, Mum,' he said, earning himself a glare from his sister. 'Have you seen what they're saying about it on Twitter?' He leaned across the table towards Celeste. 'Did you *really* have a make-up lunch with Theo yesterday? The whole of social media is aflame, wondering what's going on between you two.' His favourite conspiracy theory was that Celeste and Theo had been secretly dating for months, and the show just happened to catch a lover's tiff on film. While Damon knew for a fact that wasn't the case, it amused him nonetheless to imagine poor Theo actually *dating* his sister.

Celeste's cheeks flared red, which was an unexpected bonus. He didn't believe there was anything between his sister and the TV star. But the fact that the very idea embarrassed her, well, that suggested a lot of entertaining sibling teasing in his future.

But Celeste rallied quickly. 'Never mind my lunch. Did you *really* take Rachel for afternoon tea at the Ritz?'

'It was for work!' He needed to nip this one in the bud if he wanted to get out of Sunday lunch without a lecture from his big sister. 'She's helping out on my latest project.'

Diana turned her frown on him instead, leaving Celeste smiling smugly. 'Isn't Rachel an English graduate? How is she going to help with your…what was it? Cinema project?'

Of course the only achievement of Rachel's that registered with his mother was her academic one, even though she'd graduated seven years ago. 'The cinema project was two years ago,' was all he said. 'This is a new one.' There was no point explaining to them about the Cressingham Arcade. It just wouldn't register as important, being outside the academic world that mattered so much to them.

Celeste, however, was biting her lower lip—a sure sign that she was thinking. Damon hated it when his sister started thinking; it usually got him into trouble.

'Just…be careful with Rachel, please? I'd hate for you to, well, give her any ideas.'

Like by, say, kissing her? He didn't need Celeste to get him in trouble. He was doing fine by himself.

'It's work,' he repeated, more for his own benefit than hers. 'That's all.'

'Good. Because, to be honest, I think she's always had a bit of a crush on you. I'd hate for you to lead her on, even accidentally.'

A crush? On him? Damon had no idea where Celeste had got that impression from. Even after that night they'd spent hanging out together at university, Rachel had never treated him as anything but her best friend's little brother, rolling her eyes at his escapades the same way Celeste did.

But Celeste knew Rachel better than anyone. And if she was right…

Memories of that kiss crashed through him again, this time with a little more hope than he'd allowed himself until now.

'Just don't break her heart, okay? I know what you're like.' Celeste's words brought that hope plummeting down to the ground again. She was right; that *was* what he was like. Not intentionally, of course. But he wasn't the committed sort—just look at his career, jumping from one thing to the next. His love life was even worse. He didn't *want* to commit himself to anything, to give up the freedom to follow his whims and desires.

Whereas Rachel…she wasn't like him. She'd worked for the family business her whole life, until he came along and dragged her to Cressingham Arcade. She built perfect worlds inside her windows, with perfect mice families living perfect, normal lives.

And that was something he couldn't for a moment let her believe he was capable of giving. Wasn't that why he'd kept away from her before now?

The double doors to the dining room swung open and his father appeared, the white of his Roman-style toga backlit by the hallway bulbs against the dim candlelight on the table. In his arms was a large platter with what looked like an entire pig on it, apple in mouth and all, surrounded by jellies with apple slices and spices inside.

'Dinner is served!' Jacob announced, holding the platter high, a smug smile on his face.

Damon sank back in his chair and tried not to think about Rachel.

CHAPTER SEVEN

'WHERE ARE WE GOING?' Rachel asked as she hurried to keep up with Damon's long-legged stride along the busy London street.

'Research trip,' he answered, shortly. Which told her next to nothing at all.

They were miles away from the Cressingham Arcade—in fact, all the way down in South Kensington. As lovely as their arcade was, she couldn't really imagine that the shops there would suddenly start echoing the style—or the prices—of South Ken. So why were they there?

Unless…

One last turn and Damon came to a halt at the V&A in front of a large sign advertising its Victorian Christmas events. Suddenly things started to make sense.

'You want us to put on a Victorian-style Christmas at the Cressingham Arcade?' Rachel could just imagine all the historical inaccuracies Celeste would probably pick up on if they tried.

Damon shrugged. 'It was just an idea. I thought it might give you some inspiration for the window displays.'

He was right. Already, ideas were starting to swirl around in her brain. And who but Celeste really cared if window displays weren't one hundred per cent historically accurate? People knew what a classic Victorian Christmas looked like in their imagination, and that was what she needed to tap into. As long as it *looked* suitably vintage, that was enough. It was the perfect theme to tie all the windows of the arcade together, *and* link up to the building's Victorian origins.

She grabbed Damon's arm and dragged him towards the entrance. 'Come on. I want to see!'

The Victoria and Albert Museum had graced South Kensington's Cromwell Road since 1857, back when it was just the South Kensington Museum. Its name had been changed in 1899, when Queen Victoria herself had officially laid the foundation stone for the new building, in what turned out to be her last official public appearance. Not only was the museum named after the Queen and her Prince Consort, but it dated firmly from their era too. So it was, Rachel decided after reading all this in the information leaflet outside the museum, only right that it should host its own pop-up Victorian Christmas events over the festive season.

They stepped through the gracefully arched doorway into the entrance hall where they were immediately greeted by two women in Victorian period dress. Bonnets, bustles, gloves and all. One carried a basket filled with what looked like Christmas cards. Rachel took one, and opened it to find it full of festive facts of the sort she was sure her best friend would either enjoy or argue with.

'Huh. Did you know that the first Christmas card was sent by the founding director of the V&A, Henry Cole, in 1843?' she asked, reading from the card.

Damon smirked. 'I did not. And I imagine Theo didn't either, until Celeste argued with him about it on screen last week.'

Rachel groaned at the memory of the filming. 'Did you know she had lunch with him on Saturday?'

'Did she tell you that or did you see it on social media?' Damon asked.

'Both.' She'd had a long, weird phone call with her best friend that evening, trying to unravel the confusion of Celeste's sudden acquaintance with Theo—and Rachel's with Damon. She wasn't sure either of them was making much more sense just yet.

But then they turned to enter the John Madejski garden, a rectangular outdoor space in the centre of the museum, with a small lake in the middle, and Rachel forgot all about Celeste, mesmerised by the sight in front of her instead.

The whole quadrangle had been sent back in time, transformed into a Victorian London Christmas market. There were wooden stalls, chestnuts roasting, mulled wine sellers—all in period costume, of course—and vintage entertainment for the kids at the far end. The stalls were selling everything from wooden toys to Christmas crackers.

'The department store of its day?' Damon murmured, as she stared around her, wide eyed.

'I think they might have had department stores already back then,' she whispered back. 'But I like this more.'

'Me too.' He flashed her a quick grin. 'Come on. Let's go and explore.'

Maybe it was the period surroundings, but it felt perfectly natural to take Damon's arm when he offered it. As if she were some kind of Victorian gentlewoman, with hat and fur stole, taking a turn around the quad with her beau—rather than the truth: that she was a scruffy, single twentysomething, with a bobble hat pulled down over her curls and wearing mittens that unbuttoned into fingerless gloves. Her jeans, boots and festive sweater were hardly anything a Victorian lady would be caught dead in, and she'd been meaning to replace her duffle coat for the past two winters, but every time she tried on new coats her stepsisters decided to help so she always abandoned the idea.

But if she didn't really fit into this world, she couldn't help but see Damon as part of it. Sure, he wasn't wearing a hat or carrying a cane or whatever it was Victorian gentlemen would have done. And his hair was probably a little longer than would have been acceptable, just starting to curl over the tops of his ears, and waving over his forehead. But his smart black woollen coat and grey scarf, the suit underneath it, the shoes that somehow still looked polished despite the muck and mush of London's streets after half an inch of snow the night before, they all screamed gentleman.

Rachel had no idea what he was doing here with her.

Well, except for his job, of course. This wasn't about her, it was about the Cressingham Arcade, and how they were going to put it on the map. She had to focus on that.

Celeste had said as much when they'd spoken over the weekend. Rachel had been burbling on about the Cressingham Arcade and what Damon was trying to do there and how she was going to be involved and, even though she'd tried to keep her conversation work focused, there must have been something in her voice. Maybe she had said Damon's name too many times, or in a too specific way. A not work way. Because Celeste had heard everything she wasn't saying, no matter how hard she had worked at not saying it.

'Rach…you know what my brother's like, right? I mean, I think it's great you've found *something* to be excited about, something more interesting than your stepmother's shop. Just be careful, yeah? Make sure it's the work you're excited about, not Damon.'

Because Damon would never be interested in anyone like her. She knew that, better than anyone. She'd laughed off her friend's concerns, reassured her that she knew *exactly* what Damon was like, and she wasn't stupid enough to even fantasise about getting involved with someone like that, thanks.

She wasn't sure Celeste had believed her. She wasn't sure she believed herself.

Not after that kiss. Or the mice and the butterflies and that moment on the balcony...

She shook her head, and tried to refocus on the Victorian market as they paused in front of a small group of carol singers, looking like the image from the front of a Christmas card.

Both of those occasions had happened in the dark, at night. Maybe that was what made the difference. Anything seemed possible in the darkness, didn't it?

It was daytime now, and she was seeing clearly again.

Time to focus, Rachel.

She turned back to the carollers and thought about window displays—and definitely not about Damon's lips on hers.

Rachel was totally engrossed by the carol singers. Damon smiled as he watched her focussed stare, her slight frown enough to put one of the choristers in the front row off her line, not that Rachel had noticed. He almost hated to disturb her focus.

He wondered what she was thinking as she listened. Or what she was visualising. A new window display, perhaps? One with carol singers? That could work. Or maybe he should see if he could hire these guys to sing at the reopening. That would definitely go down well with Lady Cressingham, at least. She was a big music fan, he'd learned, although he suspected their tastes differed somewhat. He'd dated an opera singer once, but that was about as close as he'd got to a love of classical music.

Damon touched Rachel's elbow lightly and, when she looked up at him, gestured towards the stall next to them, which was selling hot chocolates and other treats. Her eyes lit up and she nodded so he left her to enjoy the music and joined the queue for drinks instead.

He wasn't entirely sure what had prompted him to invite Rachel to join him on this expedition today. In truth, she wasn't joining him at all. There was pretty much no chance he'd have come here in the first place if it weren't for her. And it wasn't as if he didn't have a mountain of other work to do that wasn't going to magically happen through the power of hot chocolate.

And yet. Here he was.

He'd spotted an article about the event online while catching up on the business news that morning, and just like that he'd abandoned his whole schedule for the day. Luckily, the schedule had been pretty light in the first place, and didn't involve moving any actual meetings—just a phone call that his virtual assistant had pushed back a few hours. But still.

Damon knew he had a reputation for being spontaneous, for acting on whims and not getting tied down to one project, one person, one future. And that reputation was well earned, he wouldn't even try to deny it. But he also knew he wouldn't have been so successful in his career if he couldn't stick with a project through to the end, if he didn't honour his business commitments, show up on time, and prove himself reliable within the context of his work. His family might not see it, his fleeting girlfriends might not appreciate it, but his business was one thing he *was* committed to.

And he'd blown it off to take Rachel Charles to a Victorian Christmas market.

Shuffling forward one more place in the queue, he tried to cut himself a break. *Technically*, this was work. He was working with a colleague to find the best way to promote Cressingham Arcade, exactly as he was contracted to do.

Nobody, not even Lady Cressingham, could find a way to object to that, surely?

Except, when he'd seen Lady Cressingham at the arcade that morning, just arriving as he left the small office, she'd raised her eyebrows and given him a knowing look when he'd confessed where he'd be spending the afternoon. And of course he didn't *need* to be here. He could have just told Rachel the event was happening and let her attend on her own.

Damon glanced back over at where Rachel was watching the carol singers, her dark curls escaping from underneath her cream bobble hat, her arms wrapped around herself, wearing that adorable green duffle coat. She probably didn't care if he was here or not. But that wasn't the point.

The point was, he'd *wanted* to bring her.

He'd wanted to see her eyes light up as she spotted the market, wanted to hear her waffle on about the first ever Christmas card, and where the tradition of Christmas trees really came from. The exact same information he'd automatically tune out if Celeste were imparting it, he happily absorbed and discussed with Rachel. Why?

'Sir? Hot chocolate?' Damon blinked, and realised he'd reached the front of the queue. The girl behind the counter had an edge in her voice that suggested it wasn't the first time she'd asked.

'Yes, please. Two. With marshmallows. And cream. And, well, everything, please.' He handed over a twenty-pound note with his patented charming smile and watched as the server's hostility melted away.

If only it were as easy with Rachel.

Oh, it wasn't that she was actively hostile to him—she never had been, not even when he *knew* she was disapproving of his antics when he had visited them in university. Rachel wasn't really the hostile sort. She just…faded into the background, and let the world happen around her instead. Had he ever realised that before? He wasn't sure. It seemed to him that throughout their whole acquaintance, Rachel had just sort of been there, never drawing attention to herself, never making a fuss, never speaking up, not when Celeste or her family or even Damon himself was there to do it for her.

He'd never really paid her much attention, except as his sister's best friend. Apart from that one night when they talked until the sun came up.

And that was why, he admitted to himself. That was why he'd pushed her to the sidelines of his mind the same way she kept to the sidelines at parties. Because it was too easy to open up to Rachel, too easy to let her in. Too easy to fall for her.

So he'd kept away. Until now.

What had changed? The obvious answer was that he'd kissed her, Damon supposed. Except he'd kissed a hell of a lot of women, and never once had it compelled him to take them to a Victorian Christmas market before. Or show them all his favourite secret places at Cressingham Arcade under the cover of darkness.

And anyway, he knew it hadn't started with that kiss. It had started hours before that. With a dress, a window and a mouse.

He could pinpoint precisely the moment he stopped forcing himself to see Rachel as nothing more than a quiet extension of his sister. It wasn't when he had realised her stepsisters were trying to humiliate her, so he'd bought her the dress. It wasn't even when he had seen her in that dress and thought how bloody gorgeous she was. It was in between.

It was the moment he'd bent down to look in that shop window and seen a whole hidden world, one that Rachel had created and only shared with those willing to look a little deeper, a little longer.

And he'd been looking deeper and longer at her ever since. He couldn't stop himself any more. Those damn mice had broken down a wall he'd spent the best part of a decade building higher.

He'd spent days thinking about Rachel and that dress, that kiss, that moment on the balcony looking at the butterflies…and he wasn't an inch closer to knowing what to do about it. Especially since he didn't know what *she* wanted him to do about it.

If it was anybody else, he'd ask her outright. But Rachel wasn't just anybody. And for all he knew, actually asking her if she wanted him to kiss her again would only make the situation worse, especially if he embarrassed her or flustered her. She wasn't like the usual women he dated, and he was at a loss to know how to handle her.

Except for the fact that he knew he had to be careful. Not just of her heart, but of his too.

He wasn't about to change his whole life and philosophy just because Rachel Charles made cute window displays. Or even because she kissed like his dreams and because he loved listening to her talk.

It was too easy to let Rachel into his mind, and his heart. It might be hard to get her out again when he wanted to go back to his real life, once this project was over.

Telling the server to keep the change—and earning himself a genuine smile in the process—Damon took the two cups of hot chocolate, laden with chocolate shavings, marshmallows and a lot of whipped cream, and headed back to where he'd left Rachel. She'd barely moved, he realised, still mesmerised by the music. Or so he assumed, until he got close enough to realise that she was muttering to herself under her breath.

He knew he shouldn't listen. That he should tell her he was there. But then, Damon had never been very good at doing what he *should* do.

He edged closer, just enough to make out the words as the carollers finished one song and prepared to break into another.

'Do not read anything into the fact he's buying you a hot chocolate. This is work. It's just cold and he's nice. That's all. Do *not* read anything into it.'

Huh.

Maybe he wasn't the only one who'd been obsessing over the last week…

And maybe, just maybe, if he was careful, he might be able to find a way to do something about that. Before he drove himself crazy.

'Hot chocolate?' He smiled as Rachel spun around, horror in her wide eyes, careful to give her no sign at all that he'd overheard her personal pep talk. Instead, he held out the cup and she took it, the horror giving way to wariness, then a smile that made his pulse tick just a little faster as she spotted the whipped cream and toppings.

'Thanks.' Her voice was warm in the freezing air, a little husky even. Sexy. Damon couldn't help but imagine some of the other ways he could make her sound like that, given half the chance.

But not yet, he reminded himself, as Rachel turned back to listen to the carollers begin their next song.

He needed to think this through. For once, he couldn't just rush in. Not until he was completely sure he had a way back out of it again.

It hadn't even been a full week since Rachel started work at Cressingham Arcade, but already the place was starting to feel like home.

Changing her shifts at Hartbury's had given her plenty of free afternoons—and evenings—to spend at the arcade, figuring out what made the place tick, why it was special, and getting new ideas for how she could communicate that to Londoners at large. She'd spent time with each of the shopkeepers individually, looking through their stock, discussing display ideas, taking photos with her heavy Canon camera, and then spending hours looking through them on her laptop screen in Damon's office after the arcade was closed.

Yes, Damon's office. Her cheeks felt warm just thinking about how many evenings she'd spent sitting opposite him in that tiny room, each working on their own laptops on opposite sides of the small desk, as if they were partners, or a pair—

Rachel pulled herself up sharply. Four nights. Less, really, since tonight was only halfway done, and she wasn't even in his office. Three and a half, then, since they'd returned to the arcade after the Victorian market and got to work. That was definitely not enough nights to start getting moony about.

Although…

As much as she was trying to be reasonable and rational about it all, and remember Celeste's warnings—not to mention her own common sense—she had to admit, Damon had seemed…different, this week. Before the fake New Year's Eve party their interactions had been limited at best. They were friendly, of course, but she wouldn't have really called them friends.

Now… Now he knew how she liked her hot chocolate— with as many toppings as possible—and would bring her one from the coffee shop just outside the arcade whenever she was working late. He'd pore over images with her, deciding which ones best represented the shops, even when she was trying to decide between two almost identical photos. He'd listen to her ideas and smile and nod and he didn't talk over her or try to change the subject.

And yes, she knew that all of those things were work related—well, apart from the hot chocolate, perhaps, although for all she knew he was only providing that because he felt guilty about her working late. She knew she should keep reminding herself that this was a working relationship. That Damon had never shown any sign of returning her crush in the ten years she'd known him, apart from that one misguided kiss at fake midnight.

But still…it *felt* different. And Rachel wasn't at all sure what that meant, or what to do about it.

Which was why she was hiding out in the large bay window of the first shop in the arcade—the new stationery and invitation shop, owned by Penelope—fiddling with the first of her displays. Penelope had long since disappeared with her boyfriend, Zach, a huge Viking of a guy with the most besotted smile Rachel had ever seen on a man, leaving Rachel in peace and quiet to create. Or, as she was doing now, procrastinate.

She'd finished the window almost an hour ago, according to her initial design. It looked exactly as she'd pictured in her head too. From the Victorian writing desk in the corner, with inkwell and parchment, to the vintage-style papers she'd used to create the decorations that hung from the ceiling into the window. A Christmas tree made out of paper covered in swirly calligraphy—thanks to Penelope's notebooks and the photocopier in the office—sat in the centre, surrounded by boxes wrapped in the Victorian Christmas card design wrapping paper she was selling inside. A stack of style notebooks from the stock with one open on top, a perfectly matched pen sitting on the page titled 'Christmas Wish List'. There were fairy lights strung around giving it a magical air and the wooden floor sparkled with added stars and glitter too. It looked beautiful.

And yet…

Rachel sighed. It wasn't right. It was everything she'd planned, but maybe she'd got the plan wrong. She'd felt so inspired after the Victorian market and she'd been full of plans to make each window specific to the business, but still with a period twist—just as she'd done for Penelope's shop.

So what was wrong with it?

She stepped back into the shop and squinted at it, trying to identify the problem. But of course, she was looking at it from the wrong angle. She needed to go out into the arcade and look in, really. Except, if she went out she might bump into Damon and that was something else that wasn't quite right. So she stayed where she was and glared at the display until a rap on the window made her jump.

Clutching a hand to her chest, Rachel looked up to see Damon grinning at her through the glass. He beckoned her outside and she went. Apparently avoiding having to deal with this…weirdness between them wasn't an option any more.

Standing shoulder to shoulder, they both looked in at the window display.

'It looks great,' Damon said, and Rachel pulled a face. 'No, it really does. It's perfect for Penelope.'

She could hear the 'but', even if he wasn't saying it. He'd given her this chance and she'd let him down already. Her first attempt at something outside the family business and she couldn't do it.

Steeling herself, she said it for him. 'But?'

He glanced down at her, his expression serious. 'Where are the mice?'

Realisation flowed through her like mulled wine. Of course! *That* was what was missing!

'I was trying to do a grown-up window, something new. And I focussed so hard on the shop and Penelope and the arcade and the Victorian details…'

'You forgot to put some of *you* in it,' Damon finished, with a gentle smile. 'But that's why I hired you, remember? Because I wanted *your* style. I want *you*.'

Oh, and didn't those words hit her right where it tingled?

But he didn't mean it like that. He meant the window display. Narrowing her eyes, Rachel studied it again, this time letting her imagination overlay reality, until she could picture exactly how it should look. Tiny felted mice, maybe in brightly coloured jackets, scurrying over the parcels, tightening ribbons and tying bows, or lifting a pen to write their own wish list in a mini notebook on top of the real one. The whole scene brought to life the way she hadn't been able to make it tonight. It would take her a while to make enough mice, but felting the creatures was relaxing and she could do it in front of the telly in her bedroom, so it would be fine. And it would be worth it.

Because the display really would feel like hers.

She wouldn't hide the mice away this time; she didn't need to. But maybe she'd leave a hint for the children to look for the secret mice Damon had shown her, just for fun.

Bouncing on her toes a little, she turned to Damon, beaming. 'I know *exactly* how it needs to look now. And I can carry it through to the other windows too...' A Victorian-style mouse Christmas. It would be perfect. She couldn't wait to get started.

Damon had other ideas, though.

'Great! In that case, I'm taking you for dinner.' Her breath caught at his words. What was this? A date? Or just a working dinner? Then he went on, 'You've been at this for hours; you need more than just hot chocolate tonight,' and she understood.

He was looking after her, probably at Celeste's request. That was all.

She looked back at her window, and thought about her mice. Then she thought about dinner with Damon. Old Rachel would be hiding away making mice already by now, staying far away from temptation or opportunity or potential embarrassment.

But ever since that kiss, she hadn't felt so much like Old

Rachel any more. She felt like someone new. Someone who, perhaps, might take a chance once in a while.

Gesturing down at her leggings and jumper, she smiled ruefully at Damon. 'As long as you're not planning on eating anywhere with a dress code.'

His smile was warm, friendly. 'Don't worry. I know the perfect place.'

CHAPTER EIGHT

DAMON WATCHED RACHEL'S face light up as they approached the café with its outdoor tables and heaters, and the chairs with the rugs and blankets layered over the back for warmth. He'd been right. This was perfect for…whatever the hell this was between them.

As much as he'd love to treat her to a fancy restaurant— one of the stupidly expensive ones where paparazzi took photos of every patron because, really, they had to be *some-one* to be dining there, even if the person behind the camera didn't recognise them—that wasn't them. It wasn't Rachel and, honestly, it wasn't really him either.

Luciana's, however, was.

'Ah! Mama's best customer, here again.' Tony, Luciana's twenty-something son, rolled his eyes at Damon as he led them to his usual table. 'Do I need to worry about my mother's virtue?'

'Only her lasagne,' Damon assured him.

Tony clicked his tongue as he pulled out a chair for Rachel. 'I won't tell her you're only interested in her for her food. It would break her heart.' Handing them both menus, he disappeared to deal with another couple of customers looking at the board by the entrance.

Damon turned his attention back to his dinner companion, and found her staring at him.

He paused in taking his own seat. 'Is this…is this okay?' Maybe the thing about no dress code had been a joke. Maybe she really had been expecting one of those fancy restaurants. But no, she'd looked excited when they arrived. What had changed?

'It's perfect.' Rachel shook her head, just a little. 'I love Italian, and this place is darling. Plus no one is going to notice the dust from the window all over my leggings once I'm snuggled under this blanket.'

Damon sat, still not convinced. 'Then what is it? You look…confused.' Was that the right word? He wasn't sure. He was normally good at reading people—their expressions, their moods, even their thoughts, to a point. But Rachel seemed to surprise him at every turn.

'I just assumed you brought me here because, well, you thought it was more…my level, I guess. The sort of place I'd belong.' She shrugged as if her words meant nothing, but Damon could hear the echoes of pain in her voice. 'I never imagined it would be somewhere you'd come regularly.'

He didn't push her on her original assumption—he could tell she was uncomfortable about having to say it out loud in the first place. But he did question the second part of her statement, not least because it echoed his own thoughts from earlier.

'You thought I only frequented the uber-fashionable London restaurants, huh? The ones where people go just to be seen?'

Rachel raised her eyebrows, just a little. 'Given how many times you *have* been seen at them, can you blame me?'

That was more like it. Those sparks of amusement, of life, that he'd grown used to seeing in Rachel over the last week or so were back.

'Trust me,' he said, setting aside the menu. He already knew it off by heart anyway. 'I only go to those places because the people I'm dining with want to eat there. When it's just me, I come here and eat Luciana's lasagne. Or sometimes her risotto of the day. It's comfort food for me.'

And so unlike the elaborate dishes his family insisted on cooking—or the ready meals or cereal he'd grown up on, since when they weren't trying to impress each other, or other people, his parents were generally too busy to bother cooking at all.

Luciana cooked food she liked and gave it to people hoping they would like it too. It was that simple and refreshing.

'How did you find it?' Rachel wasn't looking at the menu either, he realised. She was focused entirely on him.

'I stumbled on it a few years ago and promptly offered over my soul in return for a regular table and lasagne whenever I needed it.'

That earned him a thwack on the head with the menu from behind. He didn't need to look up to know who was responsible for it.

'Luciana, my love.' With a quick smile at Rachel, he turned around to charm the restaurant's owner, head chef, and matriarch of the family business back onto his side again. 'You know I think it was a perfectly fair price for lasagne as incredible as yours.'

Luciana rolled her eyes. 'Like I'd want your soul. Who knows where that thing has been?' She shot Rachel a sympathetic look. 'All I accepted from him was the occasional suggestion for improving our business. Mostly stuff I'd have done anyway, but he looked like he needed feeding, poor little boy. Now, are you two ready to order?'

Rachel appeared to stifle a giggle at the 'poor little boy' comment, but he was pretty sure she could read between Luciana's lines as well as he could. The restaurant had been on the verge of closure before he'd walked in that first night. The fact it was now bustling and busy on a Thursday night in December, with even all the outdoor tables occupied, brought him more satisfaction than any of the bigger, more corporate projects he'd done recently.

They both ordered the lasagne—Rachel without even looking at the menu.

'You didn't want to see what else there was on offer?' he asked as Luciana retreated back to the kitchen.

Rachel shrugged. 'You said the lasagne was best. I trust your judgement.'

It was a throwaway comment, Damon knew, one that didn't mean anything more than that she fancied lasagne. But still, hearing Rachel say she trusted his judgement... it meant something more to him, somehow. That someone from outside his business world, someone who was more connected to his sister, his family, than his corporate achievements, trusted his judgement...

Damon smiled, slowly. 'You won't be disappointed,' he promised.

And he really hoped he could keep it, long after the lasagne was finished.

Luciana's was Rachel's new favourite restaurant. By the time she'd swallowed her first mouthful of lasagne she'd already decided she'd be coming back again, soon and often. With or without Damon.

But, oh, she hoped it was with.

She didn't exactly have a lot of experience of dating. She'd been on a few dates, of course, but they'd mostly been awkward affairs she'd been happy to get over and done with. But tonight? Sitting in a tiny pedestrianised square in London, at a café table with a fluffy blanket around her shoulders, eating lasagne, sipping red wine and laughing about the world...it felt like every romantic fantasy she'd ever had. Which probably said more about the feebleness of her fantasy life than she'd like.

She'd been so sure that this was just another 'friends

and colleagues' dinner. But as the evening wore on and the wine took effect, she wondered. She looked into Damon's laughing eyes and remembered for the millionth time how it had felt to kiss him after so many years of imagining it.

And she wanted it again.

'So, what do you want to do now?' Damon asked as she finished off the last spoonful of tiramisu. 'Ready for home or…?'

He trailed off. It didn't matter, though. Rachel could hear worlds of possibility in his words.

She should go home. She had dozens of felt mice to make, not to mention the fact that she was behind on the Hartbury's social media because she'd been giving so much time and attention to the arcade.

More than that, she knew that going home now was the least risky strategy. The one that protected her heart and stopped her getting *Ideas*, with a capital I. The longer she spent with Damon this way, the closer she got to believing there could be something more than friendship between them.

And yet…

'Or?' Rachel picked up her almost empty glass of wine. It had to be the alcohol giving her the confidence to ask what her other options were. Heavens knew she'd never manage it on her own.

Damon's smile turned warmer somehow. More seductive. She could feel herself falling into his eyes…

'Carol singing.' He pushed his chair back from the table, leaving her blinking.

'What?'

'It's still early.' Holding out a hand, Damon pulled her to her feet. 'And they're singing carols in Trafalgar Square this evening. If we leave now we could just about make it. Come on!'

He flung some notes down on the table, waved a good-

bye to Luciana and her son, and dragged Rachel back out
onto the busy London street that had seemed miles away
while they ate.

Carol singing. Really?

'So is this something else you secretly do all the time?'
she asked as they hurried along the pavement, while she
tried to match his long stride with her much shorter legs.

'Only in December,' he deadpanned. Then he smirked
at her. 'No, it's not. But…'

'But?' she pressed, when it became clear he wasn't going
to finish the thought.

'But I wasn't ready to say goodnight to you just yet.'

Suddenly, the December air no longer seemed cold.

There was such heat in his eyes as he looked down at
her, Rachel felt it flooding through her skin into her blood.

That heat. Even Rachel knew what it meant, although
it wasn't something she was used to seeing in men's eyes
when they looked at her. She could feel the truth of it in
her bones, and the relief of knowing she wasn't the only
one soothed her jagged edges.

She knew Damon charmed everyone. Knew his easy
smiles and his warm looks didn't mean anything. Understood that even their unexpected kiss was just another part
of who Damon was. Celeste had warned her but she hadn't
needed to, not really. Rachel had watched Damon through
their university years, and after, from the periphery as always. She knew who Damon was.

But she'd never had it turned on her before. All that
charm. Those smiles.

Right now, she understood all those girls who fell for
him one weekend then spent the next week crying on the
sofa in their flat after he let them down.

She wasn't one of those girls, though. She knew better.
And not just because she knew Damon. She'd been here
before. With Tobias, Gretchen's friend, who'd turned on

the charm and turned out to be a liar. Or maybe just a coward. With other men who thought she might be a good way to get closer to her stepsisters—and presumably their bed sheets. Apart from Tobias, she'd never been stupid enough to believe any of them. But that didn't mean they hadn't tried. Gretchen and Maisie were beautiful, rich, desirable. Rachel knew she was none of those things, and so did the men who lied to her and tried to convince her otherwise, just to get close to the women they *really* wanted.

As if being close to Rachel would give them an advantage when it came to her stepsisters. It was laughable, but Rachel supposed the guys didn't know how much Gretchen and Maisie despised her.

Oh, they tried to hide it. Tried to pretend they were fond of her, in a 'poor Rachel' way. That they were helping her with their hideous clothing suggestions. Maybe they really thought they were. To start with, Rachel had believed it too.

She knew better now, even if she didn't say so. Always keeping the peace for her father's sake, that was her. He was all she had left; she couldn't risk anything else.

But Damon… She knew Damon. He wouldn't try to hurt her. He wasn't trying to get close to her stepsisters. He genuinely seemed to enjoy her company. The charm and the smiles…they were just a part of him, something he couldn't switch off. He'd used those on her back in university too; that was what had kickstarted her crush after that night they'd spent just the two of them. But the connection between them, the fizz and the pull she'd felt since their kiss, that was something else.

Something she was starting to believe he might feel too.

It defied explanation but that didn't mean it wasn't happening.

Damon Hunter wanted her. Whether he meant to or not.

Now she just had to decide what to do about it—and how to protect her heart in the process.

Because wanting, she knew only too well, wasn't loving. And it would be all too easy for her to fall if she wasn't careful.

But it could also be something else. The next step to finding her freedom…?

She'd already jumped, hadn't she? Taking the job at the Cressingham Arcade, preparing for a life outside the claustrophobic family bubble she'd been caught in for too long. One where she could chase her own dreams, for a change, rather than always keeping the peace and keeping quiet.

Perhaps a fling with Damon was just what she needed to give her the confidence to take the next move towards the future she'd been dreaming of for too long.

Carol singing. What the hell had he been thinking?

Well, he knew the answer to that. He'd been thinking that he wasn't ready for the evening to end—and that Rachel wasn't exactly the sort of girl he could just invite up to his flat for a nightcap. And now, here they were, crushed into the crowd at Trafalgar Square, singing carols. Or silently mouthing the words in his case. It was nobody's Christmas miracle hearing his appalling singing voice.

Rachel had been thoughtful on the walk over, quieter than he was used to, although even that thought stopped him in his tracks. Rachel had *always* been quiet and thoughtful. That was who she was. But this week, working together, eating together, drinking hot chocolate together…he'd seen a different side to her. A more lively, talkative one that he suspected few people besides Celeste ever really got to see.

It made him feel…privileged. Special.

Lucky.

She wasn't quiet now, either. Holding up her carol sheet, she was singing loudly, her voice ringing in his ears despite all the others around them, beautiful and clear. Her eyes shone with festive joy and Damon silently thanked whatever impulse had led him to bring her here.

Maybe it had been memory. A long-hidden memory of a Christmas at the university, swinging his legs sitting on his mother's desk while he waited for her to finish up work. He wasn't sure where his father had been—away, perhaps. That had been the case more often than not, back then. But it must have been Christmas, because he'd heard carols ringing down the hallways and he'd wanted to hear more. He'd slipped off the desk and followed the sound, finding the university choir rehearsing for their Christmas concert. He'd stayed and listened, mesmerised, until his mother had found him.

She'd dragged him out of there and her words had stayed with him every bit as much as the music. *'There's no point listening to that. None of our family have ever been able to hold a tune in a bucket. You're not going to be a famous musician, Damon, so don't waste your time.'*

Because in his family, the only things worth time were the things they could excel at. Could be the best at.

Damon hadn't wanted to be the best. He'd just wanted to listen to the music.

He pushed away the thought and focussed on the here and now. The carols filling the square. And Rachel, singing unselfconsciously next to him.

He wanted to see this Rachel more often. The one who sparkled when she smiled at him. The one who pulsed with delight at hidden mice and butterflies. The one who melted in his arms when he kissed her.

He definitely wanted to see more of that one.

But how could he without ruining the friendship and working partnership they'd built up? Without hurting her when she realised he couldn't live up to whatever she was expecting from him?

Rachel didn't do meaningless flings, Celeste had been

clear on that. And could anything between them be meaningless anyway? They'd been friends for a decade, even if
mostly through Celeste. That had meaning.

He didn't do serious, or commitment, or anything that
tied him down beyond his limited attention span. So, as far
as he could see, he was right back where he'd been nine
years ago, when he'd pulled away from her after a night of
closeness, because he knew how easy it would be for him
to get drawn into Rachel's orbit—and how hard it might
be to escape from it, afterwards. They were at an impasse.

An impasse that had resulted in carols in Trafalgar
Square, somehow.

A sharp elbow in his ribs, mildly painful even through
two layers of coats, broke his train of thought.

'You're not singing,' Rachel said, speaking out of the
side of her mouth, her eyes still on her carol sheet.

'Trust me, that's for everyone's benefit,' he murmured
back. 'Have you ever heard me sing?'

'No, actually.' She turned her head to study him, looking honestly surprised to have found some new aspect to
his character that she hadn't considered before. 'Are you
really dreadful?'

'Terrible,' he admitted.

'Worse than Celeste?'

'Well, I wouldn't go that far…'

Rachel laughed at that, then turned back to her carol
sheet as the introduction for the next song was played by
the small band at the centre of the square. She shivered a
little as she did so, Damon noticed.

'Are you cold? Shall I fetch you a hot chocolate?'

She glanced back at him again. 'No. I'm still full from
the tiramisu.'

'Do you want my coat?'

Her brow creased with confusion. 'No, because then
you'll freeze. I'm fine, Damon.'

Except she wasn't. He touched a hand to her face and found it icy. Clearly she was frozen, but she didn't want to leave. And for reasons he wasn't studying too closely right now, it was very important to him that Rachel not be cold. Or uncomfortable. Or unhappy at all.

Well, if she wouldn't take his coat, he'd just have to warm her up another way.

He moved slowly, giving her plenty of time to object if she wanted to. The slightest sound or reaction from her and he'd have given up the idea completely. But as he stepped into her space, standing behind her, and wrapped his arms around her waist, he felt her melt against him. As if she was meant to be there.

'What are you doing?' she whispered, missing the next line of the carol.

'Keeping you warm, so you can keep singing.'

She didn't respond to that. But a moment later he heard her sweet voice raised in song again and he smiled.

By the time the carols were over, Damon knew it was time to call it a night. That he should be seeing Rachel home safely, then going home to bed himself. Alone.

He just didn't want to.

And he was starting to think that Rachel didn't want to, either.

She turned around within the circle of his arms until her breasts were pressed against his chest and she was looking directly up into his eyes. He could loosen his hold, he supposed, but that might mean she moved further away. He really didn't want that to happen.

'So,' she said, her voice soft, the cold air turning to steam around her words. 'What's next?'

'You're not tired?' he asked, desperately hopeful.

She shook her head. 'I don't want to call it a night yet. Do you?'

'No,' he admitted. He had a horrible feeling they were going to have to talk about it at some point. And that talking would probably bring it to an end. But for now... 'How about we grab a drink?'

'Good idea.'

It was easy enough to find a pub with a small corner table free where they could warm up some more and talk without interruption. Damon fetched them both drinks then eased his body between the wall and the table to sit in the narrow booth seat across from Rachel.

She took her glass of wine, her brow furrowed as she stared down at it, her lower lip caught between her teeth. Slowly, she twisted the glass round and round on the wood of the table, obviously lost in thought.

And he... well. He just watched her think. Because he liked looking at her. Because he liked imagining what *she* might be imagining. Wondrous scenes for the arcade windows, perhaps. Or remembering the carols in the square. Or Luciana's lasagne.

Or even, maybe, him.

Was that just wishful thinking? Damon had assumed so, until Celeste's comment at Sunday lunch about Rachel having had a crush on him. And since then he'd been watching very closely. If she had, she had hidden it well—until tonight.

Tonight, she'd sunk into his embrace as if it was where she belonged. And every moment she'd stayed there, that hope had grown. And when she'd said she wasn't ready to call it a night...

He'd been afraid that talking about what he felt growing between them would make her shut it down. Now, suddenly, he was afraid that ignoring it might scare it away. Or let Rachel think her way out of acknowledging it at all.

She doesn't know how to ask for what she wants.

The realisation hit hard but he knew instinctively it was

the truth. Just as she hadn't been able to tell her stepsisters which dress she actually liked, or how she hadn't put any of her mice in the window at the arcade until he'd suggested it. When she'd recounted the story of asking for fewer shifts at the department store, what had struck him most was how unusual it had been for her to ask in the first place. And how her family hadn't seemed to listen anyway.

Well. That was going to be a problem. Because there was no way Damon was going to do *anything* about the attraction between them unless she told him she wanted him to.

Which meant getting her talking.

'What are you thinking about?' It was a classic, but it made Rachel's gaze shoot up to meet his.

'What do you mean?' She sounded flustered, her eyes wide, and suddenly he wondered if anybody *ever* asked her what was on her mind. Seemed to him, mostly they wanted to tell her what they *thought* she should be thinking instead.

He wasn't going to be that guy.

'You look like there's something on your mind, that's all,' he said nonchalantly, hoping it wasn't obvious how desperate he was for that something to be him. 'Want to tell me what it is?'

He could see her steeling herself to speak, as if her courage were a coat she was pulling on. For half a second, he felt bad for making her do this, then he realised that, no, that wasn't how he felt at all.

He felt proud of her for trying. For whatever she said next. For having the guts to ask for what she wanted, when no one in her life ever seemed to have listened before.

Then she said, 'I want you to come to my work Christmas party with me tomorrow night. Will you?' And he started rethinking everything all over again.

CHAPTER NINE

WHY HAD SHE asked that? Oh, *why* had she asked that?

Rachel considered just hiding under the pub table but, really, the words were out now so what was the point?

It was obvious that whatever Damon had been expecting her to say, it hadn't been that. All the same, he rallied rapidly and tossed her a smile as he picked up his pint.

'That depends,' he said, before taking a sip.

'On what?' He probably had plans. *Of course* he'd have plans. It was a Friday night two weeks before Christmas. *Everybody* had plans. Hell, even *she* had plans, which meant that there couldn't be another person in London who didn't.

'Will you wear the dress I bought you?' He raised one eyebrow as he asked, a smirk hovering around his lips.

Rachel's breath caught, rendering her unable to answer. Which was just as well, since she had no idea what to say. It felt like a tease, like a joke she was too socially awkward to understand, and from anybody else, especially the guys in her stepsisters' social circle, she'd be certain it was.

But this was *Damon*. And as much as he might look and act like those guys on the surface, she was almost certain that underneath he wasn't. Almost.

She took a chance. 'Do you…want me to?'

He grinned. 'Definitely. You looked gorgeous in that dress last week.'

When he'd kissed her. Oh, no.

'Then…yes, I could wear that dress.'

'Then it's a date.' His grin suddenly faltered. 'Wait. That's not what I meant.'

Of course not. As if Damon Hunter would ever go on an actual date with her. At least he was sweet enough to make sure she hadn't got the wrong idea. *Unlike Tobias.*

'No, of course, I didn't think—' she started, shaking her head as if she could simply shake away any idea of a relationship with Damon.

Then she realised he was still speaking.

'Unless you wanted it to be a date.'

Her head shot up, her gaze hitting his, looking for any hint of deception or humour in his eyes.

She found none.

'What do you mean?' Because none of this was making any sense to her any more.

Reaching across the table, Damon took her hand. 'I'm saying this all wrong.'

'What happened to that patented Hunter charm?'

'Apparently it doesn't work with you,' he said, and Rachel just about resisted the urge to tell him how very, very wrong he was about that.

She sighed. 'Did you mean that I might want it to be a pretend date?' It was her best guess, the only way she could really make sense of his contradictory statements. 'You know, to make it look like I actually have a date in front of my stepsisters?' Because actually that didn't sound so bad.

But Damon looked horrified at the very idea. 'No!'

'Why not?' Rachel asked, before she could stop herself. 'It sounds like just the sort of fun trick I'd have thought you'd love, from Celeste's stories.'

She laughed, as if it could cover how painfully awkward this whole conversation was.

Damon didn't laugh, though. Instead, he reached across

the table and took her hands in his. 'Because it wouldn't be pretend. I want—' He broke off, and sighed. 'I promised myself—I promised Celeste, come to that, and she's much scarier than my own guilt—that I wouldn't do anything that could hurt you. After that kiss, I told myself that the only way it could happen again was if you asked for it. But I realised tonight…you'd never ask, would you?'

Eyes wide, Rachel shook her head. She *wouldn't* ask. Because she couldn't imagine for a moment that he would say yes. Even on the walk over, imagining a fling with him, at least half her brain had still been assuming it was a fantasy brought on by too much wine and lasagne.

'But I wanted you to. And it turns out… I'm still no good at obeying the rules, even the ones I set myself.' He took a deep breath and Rachel was amazed to see something that looked like nervousness in his smile. 'So, Rachel Charles, I'd love to go to your work party with you. As a friend, or a colleague if you'd like. Or as your date, if you'll have me.'

Her world spun and it had nothing to do with the wine. Damon Hunter had asked her on a date. Her decade-long fantasy was becoming reality, and her first thought was…

What's the catch?

Because as much as she liked Damon, she knew she wasn't his usual type. He looked as blindsided by this weird attraction between them as she was. And that, more than anything, reminded her of a truth she'd already internalised.

I could get hurt here, if I'm not careful. Heartbroken.

And that wasn't a risk she was willing to take. This couldn't be like Tobias again, with him in control, the one deciding when they were together or not, the one keeping her a secret from all his friends. She didn't believe Damon would disown her in public the way Tobias had, pretending it was all a great joke. But she also knew Damon had the power to hurt her in other ways. She'd wanted him for so long, how would she feel when he didn't want her any more, after she'd tasted what being with him could be like?

I can protect my heart. As long as I know what I'm getting into.

Rachel always had a plan, and she plodded through it one step at a time. It might be boring but it was what she needed here too.

Next to freedom, the thing she wanted most was everything that Damon could offer her. But it had to be on her own terms. Her plan, not his.

Which meant she had to suck it up and ask for what she needed. Damon had done the hardest part for her. Now she just had to make sure she protected her heart well enough that, when the clock struck midnight on this thing between them, she wasn't left broken in a corner somewhere regretting her life choices.

She had to speak up for once.

Releasing her fingers from his grip, she reached for her wine, took a fortifying sip, then made herself say the words.

'If this is going to be a date, there have to be ground rules.'

He looked amused at that. She just hoped he was still smiling by the time she'd finished.

The Hartbury's Christmas Party was supposed to be the highlight of the department store's staff calendar, but as far as Damon could see that didn't say much for the rest of the year's events.

'They don't even bother to hire somewhere for the party?' he muttered to Rachel as they joined the queue to get inside the department store.

Rachel shrugged. 'Hannah always says there's no point, since they already have all this space, and venue-hire costs are astronomical at this time of year. Although Dad did try to persuade her to move it a couple of years ago after one of the seasonal workers was sick inside one of the display mannequins.'

He shot her a confused look. 'Inside?'

She nodded. 'They're hollow, you see. Apparently he just took the torso off, threw up down the legs, then put it back on again. We didn't find it for days after the smell started to spread.'

'That's…horrible.'

'Yep. And if that didn't convince her to move the party somewhere else, I don't reckon anything will.'

The queue was filled with staff members who spent all their working days at the shop and who were now heading back there in their glad rags for the party. Damon wasn't sure he'd have bothered, if he were them.

But he wasn't really thinking about them. He was thinking about the woman standing beside him, holding his hand in her gloved one.

Holding hands. He felt about fourteen again, obsessing about a girl's hand in his. Rachel did that to him. Stripped away all those years of experience and left him uncertain and unsure again in a way he hadn't even been when he *met* her, all those years ago.

He wasn't sure he liked it.

But he liked *her*. Which was why he was happy to be here, at her side, despite his awful sense of foreboding about this party as a whole. And despite—or perhaps because of—her ground rules.

He'd been afraid she'd expect too much from him, things he wasn't able to give, like promises and commitment. Instead, she'd leaned across the table and asked for the opposite.

'*This is a Christmas fling,*' she'd said, her face serious. '*I am not expecting for ever, and I know you're not either. This is fun, that's all. Because there's obviously something between us and I think I'd like to explore that a bit. But we both have to be very clear on one thing: this is over the moment the last Christmas cracker has been pulled.'*

'Are you sure?' he'd asked, hardly able to believe she was speaking his own thoughts to him so clearly.

She was giving him the way out he needed, setting the boundaries that would allow him to move on when he needed to. Because he always needed to, he knew that about himself.

Her answering smile had lit him up inside.

'Very. I've never had a proper fling before—not one that counted. You can be my first.'

Except, of course, fling clearly meant something different to Rachel than to most people. And he wasn't going to push her a second faster than she wanted to go. So he'd put her in the taxi with a chaste kiss goodnight, and now here he was, one night later, holding her hand like a prom date.

But it would be worth it. Even if he never tempted her up to his bedroom before she called time on their fling, it would be worth it, because he would get to spend time with Rachel.

Christmas turned him sappy, apparently. Who knew?

The queue shuffled up along the street as the doors to the store were opened. 'I don't see your stepsisters in this queue,' he said as they moved with the tide.

'They'll be inside already,' Rachel replied, absently. 'They're family.'

'So are you,' he pointed out, but she just shrugged. He frowned. Seemed to him Rachel spent a lot of time not making a fuss about her awful family even when she really should.

Maybe he could help her start.

Finally they reached the front where the big double doors were propped open. Just inside, Rachel's father, stepmother and stepsisters were standing to receive their guests, handing each an envelope that Damon sincerely hoped contained a decent Christmas bonus for staff members.

'Rachel! You came! We weren't sure, after the dress debacle…' Maisie trailed off as Damon stepped out of the shadows behind his date and into full sight. 'And you brought a guest!' She elbowed her sister in the ribs and Gretchen turned to join them instantly.

'Oh, Damon, how kind of you to accompany Rachel *again*!' Gretchen simpered, making every hackle Damon possessed rise up. Whatever hackles were.

'I couldn't let my girlfriend attend her Christmas party alone,' he said, coolly. 'What kind of boyfriend would that make me?'

Both Gretchen's and Maisie's eyebrows shot up in symmetrical surprise.

'Boyfriend?' Maisie echoed. Then the stepsisters exchanged a knowing look. 'Oh, of course. Boyfriend. Just like Tobias was your boyfriend, I suppose? Well. Come on in, then!' She handed Rachel her envelope. 'Enjoy the party, you two…lovebirds!'

Damon could hear them snickering behind him the whole walk to the temporary cloakroom that had been set up in the foyer.

'What was that about?' Rachel was tense beside him, almost rigid inside her coat, but she sighed at his question.

'They think it's an act,' she said, sliding her coat from her shoulders.

Damon took a moment to admire Rachel in that curve-clinging dress he'd bought on a whim—was it really less than two weeks ago? It seemed longer, somehow. But she still looked as beautiful, and as tempting, as she had in it at the TV studios that night.

The last time—the first time—he'd kissed her properly, and the moment he'd started losing his mind.

He frowned as her words caught up with him. 'An act?'

Handing their coats over to the cloakroom assistant and taking their ticket, he led her away towards the bar. 'What kind of an act?'

Rachel rolled her eyes. 'Isn't it obvious? They think you're here as a pity date, pretending to be interested in me just so I'm not embarrassed by coming to the party alone. Even though I've come on my own for the last seven years.'

Seven years. She hadn't had a date at Christmas in seven years. And yet, all Damon could think about was who she'd brought seven years ago. Someone she cared about? Someone she loved?

He shook the thought away. Was this why she'd latched onto the idea of a pretend date when they'd been talking last night?

He ran back over her stepsister's words in his head. *Tobias.*

'*Just like Tobias was your boyfriend...*' That was what she'd said.

'Who's Tobias?' he asked as they approached the bar.

Rachel's steps faltered just for a moment, then she carried on walking. 'My sort-of ex-boyfriend.'

'Sort-of ex?' he repeated. 'How does a person have a sort-of ex-boyfriend? Surely you're dating or you're not.'

'You'd have thought, wouldn't you?' Rachel said, her voice too light and cheery. She didn't want to talk about this, obviously. But he had a feeling she needed to, so he pushed all the same.

'Rach. Tell me about Tobias and I'll buy you the biggest glass of wine they sell here.'

She sighed. 'The glasses are all the same size—and the wine will be warm and you'll hate it. Besides, I have our drinks vouchers right here.' She waved the envelope he'd optimistically hoped, on behalf of the staff, would contain something more than a voucher for warm white wine.

'Then tell me because I want to know. And because I think you'll feel better for telling me.'

She gave him a disbelieving look at that. He waited and she eventually started to talk.

'Tobias was—is—a friend of Gretchen and Maisie. The same social circle, you know. We met by accident at one of the parties they threw at the house once, a year or so ago now, when Hannah and Dad were away. I normally try to stay out of the way when they're happening; I mean, I'm six years older than Maisie, and four years older than Gretchen, and we don't exactly have the same interests and friends, right?'

'I wouldn't imagine so,' Damon said, dryly.

'But that night they'd ordered the really good pizza, and I was starving, so I popped down. And Tobias…well, he seemed kind of on the outside too. So we got talking, and we actually got on well.'

'So far, so good. Why do I suspect this is all going to go wrong?'

'Because you've met me?' she guessed.

'I am one hundred per cent sure that whatever happened next is not your fault.'

'No, I guess not,' she admitted. 'Except for the part where I really should have known better.'

'What happened?'

'Long story short? We grew close. We were together for months. Except he was very, very careful to make sure that my stepsisters and their friends never saw us together. Which was easy, since I was never all that keen to be around them anyway. So much so, in fact, that it took me a while to notice.' She shook her head. 'I was naive. I should have realised sooner.'

'Realised what, exactly?' Damon could already feel the blood pounding at his temple. Just as well for this *Tobias* that he wasn't here tonight.

'That he was embarrassed to be seen with me.' Rachel shrugged, smiled a self-deprecating smile, and apparently remained unaware how much he wanted to punch her ex-boyfriend. Which was probably for the best. 'When we finally got caught out last summer—Gretchen, Maisie and a whole gang of friends walked in on us kissing—he laughed it off. Pretended it was all a big joke. That seducing me had been a sort of fun pastime, something to laugh about with his friends afterwards.'

Okay, now his blood really was boiling. 'That utter, utter bastard.' He wanted to touch her, to hold her, but he was too tense with anger.

Rachel, strangely, didn't look angry at all. Just said, 'I felt sorry for him, to be honest.'

At those words, his anger started to ebb away.

'Sorry for him?'

'Yeah. I mean, he cared more about what Gretchen and Maisie and everyone thought of him than what he actually wanted. And in some ways, he did me a favour.'

Okay, pity for the guy he could *almost* understand. But a favour? His scepticism must have shown on his face because she went on, unbidden.

'I mean, he showed me how small my life had become, stuck in that house, with those people. I've let them define me and my dreams for too long. Seeing Tobias choose their image of him over who he really was…that was what made me decide to finally stop doing that. To move out, find a new job, chase my own dreams for a change.' She sounded so strident, so determined, that Damon was almost fired up on her behalf.

Except that six months later she was still living there, still working at Hartbury's. 'What happened?'

Rachel's voice was small as she answered. 'Dad had a heart attack. He hadn't been feeling right for years—that was what always stopped me before. And then Hannah pointed out that me rowing with Gretchen and Maisie hadn't helped his stress levels. Might even have caused… Anyway. I just… I couldn't leave until I knew he was okay. We're just waiting on some last test results…'

'But you took the job at the arcade with me anyway.'

She looked up, her gaze locking onto his. 'It was too good an opportunity to pass up.'

The longer he held her gaze, the more he believed that she was saying something else. That *he'd* been the draw, not the job.

Then she looked away. 'Anyway, that's what happened. And that's why my stepsisters were so amused to see you with me. They think it's all pretend—a pity date or something.'

Because they didn't believe that any man would choose Rachel over them. Idiots.

'We're just going to have to show them this is no pity date, then, aren't we?' He couldn't change the heartbreak she'd felt last summer; he couldn't promise her anything beyond Christmas, either. But he could do this.

Rachel blinked up at him. 'And how, exactly, do you plan to do that?'

He felt the smile spreading across his face. 'Just trust me, yeah?'

She bit her lower lip, white teeth in plump flesh, and a shimmer of heat flashed through him. Proving this wasn't fake wasn't going to be a problem at all, not with the way he felt about Rachel in that dress.

'Okay,' she said.

And the game was on.

CHAPTER TEN

THE HARTBURY'S CHRISTMAS party was as awful as it always was, objectively speaking. As always, they had tiny drinks vouchers in the envelopes provided at the door, ready to be exchanged for warm, weak wine and nothing else. As always, it was filled with people who already spent all day in each other's company, and really just wanted to get drunk and not have to talk to each other any more.

Being there with Damon was a definite improvement, though. He was attentive and boyfriendy without going over the top. Rachel could feel Gretchen and Maisie—not to mention plenty of others in the room—watching them as Damon led her onto the dance floor, or fetched her drinks, or just kept one hand casually at her waist as they spoke with other employees.

In fact, she even managed to relax in a way she'd never expected to. Until she spotted her stepmother crossing the room towards them, and saw the moment Hannah realised Rachel wasn't wearing the dress she'd bought her. She wouldn't have noticed when they arrived, not while she still had her coat on. But now there was no hiding it.

'Here we go…' she murmured.

Damon, handing her a glass of lukewarm wine, followed her gaze. 'Your stepmother?'

Rachel nodded. 'I'm not wearing the dress she bought for me.'

'I imagine because it was hideous?'

'Basically.'

'Okay, then.' Beside her, she felt him straighten his posture, and saw him paste on his most charming smile. *Battle armour*, she thought, wondering why she'd never noticed how often he used his charm as a defence before.

She tried to smile too, but it was hard in the face of Hannah's frown. 'Rachel, I think someone has caused some... unfortunate damage to one of the windows. Can you clean it up?'

'I—' Rachel started, glad that Hannah seemed too preoccupied by whatever had happened to the window display to have noticed the dress, but Damon interrupted her.

'Ms Hartbury? So nice to meet you. I'm Damon Hunter, an old friend of Rachel's.' The smile he shot her way as he said it made Rachel blush and caused Hannah to pause and turn her full attention to him instead.

'How nice of you to accompany her tonight,' she said, with the same scepticism her daughters had shown. 'I wasn't aware Rachel was bringing anybody.'

'It was kind of a last-minute thing,' she said hurriedly, drawing Hannah's attention back to her. Which was a mistake.

'You're not wearing the dress I bought you.'

'Oh, well. Um...you see...' Rachel tripped over her words, trying to find the ones that might appease her stepmother.

'That's my fault, I'm afraid, Ms Hartbury.' Damon's voice was smooth, but not exactly apologetic. 'I saw this one in your shop and couldn't resist buying it for Rachel. Don't you think it's just perfect for her?'

The way Hannah's gaze zipped up, down and back up again over Rachel's outfit, she suspected her stepmother thought the exact opposite. Neat and slim, like her daughters, Hannah had always frowned about Rachel's curves, as if the body shape she'd been born with—the one she had inherited from her mother—was something to be ashamed of. Embarrassed of, even by association.

Damon *liked* her curves, though. He'd bought her this dress to show them off before they'd ever even kissed.

That thought made Rachel stand a little straighter and smile a little more. 'It's very "me", don't you think?'

'I suppose,' Hannah said, doubtfully.

'Is this thing on?'

Rachel jumped at the sound of her father's voice, coming across the PA system. Turning, she found him standing half in one of the windows, talking into the microphone.

As the rest of the partygoers turned their attention on him too, he smiled and stepped down, holding the microphone out for Hannah, who was already striding towards him.

'What now?' Damon whispered.

'This is Hannah's traditional motivational speech for the workers.' Rachel patted his arm. 'It's about as awful as it sounds.'

As always, Hannah stood up at the front of the store, half on top of Rachel's window display, and made a horrible speech about teamwork and the shop being like a family—even though all the seasonal workers would be unemployed again in a couple of weeks. Rachel held onto her warm wine and willed it to be over.

Of course, then Hannah dragged Rachel's father and Gretchen and Maisie up front while she talked, speaking about the whole family being a team together too. Rachel was perfectly used to being left out of that sort of thing— and happier, to be honest—but she felt Damon tense beside her as Hannah threw out a casual mention of her existence.

'Oh, and thank you to my stepdaughter, Rachel, of course, for her work on the window displays again this year.'

Nobody turned to find her. Nobody clapped. But then, Rachel hadn't expected them to.

Hannah was about to move on to the next part of her talk, the part traditionally dealing with expected behaviour at the party—no vomiting in the display mannequins—when a sound cracked through the room. Two hands, clapping.

Damon's hands.

He was applauding *her*. Her window displays. In a way that no one else would have even thought to.

Rachel could feel the heat flooding her cheeks, the embarrassment of being the centre of attention in a family and in a place where she was always an afterthought. She'd never wanted this, never wanted to be looked at, to be noticed, even.

But now it was Damon doing the looking, the noticing… and it turned out she didn't mind it half as much as she'd imagined she would.

Of course, when one person started clapping, human nature dictated that others would follow. And soon the whole room was applauding her little windows—even her stepsisters, for all they looked as if they'd rather be having their fingernails pulled out.

It was too much. Rachel twisted towards Damon to tell him to stop, but the thing had a momentum beyond him. He pulled her into his body, pressing a kiss to the top of her head, and she just knew everyone was watching.

'Look at me,' he murmured, and she couldn't help but obey. She met his gaze with her own, and had only a moment to recognise the warmth there before his lips lowered to hers.

She was kissing Damon Hunter. Again.

It shouldn't be such a surprise; they'd agreed to a fling, after all, hadn't they?

And yet…oh, and yet…

Rachel sank into the kiss, letting the world around them

fall away as his tongue teased her lips. This wasn't a deep, passionate kiss, she realised—it was a show kiss, meant to show her family and colleagues that he was here as her real date tonight. That he wanted to be with her. That he liked her dress, her curves. That he liked *her*.

All the same, Damon's hands gripping her hips, holding her tight against him, and the small growl she heard from the back of his throat told her he wasn't *quite* as unaffected by this as he might pretend to be.

Good. If her entire self was melting and reforming under his kiss, a growl was the least she could expect from him.

Someone, somewhere, maybe very far away, let out a whoop, breaking through the delicious bubble of solitude she and Damon had built around themselves. Then the real world began to leak in, starting with Hannah's voice over the PA system again, and Rachel pulled away from the kiss.

'Yes, well. Anyway, of course we want you all to enjoy yourselves tonight,' Rachel's stepmother said, somehow managing to make enjoyment sound like a punishable offence. 'But here at Hartbury's we do have certain standards to maintain.'

'I'm guessing we fail to meet the standard,' Damon whispered, and Rachel stifled a laugh. 'I think we proved our point, though. So… Want to get out of here?'

She did. Except the party was only halfway through. And she hadn't cleared up whatever mess was in one of the window displays. Could she really just walk out right now? In the middle of Hannah's speech?

'I didn't sort out the display,' she hedged, glancing towards the door.

Damon raised an eyebrow but didn't deign to answer that one. Instead, he ran his hand up over her hip, to her waist, then back down again. An innocent enough touch in public really, but one that shot through her body as if he'd been touching her somewhere else entirely.

And if she went home with him now, maybe he would.

Oh, hell. The cleaners would be in soon enough anyway. And it really wasn't her job...

'Let's go,' she said, and Damon smiled.

Somehow, it took both too long and too short a time to get back to his penthouse apartment. Damon had left the car in the secure garage under his building, figuring he might want a drink or two to get through the party, so they had to hail a black cab. They fell into the back of it together, Damon reluctant to let go of Rachel's hand even for a second, in case she slipped away.

Thankfully the driver wasn't the chatty type, but Damon found he couldn't make conversation with Rachel either. The tension, the chemistry between them, filled the cab until it was almost a visible fog. What could he say beyond 'I need to make love to you or I'm going to lose my mind'? Somehow he didn't think Rachel would appreciate him saying that in semi-public.

So yeah. He needed to get there quickly so he could say the words and, hopefully, follow through.

Which was the thought that made him think maybe he needed more time in the cab after all. Because this wasn't a one-night stand, wasn't a casual fling he was bringing home and would see for a few dates before they went their separate ways for ever.

This was Rachel.

And for all that she'd insisted that this *was* just a Christmas fling, and for all that he'd enthusiastically agreed to that, he hadn't considered how things would work after. Once things were over but they were still in each other's lives. They were friends, he hoped—through Celeste even if not in their own right. They were working together and he hoped that would continue past Christmas. The Cressingham Arcade would need social media support year-round, not to mention spring windows, summer windows, autumn windows… In fact, the odds were good that Rachel could be still working with the Arcadians, as he liked to call them, long after he'd moved on to his next project.

It was more than just that, though. More than friendship or working relationships. He *knew* Rachel. However determined she'd tried to sound suggesting the fling, her voice had wavered ever so slightly. This wasn't how she did things. Rachel Charles didn't have flings; she didn't fall into bed with just anybody. She was careful, especially after her past experiences. She'd chosen him and that meant he had to live up to her expectations. Not just in bed, but out of it too.

He couldn't hurt her; that was the first rule he'd set for himself. So he always had to be upfront about what he could give, and what he couldn't. So far, that had been easy enough.

But the next stage… Rachel wasn't good at speaking up, at asking for what she needed. He *knew* that. She was not used to being seen, or heard.

He saw her.

And he'd hear her, if she talked. But what if she didn't? What if she didn't tell him what she needed and he wasn't good enough to guess? He wanted her so badly that chasing his own pleasure was a necessity. But he wouldn't push her too far, ask for too much, or take her anywhere she wasn't comfortable.

So how did he make sure of that?

Rachel's hand landed hesitantly on his thigh and he looked up to see her chewing on her bottom lip.

'Okay?' His voice came out hoarse, embodying the strain on his whole self not to kiss her again right now.

'You looked like you were thinking hard,' she said, softly. 'I just wanted to say, if you've changed your mind… you know, about the whole Christmas-fling thing—'

'No!' Damon shouted, loud enough to make the silent

taxi driver glance up at his mirror to check everything was okay. He tried to lower his voice as he carried on. 'Definitely not. Trust me. It is taking every bit of my self-control not to kiss you right now.'

'You could, you know,' Rachel replied, smiling prettily.

Damon shook his head. 'No. Because if I start kissing you, I won't be able to stop there.'

Her cheeks flared pink, even in the dark of the cab. 'Oh?'

'Yeah.' He met her gaze, letting all the wanting and the needing show in his eyes, and watched as her cheeks grew darker.

The cab stopped abruptly and, when Damon glanced out of the window, he saw they were at his flat. He still hadn't figured out exactly how any of this was going to work, but he knew one thing for sure: he was going to find a way to *make* it work.

No, *she* was. Because that was the answer, wasn't it? He had to surrender himself to what she needed.

He could do that.

Tossing some notes at the driver, and not waiting for any change, he opened the door and drew Rachel out behind him.

'Before we go up,' he said as they stood on the pavement, 'I want one thing to be very clear. You're in charge here, okay?'

She blinked at him. 'Um…okay? I don't really…'

'Once we get into that flat, nothing happens that you don't ask for. You can have basically anything you want, within reason. But you have to ask for it. Okay?'

He watched the war behind her eyes, the conflict of wanting what he was offering, and having to go against her own nature to get it.

But Damon knew that you only got what you asked for in this world. And if she wanted him, Rachel was going to have to learn to ask.

* * *

Damon's flat was everything she'd expected: expensive, stylish and soulless. At least, that was as much as she could tell from her brief glimpse around it as she stumbled through the door. After that, all she could focus on was Damon himself. Decor could wait.

'So…?' Damon stood before her, a wicked smile on his face. Her back was against the front door, the wooden frame something solid in a world that seemed to be shifting under her feet.

There was too much space between them, she realised, watching him. He was holding back, staying away. Waiting.

Waiting for her.

'Once we get into that flat, nothing happens that you don't ask for.' That was what he'd said.

And now he was making good on that promise.

Rachel swallowed, her mouth suddenly dry. With want—yes, definitely. But with fear too.

Asking for what she wanted sounded like such a simple thing to do. After all, she knew *exactly* what she wanted from Damon. She'd been fantasising about it ever since their kiss at the fake New Year's Eve party. She'd imagined every single way he would touch her, kiss her, make love to her.

Knowing what she wanted wasn't the problem—in fact, it rarely was, in her life. She *knew*. She was just…oh, hell, she was scared to want it.

Scared to ask, in case the person who could give it to her said no. Scared to admit how *much* she wanted of the world, in case the world laughed in her face and asked her who she thought she was to demand such things. Just as it had when she'd asked the universe to save her mother. Or when she'd asked Tobias to love her, just as she was.

Scared of her own desires. Scared of screwing it up. Scared of a broken heart, further down the line.

The world was a terrifying place outside her bubble and

outside the tiny perfect realities she created in her windows. Asking for more than she had, well, that had always seemed like rudeness. Entitlement. As her stepmother had told her often enough, she was lucky to have a nice home, a job, a family who accepted her, after her own mother had died. She was lucky. She still had her dad, at least.

What right did she have to ask for more?

And the last time she *had* asked, the last time she'd believed she deserved more love and affection than she was given…well, that had led to the whole debacle with Tobias. Was it any wonder she was scared to ask for more than her little life already gave her?

But she had, she realised suddenly. She'd *already* asked for more. Already stepped outside her bubble into the world of the Cressingham Arcade. She'd asked to change her shifts and the world hadn't ended. She'd taken Damon to the Christmas party, worn the wrong dress and, snide comments from her stepsisters aside, nothing terrible had happened. In fact, quite the opposite.

She'd asked Damon for a Christmas fling and he'd said *yes*.

'Rachel?' he asked now, a worried frown creasing his brow. She'd been thinking too long. Years too long, perhaps.

Now it was time to speak.

'I want you to kiss me,' she said, proud that her voice barely wavered at all.

Damon's frown disappeared into a warm smile and he stepped closer, his hands moving to her waist as if they belonged there. Maybe they did.

'Like this?' He pressed his lips to hers almost chastely, then pulled back.

She swallowed. 'No. Like this.'

Resting her palms against his shoulders, and hoping they weren't too sweaty, she stepped up into his space, until she could feel him sucking in a breath at her closeness. His whole ribcage moved, and, boy, did she love that she could affect him that way.

The power rush gave her the confidence to continue, reaching up on tiptoes and kissing him. There was nothing chaste about what she wanted from him, or about the kiss. The moment their lips touched, she felt the heat between them ignite and there was no holding back any more. It was as if, having decided to give in, her body was going to take full advantage of the opportunity and go for everything.

And despite Damon's obvious determination to let her lead the way, she could tell he was barely holding back from taking everything he wanted too.

Well, she wanted him to take it.

Breaking away, reluctantly, she tried to catch her breath—gratified to see that he was panting too.

'Too much?' he asked.

She shook her head. 'Not enough. Bedroom. Now.'

Rachel knew what she wanted. And she was ready to ask for it.

CHAPTER ELEVEN

RACHEL DIDN'T KNOW how many hours later it was. Damon's bedside clock had been sacrificed to a particularly enthusiastic manoeuvre some time ago and her phone could, quite honestly, be anywhere. It didn't matter. Time had ceased to have any importance here in the cocoon of Damon's bedroom.

He'd made love to her with a thoroughness that shouldn't have been sexy, but really, really was. His attention to detail and focus in this particular area had been unsurpassed. But he'd been true to his word and had made her ask for every single step of it. She'd used words she hadn't previously even admitted to herself that she knew just to get where she needed to go.

And he had got her there. Twice.

'You okay?' Damon's voice was warm, private, and a little husky as he pulled her closer into his arms.

'More than.'

'Good.' He paused for a second, then asked, 'Do you need to get home tonight?'

She tried not to freeze but it was hard, even in the warmth of his arms. *It's just a fling, Rach, remember? Maybe flings don't stay the night.*

She wouldn't know. She'd never had one before.

Suddenly, she felt as if she'd gone from having all the power to having none at all.

Just ask. Wasn't that what Damon had been showing her tonight? All the things that could be hers if she just asked for them?

She swallowed. 'Do you want me to go?'

His arms tightened around her. 'No. I'm hoping I can keep you here all night so we can do that again once I've recovered from the first round. I haven't even shown you my walk-in shower yet. I bet you can think of a few things to ask me to do in there.'

Her mind was already whirring with the possibilities while her body relaxed with the knowledge that he didn't want her to leave. 'I can stay.'

'Good.' He pressed a kiss to her curls. 'Your family won't miss you? I can probably track down your phone if you want to call them...'

Pulling back slightly, she raised her eyebrows and gave him a look of disbelief. 'You saw them tonight. Do you honestly think they're going to notice I'm not there?'

'Well, maybe not your stepsisters. Or your stepmother. Your dad?'

She shook her head. 'Probably not.'

That, of course, was the part that hurt the most. Hannah, Gretchen and Maisie...they weren't blood family. They didn't choose her; she just came as a package deal. She could cope with them not caring.

But her dad... He loved her, she knew that. Every bit as much as she loved him. But he was torn between his love for her and his new family.

'He, well...when my mum died, he was an absolute wreck. People started telling him he had to pull it together for my sake. That I needed a family. A new mum, even. So he remarried to give me that. But instead, Hannah and the girls became his new family.' The memories hurt. She swallowed and forced herself to continue. 'He desperately wanted me to fit in with that too, to start with. He'd talk about how we'd be a proper family again, now we were all together, instead of it just being the two of us.'

'And you? Did you want that "proper family"?' It was as if now he'd touched her so intimately, seen every bit of her on the outside, he'd gained the ability to see inside too. Into her mind, into her heart.

She'd have to be careful with that. She knew what happened when people saw too deeply.

'No. I didn't.' She shifted just a little away from him. Still close, still in his arms, but not quite so intimate. 'I was happier when it was just the two of us. Mum...she died when I was twelve. I was old enough to remember what a real family felt like. And this...it wasn't that. Suddenly there were three other people and we lived in a new house—a bigger, better house, as Dad kept pointing out. But for me... I never felt like I was a part of it. I was fourteen when he remarried, raging at the world and, well, I guess I stopped trying to fit in at all.'

Would she have had a better relationship with her stepfamily if she'd made more of an effort to be part of it? Perhaps. But she knew herself too well now to believe that she could ever have been the sort of person that Hannah and her daughters valued. She would always have been lesser—less important, less beautiful, less rich. At least this way she got to be less on her own terms.

And right now, here in bed with Damon, she didn't feel less at all. She felt mighty.

'What about you?' she asked, suddenly keen to turn the conversation away from herself. 'I remember, when you used to come and visit us at university...'

'I'd get drunk and rant about my parents?' Damon finished for her, then sighed. 'Yeah, well. All teenagers do that.'

'True.' But somehow, she'd always suspected it was more than that with Damon and Celeste's family. The siblings

were so different in so many ways, but Rachel had watched
them closely enough to find the similarities too.

'My parents are…academics. Which isn't a bad thing.
Except sometimes it feels like that's all they are. That even
as kids Celeste and I were more like experiments, more
academic curiosities than children. They are intelligent
people and they expected us to be the same. Celeste never
let them down there; she was as focussed on an academic
career as they were. But I knew pretty early on I wasn't
going to make that cut.'

Rachel wasn't sure she believed that. 'You're an intelligent guy, Damon. If you wanted to be an academic like
your parents—'

'Ah, but that's the thing. I really didn't.' Sighing, he
rolled further onto his side to look her in the eye. 'I saw
how single-minded it made them all. How they ignored the
whole rest of existence outside their little bubble and… I
didn't want to be that way. I wanted to explore the world,
meet new people, do new things. I didn't want to be tied
down to one career, one obsession, my whole life.'

'That makes sense,' Rachel admitted. 'I guess some people know from really young what they want to do and be.
Then for others…it takes us a bit longer.'

'Yeah. My parents never really understood that. Or me.'

'I think that's their loss,' Rachel told him. 'So is that
why you work for yourself? Why you take a different sort
of project every time?'

*Why you never date the same woman more than a hand-
ful of times?*

Damon shrugged. 'I like variety. In all things.'

She heard the hidden message, whether he meant her to
or not. She was a novelty, something new and interesting to
pass the Christmas season. Once it was over, so were they.

Just as she'd told him she wanted. Just as she still
should want.

And she would.

She'd take what she needed from this thing with Damon, then move on. Explore the wider world of possibilities he'd opened up for her.

Figure out what she wanted and ask for it.

Starting now.

'So, speaking of variety…' She moved closer, her whole body pressed up against his. 'Tell me more about this shower of yours.'

Damon grinned. 'Better than that, I'll show you.'

It should have been awkward afterwards. It usually was. Certainly, mornings after, in Damon's experience, had never been less than mortifying.

More often than not he tried to avoid them happening altogether. He'd sneak out of women's beds and apartments late at night and head home. If they came back to his and somehow ended up staying the night, which didn't happen often in the first place, he had a routine for the following morning. He'd get up early, shower and dress, and be ready to claim an early morning meeting when they finally roused. He'd leave them with coffee, breakfast, and occasionally plans to get together in another week or so. Once or twice he'd even followed through on the plans without cancelling.

The point was, waking up in his king-sized bed to the weak winter sun already fighting its way through the window, Rachel propped up on one elbow watching him, should have been awkward. Beyond awkward. Alarm bells should have been ringing. He should have been bounding out of bed and racing for the shower, ready to escape. His heart should have been pounding with fear that she'd read more into what had passed between them than was really there.

Instead, as he opened his eyes and she smiled down at him, he smiled back.

He checked in quickly with his body—pleasurably aching—his mind—quiet, for once—and even his heart—still beating. The world seemed...fine. Right, even.

'Good morning,' Rachel murmured.

'Very,' he replied, then kissed her.

And as one kiss turned to another, he decided that perhaps he was overthinking this after all. Maybe he could just enjoy being with Rachel, letting her ask for what she wanted and needed for once in her life, then leave her in a better place once Christmas was over. A place where she believed in herself, and had the confidence to show that to others.

The fact that he got incredible sex and lots of time with the most fascinating woman he knew was just an added bonus. Right?

Because in one night together, he'd already opened up more than he had with anybody since...well, since the last time he talked all night with Rachel, nine years ago. And he felt as if he'd seen the real Rachel again too. The passionate, open woman hiding behind the shy and reserved exterior she showed the rest of the world. He felt as if he'd gone through the window, into the deeper world she concealed inside, and he didn't want to leave.

So he pushed aside the part of his mind that reminded him how much this had scared him last time he'd grown close to Rachel. This time was different.

This time, he had an exit strategy. He could enjoy this, just until Christmas was over.

Five days later—five blissful, sex-soaked days later—came the first real test of their fling.

The days in between had been filled with waking up with Rachel, having breakfast with Rachel, walking to work with Rachel, working at the arcade with Rachel, having dinner with Rachel, going to bed with Rachel, making love to Rachel...

But he couldn't think about that last part now. Couldn't risk today's companion reading his mind, like some sort of witch.

Because today he wasn't working with Rachel, or doing anything with Rachel.

Today, he was Christmas shopping with his sister.

Across a rack of historically patterned scarves in the British Museum shop, Celeste narrowed her eyes at him. 'What is going on with you today?'

'Nothing,' he lied.

One eyebrow raised sceptically, she checked her watch. 'Well, there's nothing for Mum here. Come on, let's try the bookshop.'

If they ended up in the museum bookshop they would never, ever leave. 'What about this scarf?' he asked, grabbing the first item that came to hand.

Celeste cast a cursory gaze over it, then shook her head. 'That pattern is generally accepted to be from the right era, I admit, but Mum's latest research suggests it might actually be later, so it'll only cause an argument between her and Dad. Come on. Bookshop.'

Damon blinked down at the apparently controversial scarf. It looked like a nice pattern to him. *And this is why I don't go shopping for our parents' presents on my own*, he reminded himself as he hurried to catch up with Celeste.

They'd instigated the annual shopping trip for their parents' Christmas presents five years ago after a particularly disastrous round of gifts from Damon one year. *He'd* thought the racing wind-up monks were hilarious, but apparently not according to the rest of the family. Similarly, the British History tie that turned out to have some dating errors on it. In his defence, he'd already tried things like spa vouchers his mother never remembered to use before they expired and experience gifts for his father that apparently he didn't want to experience. He'd been running out of ideas and, frankly, enthusiasm. Especially since Celeste always managed to find the perfect—and historically accurate—gift for them both.

Celeste had insisted that next year they'd go shopping together for joint gifts. She'd said it at the Christmas dinner table so he'd been able to see the matching looks of relief on their parents' faces.

Sometimes he didn't know why he bothered buying them anything at all.

The museum bookshop curled around the centre of the circular Great Court, filled with all sorts of literature from academic tomes to light-hearted romps through history. Celeste obviously bypassed all the books he thought looked vaguely entertaining and went instead to the more academic end of things, eventually settling on a large, coffee-table photo book of archaeological digs through the ages.

'This will do for Dad,' she said, turning decisively towards the till. 'He'll enjoy criticising the older techniques. Now, once I've paid for this you can buy me a coffee and tell me what's going on with you and Rachel. Then we can go to this arcade of yours and look for something for Mum.'

Damon winced. He knew that tone. That was Celeste's *no arguing* tone.

'I'll go and get in the queue for the coffees.' At least that would give him a chance to figure out what he was going to say.

He was walking around the Great Court heading for one of the coffee stations when he was distracted by something in the children's shop. A small felt mouse, dressed in Victorian costume, singing from a tiny carol book. Smiling to himself, he picked it up, examining the details and imagining Rachel's smile if she saw it.

He glanced back over his shoulder but there was no sign

of his sister yet. Celeste was bound to get distracted by the books on her way to the till. He had time.

Decision made, he paid for the mouse, then continued to the café.

He might not be any good at shopping for his parents, but at least there was someone in the world he knew a good gift for when he saw it.

'So,' Celeste said, easing herself onto the bench across the table from him ten minutes later. He pushed her coffee towards her, hoping it might mellow her somehow. 'You and Rachel.'

'You've spoken to her?' He needed to know what she already knew before he could figure out his line of defence.

'No. That's how I know there's something going on. She's dodging my calls.'

Damon winced. 'Not dodging. She's…been busy.'

'With you.'

'Well, yes. We're working together.'

Celeste pinned him to his seat with her steeliest gaze. 'And is that all you're doing together?'

'Isn't this a conversation you should be having with your best friend?'

'I'm trying to have it with my brother. Damon, I warned you not to mess her around—'

'I'm not!'

'Oh, so this is true love at last?' Celeste scoffed.

'I didn't say that.'

'Of course not. You wouldn't ever. And Rachel *deserves* true love.'

I know that.

Worse, he knew he wasn't the person who could give it to her.

'You have no focus, Damon. You can't commit to any-thing.' His mother's voice was echoing Celeste's implications in his head.

Damon sighed. 'Look. If I promise you that I know what I'm doing, will you let this drop?'

She raised both eyebrows at that. Never a good sign. 'That depends. *Do* you know what you're doing?'

The lie was on the tip of his tongue. How hard was it to just say *yes*? To blithely promise that he had everything in hand and there was no need to worry, just as he did for work projects all the time? Even when things were a little off course, he always managed to bring them back round again. He'd do the same this time.

So he hadn't planned on a festive fling with his sister's best friend. But now he was there…he could hardly imagine this Christmas happening any other way.

'*Do you?*' Celeste pressed.

'I hope so,' Damon replied, and prayed that would be enough.

Rachel was just putting the finishing touches to the window of Jasmine's Bridal and Formal Wear Boutique when she heard her best friend's voice behind her.

She froze, one hand still holding a small posy of holly, mistletoe and white roses she'd begged from Belinda the florist but had yet to find the perfect place for. If Celeste was here that meant Damon was probably back too, which was good because she hadn't seen him all day.

But if Celeste was here it was also bad. Because it probably meant she'd realised Rachel had been avoiding her all week.

Quickly, Rachel tucked the posy into the hands of a bridal mannequin dressed in an icy lace wedding dress— with tiny mice pulling tight the ribbons of her bodice—and ducked out of the window into the shop. Jasmine was still behind the counter, humming to herself as she worked. Rachel thought she was making a tiara, although she wasn't entirely sure. She also had bigger issues.

'Avoiding you?' she whispered to herself, practising the upcoming conversation under her breath. *'Why would I be avoiding you?'* She added a tiny laugh at the end, hoping it sounded genuine.

Behind the counter, Jasmine looked up, staring straight at her. 'If you're trying to sound convincing, you need a lot more practice than that.'

'No time,' Rachel said as the door to the shop swung open.

'There you are!' Celeste swept into the shop, elegant in her soft white woollen coat, her dark hair tucked up in the sort of clip Rachel's curls would escape from in a heartbeat. She wrapped one arm around Rachel in a perfunctory hug, the other arm weighed down by an enormous black hand-bag. Knowing Celeste as she did, it was probably full of reading material and notes rather than Christmas shopping.

'Hi, Celeste.' Rachel met Damon's gaze over his sister's shoulder. He had the beaten-down look of a man who knew he couldn't win the fight he was in.

People often had that look around Celeste. Normally she wouldn't read too much into it, except this time…this time, she was pretty sure the fight was about *her*.

'I thought you two were shopping at the British Museum today,' Rachel said, stepping back. She held her hands clasped in front of her, trying desperately not to fidget. Celeste was her best friend, for heaven's sake. Why was she nervous now? Especially when she'd spent almost a whole week with Damon, learning *not* to be nervous about asking for what she needed.

She straightened her spine and looked over to see Damon giving her an approving smile.

'I wanted to see this arcade that's got you and Damon so busy this month,' Celeste said, glancing around the boutique. 'You know me, I'm not much of a shopper.' It was one of the things that had drawn Rachel and Celeste together at university when everyone else was spending their student loans on new clothes. 'But this place is stunning. I can see why you both love it. And your window displays are amazing.'

'That's why I had to have her. For this project, I mean,' Damon added hurriedly as Rachel's eyes widened. 'I knew she'd be perfect for the Cressingham Arcade.'

Celeste still had her back to her brother so he couldn't see her raising her eyebrows in an amused expression. But Rachel could. She'd had years of translating Celeste's every slight frown or eyebrow lift, every half-smile or concerned look. And Celeste could read hers too. Between them, they could have an entire conversation across a library and know when the other needed rescuing from an overenthusiastic fellow researcher. It also worked well on their rare nights out in pubs and clubs. It was how Rachel had known that her friend was overcompensating for nerves as she argued with Theo at the filming.

And right now, she knew Celeste was saying, *He thinks he's so subtle, but he really isn't.*

She smiled in agreement, and Celeste's expression changed—a slight furrowing of the brow, a small, sideways half-smile, concern in her eyes. *Are you okay? With everything? Do I need to beat up my brother? Because I will.*

Rachel knew it. But there was no need.

Damon had been perfect all week. Alarmingly so, in fact. She'd expected him to freak out when they woke up together on Saturday morning, but he hadn't. In fact, he'd been so okay with it that they'd barely been apart since. She'd actually been the one who was unsure about that, suggesting that maybe she should go home at least *sometimes.* But Damon had asked her why she'd want to and she hadn't been able to think of a good reason so she'd stopped by the Hartbury family home long enough to pack a bag and that was about it. She wasn't sure if her family had noticed.

The thing was, she reasoned to herself in the dark of the night, she only had this Christmas with Damon. A festive fling, that was all.

So she might as well make the most of every minute of it.

Celeste was still watching her, waiting for her response, that furrow of a frown line growing deeper with each passing second. Rachel wondered what Damon had told her. She'd have to ask him later. But for now, she needed to reassure her best friend that she knew what she was doing, that she wasn't about to get her heart broken. Probably.

So she smiled, eyebrows neutral, gave a slight nod and watched Celeste relax. Mission accomplished.

Celeste clapped her hands together as if they'd had an actual conversation, instead of a weird eyebrow discussion. 'Great! Well, in that case, Damon, I assume you're bringing Rachel to the traditional Hunter Christmas Eve party this year?'

Damon, understandably, looked a little lost at the sudden change of topic. 'Uh, we hadn't talked about it. But, if you'd like to come… I'd love to have you there.'

She hadn't had as many years translating Damon's expressions and hidden words but, after the last week, she liked to think she was getting better. So she heard the truth in his words and hoped she understood them.

He didn't want to go to the family party, she knew that. But if he had to be there, he'd rather be there with her at his side. And that felt pretty wonderful. It felt like…hope.

'Okay,' she whispered, and watched the smile spread across his face.

'In that case, you're going to need something to wear.' Celeste spun slowly around, taking in all the beautiful evening dresses and wedding gowns the boutique racks held. 'I'm fairly sure you can find the perfect dress here, don't you think?' She smiled at Jasmine, who darted out from behind the counter and grinned as she sized Rachel up.

'We absolutely can,' she promised. 'I'm thinking something red. The colour of a really good red wine.'

'My favourite,' Damon said, moving behind Rachel. He lowered his voice so only she could hear. 'I'm thinking something that slides off your shoulders all the way to the floor the minute we get home again.'

Her cheeks warmed at that, but Celeste didn't seem to notice.

'Perfect,' she said, and turned to them both. 'And after that, we need to go out for lunch, so you can both meet my sort-of date for the party too.'

Rachel and Damon exchanged a look, one that Celeste could probably have read effortlessly if she hadn't already been looking through dresses with Jasmine with more enthusiasm than Celeste had ever shown about anyone's wardrobe, including her own, previously.

Celeste had a *date*?

CHAPTER TWELVE

CELESTE HAD SPENT all morning grilling him about his relationship with Rachel, and now this? She'd avoided all of his questions under the premise of concentrating on choosing the perfect dress for Rachel—which they had—and then been tight-lipped all the way in the cab to the restaurant she, or rather her date, had apparently booked for the four of them.

'Do you have any idea who she's been seeing?' he murmured to Rachel as Celeste paid the driver.

She shrugged. 'None. To be honest, I haven't been paying a lot of attention to the world outside the Cressingham Arcade for the last week.'

'Apart from the world inside my apartment,' he pointed out, mostly just to watch the pink spread across her cheeks as she remembered all the places in that apartment he'd kissed, touched and made love to her over the last five days.

She gave him a secret smile, one he'd come to know and adore since they began their festive fling. He returned it, then looked up to find Celeste watching them, her expression speculative. Damn.

He really didn't need her getting ideas that this was anything more than he'd told her it was, more than he and Rachel had *agreed* it was.

Well, he thought as Celeste swept into the restaurant,

this lunch would have to be his chance to convince her of the truth. And tease her mercilessly about keeping her new boyfriend from them. Not enough to scare the poor guy off—although, if he was dating Celeste, he had to have a higher tolerance for terror than most men anyway. It would probably take a lot more than an amused little brother to ruin things.

Then he saw Theo Montgomery sitting alone at a table for four and realised that this double date was going to be even more bizarre than he'd imagined.

'Is that…?' Rachel trailed off, her mouth still slightly open with astonishment.

'Apparently. Something you want to tell us, Celeste?'

'Just…pretend this is all totally normal, okay?' His sister straightened her spine, pasted on a smile and led them across the restaurant to Theo's table.

Damon watched in astonishment as Theo stood, smiling, and embraced Celeste, kissing her right on the lips. And Celeste, against all possible odds, returned the kiss, blushing prettily as she stepped away afterwards.

Was he in another dimension? It seemed possible. And more likely than Celeste and Theo actually being in love and not bickering with each other.

'Sweetheart, you remember my brother, Damon? And his girlfriend, Rachel?'

Okay, Celeste had definitely never called anyone 'sweetheart' in her life. Something was definitely going on here—Wait. Did she call Rachel his girlfriend?

It was too late to correct her now, he supposed, while Theo was hugging Rachel in welcome, and holding out a hand for him to shake. Damon took it then moved closer to the table, pulling out Rachel's chair first instinctively, only realising he'd done it when he saw Theo doing the same for Celeste.

What followed had to be the most surreal meal of his

life, and he said that as someone who had experienced his father's attempts to recreate an Ancient Roman banquet, complete with honeyed dormouse. Watching Theo and Celeste be not just civil, but actually affectionate with each other, to the point of Theo feeding her some of his starter from his own fork, was just baffling. As far as he could tell, Rachel was equally confused, although she managed to keep up something of a conversation with Celeste.

Damon tried to chat with Theo but, to be honest, his mind was occupied by other things. Like Celeste calling Rachel his girlfriend.

Girlfriend implied long term—certainly past Christmas. It implied deeper feelings than Damon was willing to commit to. And worse than that, it gave people—namely Rachel—ideas.

He needed to talk to his sister, make the situation even clearer than he had over coffee that morning. Hadn't she been the one who'd pointed out that Rachel deserved more than him? So why was she suddenly pushing like this, inviting Rachel to the family party, calling her his girlfriend?

Although having Rachel at his parents' Christmas Eve party with him was the only thing that could make the night bearable, as far as he was concerned.

Still. It wouldn't do for anyone to get ideas, that was all. Especially not him.

It wasn't until the puddings were eaten that Theo suddenly sat up straighter, leaning around Celeste to watch something out of the window, then collapsed back into his seat with obvious relief.

'He's gone?' Celeste asked, shifting her chair away from Theo's to a more normal distance.

Theo nodded. 'Finally.'

Beside Damon, Rachel frowned. 'Who's gone?'

'Our reporter stalker,' Theo said, with a tired smile.

'Come on, let's grab after-lunch drinks in the back bar where it's more private. Then we can explain.'

The back bar was cosy, warm and empty. Theo spoke briefly to the head waiter on their way in and he nodded, then shut the door behind them, returning moments later to enter, after knocking, with a tray of coffees and liquors. Then he departed again, leaving them in peace.

It didn't escape Rachel's notice that, now they no longer had an audience, Celeste and Theo were sitting as far away from each other as they could manage while still at the same table.

Damon had noticed too. He looked between them once, twice, then just asked. 'What the hell is going on here?'

Rachel let out a breath and took a seat—one next to Celeste, just in case her friend needed her. She hadn't seen any hint of this, whatever *this* was, in Celeste's manner when they'd been dress shopping at the arcade. And surely if something really weird was going on Celeste would have told her?

When? her mind asked rebelliously. *When you were avoiding her calls because you were in bed with her brother and you knew she wouldn't approve?*

Okay, fine. She'd been a rubbish friend this month. But now she was here, she was every bit as curious as Damon as to what was going on.

'Do you want to explain, or shall I?' Theo asked Celeste, his upper-class tone lazy.

'I'll do it,' Celeste replied, sharply. 'You'll get it wrong.'

'Probably,' Theo agreed easily. 'I'll pour the coffees, then.'

'So, Damon, I know you watched the car crash that was our festive TV quiz. Rachel, I assume you did too?' Celeste asked.

Rachel nodded, although in truth she'd only been able

to bear watching the highlights on the Internet after the event. They were definitely bad enough.

'It didn't go down particularly well with the Internet fans. Or my agent,' Theo said.

Celeste shot him a look that Rachel interpreted as, *Who is telling this story, you or me?* Theo had obviously spent enough time with Celeste to read it too as he shut up and let her continue.

'So Theo called me and asked me to help him rehabilitate his reputation.'

'And yours,' Theo interjected.

Celeste rolled her eyes. 'My reputation is based on my research, my publications, my education and my brain, not my ability to be pleasant on television. Unlike yours.'

'Your reputation with TV companies, however, is based *entirely* on that,' Theo pointed out, apparently unruffled by the accusation that he was just a pretty face.

Celeste ignored him.

Rachel snuck a look across the table at Damon, who was glowering at both of them. For all that he was the younger of the two siblings, she knew he could still be fiercely protective of his big sister. If he thought Theo was using Celeste…

'So what happened next?' she asked, keen to move the conversation along before the two of them descended into bickering again.

'We agreed to a few public appearances together, as friends,' Celeste said, as if it were the most normal thing in the world. Maybe it was in *Theo's* world, but Rachel knew for a fact that Celeste had never once in her life pretended to be anything she wasn't.

And now she was pretending to be Theo's friend? Girlfriend, even?

'It got a little bit out of hand from there,' Theo admitted. 'There were these stories online…'

'People thought we were faking it,' Celeste explained.

'Which you were.' Damon, Rachel noticed, was still glowering as he spoke.

'So we had to prove that we really *were* okay with each other,' Celeste went on, ignoring her brother. 'By pretending we were in love.'

'So you're mortal enemies pretending to sleep together for the cameras,' Damon said, dryly. 'The miracle of modern love, huh?'

'Like you can talk,' Celeste scoffed, then turned to Theo. 'This one spent all morning telling me how he and Rachel are just colleagues who sleep together. Apparently they're having a "festive fling".'

Oh.

Oh.

There was nothing about the words that were untrue, Rachel knew that. It was exactly what they'd agreed—a festive fling, nothing serious. Just something that would make the time while they were working together more fun.

And yet, every syllable of Celeste's words seemed to slice off another section of her heart.

She knew she couldn't let it show. This was like Tobias all over again, even if it shouldn't be. Tobias had lied to her, let her believe that what he felt for her mattered to him. Damon had never done that. He wasn't hiding her away, he wasn't ashamed of his attraction to her. He liked her, wanted her, desired her, enjoyed her company. All of that was still true, and he'd never promised anything more. She couldn't hold this against him.

But she could still feel the other three watching her, waiting to see if she'd fall apart, as she had when she'd realised the truth about Tobias.

Not this time. This time she was stronger. This time, she knew she'd be okay.

Yes, she might have very stupidly fallen for a man who had told her upfront he wasn't in this for the long haul, but she'd told him the same. Now she just had to suck it up and deal with it.

Even if she was realising, rather too late, that she might be just a little bit in love with him.

Rachel forced herself to smile, just as Celeste said, 'Sorry, Rachel, that came out wrong.'

'No, it's true.' She reached for her liquor. That might help. 'He's my festive fling. Right, Damon?'

'Right.' But even he didn't look convinced.

She took a sip of her drink and reminded herself to keep breathing.

She'd figure this out. Find a way to save her battered heart.

But if she only had one more week with Damon Hunter before their Christmas romance was over, she wasn't going to waste any of it moping about. She was going to enjoy every second.

Four days after the double date from hell, the Cressingham Arcade officially opened to the public, not that it had been fully closed all along. But the scaffolding and cordons were gone, the floor tiles were repaired, the window displays were beautiful—apart from Mr Jenkins's jewellery shop, because the old codger had kept putting off letting Rachel in to arrange anything—and Rachel's social media campaign had built to such a frenzy that there were actual queues waiting outside the arcade at opening time.

'I can't believe we really did it,' Rachel said, her eyes wide with astonishment as Lady Cressingham formally opened the gates for the first time.

'I can,' Damon told her, but he was watching her, not the crowds.

She'd made this happen. He hoped she knew how incredible that made her.

He tried to show her, that night in bed. Tried to tell her

how amazing she was. But that connection, the one he'd felt since the first time they kissed…it seemed closed off. As if he couldn't get through to her any more.

Was it because they were coming to the end of their time together? Probably. It made sense to try and pull away before they had to, to ease the ending. He should probably be trying to do the same thing.

But he couldn't. Because every time he thought about not waking up to Rachel's face smiling at him, he felt as if he couldn't breathe.

But he was going to have to figure it out, he resolved, in a stern pep talk to his reflection in the kitchen window of the Hunter family townhouse, three days later. Because tonight was Christmas Eve and, after tomorrow, their festive fling would be over. Which meant he'd have to spend the dying minutes of it here, in his parents' town house. His least favourite place in the world.

He fingered the felt mouse in his pocket, the one he'd bought at the British Museum. He hadn't found the right moment to give it to Rachel just yet, but he supposed he'd better find it tonight.

It might be his last chance.

'What are you brooding about in here?' Celeste asked, walking into the kitchen and catching him glaring at the drinks trolley.

'Who says I'm brooding?'

'Anyone who can see you.'

'Which is…' Damon looked ostentatiously around them '…basically just you.'

Grabbing a tea towel from the counter, Celeste swatted him lightly with it, the way she used to when they were kids. 'Is it Rachel?'

'Is what Rachel?'

That earned him an eye-roll. 'Is it Rachel that's making you so broody?'

'If I were brooding—and that's a big if,' he added as Celeste made her *I knew I was right* smug face. 'If I were, there would be no reason for it to be about Rachel.'

Except, of course, it was. And his sister wasn't falling for any twisted non-answers he might give, unfortunately.

'So, which is it?' She hopped up onto the kitchen counter and ticked the options off on her fingers. 'You're bored of her already and regretting asking her to come tonight because it will end your chances of picking up someone else.'

'No.' Damon grabbed the ice tray from the freezer and started bashing the cubes out into the ice bucket, as his mother had asked him to before his broodfest had started.

'Okay, good, because I really would have snapped that towel at you if you had. Okay, option two: you're worried that she's falling in love with you, and you're going to hurt her when you end things *just like I said you would*.' The last part was loud enough that Damon half expected his parents to come rushing in to see what they were arguing about.

Except since they'd rarely ever done that when they were kids, it seemed unlikely they were going to start now. Not when they were each busy in their own private rooms, preparing for the party ahead.

'That's not the problem,' he said, curtly. 'Now, if you don't mind, I've got a list of tasks to finish before Mum comes down—' Damon tried to move towards the door, but Celeste swung her long legs up to rest on the counter opposite, blocking his way out of the narrow galley kitchen.

'In that case, that only leaves option three.'

'Which is?' he asked impatiently, even though he didn't really want to know.

'That you don't want to end it at all. That you've fallen for her. Properly.' There was a hint of awe in Celeste's voice at the very possibility.

'Don't be ridiculous,' he said, even though his heart was beating too fast at her words.

'I don't think it's ridiculous. I mean, Rachel is far too good for you, but other than that—'

He pushed her legs out of the way and stepped through. As if he didn't already know that. 'Unless you and Theo are going to come clean tonight that your whole relationship is a lie—or announce that you're actually madly in love and planning the wedding—please stop lecturing me about my situation with Rachel, okay?'

She bristled at the mention of Theo, just as he'd known she would, and he escaped without further comment from her. Their whole lives, the easiest way to distract Celeste had always been to bring up her own shortcomings.

It made a change from thinking about his anyway.

CHAPTER THIRTEEN

CHRISTMAS EVE. How was it Christmas Eve already?

The last week had seemed to go both too fast and too slow for Rachel. Every day was so busy, between the opening of the arcade, her shifts at Hartbury's, and spending her evenings and mornings with Damon, the time had flown by. Counting down to the moment her life went back to normal, the way it had been before Damon Hunter had swept her onto a dance floor at fake midnight and kissed her.

And yet, at the same time…every moment she'd spent with Damon had seemed to last longer. Maybe because she was so determined to remember every last second. Or perhaps just because she could already feel the distance growing between them.

Now, as she finished up her last shift at Hartbury's before it closed for Christmas, she wondered how, exactly, she'd be able to go back to that old life. She wasn't the person she'd been then. How could she be, when she'd lived a whole life's worth of missed romance and seduction in less than a month?

The bell had rung to announce closing time almost fifteen minutes earlier and the children's-wear floor she was covering that afternoon was empty. Time to get ready for Damon and Celeste's parents' party—and to say goodbye to her festive fling for good. Just until Christmas, that was what they'd decided—what she'd insisted on. And now Christmas was here.

At least she was going to see it out in style. Grabbing the bag she'd brought from her little closet office, she headed for the changing rooms to get ready for the party. It didn't take long to wriggle into the silky, wine-red dress she'd chosen from Jasmine's collection, although she decided to save the high heels until she'd found a taxi, just in case. Her dark curls didn't need much more than a fluff—they were going to do whatever they wanted anyway so she might as well just let them get on with it.

She was halfway through putting her make-up on when she realised she was no longer alone.

'Another party, Rachie?' Gretchen asked. Rachel spun to find both her stepsisters watching her from the doorway to the fitting room. 'You're getting to be quite the party animal, aren't you?'

'Compared to who?' Rachel asked, without thinking. But really, she'd been to two parties that month, and one of those was the shop one.

Maisie's smile twisted a little, making her beautiful face a little uglier. 'We're just worried about you, Rachie. Don't think we haven't noticed you staying out until all hours— or worse, not coming home at all.'

'You don't need to worry about me,' Rachel said, stiffly. How could she have believed they wouldn't notice? Of course they would. Mostly to give them ammunition to cause trouble for her later.

'But we *do*! You're our sister after all.' Gretchen swept into the changing room, casting an eye over Rachel's outfit. Rachel fought the urge to scream *step*sister at her.

'It's Damon, isn't it?' Maisie followed her sister, as always, until between them they were almost surrounding her, blocking her between the mirrored walls and themselves. 'You're falling for him.'

'And that worries us too,' Gretchen added. 'You're so naive when it comes to love, Rachie.'

'Remember Tobias?' Maisie added, as if Rachel were *ever* likely to forget that particularly humiliating episode.

'We just don't want something like that to happen to you again, is all.' Gretchen reached out to touch the silky fabric of her dress and Rachel flinched away. 'I mean, dressing up to try and impress him? It's just not you, Rachel.'

'You know he's using you, right?' Maisie said, bluntly. 'I mean, why else would he be interested? He's got you working over at that arcade everyone's talking about, hasn't he? I've seen the social media campaign.'

'Luckily for you, I don't think Mum has.' Gretchen raised an eyebrow as she spoke. 'And of course *we* wouldn't show her.'

Yes, you would, Rachel thought. *Why haven't you?*

Maisie shot an irritated look at her sister. That was unusual too; they were always so in sync.

'The point is, now the place is open he won't need you any more, Rachel. And we don't want you going out there embarrassing yourself again, like before.' Maisie's gaze was wide and guileless and Rachel didn't buy it for a minute.

Unwilling to look either of them in the eye a moment longer, Rachel found herself staring at her own reflection, along with her stepsisters'. The two of them loomed over her in their heels, their immaculate outfits, hair and make-up as intimidating to her as always.

For just a second, she let it get to her.

Were they right? Had the festive fling just been a convenient way to keep her onside while they worked on the project?

Just colleagues who sleep together.

No. She knew it was more than that because she'd seen the passion in Damon's eyes when he watched her, felt his need for her in his touch. She'd laughed with him, talked with him, relaxed with him—and felt more herself than she had done in years, just from being in his presence.

With Damon, she'd found the courage to ask for what she needed—and now she hoped she'd continue to have that strength without him.

Because Gretchen and Maisie were right about one thing. After tonight, it was all over between them.

Unless it isn't.

The possibility welled up in her too fast, too strong for her fear to stamp it down.

Because she *knew* Damon wasn't giving up on them for any of the reasons her stepsisters were suggesting. Their fling was ending because that was what she'd asked for. And if she wanted something different now...

Well. She had to ask for that too.

He might say no.

She felt the truth settle in her heart, and knew there was a very good chance he would. Damon Hunter didn't settle down, didn't choose one path if it closed off all the others. He liked to keep his options open and what she wanted from him was the opposite of that.

She didn't want a festive fling.

She wanted Damon forever. Hers.

Which meant she had to tell him that. Tonight.

Spinning around, she grabbed her bag and figured she'd sort out her make-up in the taxi using her phone camera.

'Where are you going?' Gretchen called after her.

'Didn't you listen to anything we said?' Maisie yelled.

Rachel turned and walked backwards for a few steps as she replied, glad she hadn't put her heels on yet.

'I listened,' she said. 'And I know you're wrong. So, if you'll excuse me, I'm off to find my own life, for a change.'

Then she turned her back on them and headed for the doors.

His mother was complaining about something but Damon had tuned her out minutes ago. Or years ago, perhaps. All he knew was that there was something wrong with the ice—inexplicably, since surely ice was ice?—that Celeste was still glaring at him across the room, and that his father was deep in conversation with Theo Montgomery. Or, more accurately, his father was talking, at length, and Theo was listening politely.

Oh, and Rachel wasn't there yet. He was definitely aware of that.

'And I don't know *what* your father is finding to talk to *That Man* about,' his mother said as Damon tuned back in.

'I think *That Man* is just a convenient audience for Dad to practise his latest lecture.' Theo Montgomery had gone down about as badly as expected as a boyfriend for Celeste. It wasn't as though she'd brought many home before now, but Theo was definitely at the bottom of the list. He didn't even *have* a PhD.

His mother sniffed. 'I don't know what happened to that nice boy from the Philosophy department.'

'I think you and Dad scared him off after his first Sunday dinner,' Damon said mildly, safe in the knowledge that his mother wasn't listening to him anyway.

'At least he knew what he wanted, knew what *mattered* to him.' His mother gave him a sideways look. 'Which is more than we can say for some people.'

Yes, yes. Because he was hopelessly uncommitted. His parents' motto was practically, *If you don't know what matters to you, then you don't matter at all.* He was used to not mattering. It didn't bother him any more.

Where was Rachel? Tonight was the last night of their festive fling; that was the deal. And he didn't want to miss a moment of it. So where was she?

He scanned the room again in case he'd missed her, although he couldn't see how that was possible. But he did realise suddenly that his sister was missing. Which meant...

Turning his back on his mother—not that she noticed—he focussed on the door that led in from the main hallway to the living room and dining room, which had all been opened up for the party. Any moment now...

There.

Even though he'd been preparing himself for it all day, the sight of Rachel in that wine-red dress still took his breath away. Her hand tucked through Celeste's arm, she entered the room smiling and he could sense the other guests turning to look at her. Even with the dress she still looked just like the same Rachel he'd known for so long, her curls rioting around her head, her make-up minimal, her figure gorgeously curvaceous. But there was something new about her too. And that was what was making everyone stare, where before they might have overlooked her.

Damon wasn't conceited enough to believe that the difference was him, but it *was* visible. As she walked towards him, it clicked.

It was her confidence.

She wasn't looking at the ground, avoiding everyone's gaze. She wasn't clinging to the walls hoping no one noticed she was there, hoping no one asked her anything.

She had her head held high, a secret smile around her mouth—the smile of a woman who knew what she wanted and intended to get it. And she was heading straight for him.

Suddenly, the pain in his chest wasn't from lack of breath. It was pangs of fear. Because he knew that look; he'd seen it before on other women's faces. That was the smile of a woman who thought she had him where she wanted him. Who thought he couldn't possibly let her down now.

He'd let them all down, every one of them. Starting with his parents, then his sister, then every woman he'd ever dated, he'd let down every single person who'd ever looked at him that way. With expectation. Because that was what he did.

And as much as he might hate himself for it, he knew he was going to do the same thing to Rachel. Because that was just who he was. Damon Hunter, commitment-phobe, flake, unreliable guy.

Why on earth had he thought he could be anything different, even for a moment? That he could get out of this festive fling with everyone's heart and pride intact?

You don't want to end it at all. You've fallen for her. Properly.

Those weren't his words, weren't his thoughts. They were Celeste's. And if he'd never listened to his sister before, he wasn't going to start now.

He and Rachel had made an agreement: a festive fling. And he was sticking to it. That was all there was to it.

Maybe his decision showed on his face because as he straightened his spine and tried to smile, Rachel stumbled, just a little. Celeste caught her arm and he saw Rachel murmur something to her. His sister nodded then, Rachel steady again, and peeled off to head towards Theo. Damon stopped paying her any attention at that point.

He couldn't see anything but Rachel. And how everything good in his life was about to blow up in his face.

Oh, goodness, she wasn't sure if she could do this. Just the look on Damon's face as he watched her...he knew what was coming, she could tell. He was figuring out how to let her down gently.

Because what she was about to do wasn't what they'd

agreed. It wasn't *fair*. And she was going to do it anyway, because it was a hell of a lot more honest and important than any agreement about a festive fling.

'You okay?' Celeste murmured as Rachel slipped, one of her high heels skidding on the Hunters' parquet flooring.

'No.' She grabbed onto Celeste a little tighter while she found her balance. 'But I will be.'

'Do you want me to come with you to talk to him?'

Because of course Celeste knew what she was going to say. She was transparent. The moment Celeste had opened the door she'd taken one look at her and said, *'Oh, my God, you're in love with my brother.'*

That was what happened when you only had one good friend your entire adult life. They could tell *everything*.

'No,' Rachel told her now. 'I need to do this alone.'

'You're sure?'

Rachel looked again at Damon. He looked as if he was steeling himself for a horrible scene. Maybe he was. She'd never had this kind of conversation before. Never had this kind of confidence before. She didn't know how it was going to go.

But she still wasn't strong enough to do this with too much of an audience.

'Sure. Besides, I need you to do something else for me.'

'Anything,' Celeste said.

'Distract the rest of the room?' The party wasn't so big that the small crowd would be able to ignore any argument between her and Damon. Apparently the Hunters' idea of a party was more like everyone else's idea of having a few friends round. Or maybe they just didn't have that many friends. 'Just while I get Damon out of here. I don't want an audience for this.'

Celeste shot her a crooked smile. 'On it.'

Rachel took another breath and continued on towards her doom.

Damon smiled as she reached him, obviously hoping he could pretend there was nothing unusual going on here.

'Hey, you look beautiful,' he said. 'Can I get you a drink? Or there are some nibbles over here—'

'Damon.' Her voice didn't even sound like her own. It had authority. Confidence. Surety. All the things she'd never had before in her life…before him.

And now, because of them, she was going to lose him. She could see it in the desperate gleam in his eyes, the way his shoulders slumped as she said his name.

He didn't want her to do this any more than she wanted to do it. But because of him, because of all that she'd learned about herself in the time they'd spent together, she had to.

'I bought you something,' he said, desperately. Fishing something out of his pocket, he held it out in the palm of his hand.

Rachel stared at it. A small felt mouse in a perfectly fitted red jacket holding a carol sheet in front of him.

She loved it. But she didn't take it. Not yet.

'We need to talk,' she said, instead.

'I know.' She heard defeat in his voice as his fist closed around the poor mouse. 'Come on.'

She followed him into the kitchen, aware that there was some sort of commotion drawing attention behind them, but unwilling to take her eyes off Damon for a second to find out what it was. Theo and Celeste, she imagined. And actually, she didn't want to imagine that any more than she had to.

The kitchen, at least, was quiet, cool and drama free. She'd expected they'd stop there, but Damon kept walking, all the way to the back door, which he opened and drew her out into the bitter December night. She shivered as she followed him across the grass to where a small swing seat hung from a tree at the end of the long, narrow garden.

Shrugging off his jacket, Damon wrapped it around her shoulders, then motioned for her to sit.

'Tonight's the last night of our festive fling,' he said wistfully as he sat beside her. And for a moment, Rachel felt a spark of hope deep inside her. Then he flashed her a quick smile and added, 'We made the most of it, didn't we?'

Yes. So much so that I fell head over heels in love with you.

He was trying to take control of the conversation, talking over the spaces where she would have spoken, the way her family had done all her life. The way *he* never had before.

He's scared, she realised. But why? What could he have to be scared of? The worst that could happen was that Celeste would be cross with him for breaking her heart. If he felt nothing for her beyond their fling, what was there to be scared of?

Unless he was scared because he *did* feel something, and he didn't know what to do about it.

Rachel felt that hope flare up again. She just hoped Damon was brave enough to feel it too.

CHAPTER FOURTEEN

'In fact, I was thinking, maybe we could still get together, now and then, if you wanted. Just casually, of course.' Damon was talking for the sake of talking and he knew it. But if he stopped, he knew Rachel was going to ask him for something he didn't know how to give. So he just kept going. 'It seems a shame to give up such great chemistry completely, right?'

Please, let it be enough. It's all I know how to give you. Please.

He just needed time. He wasn't an idiot. He'd known long before Celeste brought it to his attention that he was in over his head here. That what he felt for Rachel wasn't like anything he'd felt before. That was why it was so terrifying.

Hell, he'd known nine years ago that if he got too close to this woman he'd fall. At eighteen he'd been smart enough to run the other way.

Apparently, growing up had made him stupid.

He needed time to figure out what it meant. How it fitted in with who he was. How he could still be *him*, when he felt this way about her.

'I think a spring fling has a nice sound to it anyway, don't you?' He flashed his best, most charming smile, and hoped.

But Rachel wasn't smiling. He knew that, even in the

pitch dark of the winter night, with only faint lights from the windows, the moon and the street lights behind them to help him figure it out.

He stopped talking. People had been talking over Rachel, talking *for* her, for too many years already. He might be a complete arse but he wasn't going to be another of *those* people.

However hard it was, he needed to listen to what she had to say.

'Damon. That's what I came here tonight to tell you. I don't want a fling, festive, spring or otherwise, with you.' She paused, taking a breath, and Damon resisted the urge to interrupt her. Just. 'I'm in love with you. I know that wasn't the deal we made, and it definitely wasn't what I planned but… I knew it was a risk. I've, well, had a crush on you basically the whole time I've known you. I knew I should stay away to protect my own heart, I knew that you didn't do commitment, that you weren't offering anything beyond this Christmas. But the way I feel when I'm with you… Damon, you make me feel like I can do anything, and I want more of that feeling.'

'You *can* do anything,' he told her, because it might be his last chance. 'You're amazing.'

'That's what made me believe I could do this.' She met his gaze with her own, and even in the half-light he could see the steely determination in it. 'You taught me to ask for what I wanted. So I'm asking. I want *you*, Damon. Not for a fling, or for a season. Forever. I want you to love me the way I love you. I want us to be together. And I think deep down you might want the same thing too. So I'm asking…do you?'

It was as if his world had frozen.

So many years, so many people, jobs, opportunities, and nobody had ever asked him to stay, to commit. Not outright like that. Oh, people had hinted, made suggestions, always couched in terms that allowed them to save face if he said no. And he had always said no, because that wasn't who he was.

For the first time, the smallest corner of his heart wanted to say yes.

But he couldn't.

So he tried to negotiate.

'I'm not ready to say goodbye to you yet, if that's what you mean. So maybe we could—'

'It's not what I mean,' she interrupted him, proving once and for all that she wasn't the shy, easily intimidated Rachel everyone else seemed to think she was. 'I'm not asking you to propose marriage here and now or anything, but I need to know if you're willing to give a relationship between us a proper shot. To admit that this isn't just "colleagues who have sex" or even a festive fling. That what we have *matters*. It's special, and it means something, and you're willing to commit to finding out where that leads us. If you can't do that—'

'I don't commit,' he said, automatically. 'You know that.'

Was it the moonlight that made her expression look so pitying? He hoped so.

'Because you have to keep your options open, right?' She nodded and got to her feet, shrugging off his jacket and laying it on her empty seat. 'Okay, then. Well, in that case, thank you for my first festive fling. It honestly changed my life. I'll see you at work next week.' And with that, she turned her back on him and walked away, taking that part of his heart he'd been ignoring for so long with her.

'Wait!' he called, but while her footsteps slowed, just for a moment, when he couldn't find any more words to follow up with, she didn't stop.

She left him sitting there in his parents' garden, feeling like the biggest idiot known to man.

A feeling that didn't dissipate when his sister appeared

a few minutes later, and sat down beside him on the swing, crushing his jacket.

'You are the biggest idiot known to man,' she said.

'I know.' But what else could he have done? Rachel was asking for something he wasn't able to give. Saying no now was far easier on everyone than going along with what she wanted, only to break her heart later when she realised he wasn't the man she'd hoped he could be.

'Let me guess.' Celeste kicked off the floor with one foot, making the old swing seat sway forward and back. 'She asked you to commit and you said no.'

'Basically.'

'Why? Because you wanted to be free to sleep with as many other women as possible?'

'No!' He was pretty sure he'd never find another woman like Rachel anyway. 'Because I'm not that guy. I'd let her down, in the end, when she realised that.'

He needed to keep moving, keep things interesting, seek out new variety in his life. He couldn't afford to become as tunnel-visioned as his parents had always been. He couldn't pass up all the other opportunities that might come his way. Not other women, other relationships. Those were the last things on his mind right now. But committing, settling down, that meant saying no to other things, didn't it? Meant always asking permission, always consulting someone else…

The way his parents never had.

They'd single-mindedly pursued their own interests and expected their children to be interested in the same things. He'd spent his whole life knowing he wasn't good enough for them because he didn't have that same passion for one subject. They'd chosen what mattered to them and gone after it, while he'd tried to take a different path by seeking variety in all things.

In fact, he'd chased constant change the way they'd

chased their careers, to the point of ignoring all other options...

He'd thought he was so different from them, but what if he was just making the same mistakes in his own way? What if he'd been so fixated on moving forward that he failed to recognise the one thing worth standing still for?

Love.

'Damon?' Celeste actually sounded concerned, which meant he must look worse than he felt.

'I'm okay.' A lie, but then, she'd know that too.

'For what it's worth? I don't think you'd let her down, little brother.' Standing up, she pressed a quick kiss to his hair, something he couldn't remember her doing since he was a child. 'In fact, I think you've got a better handle on this love thing than most of us. You just need to be brave enough to go after it.'

Go after it. Go after her.

As he watched his sister walk away, the same way her best friend had not so long ago, the pieces started to fall into place in Damon's head.

And suddenly, he knew what he had to do.

Rachel was not going to cry. She was absolutely not crying. She was not—

'Need a tissue back there, love?' The taxi driver reached back between the front seats and handed her one anyway, which was just as well, as she couldn't really talk much through her sobs.

'Christmas can be tough,' he added sagely as she blew her nose. 'Now, let's get you where you need to be.'

Theo had put her in the cab, bless him, and when the driver had asked her where she wanted to go she'd only hesitated for a moment.

She couldn't go home, not knowing that Hannah, Gretchen, Maisie and her dad would be there, playing happy Christmas Eve family. Not when her stepsisters would know instantly what had happened—and wouldn't hesitate to tell her that they had told her so. She needed a little time to herself before that happened.

She'd thought briefly of the department store. It would be empty, she had a key, and she could hide out in her little cupboard office until she felt ready to face the world again.

Except that was going backwards, back to who she had been before. And she wasn't going to do that.

In fact, she'd sent her resignation letter to Hannah by email before heading to the party, just to ensure that she couldn't.

So, with her past behind her, and the future she'd hoped for out of reach, that meant there was only one thing to do.

Build a new future.

'Cressingham Arcade,' she'd said. 'Take me to the arcade.'

Because while the arcade would always be intrinsically linked to Damon in her mind and in her heart, it was also the place where she'd found her professional courage. It was where she'd realised for the first time that her window displays were something people valued, rather than something she was allowed to do as a favour from her stepmother. Where, working with the shopkeepers, she'd finally been able to put into practice all she'd learned in her years of studying, to bring to life all the ideas she had for bringing local businesses to the public eye. She'd been able to help people because she had skills and knowledge they didn't. Ones they valued.

She'd never felt that way before. And she wasn't going to give it up just because Damon wasn't brave enough to face up to what he felt.

Besides, there was one last window she still hadn't managed to transform. And she wanted it done before Christmas morning.

The arcade was in darkness, of course, but as she let herself in she realised it wasn't actually empty. At the far end of the passageway there was a light on inside one shop. The shop she'd come to visit.

'Mr Jenkins?' Rachel leaned against the open doorway and looked in at the older man sitting hunched over at his desk.

He looked up, apparently unsurprised to see her. 'You're here to finish that window display, I suppose.'

'If you don't mind.'

Mr Jenkins waved a hand towards the window. 'What do I care? It's only my shop.'

That, Rachel decided, was practically an excited request for help, coming from Mr Jenkins.

'I'll get to work, then.'

The display had been building in her imagination for weeks, ever since she'd first visited the shop. Working under Mr Jenkins's watchful eye—for all that he pretended he was paying her no attention at all—she quickly brought together all the elements she'd dreamt of.

There were her mice, of course—those featured in every window, in one way or another. And elements from the other shops in the arcade too, like silk flowers from the florist's, a lace veil from the bridal boutique, beautiful papers and pens from the stationer's, all to display Mr Jenkins's jewels on. But most of the display elements came from the jeweller's itself—not just the rings and necklaces and gems, but the vintage typewriter he kept behind the desk, and the black and white photo of a beautiful young woman from the shelf above it.

'My late wife,' he said, gruffly, when she asked if she could use it. 'She always liked putting on a show. Reckon she'd like to be in your window too.'

It was more than an hour later that she finally stepped

outside the shop, stretched out the kinks in her back and neck, and stood back to admire her handiwork.

There, sprawling from left to right across the window display, was the story she wanted to tell. A love story, of course. One that spanned years and continents—courtesy of the vintage clocks and map Mr Jenkins had squirrelled away in a cupboard. One written in piles of letters—delivered by mice, naturally—and culminating in a stunning engagement ring.

Suddenly, one last mouse appeared. A mouse in a red jacket, singing Christmas carols, placed next to the ring by a hand she recognised, although the face attached to it was hidden by the shadows of the shop.

He must have come in the back way, her mind noted absently. *Mr Jenkins hates it when he does that.*

But the thought was so surreal, she couldn't quite process it, let alone begin to hope. Maybe she was imagining things. That made more sense than the alternative right now, given the way the rest of the evening had gone.

Rachel stared at the mouse as the hand pulled away, even as she heard the shop door open, and someone join her outside.

'It's perfect.'

At the sound of Damon's voice, the spell broke, and she spun around, the display forgotten.

'What are you doing here?' Anger rose up in her, unexpected and unbidden. This was her future she was chasing. Couldn't he give her one night to move on from their fling?

But Damon shifted his weight from one foot to the other, his expression nervous in the faded yellow of the arcade's vintage lighting.

'I'm here to follow your lead,' he said. 'To finally admit what I want…and ask for it.'

Anger faded. Instead, that flicker of hope, the one she'd swallowed down and tried to ignore as she'd walked away from him, returned. 'And what do you want?' She kept her tone neutral, free from emotion or influence. He needed to tell her, this time. To ask for what he wanted. What they both needed.

'You. If you'll have me.'

'Why?' She hoped his reasons were good. Because it was taking everything she had not to jump into his arms right now.

'Because…because I realised I've been trying so hard not to be my parents I turned into them anyway. Because I never thought I could matter to someone the way I want to matter to you. Because when I'm with you, I don't feel like my worth is weighed out in my achievements or my focus. Because…' He paused, and motioned to the window behind her, turning her around to look at it herself. 'Because I see these perfect worlds you create and I want to make them real for you. I want to give you everything you ask for, everything you can imagine.'

Rachel didn't look away from the window, from the story she'd told there, knowing that the minute she met his gaze again she'd be in his arms. She needed answers first. 'But… you told me no. You said you couldn't. What changed?'

'The world,' he said simply. 'It's so much emptier without you in it.'

'Good answer,' she muttered. 'So, what exactly are you asking for? Another fling?'

She held her breath until she saw him shake his head in the glass of the window. And then, to her astonishment, she saw his reflection drop down to one knee.

Rachel spun around to face him. 'No.'

'Yes,' he said, with a grin. 'I hope.'

'You hate commitment. You hate being tied down to *anything*. Why would you propose to me?'

Damon took her hands in his and tugged her closer. 'Because you don't tie me down. You make me feel like I can take on the world. So, Rachel Charles, will you do me the incredible honour of being my wife?'

It was crazy. She knew it was crazy.

But at the same time…it felt completely right.

She wanted this.

'I'm a little surprised you're not making me ask you,' she joked.

'Feel free.'

Laughing, Rachel dropped to her knees in front of him, mirroring his pose. 'Damon Hunter, will you marry me?'

'In a heartbeat,' he said, and kissed her.

She could feel a lifetime in that kiss. A whole story waiting to be written. She never wanted it to end.

Then Mr Jenkins coughed loudly behind her. 'Suppose you two had better come in and pick a ring, then.'

Rachel met Damon's gaze and found everything she was looking for there. This wasn't a dream.

This was her, awake to her own life at last. To all the possibilities that might give her.

Give *them*. Together.

'Come on,' Damon said. 'You get to choose the ring.'

'Damn right I do,' Rachel replied. 'And then we can go and tell Celeste she gets to be maid of honour. And she's not allowed to wear black.'

Because if she was starting her new life, there was no one else she wanted beside her than the man she loved and her best friend.

She just hoped that one day Celeste would find the kind of forever love that she had. And that when she did, she'd be brave enough to ask for love in return.

* * * * *

A TEMPORARY CHRISTMAS ARRANGEMENT

CHRISTINE RIMMER

For MSR, always.

Chapter One

The drive from Portland to Valentine Bay started out just as Lincoln Stryker had been certain it would. Both kids seemed happy. Linc had everything under control.

A glance in the rearview mirror revealed five-year-old Jayden in the car seat directly behind Linc. The boy gazed dreamily out the window.

Jayden was a talker. He might be lazily watching the world go by, but he didn't do it silently. Not Jayden. He chattered nonstop. "Uncle Linc, I hope the nice ladies next door are home. Did you meet the nice ladies?"

Had he? Linc had no clue. Probably not. "At the cottage, you mean?"

"Yes. They are Harper and Hailey and I like them a lot."

"I don't think I've met them." Linc hadn't been to his family's seaside cottage in more than a decade. His hazy, fond memories of the place didn't include the neighbors.

And as it turned out, Jayden didn't care if Linc knew the "nice ladies" or not. The little boy babbled on, "Harper and Hailey are sisters and they are so much fun. I was only four last Christmas, but I 'member. I 'member everything. I 'member they came over to play and they helped me make a snowman—and that 'minds me. There should be snow, Uncle Linc. There should be snow, and Harper and Hailey can help me make a snowman. Will you help, too?"

Linc took his eyes off the road long enough to cast a quick look over his right shoulder at two-year-old Maya in the other car seat. She was already asleep, her plush stuffed pig, Pebble, clutched in her chubby little arms.

"Uncle Linc, will you help me make my snowman?" Jayden asked more insistently.

Linc faced the road again, caught Jayden's eye in the rearview and winked at him. "Absolutely, I will."

"Good. And don't forget the Christmas tree…"

"I won't."

"I 'member last year we had a tall one."

Linc felt a sharp pang of sadness. "I'm sure you

did." Megan—Jayden's mom and Linc's only sibling—had always required a real tree, a tall one.

"I want one like that this year, too, Uncle Linc."

"A tall one, it is." Megan Hollister had loved Christmas. For all her too-short life, she'd insisted that the holidays should be spent at the Stryker family cottage on the coast.

"We have to put on all the lights," Jayden said. "All the lights and the red shiny balls and the little toy soldiers and the angel on the very top…"

Linc pushed his sadness aside and focused on the wide, gently curving road ahead as Jayden happily chattered away. The kid was intrepid in the best sense of the word. Nothing got him down.

And Linc would do everything in his power to make sure that Jayden—and Maya, too—had a good Christmas this year, the kind of Christmas Megan would have given them if she were still here. It was going to be Linc and his niece and nephew, from Thanksgiving through New Year's. Family only, the way Megan would have wanted it.

The kids' grandma Jean had tried to convince Linc that he would need a nanny at the cottage, especially if he hoped to work remotely. Jean Hollister was a wonderful woman. Jayden and Maya adored her—rightfully so. But Jean didn't know everything.

Linc and Jayden and Maya would manage just fine. No nanny required until after Christmas, when they returned to Portland and Linc went back to the office full-time.

"Uncle Linc, I'm hungry…"

"You think maybe you can hold on until we get to the cottage?"

"I'll try…" Jayden lasted exactly three minutes. "Uncle Linc, my tummy is *growling*…"

They were just passing Hillsboro, so there were still plenty of fast-food places with drive-throughs. Linc pulled into the next one.

As he rolled down the window to put in Jayden's order, Maya jolted awake with a startled little whimper. She fussed as they moved on to the pickup window, where Jayden's snack waited.

A few minutes later, they rolled out onto the road again. Maya had not stopped fussing. But with any luck, she would be lulled back to sleep by the ride.

Ten minutes later, Maya's whines had turned to all-out wails. Linc pulled off at the next opportunity and checked her diaper. It was wet, so he changed it.

Jayden waited until they were back on the road to mention that he really, really had to pee.

It went on like that. One thing after another, a classic car-ride-with-the-kids experience. What with stopping to offer comfort to whichever child was upset, change a loaded diaper, get Jayden another snack and then, soon after, yet another potty break, the hour-and-a-half drive took almost twice that long.

When Linc finally pulled the Range Rover in at the cottage on the wooded bluffs above the ocean in Valentine Bay, it was after three and the shadows had grown longer. It would be dark by five.

And Maya had started crying again.

Jayden just kept on talking. "We're here! I want to see the nice ladies. I want to go get the Christmas tree..."

"One thing at a time, Jayden." In the phone holder, Linc's cell lit up. Again. He let it go to voice mail. Already, he'd ignored several calls from the office, where they damn well ought to be able to get through one day without him.

He needed to unload the car, get the kids inside; settle them down a little; turn on the water, the power and the heat; and put something together for dinner—and okay, fine. Maybe he should have listened to Jean and considered bringing help.

At the very least, he could have called the property manager to get the water running, the lights on and the place warmed up.

But he hadn't. Because it was tradition, after all. The Strykers might be one of the wealthiest families in Oregon, a fortune built on four generations of running Stryker Marine Transport coupled with smart investment strategies, but when Christmastime came around, having money running out their ears didn't matter.

At the cottage, Linc's family did for themselves. His happiest childhood memories were in Valentine Bay. At the cottage, he and Megan had almost felt like they belonged to a regular family, the kind where the mom and dad actually cared about each other and spent time with their kids.

And damn it, he could do this.

He *would* do this.

He just needed to take it one step at a time.

First up: try to settle the wailing Maya down a little.

Jayden announced, "I'm gonna get out and—"

"Jayden."

"What, Uncle Linc?"

"I need you to stay in your car seat for a few minutes. Will you do that for me?"

Jayden wrinkled his nose, like the idea of staying put smelled bad. "There's french fries under my butt."

"We'll deal with that, I promise. For right now, though, just sit tight."

Maya had sailed past crying and straight on to wailing. "Unc Winc!" she screamed, and threw her beloved stuffed pig on the floor.

"She's hurting my ears!" whined Jayden. Ever resourceful, he stuck his fingers in them. "There." He let out a long sigh. "That's better."

Linc flashed the boy a big thumbs-up, after which he climbed from the car, ran around to Maya's door and extricated the unhappy toddler from her seat. "Here we go, sweetheart." He hoisted her into his arms.

She grabbed him around the neck and screamed all the louder, burying her sweaty little face in the crook of his shoulder, smearing him with snot and unhappy tears.

He stroked her dark, baby-fine curls and soothed, "Shh, now. It's okay…"

Pulling open the front passenger door, Linc laid her on the seat and somehow managed, through her layers of winter clothing, to get two fingers down the back of her diaper. It was a bold and dangerous move, but it turned out all right. She hadn't soiled her diaper, which meant her two-year-old molars were probably acting up again.

Maya confirmed the problem, pressing small fingers to her jaw. "Hurt, Unc Winc." She needed a cold washcloth to chew on, but he couldn't give her one until they were inside the cottage and he'd turned on the water. Jean had taught him to stick his fingers in her mouth and massage the area. But he hated to do that without washing his hands first.

"I'll help," announced Jayden, and snapped himself out of his car seat before Linc could order him to stay put.

Which was okay, come to think of it. "You're the best, Jayden. Get that blue chew thing out of the front of her diaper bag…" It was soft silicone and shaped to fit in the back of her mouth.

Jayden crouched in the footwell to dig around in the bag. "Got it!" Beaming proudly, he handed the teething toy over the seat to Linc.

"Great job—now, stay close," Linc warned.

When left to his own devices, Jayden sometimes went off "adventuring."

"I will, Uncle Linc…"

"Thanks." Linc gave the screaming little one her chew toy. She knew what to do, sticking it into her mouth with a sad little moan, holding the soft handle while chewing the business end into the spot she needed it, all the way in back. The silence that followed was golden. "Better?" he asked.

Her expression relaxed and she made a soft, contented sound as she worked the toy inside her mouth.

He glanced over the seat at Jayden again. "Can you hand me Maya's baby sling?"

"Yep." The little boy dug out the sling and passed it to Linc.

Linc thanked him enthusiastically and then got down to the business of putting Maya into the sling, all nice and cozy against his chest. She was still small enough to carry that way—though she wouldn't be for long. He spoke to her softly as she chewed on the blue toy and stared up at him with so much trust in those big brown eyes.

Megan's eyes…

The sadness dragged at him again. He refused to surrender to it. Megan and Kevin were gone. But they lived on through Maya and Jayden—and Linc would do whatever it took to give his niece and nephew a happy childhood and a decent start in life.

Maya, attached to the front of him now, chewed

away on her teething toy and reached up her free hand to gently pat his cheek.

His heart suddenly too big for his chest, he smiled down at her. "Okay, then, sweetheart. Let's go on into the…"

Was it suddenly much too quiet?

He glanced into the back seat, where Jayden's door gaped wide-open. The boy was no longer crouched in the footwell and, except for a few smashed fries, his car seat sat empty. "Jayden?"

No answer.

"Jayden!"

Silence.

Maya stared up at him, eyes wide as saucers. She made a tiny, anxious sound. "It's okay," he soothed her, rubbing her back as he turned in a circle, his gaze probing the shadows between the giant Douglas firs that loomed all around. "Jayden!"

Again, no answer. Linc's heart pounded the walls of his chest and his pulse roared in his ears.

He'd only taken his attention off the kid for a minute or two, tops. And yet somehow, in that those minutes, he'd vanished.

"Jayden?"

Still no answer. Linc tamped down a hard spurt of adrenaline-boosted terror. No reason to lose it yet. Jayden couldn't have gone far.

In the rambling family-owned cottage she used to share with her sister, Harper Bravo stared into the wide-open fridge and tried to decide what to have for dinner. Nothing looked good. She was just about to check the freezer when the doorbell rang.

Company. Her mood brightened. Harper had yet to become accustomed to living alone. She would love a little company, even old Angus McTerly, who lived two cottages south and had no doubt lost track of his wandering dog, Mitsy.

But it wasn't Angus. She pulled the door wide and found little Jayden Hollister, whom she hadn't seen since last Christmas, waiting on the step.

"Hi, Harper." He threw his arms wide and beamed up at her from under the blue hood of his down jacket. "It's me!"

"Jayden. What a surprise."

"Is Hailey here, too?"

"Um, not right now." The boy, who'd grown a good three inches since the last time she'd seen him, appeared to be on his own. Whoever was supposed to be watching him probably wondered where he'd gotten off to. "Jayden, are you all by yourself?"

He tipped his head to the side and looked up at her through a fringe of thick, dark eyelashes. "Not ezackly…" And he launched into a chatty little monologue about his uncle and his sister and how they were all in the car for "a reeeely long time." From there, he segued into how he hoped it would snow and there could be a snowman like last year. "And we will be here all the way to New Year's Day, Harper, so can I be in the Christmas show again and

you can make me an elf suit like you did before?"
Harper and her sister Hailey put on several community events a year at the Valentine Bay Theatre
downtown—and Jayden had quite the memory for
a five-year-old.

"Did you say your uncle is here with you?"

"Yes!"

"Let me check with him about the Christmas
show, okay?"

"Okay!"

She stuck her phone in her pocket and grabbed
her old wool Pendleton from the hook by the door.
When she wiggled her fingers at him, Jayden took
her hand. "Tell you what. Let's go on back to your
cottage, shall we? Your uncle is probably wondering where you are."

"All right, let's go!" Jayden skipped along beside
her as they took the narrow, tree-lined path that led
to the next cottage north of hers.

Halfway there, a handsome and harried-looking
man appeared from around the next bend. He had a
second child strapped to his chest in a baby sling—
undoubtedly Maya, who was about two years old
now. And the hot guy? The uncle in question, the one
who took guardianship of the children when their
parents had died so tragically last January.

Like most people in town, Harper had read about
the plane crash in the news. Such a heartbreaking
story, and it must be so hard for the family—the two
innocent kids, especially. But for the uncle, as well.

He'd lost his sister and his brother-in-law. Harper understood that kind of loss from firsthand experience.

"Jayden!" The uncle sounded as frantic as he looked. "There you are. You scared me to death." The little girl in the baby sling started fussing, and Jayden, alarmed at the uncle's wild-eyed expression, stopped stock-still on the path.

"Hi, I'm Harper." She spoke in a cheerful, non-threatening tone and plastered a big smile on her face, hoping the uncle would take the hint, lower his voice and stop scaring the kids. "Jayden and I are friends," she said brightly. "We know each other from last Christmas. Are you staying at the Stryker cottage?"

The uncle turned his angry glare on her. "Where else would we be?"

Still in her child-soothing voice, she suggested softly, "You need to smile. Because a smile would be so much less scary than your face right now."

Linc finally got what the woman with Jayden was trying to tell him. "Uh, right." Bouncing Maya gently to calm her down, he drew a deep breath and rearranged his expression to something he hoped came off as not quite so freaked. "I apologize for the scariness. I was worried…"

"I completely understand." The woman—Harper?—softened her smile. Linc found himself thinking how pretty she was, with long, thick blond hair and enormous pale blue eyes in a heart-shaped face.

He introduced himself. "I'm Linc Stryker, the kids' uncle and guardian."

"Great to meet you, Linc." She cast a downward glance at the wide-eyed Jayden and then arched an eyebrow at Linc.

He took her meaning and spoke gently to the little boy. "Jayden, I'm sorry for using such a loud voice. But remember, no adventuring without an adult."

Jayden gave him a slow and very serious nod. "I'm sorry, too, Uncle Linc. I shouldn't have left like that, and I won't do it again—and I wasn't adventuring, not really. I just wanted to say hi to Harper and Hailey."

"I get it. But leaving without telling me where you're going is not okay."

"I know, Uncle Linc. I *promise* I won't do that again."

"Excellent."

Right then, Maya whined, "Unc Winc, I hungwy!"

He dropped a kiss on the top of her curly head. "Okay. Let's see what we can do about that." He held out his hand for Jayden, who let go of Harper to take it. "Thank you," he said to the blonde.

"Anytime." Her soft mouth bloomed in a radiant smile as he turned to take the kids back the way they'd come.

Harper felt weirdly stunned.

The uncle was way too attractive, tall and broad shouldered with caramel-brown eyes and full lips and a sculpted jaw dusted with just the right amount of scruff—and where were her manners?

Linc Stryker could clearly use a hand.

"Wait." When he paused and glanced back at her, she offered, "Let me help. What can I do?"

Linc turned fully around again and grinned at her, a slow grin that caused the muscles in her belly to tighten and warmth to flare across her skin. "I've been trying really hard to pretend that I've got this."

"Pretend? No way. It's obvious to me that you know what you're doing."

He scoffed. "If you say so."

"I do. Now and then, though, you need to let a neighbor give you a hand."

"You're sure?"

"Honestly, I'm happy to help."

"Hungwy, hungwy, hungwy," chanted the little one in the baby sling, reaching up to capture Linc's face between her hands.

He caught the teething toy she'd dropped and bent to whisper something to her. When he glanced up, he aimed that sexy smile at Harper again. "Help would be wonderful."

"So, what can I do?"

"I hate to ask…"

"Just tell me."

"Well, if you would maybe come on back to the cottage with us? I would owe you big-time if you could keep an eye on the kids until I can unpack the car and get the power and the heat turned on…"

* * *

The Strykers' charming, gray-shingled two-story vacation house was a cottage in name only. Harper guesstimated the size at around four thousand square feet, with a beautiful, modern kitchen and lots of windows offering forest and ocean views.

"It's been updated since last year, hasn't it?" she asked, when they stood in the kitchen—still wearing their coats because the heat wasn't on yet. "I remember seeing workmen here, in July and August…"

Linc gave Maya back her teething toy. "I hired a contractor last summer to upgrade the kitchen and bathrooms. Then in September, I arranged for a decorator to come in. She had all the rooms painted and changed out the furniture." His warm brown eyes looked shadowed suddenly. Harper had a sense he was thinking of the sister he'd lost. "I wanted to bring the kids here for the holidays and the place needed an upgrade or two."

"It's beautiful," she said.

"I like it!" declared Jayden.

Linc seemed pleased. He ruffled the boy's hair. "I'm glad to hear it meets with your approval." He glanced down at the little girl attached to his chest and then up at Harper. "If you'll take Maya, I'll get busy unloading the car."

Harper helped him unhook the sling. When he handed the little one over, Maya didn't protest, just reached out her arms and let Harper gather her in, taking the blue teething toy out of her mouth long enough to remark, "I hungwy. Now."

"We'll fill up that tummy. Promise." Harper brushed a kiss on her plump cheek.

Linc brought in the food first—what there was of it. "It's not much," he confessed sheepishly. "I had this idea I would just take the kids out with me to get everything we needed right here in town." He set the two bags of groceries on the white marble countertop.

Harper shifted Maya onto one arm and took a quick peek inside the bags. "No worries," she reassured him. "I see bread, eggs, milk and sandwich fixings. Fruit. Perfect. Nobody will starve."

"Hungwy," whined Maya hopefully around her blue teething toy.

Harper stroked her soft hair. "We'll fix you a nice snack." She sent a quick smile Linc's way. "Turn the heat on. We're fine."

"Great." He was already turning away.

There was a booster seat at the table. She put Maya in it, peeled a banana and gave the little girl half. Next, Harper found crayons and a tablet in a kitchen drawer. She handed them to Jayden and asked him to draw some pictures.

He had questions. "Pictures of what, Harper? How many pictures? What colors do you like? Should they be *Christmas* pictures?"

She tipped Maya's chin up. "What do you think your brother should draw for us?"

Maya swallowed a bite of banana and exclaimed, "Cwissmuss!"

Harper winked at Jayden. "You heard your sister. We want some Christmas pictures—in Christmas colors, like green and red and yellow." But why limit a guy's creativity? "Blue and purple and pink are perfectly acceptable, as well. In fact, Jayden, you should use any color in the box. I kind of love them all."

"A Christmas tree, Harper? A snowman?"

"Yes. Good ideas. Start with those." She pressed a kiss to Maya's silky hair just so she could breathe in the scent of baby shampoo and that special something else exclusive to little ones—like fresh, sweet milk and clean sheets hung to dry in the sunlight.

"More?" pleaded Maya, who had scarfed down the half banana in record time. Harper gave her the other half, found a plastic plate and a sippy cup in one of the cupboards and then supplemented the banana with dry cereal, sliced apples and milk.

Linc got the utilities turned on and the fire going in the gas fireplace. It wasn't long before the cottage warmed up enough that they could hang up their coats.

Harper kept both kids occupied as Linc got the rest of the stuff from the car and then started making beds.

As soon as Maya finished her snack, Harper

gave her back her chew toy and set her down on the kitchen floor, where she toddled around a bit and ended up plopping to her butt by the table. For a while, she just sat there cuddling the stuffed pig Linc had brought in from the car, contentedly chewing on the blue toy.

By then, Jayden had drawn a Christmas tree, a snowman and a picture of five smiling stick figures. "That's me and Maya and Uncle Linc and Gramma Jean and PopPop," the boy explained. "Gramma and PopPop just went on a boat to go everywhere around the whole world. They won't be back for a looong time."

Harper studied the smiling figures. "Are you saying your grandparents went on a cruise?"

"Yeah. A cruise. That's what they call it. They took care of us for a looong time and now they get to go on vacation, and we will be with Uncle Linc, but get to see them all the time on Stype."

"You mean Skype?"

Jayden wrinkled his nose, thinking it over. Finally, he nodded. "I think so, yes. Skype." He bent over the paper again and began to add what looked like a boat to the picture. "All done!" he announced.

Harper praised his work and then found some magnets in the drawer where the crayons had been. She hung all three pictures on the big two-door fridge. "They look great," she said. "Very festive."

Jayden frowned. "What's festive?"

"Happy and cheerful and jolly."

"Like you feel at Christmas?"

She nodded approvingly. "That's right."

Jayden beamed with pride. "Yes, my pictures are festive. And I like them, too."

"It's always nice to be pleased with your work. And now that the pictures are finished, I think we need to get started on dinner."

Jayden wanted to help, so Harper found him a step stool. He stood at the counter beside her, chattering away, munching on chips and nibbling on slices of cheese.

"I hewp, too!" insisted Maya midway through the process. She seemed pretty steady on her feet, so Harper let her stand on the other step stool, with Jayden on one side of her and Harper on the other. "I good!" announced the toddler as she chewed on a piece of bread.

"Yes, you are. Very helpful," Harper agreed.

When they all four sat down at the table, Linc praised the meal and the kids' efforts and confessed that he was having some serious trouble figuring out how to get the Wi-Fi working. "I may have to call the property manager," he added.

"I'm pretty good with anything technical," Harper volunteered. "Let me have a look at it first."

"Not only a kid whisperer, but you've got the tech handled, as well?"

"I guess you could say that, yeah." She explained her work at the Valentine Bay Theatre downtown. "I'm the theater's tech director, which means if it doesn't have to do with acting, I'm the one to talk to. We do several shows a year. With each one, we try to get the participation of every child in town."

Jayden seized the moment. "Uncle Linc, can I please be in the Christmas show? I was in the show last year and it was so much fun."

Linc turned to Harper. "So, the Christmas show would be at the Valentine Bay Theatre?"

"That's right." She gave Jayden a smile and suggested, "How about this? I'll discuss the Christmas show with your uncle later and then he'll talk it over with you."

Jayden glanced from Harper to Linc and back to Harper again. She could see the wheels turning in his head as he considered going all out to get an immediate yes.

But in the end, he gave it up. "You just let me know, Uncle Linc."

"Will do."

And then he couldn't resist one more push at the goal. "Because I really, really want to be in that show."

"I can see that." Linc was trying not to grin. "Now finish your sandwich."

After the meal, they all four cleared the table. Even Maya waddled back and forth carrying her sippy cup and *Little Mermaid* plastic plate to the sink.

"Bath time," Linc said.

Jayden objected. "We just had baths yesterday."

"Might as well freshen up after that long car ride."

Jayden moved on to bargaining. "Can I get bubbles?"

"Of course."

"Well, then, okay!"

Linc herded the kids upstairs. Harper stayed behind to wipe the counters and sweep bits of chips and apple from the floor.

With the kitchen tidy, she sorted out the Wi-Fi situation. It didn't take long to get the home network up and running.

After that, she couldn't think of anything else that needed doing immediately, though she was tempted to delay leaving any way she could. Her cottage always seemed too quiet, and it was so warm and cozy here. The kids were the cutest. And Linc was...

Well, never mind about Linc. She didn't need to go getting too excited about the temporary guy next door.

And come to think of it, maybe the kids' clothes needed stashing in drawers upstairs...

She caught herself—because putting things in drawers without being asked to do it verged on intrusive.

She'd been a good neighbor, done her bit to help Linc and the kids get settled in. Time to say goodnight.

At the top of the stairs, she followed the sounds of splashing and laughter to the hall bathroom.

"Harper!" Jayden called when she stopped in the

open bathroom doorway. He was in his pajamas and playing with Maya, who sat in the tub.

"Hawp!" Maya echoed.

They waved at her and Maya splashed with abandon, sending bathwater and bubbles flying everywhere. At this rate, Jayden would need dry pj's before heading to bed.

Linc, kneeling by the tub, turned to grin at Harper. His button-up was wet and he had a patch of bubbles dripping down his cheek. She laughed.

"What?" he demanded.

She touched her own cheek. "You've got bubbles..."

"No kidding." He wiped them away.

And then they both just stared at each other—for a while. Several seconds, at least. The sounds of the two kids laughing and Maya's splashing faded into the background.

It was just Harper and this amazingly great guy—a guy who looked like someone off the cover of *GQ* and treated his little niece and nephew like the most important people in the world.

Because they were.

"Wi-Fi's working," she said, her voice strangely breathless.

"Best news I've had since you organized dinner. We have a video-chat with the grandparents first thing in the morning. They're staying overnight in Miami, boarding a cruise ship tomorrow afternoon."

"Jayden mentioned a cruise."

"A cruise around the world, six months and thirty-three countries."

"Wow."

"Jean and Alan Hollister are the best there is. They canceled a two-week Mediterranean cruise last January to stay with me and the kids. The world cruise is my attempt to make it up to them."

Jean and Alan Hollister, he'd said. Gramma and PopPop must be Kevin's parents, not Linc and Megan's. "I'm sure they're going to love it—and the Wi-Fi is ready for your video call tomorrow. I left the password on a sticky note next to your laptop, but it's actually printed right there on the bottom of the gateway, too."

He gave a low chuckle. "See, I knew that…"

She tried not to giggle and found it a challenge to restrain herself. Something about him had her feeling like a thirteen-year-old in the throes of her first major crush. "Looks to me like you've got everything under control now."

"I hope so." He'd barely finished the sentence when Maya gave a gleeful screech and let loose a volley of wild splashing. Jayden splashed her back. "Whoa!" Linc swiped bubbles off his forehead. "How 'bout we keep the bubbles in the bathtub, guys?"

"Sow-wy," said Maya, looking completely angelic, with her curly hair sopping wet and topped with bubbles.

Linc's amber gaze fell on Harper again. "I have

no clue where you got the idea that I'm running this show."

"Hey. The kids are happy, and the beds are made. The Wi-Fi is working. Everybody's been fed. You're on top of this situation, and my job here is done."

The corners of his sexy mouth turned down just a fraction. "Wait. You're not leaving? You can't go yet."

"Yeah, Harper!" Jayden backed him up. "We still have stories. You have to stay for story time."

"Stow-ie!" shouted Maya, and then tossed her rubber frog in the air. It plopped back into the water with a splash. "Oopsy." She tried to look contrite but didn't really succeed.

Linc gave his niece an indulgent glance and swung those melty eyes back on Harper. "Are you vulnerable to a bribe?"

Absolutely. "Hmm. What's on offer?"

"Later, there will be wine—or vodka, if that's your preference."

"You have wine?" There hadn't been any in the grocery bags he'd brought in.

"I do. I just haven't brought it in from the car yet. The way I see it, so what if we only had sandwiches for dinner? At least I didn't forget the liquor."

It happened again. They stared at each other. It felt like…infinite possibility, somehow. Like she was floating on air, walking on rainbows. Like all the corny, lovely things a woman feels when she meets a certain special man.

And she really needed *not* to get carried away here. Linc was a great guy. They had a neighborly thing going on, not a budding romantic relationship.

But reading stories with the kids? That sounded like a lot more fun than returning to her empty cottage and going over the list of props she still hadn't found for the Christmas show. "Hmm. Wine. It just seems wrong to say no to wine…"

Those gorgeous eyes gleamed at her. "I think you've earned it."

"True. I've been such a good neighbor."

"The best." The kids laughed and chattered together as Linc and Harper continued to gaze at each other. His voice low, with a delicious hint of roughness, he coaxed, "Stay…"

Chapter Two

They had story time in the master bedroom, all four of them together on the king-size bed.

After *The Name Jar, Dragons Love Tacos* and an older book of rhymes by Shel Silverstein, both kids were droopy-eyed and yawning. Jayden asked Harper to tuck him in and Maya held up her arms for Linc, who scooped her against his broad chest and carried her to the bedroom across the hall.

Jayden took Harper's hand. "This way."

In his room, Harper pulled back the covers on the bottom bunk. He wiggled between them and stretched out with his head on the pillow. She tucked the Star Wars comforter in around him.

"Harper?"

"Hmm?"

"Sometimes in the nighttime, I miss my mom."

She smoothed the thick, dark hair from his forehead and whispered, "I really did like your mom a lot."

"She died. My daddy died, too." His eyes were wide and soft and full of hurt. "It makes me feel sad."

She laid her palm gently on the center of his small chest. "I remember that they both—your mom and your dad—loved you so much."

"I 'member that, too." His little face was so very solemn.

"That's good. Because when somebody loves you a lot, you never lose them. Not really. You always have them, the good memories of them, in your heart."

"Harper, I 'member *everything*."

"Keep those memories. Treasure them."

"I promise I will."

"Excellent. Do you have a prayer you like to say at bedtime?"

He closed his eyes and whispered, "Dear God, thank You for another good day. Please give us a tall Christmas tree and make the snow come down so I can have a snowman. Bless Uncle Linc and Maya and Gramma and PopPop. And Mom and Daddy up in heaven…" His dark lashes fluttered as he sneaked a peek at her. "And Harper, too. Amen."

"Amen." She bent to brush her lips across his forehead. "'Night."

"G'night—and Harper?"

"Yes?"

"Don't forget the Christmas show…"

"I won't forget. I'll talk to your uncle tonight."

When Harper got downstairs, she found Linc in the kitchen pulling bottles from a box.

He held up a bottle of red and another of Ketel One. "Pick your poison."

"Wine, please."

He put the vodka back in the box. "Let's go in by the fire," he suggested, after he'd opened the wine and she'd found two stemless glasses in one of the cupboards.

In the living area, they sat on the sofa and he poured them each a glass. "It's good," she said after her first sip.

They sat in silence for a bit. She hardly knew him, and yet it was easy to sit with him and say nothing, to simply enjoy the warmth of the fire and the rich, dark taste of the wine.

Her thoughts went to the little boy upstairs and the things he'd said before his bedtime prayer. "While I was tucking him in, Jayden said how much he missed his mom and dad…" She waited for a response.

None was forthcoming. Linc stared at the fire and took another slow sip of wine.

Okay. Now she did feel awkward. "The kids seem to be doing really well."

He slanted her a wry glance. "Given that they lost both their parents ten and a half months ago, you mean?"

"Yeah." She wanted to reach out, touch his hand, pat his big shoulder. But that seemed presumptuous, somehow. Instead, she struggled with how to offer her condolences. "I'm so sorry, Linc. That you lost them. I met them last year, over Christmas."

"Yeah. I figured you must have gotten to know them a little. Jayden mentioned hanging out with you and your sister last year."

"I thought they were wonderful, both Megan and Kevin. So in love. Good parents, completely committed to their family, to the kids..."

"Yeah. It's been hard, losing them. Jayden acted up some at first. There were angry outbursts, essentially out of nowhere, and sudden bouts of crying. I talked it over with Jean and Alan. We decided to send him to a therapist. That helped."

"Right now, he really does seem happy, overall."

"Yeah, he's coping, I think." Linc had resumed staring into the fire. "I didn't get together with my sister and her family enough before the crash. I regret that now, that I didn't make the time to fly down to Sacramento now and then..."

Anything she might have said felt either inadequate or shallow, so she said nothing.

He didn't seem bothered by her silence. "I don't

know how I would have made it these past months without Jean and Alan," he said. "They left their cozy place in Carmichael, California, and moved in with me in the West Hills to help me look after the kids."

There were a lot of big houses in the West Hills of Portland. Harper had no doubt that Linc's was one of them.

He said, "Having their grandparents taking care of them gave Jayden and Maya time to adjust to the new normal, I guess you could say." He shifted his gaze down and seemed to contemplate the dark color of the wine. Shaking his head, he took another sip. Then a grim laugh escaped him. "Kevin loved that damn plane of his. It was his pride and joy..."

"I heard about what happened." The Hollisters had left the kids with the grandparents in Sacramento and flown off for an overnight getaway in Monterey. They'd crashed in the Santa Cruz Mountains and were killed instantly.

"It was a shock," he said. "To everyone. I don't really think we're over it yet."

Again, she had to resist the urge to reach out—clasp his arm, pat his shoulder. "Something like that, you never really get over. But it does get better—you know, over time."

He turned his gaze on her, his eyes darker than before, more bittersweet chocolate than caramel. "You sound like you're speaking from experience."

"Yeah, you could say that..."

The way he looked at her—as though she fascinated him. How did he do that? He made her feel *seen* in the truest sense of the word. "Tell me," he commanded.

She shifted on the cushions and took another sip of her wine. "When I was five, my brother Finn got lost in Siberia. Then, when I was seven, my parents died." She chuckled at the look of disbelief on his face. "My parents were big on travel. Finn was eight when he disappeared. We're still looking to this day, but we haven't found him. Yet. Two years after we lost Finn, my parents headed off on a romantic getaway, just the two of them, to Thailand. As my oldest brother, Daniel, always explained it to the rest of us, the Thailand trip was supposed to be a way for them to reconnect with each other, to try to move on a little after Finn went missing. They arrived right in time to be killed in a tsunami."

"That's horrible."

"It was, yeah. But we got through it. There were eight of us at home then, including Daniel. Daniel took custody of the rest of us. Our ancient great-aunt, Daffy, and great-uncle, Percy, were always there to help. Daffy and Percy are the Bravo family's Gramma Jean and PopPop, I guess you could say."

He was still watching her, his expression hard to read. "Thank you."

"For…?"

He gave a half shrug. "Sometimes I forget I'm not the only one who ever lost a sibling. I get feeling down, remembering all the ways I wasn't there for Megan when I should have been, worrying the kids will never fully recover from losing her and their dad. But you've made it through more than one personal tragedy as a child and grown up with a great attitude. Not to mention, you're generous and kind, and willing to come to the rescue of the clueless guy next door. So, yeah. Thank you for all of that." He tapped his glass to hers.

"I never said I thought you were clueless."

His mouth quirked at the corners. "But you did think it, didn't you?"

"Maybe. At first. But you're good with the kids, and it's clear they love you and trust you."

His grin had turned rueful. "I have a confession to make."

She held up her wineglass in a salute. "Now you're talkin'. Spill."

"Jean tried to tell me I would need help for the holidays, but I wouldn't listen to her. I was positive I could do it all, get the cottage opened up, run to the grocery store, look after Jayden and Maya—and fit in working remotely a few hours a day, too. Today was a crash course in harsh reality."

"You might have been maybe a touch too ambitious."

"You think?" He laughed, a low sound, intimate. Just between the two of them.

She tried to remind herself—again—that she'd only just met him. He was a Stryker, an important name in Oregon, and only here for the holidays. Come New Year's, he'd be gone. Back to Portland to live in a West Hills mansion and run his family's shipping empire. She would be heading for Seattle, where she would rent an overpriced studio apartment and try to figure out what she really wanted from life.

Didn't matter, though, how mindful she tried to be of all the ways they were strangers. Somehow, in the span of an afternoon and evening, she felt as though she'd known him for years.

He smiled his devastating smile. "Jayden chattered nonstop all the way here from Portland."

"Why am I not surprised? He's wonderfully verbal."

"Verbal." Linc shrugged. "That's Jayden, all right. And my point is, all the way here, you and your sister were the main topic of his never-ending monologue. He couldn't wait to see you. He has all these plans for hanging out with you—for building snowmen and being in your Christmas show…"

"Which reminds me, I promised him I'd talk to you about the show."

"Don't worry. If you think it's a good thing, I'll say yes. I'm pretty much incapable of telling Jayden no."

"Well, I'm not arguing that you can *never* say no. But the Christmas show should be a definite yes. He starts kindergarten next year, right?" At his nod, she continued, "So next Christmas, you won't be able to stay the whole month. He shouldn't miss this chance. He'll get to be around a lot of other kids and the rehearsal schedule isn't all that demanding. You could start him next week if you want to wait until after Thanksgiving."

"Hold on. The rehearsals have already started? How will he catch up?"

"It's a series of sketches, songs and dance numbers. My sister Hailey directs the whole thing. She's amazing—and I say that with absolute objectivity."

"Right."

"I'm serious. She has the kids practice all the songs and skits separately, in small groups, and then puts everything together during the last week before the show opens. We will fit Jayden in, and he'll have a wonderful time. He'll need to be at the theater for a few hours most weekday afternoons, depending on which numbers he's in. There are two performances, both matinees, on the second and third Saturdays of December. I can hook you up for carpooling with other parents. Once you're comfortable with the process, you don't need to be there if you don't want to be. Jayden will be busy with his part in the show and there's constant adult supervision. Even Maya's old enough to participate this year."

He frowned. "She's barely two."

"I know. But if they can walk and understand basic instructions, they're in. The older kids love looking after the little ones, kind of shepherding them along. Maya can be in a couple of sketches if she's comfortable with it. That would take a little more time on your part—or for anyone you get to look after the kids. Children four and under require a supervising adult for each rehearsal they attend."

"What about the performances? She could wet her diaper, start crying…"

"Linc, it ain't Broadway. Everybody understands. You would just go up onstage and get her, take her out to the lobby to settle her down or whatever. Meanwhile, the show would go on." She set her glass on the coffee table.

He put his down beside it and poured them each more wine. "I'll tell Jayden he's in." At some point, he'd rolled his sleeves to his elbows. His forearms were the good kind—corded with lean muscle, traced with a couple of so-sexy veins and dusted with just the right amount of silky dark hair. He had gorgeous wrists, too, lean, the bones sharply defined.

And seriously? Gorgeous *wrists*? She should probably say no to that second glass of wine…

And what were they talking about…?

Right. He'd just said that Jayden could be in the show. "Terrific. He'll be so pleased."

"I'll have to think a little about putting Maya in."

"I hear you. I'll give you my number." She took out her phone, entered her PIN and handed it to him.

He sent himself a text. On the coffee table, his phone chimed. "Done." He passed her phone back and relaxed against the cushions again, wineglass in hand. "I need to ask you…"

Anything. "Yeah?"

"Last year, did you maybe babysit the kids now and then?"

"Yes, I did. It was fun—and you should see your face."

"What's wrong with it?" His slight grin let her know he was teasing her.

"Nothing wrong, exactly. But I do detect a calculating gleam in your eye."

"You're onto me." He studied her for a long count of five. "Jayden and Maya adore you. You're amazing with kids."

"Um. Thanks?"

"And I'm facing reality here, admitting that I do need a nanny while we're in town. Will you consider taking the job? Flexible hours, whatever you can manage. As I already said, you're so good with them, and you're also right next door. You could just come on over anytime you're available."

She sipped that second glass of wine she shouldn't be having and considered the idea. She did enjoy being with the kids…

He coaxed, "Say yes. I'll definitely make it worth your while in terms of the money."

Now he'd done it—found her weak spot. She needed to save every penny she could get her hands on for her upcoming move. "You have an hourly rate in mind?"

"Eighty an hour?"

She tried not to gape. His offer was a lot more

than she'd dared to hope for. "I could come in the afternoons. Mornings, I need to be at the theater. And then some days I would switch, watch the kids in the morning, go to the theater in the afternoon."

"As I said, whenever you're available, I'm grateful for the help."

He'd pretty much had her at that giant hourly rate. Still, he needed to understand that she did require flexibility in terms of her schedule. "I really can't work for you full-time."

"You already said that, and I heard you."

"You're sure?"

"Positive. Jayden and Maya love you, and you're so good with them. If you could be here every weekday for a few hours—and longer whenever you can manage it? That would give me the time I need to put out any fires at Stryker Marine."

She suddenly felt hesitant, somehow.

But why? She needed the money and he could use the help. Plus, it would be no hardship for her to spend time with Maya and Jayden.

She would have to sock away every penny she could get her hands on to achieve her goal and make her move by February, and this was a golden opportunity to fatten her malnourished bank account.

Linc leaned a fraction closer. She got a hint of his aftershave. Fresh and clean and manly. He was way too attractive. And too rich. She'd read somewhere that he'd been CEO and President of Stryker Marine Transport since he was twenty-five. "Harper."

"Hmm?"

"Just say yes."

Oh, come on. Why not? Instead of spending hours alone at her cottage, she could be here making excellent money, taking care of two great kids for this way-too-attractive man. "Yes."

His smile made her pulse speed up. "Can you start tomorrow afternoon?"

"Yes."

"Excellent. You just made my month—oh, and I have meetings I can't get out of in Portland on Thursday and Friday the first week in December. Any chance you could spend the two days there with me and the kids at my house, looking after them while I'm at the office? I would pay you for eighteen hours a day on those two days if you can swing it."

She did the math. Almost three thousand dollars for two days. She would have to work it out with Hailey and Doug Dickerson. The theater's volunteer lighting director, Doug would be stepping up into Harper's job when she left in February. "Sure. I'll make it work."

"You're a lifesaver. Don't move from that spot. I'll get you a key and grab my laptop. We'll download a simple contract, fill in the blanks to our mutual satisfaction and be good to go."

After Harper left, Linc checked on the kids. They were both sound asleep, looking so pure and innocent, untroubled by the hard realities of life. He went into the master suite and spent about thirty seconds staring at the king-size bed. The duvet was rumpled from the four of them—Harper, the kids and him—lying there together to read bedtime stories.

Linc glanced at his watch. It was barely nine.

He could get a head start on messages before he turned in, find out more than he wanted to know about how everyone at the office was getting along in his absence.

Downstairs again, he got his laptop from the office room and returned to the living area, where he sat on the sofa and started checking email and messages. Harper would be over around one tomorrow. She'd said she could stay into the evening if he needed her.

He would absolutely need her.

Maybe after the kids went to bed, they could hang out for a while, the way they had tonight. He really liked her. She was not only a pleasure to look at, she was easygoing, capable and fun. And smart. With a big heart. Low maintenance, too, in her floppy sweater, ripped skinny jeans and high-top Converse All Stars.

He'd been swimming in the wrong dating pool. There should be more women like Harper Bravo in his life.

On the coffee table next to his laptop, his phone chimed with a text. He tapped the text icon.

Imogen's profile shot popped up, a picture he'd taken at a charity gala they'd attended together last year, before Megan died and everything changed. Imogen wore a strapless red satin dress. A diamond necklace he'd given her sparkled at her throat and the big rock in her engagement ring glittered on her left hand as she coyly blew him a kiss.

Imogen was a lot like Linc's mother, Alicia— completely self-absorbed. He should have taken note of that before getting involved with her.

But he hadn't. And less than a week ago, he'd finally had to face the fact that Imogen Whitman was not the woman for him. She was the one who broke it off, but he'd been way too relieved when she did. They weren't a good match. He got that now.

He shouldn't read her text. There was no point. But he couldn't help wondering what she might pull next.

I was upset. I'm sorry for the things I said. We really need to talk.

Bad idea. They never needed to talk again. Everything had been settled. *She* needed to let it go.

He went back to dealing with his messages.

A second text popped through.

Linc. Come on. The least you can do is answer me.

He blocked her from his mind—and if she kept it up, he would block her number from his phone.

The phone rang. He should just let it go to voice

mail and then delete whatever message she left. But he was pissed off and he wanted to make himself utterly clear.

He hit the green icon and put the phone to his ear. "It's over. Stop texting me. Don't call me again."

"Oh, Linc." Her voice was soft. Pleading—which was rich. There was nothing soft about Imogen Whitman. He understood that now. "Come on. We can work this—"

He didn't hang on for the rest. Ending the call, he blocked her.

The next morning, Harper arrived at the landmark theater on Carmel Street good and early. Hailey was already there.

Harper's sister sat in her office backstage sipping a latte from their favorite coffee place, the Steamy Bean, and studying an Excel spreadsheet on her tablet. "Roman wants to close us down as soon as the Christmas show's over to start the remodel," she said without looking up. "I told him that now the theater is mine to do with as I please, I have things in the works. He'll need to renovate around upcoming projects. He says that's impossible, that the wiring alone means just about every wall has to be ripped out."

Roman Marek was Hailey's fiancé. A real estate guy, Roman was prone to larger-than-life gestures. A few weeks ago, he'd given Hailey the theater. Now he was determined to refurbish it to her specifications. They were at odds over how that would happen.

"You'll work it out, Lee-Lee." Harper used the old nickname, from when they were little—Harp and Lee-Lee, like twins, inseparable. "You always do."

Hailey sat up straight, the spreadsheet forgotten, and narrowed her eyes at Harper. "Okay. What's on your mind?" Hailey was ten months older, but they might as well have been born ten minutes apart.

They'd been a team all through childhood. Their mom had even held Hailey back a year so she and Harper could start kindergarten together. They went off to the University of Oregon together, both as theater majors—Hailey focusing on performance, directing and management, Harper on stagecraft and design—and her other great love, architecture. They finished each other's sentences. And sometimes they read each other's minds.

Harper dropped into the straight chair opposite Hailey's vintage metal desk. "I took a second job and I wanted to let you know. It's flexible, a few hours a day, after I'm done here at the theater."

"You're never done here at the theater."

"Yeah, well. I'll make it work. You know I need the money. A place in Seattle won't be cheap." She watched Hailey closely as she spoke, on the lookout for any hint that her sister wasn't really down with the move she had planned. It would, after all, break them up in terms of their partnership as H&H Productions. And for the first time in their lives, they would be living miles apart.

But Lee-Lee didn't so much as flinch. Harper

loved her all the more for that. Her sister knew what Harper needed, and she wanted Harper to have it. "I hear you. So then, you'll be making good money at this mysterious second job?"

"Eighty bucks an hour."

Hailey's right eyebrow inched toward her hairline. "Do you have to take your clothes off?"

"Oh, please. To do that, I would need more than eighty an hour." They laughed together and then Harper asked, "Remember the Hollister kids?"

"Of course." Hailey's teasing expression had turned somber. "It's heartbreaking, what happened to Megan and Kevin."

"Yeah." For a bittersweet moment, they regarded each other. Memories of the sweet couple from Sacramento seemed to hover in the air between them. Megan had had a glow about her. You could see that her life made her happy. And Kevin was kind of nerdy and a little bit shy. With a long breath, Harper forged on, "Megan's brother, Linc Stryker, took custody of Jayden and Maya. He's brought the kids to the Stryker cottage for the holidays. Last night, he offered me a job as part-time nanny while they're here in town."

"Wait." Hailey made a rolling gesture with her hand. "I need you to back it up a little. You met Megan's brother, how?" Harper gave her sister a quick rundown on the events of the day before, after which Hailey asked, "Is this brother of Megan's single?"

Harper realized she didn't know. He'd certainly

acted like he was single—hadn't he? "He's alone with the kids at the cottage. He didn't mention a girlfriend and he doesn't wear a ring, so I'm guessing, yes."

As always, Hailey saw right through her. "You like him. You like him a lot."

Had her face turned red? She willed the blush away. "I hardly know the man—I mean, he seems nice."

"Nice." Hailey wrinkled her nose like she smelled something bad.

"Yeah. Nice. And I do like him."

Hailey smirked. "He's hot, am I right?"

"Will you stop?" She'd been thinking way too much about the guy next door and she needed to cut that out. Especially now that she would be working for him. Romance in the workplace was not a great idea. She could lose a fun gig taking care of two kids she really liked—not to mention the money she now counted on putting in the bank.

"So, then." Hailey sat back in her swivel chair. "He's hot and you like him and you're going to be hanging around him a lot in the next month—for purely financial reasons."

"Enough. I've got a lot of work to do and a short time to do it in." Harper rose and turned for the door.

"Say hi to Jayden for me and be sure to give Maya a great, big kiss…"

Harper sent a wave back over her shoulder and kept right on walking.

* * *

The doorbell rang at one sharp.

Linc answered and there she was, in baggy, busted-out jeans and a black waffle-weave shirt. She carried a puffer coat the color of marigolds and she'd woven her thick, streaky blond hair into a single fat braid that fell over her left shoulder, the tail teasing the undercurve of one round breast. He wanted to grab that braid and give it a tug.

He stepped back and ushered her in. "Here. I'll take your coat."

"Thanks." She handed it over. A hint of her scent came to him—sweet and tart, like vanilla and lemons.

As he hung the coat in the entry closet, Jayden came running. "Harper, *there* you are!"

Maya trailed after him, crowing, "Hawp, Hawp!"

Harper laughed—she seemed delighted at the sight of the two kids barreling toward her. "Hey, you guys!"

She knelt to gather them both in a quick hug. They wiggled like excited puppies in her loose embrace. When she stood, she scooped Maya up on one arm and took Jayden's offered hand.

"We don't get the Christmas tree until Friday because first there's Thanksgiving," Jayden said.

"That makes sense."

"And I get to be in the Christmas show," he proudly informed her. "Uncle Linc said so."

"I'm glad."

"Me, too. And we had a Skype with PopPop and

Gramma Jean before they got on the big boat to go out in the ocean—now, come up to my room." He started pulling her toward the stairs. "I built a whole train station. Uncle Linc helped. The train tracks click together, and you can make them go everywhere, even under my bed."

"I want to see that—but hold on a minute."

"What for?"

"I need to talk to your uncle first." She planted a quick kiss on Maya's cheek. Then she turned those big eyes on Linc. "Have they had lunch?"

"We did!" Jayden tugged on her hand again, this time to get her attention. "We had eggs and toast for breakfast, and we had sandwiches for lunch, with chips. Now we're all out of chips, though," he added with a frown. "And there's no more ham. We'll have to have chicken sandwiches for dinner, I guess. I don't like chicken, not as much as ham."

Linc felt a twinge of guilt. He should have gone shopping this morning, but he kind of dreaded dragging the kids around Safeway while trying to find everything they might need for several days of meals. In Portland, he had a cook who took care of that stuff.

But this was the cottage, he reminded himself. It was family-only around here—well, except that he'd hired Harper, which made the family-only rule pretty much null and void.

Not that he regretted hiring her. No way. She was a find and would make it possible for him to get a little work done now and then while giving the kids the kind of Christmas they deserved.

As for the shopping, it had to be done, which meant that this afternoon, along with resolving the never-ending issues at the office, he would need to haul his ass to the store.

He was about to reassure Harper he would deal with the food situation when she volunteered, "Trust me to take care of it?" A matched pair of sweet little dimples winked at him from either side of her beautiful mouth.

The woman *was* a prize. As generous and helpful as Gramma Jean, and gorgeous, as well. "You're not serious?"

"The kids and I would love a trip to the store—wouldn't we, guys?"

"Yes!" the two little ones said in unison.

Harper suggested, "Just jot down a grocery list for me, if you would."

"You're a lifesaver."

She shrugged. "No problem. Does Maya need a nap?"

Did she? He had no clue. "Jean wrote it all down for me, in longhand on the pretty stationery she uses—about naps and allergies and when to do what. I'm fairly sure I brought those instructions with me from Portland…"

Harper seemed amused at his befuddlement. "Well, okay then. If you find it, let me know. Otherwise, I think we'll go for groceries soon and then we'll figure out the nap issue when we get back."

"Works for me. I'll put the shopping list together right now. Just add anything else you want or think I should have included."

"Like chips!" Jayden put in. "We could get Fritos. I *like* Fritos."

"Fweetos!" Maya echoed, clearly in agreement with her big brother.

Linc whipped out his black card and grabbed his keys from the art glass bowl on the entry table. "The kids' car seats are already hooked up in the Range Rover. You might as well just drive that."

"Works for me." Harper let go of Jayden's hand to take the card and keys. Her fingers brushed Linc's, light as a breath, sending an arrow of awareness slicing through him.

Was he way too attracted to her?

Probably.

Not that there was anything wrong with that. He and Imogen were yesterday's news, so what harm could there be in a little innocent flirting with the new nanny? It put a whole new light on the day, just having her around. He had no plans to make a move on her. None whatsoever.

As soon as she'd stuck the keys and credit card in her pocket, Jayden grabbed her hand again. "Harper. Can I please show you my train set now?"

She grinned down at his upturned face. "Lead the way, young man." He pulled her toward the stairs.

Linc remembered he had more to discuss with her. "Hold on a minute…"

She sent him a glowing smile over her shoulder. "Hmm?"

"About Maya and the Christmas show…"

"You think you might let her try it?"

"Well, I wondered if you could take her, be there for whatever practices she needs to attend—on the clock, of course? I thought you would see how she does with it, make a judgment call from there."

"I, me, Maya?" Maya had evidently understood enough of his words to get that they were discussing her.

Harper nuzzled her cheek. "Yes, you, Maya. It's going to be such fun."

"I fun!"

"You certainly are," Harper agreed. She turned that blinding, happy smile on Linc again. "That's a great idea. I'll talk to Hailey tonight, see where she can fit them both in. I might even be able to take them to their first rehearsal tomorrow afternoon."

"That works."

The eager Jayden was pulling on her hand again. "Come on, Harper…"

She laughed as the little boy led her away.

Harper's plan was to work as many hours as possible for Linc. If she put in only twenty hours a week, she could add seven thousand dollars toward her moving fund by New Year's—more, when she in-

cluded the two eighteen-hour days he would pay her
for when she watched the kids in Portland.

That day, she did the shopping, cooked the dinner
and hung around for face-washing, toothbrushing,
story time and tucking the kids in. Seven hours total.
More days like today and her moving fund would
cease to be a problem.

Linc waited at the foot of the stairs when she
came down. He looked distractingly hunky in his
dark-wash jeans and gray-blue sweater, the sleeves
pushed to his elbows—and uh-uh. She was not letting herself get carried away admiring his forearms
and mentally rhapsodizing over his manly wrists.

"So, then," she said, all business. "Tomorrow,
I'll be here at—"

"Stay," he interrupted, his warm gaze holding
hers. "Just for a little while."

She really had planned to keep it strictly professional, but for some reason, her mouth opened of its
own accord and the wrong word popped out. "Sure."

Hey. No big deal. He probably needed to talk
about something concerning the kids.

Linc offered wine. She accepted. Nothing wrong
with that. She deserved a little treat at the end of the
day. She and Hailey used to go out for beers after
work three or four times a week, back before Hailey met Roman.

Really, Harper spent too many evenings alone
nowadays. Why shouldn't she enjoy a late happy
hour with her new boss?

In the living room by the fire, he poured her a glass of wine and then some for himself. They settled back against the cushions.

For several minutes, they sipped in silence. Like the night before, it was nice, easy. Comfortable.

When she glanced at him, she saw he was hiding a grin and his eyes had a teasing light in them. She liked that light, maybe too much.

"There's a turkey in my fridge," he said.

She turned her body his way and hitched a knee up onto the cushions. "It wasn't on the list, but I kind of figured you would need a bird for Thursday. I also got cranberries for sauce and stuff for dressing. Plus sweet potatoes and string beans—all the sides you could possibly hope for."

He frowned. "Wait a minute. You're talking about Thanksgiving dinner?"

"Sorry. I assumed you would be cooking, and you said to add anything I thought you might need."

He seemed vaguely embarrassed. "Can I be brutally honest?"

Brutally? That didn't sound very encouraging. "Of course."

"I was just going to get takeout. Is that sad or what?" His brow crinkled even more. "There's gotta be a place in town that's open on Thursday. Right?"

"Yeah. But you should order by tomorrow. I'll text you some suggestions."

"You're a lifesaver."

She laughed. "Don't overpraise me. I'll become impossible to work with."

"I doubt it. You sure you don't want to move to Portland and look after the kids for me full-time?"

Why was that idea so tempting? And why was she leaning into him—close enough to smell his wonderful scent, woodsy with a hint of spice, and make out the gold flecks in his brown eyes? Reluctantly, she lowered her foot to the floor and turned her body toward the fire again. "I love taking care of Maya and Jayden. But I don't really think I'm career nanny material."

He faked a big sigh. "Go ahead. Crush all my hopes—and you know what? I'm fairly sure there's a cookbook or two around here. I'm going to grow a pair and figure out how to roast that turkey myself."

She didn't know which sounded sadder—Linc and the kids having takeout, just the three of them, on the holiday where families gathered close around a big, home-cooked meal. Or him cooking Thanksgiving dinner for the first time by himself.

Don't do it, Harp, she berated herself. *Don't you dare do it.*

But the image of him and Maya and Jayden alone with a burned turkey and some singed sweet potatoes on Thanksgiving Day made it impossible for her to keep her mouth shut. "Look. We have a huge family dinner up at my brother Daniel's house on Thanksgiving. It's the more the merrier. There will be lots of kids, plenty of great food and nice wine. Why don't you join us?"

He didn't say a word for several seconds. She just knew he was going to say no to her invitation. She should be relieved about that, but instead she braced herself to feel let down.

"I have to confess," he said at last.

"Hey." She kept it light. "It was only a suggestion. We'd love to have you, but I understand if you want it to be just the three of you."

He gave a low chuckle, an intimate sound that made her feel all warm inside. "Are you kidding? We would love to come."

Her unacceptable disappointment vanished like morning mist in sunlight. "Great."

"As for my confession, I was trying really hard to make you take pity on me. I might feel a little guilty about manipulating you—but not guilty enough to let you off the hook now that you've offered to let me and the kids crash your family party."

She slanted him a chiding glance. "You were playing me."

"And I'm so glad that it worked. I pictured you at some big family dinner, and I couldn't help wishing I could give that kind of Thanksgiving to the kids."

She whacked his rock-hard shoulder with the back of her hand. "I can't believe you set me up."

He laughed again. "It's too late now. We're invited. You can't take it back." He picked up the wine bottle, offering her more. She held out her glass. As he poured, he asked, "So what do we do with the turkey and all the other stuff you bought?"

"No worries. It won't go to waste." She indulged in a slow, delicious sip. "I'll take some of it to Daniel's, if that's okay?"

"Of course."

"We all try to bring something, so I'll bring what I bought with your money." She gave him a flirty little smile with that.

"You're a crafty one." He said it admiringly.

"Oh, you better believe it." Really, she was having far too much fun—and she probably ought to slow down on the wine.

He'd rested his arm along the back of the sofa. She could feel the weight and warmth of it there, behind her shoulders, and she liked having him so close. All cozy and companionable.

Hailey was right. It was just possible that she might have a slight crush on her temporary boss.

This girl.

What *was* it about her?

It just felt so easy with her—and yet with an edge of excitement, too.

He probably shouldn't compare her to Imogen, but he did it anyway. Had he ever had fun with his ex-fiancée? He asked himself the question and kind of wished he hadn't. Imogen could be charming and friendly when it suited her purposes.

But she'd never been someone who just liked

hanging out. For the life of him, he couldn't imagine bringing her here to the cottage. She would have been bored out of her skull within an hour of walking in the door.

He wondered at himself sometimes—at how damn oblivious he could be. Oblivious enough that he hadn't even realized how unhappy he was with the woman he planned to marry. He'd been too busy working to realize that he was turning into his father and that Imogen had all the makings of Alicia Stryker 2.0—meaning even colder and even more calculating than his mother.

And then he'd lost his sister and become the guardian of the two sweetest kids on the planet, after which he'd spent ten months living in the same house with Jean and Alan and found out what a real marriage was.

The bald truth? When Imogen got fed up with him putting the kids first and dumped him, he'd dodged a bullet. Being around Harper brought that hard fact sharply home.

He sipped more wine and wondered about the pretty woman on the sofa beside him.

She slanted him a quick smile and then stared into the fire again. It was quiet in the big room. And it felt good, just to sit here beside her, saying nothing. Harper was someone who enjoyed the moment. She didn't waste any energy looking for somewhere better to be—the latest, hottest restaurant or a trip to fashion week in Manhattan.

Was she with someone? He couldn't stop himself from wondering.

She'd never mentioned a guy…

But why would she, necessarily? It might feel like he'd known her a long time, but they'd only just met.

He didn't like wondering if she might already belong to someone. Could it be that the sole reason she sat here next to him now was because he'd asked her to stay? He *was* her boss, after all. Until the end of the year, anyway.

No.

She didn't have anyone. She couldn't. He would know if she did…

Wouldn't he?

That he even dared to assume such a thing should have been ridiculous to him.

She turned to him again. Those beautiful baby blue eyes had him thinking of clear summer afternoons and the Pacific Ocean on a windless day.

And what was his problem here, really? A simple question would resolve this issue one way or another. "Got someone special waiting for you back at that cottage of yours?"

She looked at him so steadily. "I used to share it with my sister, but now I'm there on my own."

"No boyfriend trying to talk you into moving in with him?"

Her thick eyelashes swept down and then fluttered up. "No."

Warmth radiated through him. He'd been right.

There was no one. But he double-checked, just to be sure. "Not seeing anyone at the moment, then?"

Her mouth curved sweetly in a smile that seemed a little bit sad. "Not for a while. I was with a guy at UO. We broke up my senior year."

"Why?"

She stared into the fire again. "Let's just say that he and I grew apart."

It was an obvious evasion. He hoped she might get honest about it.

And then she did. "Okay, the truth is, he and I were never all that close. I was interested in my studies, in the next design problem I needed to solve—whether as a set builder or for a project in a 3D modeling class. It was nice to have someone to be with now and then, but he wasn't exactly the love of my life."

"You sound sad when you talk about him."

"Yeah, well. Most women my age have been in love at least once. For me, there have been dates and hookups and two steady boyfriends—the guy at UO and a boy I went out with in high school. But I've never actually found that special someone—you know, the man I would drop everything for. I've always had interesting work I wanted to do, my sister for a BFF and a big family to count on. Men have kind of taken a back seat in my life, you know?"

He got that. In a lot of ways, he was the same—minus the big family and the sister who was also a best friend. He had loved his sister, but once they grew up, they'd chosen different paths. Until Megan and Kevin went down in that plane, his life had centered on Stryker Marine.

"What about you?" she asked. "Anyone special?"

He'd figured that was coming. Still, he hesitated, though he knew it would be better just to put it right out there. Rip the bandage off, so to speak.

"Trying to decide how much to say?" she teased.

He went ahead and busted himself. "You got me."

Her big eyes had grown wary. "So there *is* someone, then?"

"No—but I was engaged until recently."

She blinked. Probably not a good sign. "How recently?"

"We broke up last Friday."

Chapter Three

Last Friday?

Until four days ago, Linc was engaged?

Harper couldn't hide her dismay. "What happened?"

He didn't answer immediately. She knew he was choosing his words with care and that did not reassure her. "I realized we weren't a good match, after all."

"So you just ended it?"

"No. *She* did—and that's good. As I said, we wouldn't have been happy together."

She wanted to know more, every detail. Who was this woman? How long were they together? Why had

his fiancée broken it off just as he conveniently decided that the engagement wouldn't work?

And hold on a damn minute here…

Eighty bucks an hour, she reminded herself.

She needed to remember her goals. And her goals
did not include getting too personal with Linc. Yeah,
she liked him and she felt drawn to him.

But why take the chance she might ruin a good
thing? This great job watching the kids could blow
up in her face. She needed *not* to get too close.

The man was in flux. He'd been *engaged* until
Friday.

Exactly, a devilish voice in the back of her mind
cut in. *That could mean he not only needs a nanny
to look after his adorable niece and nephew, Linc
Stryker just might be a prime candidate for a rebound fling.*

They could have a good time. It could be just for
fun, until New Year's, in the evenings, like now,
when the kids were in bed.

And it could be good for her, too—like a Christmas present to herself. Something sweet and hot
and temporary…

No.

Bad idea. It was just too risky.

Eighty bucks an hour.

She would make that her mantra every time she
got carried away gazing into those warm brown
eyes, longing to hear all his secrets, wanting to feel

those perfect, hard arms wrapped around her and those sexy lips pressed to hers...

"Hey." He looked worried now. "You're very quiet..."

She set down her empty glass. When he moved to pour her some more, she put her hand over it. "I should go."

He tipped his head to the side, studying her. "The very recently broken engagement kind of freaked you out, huh?"

"No..."

"Don't lie." He said it so gently, and that caused an ache in the center of her chest.

Why? Nothing at all had been lost.

Yet she felt something really good slipping away.

Carefully, she guided her heavy braid back over her shoulder. "Well, I guess what you just told me did remind me that we have a great thing going here. You get help with the kids and I get to beef up my savings. Getting too close to each other could mess with the program, you know?"

"Not if we both went into it with our eyes wide-open."

A hot shiver raced down her spine. She sat back away from him. "What does that even mean?" she demanded, though she knew very well what it meant. A moment ago, she'd been thinking the same thing.

He said nothing for several seconds. When he did speak, it was cautiously. "I've offended you. I'm sorry. I really like you, Harper. Maybe too much. I find myself behaving in contradictory ways."

Her heart kind of melted. "Oh, Linc. I like *you*—and you surprised me, is all."

"Be specific." It was a command. His take-charge tone sent another giddy little shiver sliding down her spine.

She answered him honestly. "Well, a minute ago, I was thinking along the same lines as you, that maybe we could, you know, get together, just for fun, until New Year's."

Now he looked kind of mournful. "But then you realized that would be a bad idea?"

She nodded. "Too risky." They shared a long, intense look. The things they didn't say hung in the air between them. "I need this job with you, Linc." He gave her a slow nod in response. She rose. "And I'd better get going."

He walked her to the foyer, where he held her coat for her like the gentleman he was. "See you tomorrow."

"'Night, Linc." Pulling her coat closer around her, she went out into the chilly darkness.

Harper arrived on Linc's doorstep at one o'clock sharp the next day.

Her plan? To get the kids and get out.

In the evening, she would cook dinner if he needed her for that—and head straight back to her cottage as soon as the kids had been tucked in.

Absolutely no hanging around for wine by the fire.

But first, Linc had to be brought up to speed on her schedule for the day and on the Bravo family Thanksgiving tomorrow. She had the key he'd given her, but she rang the bell just to give him fair warning that she'd arrived. As she let herself in, he appeared in the arch to the living area, wearing a sweater the same honey-brown as his eyes and perfectly fitted dark-wash jeans that probably cost more than the costume budget for the Christmas show. Maya toddled along beside him.

"Hey." He gave her a cautious smile.

"Hey."

"Hawp!" Maya came right to her.

Harper scooped her up. "How you doin', pretty girl?"

"I pwetty!" She wrapped her little arms around Harper's neck.

"*So* pretty," Harper agreed. She asked Linc, "Where's Jayden?"

"In his room playing with his train set. Expect him to come barreling in here, talking nonstop, any minute now."

There was a moment. A little awkward. Too quiet. But somehow, with sparks.

Linc broke the silence. "They've had lunch."

"Terrific. So we're still on for Thanksgiving at Daniel's tomorrow?" She needed to ask. After last night, maybe he'd changed his mind about that.

"I'm looking forward to it," he replied.

She felt altogether too pleased at the news. "Great. I'll take the side-dish stuff home with me tonight."

"I appreciate this. Whatever cooking you have to do, consider it on the clock."

"No. It's Thanksgiving. I would be cooking anyway—except this year, my boss has covered the cost of all my ingredients. So thank you for that. I'm thinking we should leave about eleven or so tomorrow?"

"We'll come pick you up." He looked at her so steadily.

She imagined banked fires smoldering in his eyes. Like in those old romance novels where the men looked like Fabio and all the heroines had tumbling hair and heaving bosoms—and what were they talking about?

Focus, Harper. "Eleven, then." She made her tone brisk. "I'll be ready. As for today, I spoke with my sister and she's found slots for both kids in the show. So I would like to head over there now. I can get them started, introduce them around. Hailey and the other children will make them feel welcome. It will be fun. We should be back around five, if that works for you?"

"No problem. I've got no end of online meetings before everyone takes off for the long weekend. You think you can stay until bedtime tonight?"

"Of course." More hours. Excellent.

"About dinner…"

"I'll be happy to cook."

"I really hoped you would say that." He gave her one of those warm, grateful smiles—the kind that could so easily have her forgetting all the reasons the two of them would never be a thing.

She summoned her most businesslike tone. "No problem. As for today at the theater, Maya and I will be winging it." She met the little girl's eyes and they shared a smile. "If it doesn't work out for one reason or another, we can always come home and then go pick up Jayden later."

"Sounds good. Take the Range Rover. Keys are in the bowl there." As he spoke, his cell rang in his hand. "I need to get this…"

She had no business feeling dismissed—and yet somehow, she did. Probably because she barely knew him, and yet already, she wanted more from him than was wise, more than she could afford to let herself have. "All right, then. See you at five."

With a wave of his hand, he turned for the room he'd set up as an office, answering the call as he went. "This is Linc…Hi, David. Of course. Just heading into my office to switch to the laptop now…"

The afternoon at the theater worked out even better than Hailey had hoped. Jayden reconnected with kids he'd met last year and made some new friends.

Maya did great. Hailey's mother-in-law-to-be, Sasha Marek Holland, was there to help backstage. Sasha was amazing with the little ones. And between Sasha, Harper, Hailey and Hailey's assistant director, Rashonda Kyle, someone was always available to keep a close eye on Maya.

Harper and the kids were back at the cottage by five as promised. She made spaghetti with her favorite bottled sauce and cut up a salad to go with it. They sat down to eat at a little after six.

Too soon, it was seven thirty and she was tucking Jayden into his bed as Linc put Maya in her crib.

Downstairs, she saw that Linc's office door was shut. She gathered up the food she wanted to take to Daniel's tomorrow and then tapped on the office door.

Linc pulled it open. He had his cell phone in his hand.

"I'm out of here. I'll see you at eleven tomorrow." Did she hold out hope that he might try to coax her into spending a few minutes with him, decompressing a bit at the end of the day?

She most certainly did. Even if the expectation was completely unreasonable. Hadn't she made it painfully clear that they wouldn't be sharing wine by the fire again anytime soon?

He gave her a quick smile. "We'll be there, thanks." He put the phone to his ear as he shut the door.

Dismissed.

No doubt about it.

She returned to the kitchen to grab the bags of groceries and went home to her cottage, where she assembled a sweet potato casserole, made some cranberry relish and tried a new recipe for cheesy baked brussels sprouts. By the time she finished prepping the food, it was almost ten.

And she didn't feel the least bit tired.

She ended up in the living room, working on costumes for the Christmas show with *Little Women* on the flat-screen TV, trying not to feel sad and lonely. Practically everyone she knew was coupled up, leaving her on her own in the quiet cottage, wishing for things she couldn't allow herself to have.

It was after one when she finally went to bed. Sleep was elusive. She stared at the shadowed beadboard ceiling overhead and tried not to regret drawing the line on Linc the night before.

Linc and the kids arrived right on time the next day. He and Jayden helped carry the food she'd prepared to the Range Rover, and they set off for the house where Harper had grown up.

A big Colonial on several wooded acres perched atop Rhinehart Hill on the east side of town, the Bravo house was packed with Bravos and extended family. Jayden and Maya happily joined the other kids, of whom there were several now. They all trooped through the house in a pack, with the older ones leading the way, either carrying the little ones or making sure they didn't wander too far from the group.

Linc seemed relaxed, Harper thought. She introduced him to her ancient great-uncle Percy and her great-aunt Daffodil. He visited with her brothers and was cordial with her sisters. When Keely and Daniel's toddler, Marie, climbed up onto the sofa and cuddled up next to him, he moved his arm to the backrest so Marie could more easily lean against him and went right on talking salmon fishing with Harper's brother Liam.

"You *really* like that guy," Hailey whispered to her when they were alone for a moment in the kitchen, checking on the dinner rolls before the big push to get everything on the tables in the dining room.

"Not going there," she whispered under her breath.

Hailey only laughed. "I notice you're not even trying to deny that you're interested."

What was the point? Hailey would know she was lying.

So fine. She really liked him. A lot. He was not only yummy to look at, but he also seemed like a good person, someone who was honestly interested in others, in who they were and what made them tick. Megan had been the same way.

Harper watched him interacting with her family and wondered about his parents. They must be special, to have raised a son and a daughter like Linc and Megan. Strange that Linc's parents weren't here in town for the holidays. Linc had mentioned it was a family tradition to spend Christmas at the Stryker cottage.

Come to think of it, Linc's parents hadn't been here last year, either—well, not that she remembered, anyway. They'd probably dropped in on a day when Harper wasn't around.

The big meal went on for over an hour. There was a lot of food and the Bravos felt honor bound to do it justice.

They always took a break before dessert. Some of them put on their coats and sat out on the wide front porch, some strolled the garden paths in the backyard.

Harper checked on the kids. They seemed happy. Maya and little Marie were lying on the floor together, both of them staring dreamily up at the ceiling, chewing on teething toys. Liam's ten-year-old stepson, Ben Killigan, seemed to have taken Jayden under his wing. They sat near Marie and Maya. Ben was building something with wheels and gears from a metal construction set as Jayden peppered him with questions, each one of which Ben patiently answered.

Harper went looking for Linc—after all, he was her guest. She wanted him to be comfortable, to have a good time.

She found him out on the back porch with Hailey's fiancé, Roman. They were deep in conversation, talking real estate. Roman had a project he was developing in Portland. It sounded as though Linc might be considering an investment.

Did she imagine stepping up next to Linc and having him casually put his arm around her—like he was more than her boss, more than her guest for the afternoon?

Like she was someone special to him and he wanted her close?

Yeah, maybe.

So what? A girl had a right to a little fantasy now and then. Nothing would happen between them. She'd already made way too sure of that.

Feeling a little sad for no real reason, she went back inside to find her big brother Daniel lurking in the mudroom. He had that look—the one he got when someone in the family needed checking on.

Daniel took his duties as honorary family dad very seriously. "Hey. There you are. Got a minute?"

She wanted to be annoyed with him, but Daniel was a sweetheart, so steady and upstanding. It was hard to be mad at him. "Sure. Just don't make me drink scotch. Please." Daniel liked to take friends and family into his study at the front of the house and serve them top-shelf single malt to go with his honest concern for their success and well-being. "It's wasted on me, Daniel." *Like drinking peat moss*, she thought but had the grace not to say.

He grinned at that. "There will be options. This way…"

In her brother's study with the door closed, Harper took a seat on the leather sofa and accepted a small glass of local brandy. "Delicious," she said, after a first careful sip. "And okay. Consider me braced. You may proceed with the interrogation."

Daniel chuckled and sipped his scotch. She loved seeing him so happy. In the old days, he used to look like he carried the weight of the world on his shoulders. Not anymore, though. He'd raised seven of his siblings to successful adulthood. He loved his wife and his kids—little Marie, and the twins from his first marriage. These days, Daniel smiled a lot more than he used to.

"I just wanted to catch up with you," he said mildly. "How're you doing in the cottage now that Hailey's moved in with Roman?"

She answered honestly, "It can get a little lonely, but I'm managing." And now seemed as good a time as any to share her moving plans with him. "Actually, I've been meaning to tell you about what I want to do next year. I'm going to try a move to Seattle, look for something new workwise. Lee-Lee's on board with it. We'll miss each other, but it's time for me to try my wings, I guess you could say."

"You hope to find something with a theater company there?"

"Unlikely. I applied for a paid internship with an architectural firm up there a couple of months ago. It didn't come through, but it would have given me enough to live on. And that got me thinking that unless I want to move to New York or LA, a life in the theater may not be for me. I would rather stay a little closer to home."

"I can't help liking the idea of you staying nearby..."

"We'll see."

Daniel had a slow, thoughtful sip of his drink. "Linc Stryker seems like a fine man."

Had she known that was coming? Unfortunately, yes. "He really appreciated being invited to dinner. He was going to order takeout. Can you believe it?"

"Can't have that. I'm glad you talked him into coming. I spoke to him briefly, gave him my sympathies on the loss of his sister and her husband."

She decided to cut to the chase. "He's paying me a premium rate to help with the kids through the holidays. It's good for both of us. I save money toward my move, and he can work remotely in the afternoons."

"So it's just a job for you then?"

"Yes." Did she say that too strongly? Well, it never hurt to be crystal clear with Daniel. "I love the kids and I like to keep busy, so it's a win all the way around."

"You know I'm here, right?"

"I do, Daniel. Thank you."

"If the cottage is too lonely now—"

"It's not. I'm fine. I promise you."

He gave her a gentle smile. "I'm making you uncomfortable."

"Maybe. A little."

He set down his glass. She did the same. They rose simultaneously and shared a quick hug. "I'm proud of you, Harp."

She smiled up at him. "It means a lot, to hear you say that. Keep in mind, though, that while I appreciate any advice you give me, I'm going to do things my own way."

"I get that."

"And I...well, I do really like Linc."

"But...?"

She thought of Linc's ex-fiancée. A guy didn't get over a serious relationship in a week, and that was almost how long it had been since Linc's engagement had ended. "Truthfully, it's just bad timing, you know?"

"Because he's in Portland and you're moving to Seattle?"

She knew she'd said too much already—and yet, she just kept talking. "There's that, yes. And I *work* for him."

The gleam in her big brother's eye said it all. "Wouldn't that be shocking, you and Linc getting together? I mean, falling for the nanny. Who does that?"

"Omigod. I didn't even think of you and Keely..." Daniel and Keely had gotten together when Daniel had nanny troubles and Keely stepped in to take care of the twins.

Daniel nodded. "You never really know how things will work out. Be open to all the possibilities. That's all I'm saying."

Color her blown away. Never would she have imagined that Daniel would encourage her to give Linc Stryker a chance. As a rule, Daniel had the overprotective-big-brother act down pat. "I, um, yeah. Sure. Thanks, Daniel. I'll do that."

For the rest of the afternoon and into the early evening, Harper couldn't stop thinking about what Daniel had said.

"You want to go straight home?" Linc asked when they were on their way down the hill from Daniel's house.

From the back seat, Jayden objected, "Don't go home, Harper. I need you to tuck me in."

Linc sent her a wry glance. "You don't have to give in to a five-year-old's demands."

"I know. But it *is* Thanksgiving…" And who was she kidding? She didn't want to go home yet. She wanted to…be open to all the possibilities. Like her big brother had told her to do.

Jayden kept pushing. "Harper, *please*…"

Linc cut him off in a firm, level voice. "It's Harper's decision, Jayden."

A silence, then, so sweetly, "Sorry," from the back seat.

She and Linc shared another glance—more than friendly. Conspiratorial. Like they had secrets together.

A memory came to her. Of sitting in the back seat as a child before her parents died. It was dark out, same as now. Her mom sat in the passenger seat, her dad at the wheel. She remembered her parents turning to each other, sharing a glance, their faces in profile. She couldn't have been more than six or seven, and she had no awareness of who else was in the car at the time. What she did have, right now, was the achingly clear sense that her parents spoke to each other without saying a word.

In that moment, she'd felt such peace, firmly strapped in the back seat, her parents in front, leading the way, solid with each other, invincible together, keeping her safe...

Swallowing down the knot of emotion that had lodged in her throat, Harper said, "I think I'll go to your place first, if that works for you?"

Linc glanced her way yet again, his eyes warm, the cool, careful distance of yesterday vanished as though it had never been. "Works for me."

Like night-before-last, Linc stood at the foot of the stairs when she came down from saying good-night to Jayden. He was heartbreaker-handsome in his gray dress pants and a beautiful cream-colored sweater. "Thank you," he said. "For today. The kids loved it. I did, too."

"I'm glad you were there."

He glanced away and then back, his expression a little wary, but also determined. "I shouldn't ask..."

She couldn't hide her smile—and she didn't even try. "Yes, you should."

"Stay. Just for a little while..."

"I'd like that, yes."

"I was thinking hot chocolate, for some reason…"

"I'm in. Let's see what we have to work with."

He followed her to the kitchen, where they found milk, cocoa, sugar and vanilla—but no marshmallows. She made a mental note to add them to her shopping list.

"Here we go," she said as she raided the spice rack. "Cinnamon sticks and cayenne."

He stood at the end of the counter, looking puzzled. "Cayenne pepper?"

"Just a pinch or two. It's my secret ingredient. You're gonna love it."

Ten minutes later, they sat on the sofa in front of the fire.

"It's really good," he said after the first sip.

"Thanks. I miss the marshmallows, but still. Hot cocoa is a perfect choice on a chilly night—with or without the white fluffy goodness."

He watched her so closely, she started to wonder if she had cocoa powder on her nose. But then he said, "It's another sad milestone, you know? First Thanksgiving without them…"

"Yeah." The word escaped her in a near whisper. "The whole first year is rough."

"You're telling me that it gets better?"

"I know it's not news, but yeah." She bent forward to set down her mug. "It does."

He put his mug beside hers and then leaned back.

"I kind of set myself up for disaster with all this," he said.

"Not following. All this?"

One thick, hard shoulder lifted in a shrug. "Bringing Jayden and Maya here for Christmas at the cottage, but minus anything resembling reasonable preparation. I keep messing up. And then, there you are, saving my ass yet again. Today could have been awful, me and the kids with whatever takeout I could scrounge up..." He turned more fully toward her, bracing an elbow on the back of the sofa.

She mirrored his pose. "Stop beating yourself up. You're doing great."

He leaned a little closer. That worked for her. He smelled so good, and she couldn't get enough of the sweet things he said. "I love those dimples you have—" he brushed a touch against one cheek and then the other, causing heat to sear across her skin "—when you smile." He caught a lock of her hair and rubbed it between his fingers. "So soft..."

She leaned closer, too, into the moment, into the scent of him—cinnamon and chocolate and man. His mouth was so tempting and full, his eyes darker than before, mysteriously shadowed with tender intent.

And then he did just what she needed him to do. He leaned that all-important fraction closer and his lips were touching hers, brushing so lightly, tasting of hot cocoa with a hint of cayenne. With a happy sigh, she pressed closer.

He gathered her in, his mouth opening over hers, his teeth nipping just a little. She gave way to him gladly, letting him in with a small, throaty moan.

His arms tightened around her. They felt just right, big and strong and encompassing. She surrendered—to his touch, to the feel of his muscled chest against her soft breasts, to the wonder of those lean hands at her back.

The kiss went deeper. Lost in sweet sensation, she lay back, pulling him down on top of her across the sofa.

He was heavy and warm. His mouth felt so good pressed to hers. So good and so right.

Should there be warning bells going off in her head?

Probably.

Eighty bucks an hour was nothing to sneeze at. When the kissing was over, she could easily lose a major addition to her relocation fund.

But somehow, at this moment, a fat paycheck meant nothing.

The feel of this—his body on top of her, pressing her down, his full lips moving on hers, the taste of him in her mouth...

This intimacy, this connection with him.

It was everything, all the things she always tried not to let herself admit she'd been missing.

She might have, just maybe, started to wonder if there was something somehow lacking in her. Everybody else she knew seemed to be finding the hot magic, coupling up and reveling in it.

Like dominoes, they fell in an endless chain, to passion and excitement and love ever after—and okay, maybe she was getting a little carried away here. It was only kissing.

Thoroughly excellent, delicious, fabulous and overwhelming kissing.

But just kissing, nonetheless.

Just really good kissing and she wanted more of it.

Linc's big body covered hers so perfectly, and his mouth made love to hers and it was fireworks and a brass band, Christmas and New Year's and every good thing all wrapped up in his lips on her lips and his body touching hers.

Until, with no warning, he ripped his mouth from hers.

"Don't…" She grabbed for him to keep him there, but he braced his hands on either side of her and pushed himself back even more. Dazed and yearning, she blinked up at him.

His mouth was swollen from kissing her, his face flushed crimson. His thick hair looked wild, as if he'd been set upon by hurricane-force winds. She must have been clutching fistfuls of it. "I shouldn't have done that," he said.

She felt a hot stab of guilt. Was this about the ex-fiancée, somehow? Did he still love her and consider kissing someone else a betrayal of that love?

But why? That was over, right? He'd said so. He wasn't with anyone and neither was she.

She gaped up at him in complete disbelief. "Um, what just happened?"

He sat up and raked his fingers through all that scrambled hair, smoothing it down. And then he shook his head at her, his beautiful eyes full of regret. "This is all kinds of wrong. We went over all this the other night. You *work* for me and here I am, taking advantage of you…"

Tugging on her silk shirt that had somehow gotten all twisted around in the excitement, she scrambled to a sitting position, too, scooting back from him until her butt hit the sofa arm. "Really, Linc? Harassment? You're going to go there?"

He looked very noble, sitting so straight, his square jaw determined, his beautiful sexy mouth set. "It's a bad idea."

She knew exactly what he meant, but she asked, anyway, "What is?"

"This—us. I can't believe I just kissed you."

A girl could only take so much. She threw up both hands. "No problem," she replied sweetly. "I quit."

Now he looked kind of terrified, and she couldn't help feeling gratified about that. "Please." He put up both hands. "Don't quit, Harper. Don't do that."

Rising, she tucked in her shirt and shoved her wildly tangled hair out of her eyes. It was definitely time to call it a night. "I do not work for Stryker Marine Transport. I'm an independent contractor and you are in no way harassing me. If you were, frankly, you wouldn't be so concerned about it—but you know what? Enough. Happy Thanksgiving. And good night, Linc."

She headed for the door.

Chapter Four

Linc watched her go. Through a supreme effort of will, he did not call her back or leap up and run after her.

Oh, but he wanted to.

He heard the front door open and then shut. She was gone.

And he had no idea if he would ever see her again.

He'd messed up so bad. Two nights ago, they'd agreed to keep it cool and professional.

And then tonight...

He really shouldn't have done that, shouldn't have pushed her down and crawled on top of her and let himself get swept away in the feel of her, the scent of her, the perfection of her sweet, curvy body in his arms.

It was wrong.

Wasn't it?

God.

It hadn't *felt* wrong. On the contrary, kissing Harper Bravo had felt right in a way that not a lot in his life ever had.

Had she really quit? He didn't want her to quit. He missed her already, and she'd just walked out the door.

And what about the kids? He didn't know how he was going to explain her absence to the kids. They would be hurt that she hadn't even said goodbye.

No.

Wait.

She couldn't have quit. Harper wouldn't do that to Maya and Jayden.

She'd been yanking his chain.

Hadn't she?

It was all way too damn confusing.

For a while, he just sat there by the fire and indulged in deep thoughts about his life and his choices.

He thought of his sister, of how he hadn't spent enough time with her in the past decade or so—since their dad dumped their mom and married his twenty-eight-year-old assistant at Stryker Marine, followed quickly by their mom setting out, as she had put it, "in search of meaning." Alicia Stryker had become a globe-trotter for a while. Recently, she seemed to have settled in a villa in Tuscany. She pretty much never came home to Oregon anymore.

A few years after leaving his mom, Linc's dad had retired. Linc, young and untried, took over at Stryker Marine. The demanding work had given him yet more excuses for not spending time with his sister and her family. As for Linc's dad, Warren Stryker was now on his third wife, a woman younger than either of his children.

Linc thought how there were always reasons not to do the things a man most needed and wanted to do.

Now Megan and Kevin were gone. He could never tell them he was sorry for all the time they hadn't spent together, all the summer barbecues he'd missed, all the Thanksgiving dinners when he should have shared their table, all the Christmases here at the cottage, the ones he'd been too busy to show up for.

It all went in a circle, really. Bad choices created plenty of opportunities to make more bad choices.

Which led him back around to kissing Harper.

He was all over the damn map with her—desperate for a chance with her one minute, angry at himself for kissing her the next. Which was the bad choice?

The more he sat there and stared at the fire, the more he found himself thinking that the bad choice had been to *stop* kissing her…

* * *

Linc didn't get a lot of sleep that night.

Sometime after three, he finally drifted off. It seemed he'd just shut his eyes when he heard knocking on the bedroom door.

Jayden called out, "Uncle Linc, it's morning! Can we have pancakes and then go get our tree?"

The knocking and happy shouting woke Maya. On the nightstand, the baby monitor erupted with the sounds of her fussing.

"Uncle Linc, you know what?" Jayden called through the shut door.

"What, Jayden?"

"We should have *blueberry* pancakes. I really like them!"

Linc groaned and plopped his pillow over his head—but only for a second or two. Then he tossed the pillow aside and called, "Come on in, Jayden. The door's open…"

At which point, Maya cried, "Unc Winc, I wet!"

And that had him worrying about potty training. Should he be on that with Maya by now? Had Jean left him a note about it on the list of how-tos that he still hadn't found?

Didn't matter, Linc decided. His niece would hardly be damaged for life if she didn't start potty training until the new nanny he planned to hire when they returned to Portland came on board in January.

And just thinking the word *nanny* had his mind

circling back to last night and what had happened with Harper.

In his measly few hours of restless sleep, he'd come to a decision. If she didn't show today, he would track her down and get things worked out with her. Whatever she wanted, he would provide it.

More kisses? Definitely.

Strict respect for the accepted boundaries between boss and employee? Of course, if those were her terms.

A raise?

Sure, why not?

Jayden pushed the door open enough to stick his face in. Why did kids always look so happy and wide-awake in the morning? "Maya wants you."

He shoved back the covers and grabbed for the pair of sweats he'd thrown across the bedside chair.

The diaper change took a while. Jayden wanted to help and that seemed like a good thing, but during the process, Maya peed some more, which horrified Jayden—at first. The look on his little face was so comical, Linc let out a snort of laughter. And Jayden thought *that* was funny, so he started laughing, too.

Maya lay on the changing table, kicking her fat little legs, staring up at them as she chewed on her blue teething toy. After a few seconds, she seemed to decide that if the guys were laughing, then fine with her. She pulled her blue toy from her mouth and chortled right along with them.

Eventually they all settled down. Linc cleaned

up Maya and laid her on a fresh diaper. He showed Jayden how to position the tabs—not too tight and not too loose. Then he put Maya in her favorite pink fleece pants with the pink fleece top and the Minnie Mouse trim. Jayden helped with her pink socks and little white shoes.

Once she was fully dressed, Linc scooped her up, kissed her forehead and set her on her feet as Jayden pushed the chair he'd been standing on back under the kid-sized table in the middle of Maya's room.

They all three went downstairs to the kitchen, where Jayden headed straight to the freezer drawer.

"We got blueberries, Uncle Linc!" he crowed, holding the bag high.

"Excellent," Linc replied as he put Maya in her booster seat. He probably shouldn't be surprised about the blueberries. Harper had done the shopping, after all, and Harper thought of everything.

"Miwk, pwease?" asked Maya.

"You got it." Linc gave her a sippy cup of milk and some dry cereal to keep her busy while he got the pancakes going.

As usual, Jayden wanted to help. He stood on a step stool and poured the ingredients into the mixing bowl after Linc had measured out the right amounts of everything.

After mixing the batter, Linc put the dishes and flatware on the table and asked Jayden to set the places. Linc got busy at the griddle. He was flipping the first batch when he thought he heard a noise in the front hall.

Glancing that way, he saw Harper standing in the open arch that led back to the front door. He was so happy to see her, he almost flipped a pancake over his shoulder.

"Harper!" cried Jayden as Maya called, "Hawp!"

"Hey, guys. What's cookin'?"

Jayden launched right into how there were pancakes and he'd found the blueberries and he couldn't wait to go get the tree. In the meantime, Maya waved her sippy cup and brandished a fistful of cereal.

Jayden collected more flatware from a drawer and set a place for her as Harper took a couple of juice boxes from the fridge, putting one at Jayden's place and offering Maya the other. The little girl handed over her empty sippy cup in exchange.

Linc became so absorbed in watching them, he almost burned the pancakes, but got them off the griddle and onto the serving platter just as Harper came toward him again. She stopped a few feet from him to pour herself a cup of coffee from the coffee maker on the counter near the cooktop. Their eyes met. She gave him a devilish smile, and he almost dropped the plate of pancakes.

"Nothing going on at the theater today," she said. "Thought I'd come early." She set down the pot, picked up her mug and had a slow sip. "If that's all right…"

He couldn't agree fast enough. "Yeah. All morning, all afternoon and into the evening." The words came out low and rough, though he'd meant to sound easy and carefree. "We really need you today. There will be lots of overtime."

Harper tried not to grin too widely. Last night had been awkward, but this morning he talked about overtime. It could have been worse.

"I love overtime," she said. "Here. Give me that."

He passed her the platter. She carried it to the table and began helping the kids with butter and syrup and cutting the pancakes into bite-size bits.

It had been a cold night—no snow, but frost glittered on the porch railings and rooftops. After breakfast, they headed out to find the right tree. Harper knew the best tree farm. By eleven, they were strapping a gorgeous, thick Fraser fir onto the rack atop the Range Rover.

Back at the house, they brought it in and put it in the stand in front of one of the big windows in the living area. Jayden stood awestruck, gazing up at it, declaring, "It's even bigger than last year!"

After a break for sandwiches and chicken noodle soup, Maya took a nap. Jayden, Linc and Harper trooped down into the storage area off the garage to bring up the endless boxes of decorations stacked under the house over the past thirty-plus years of Stryker and Hollister family Christmases.

Maya woke up after an hour or so and Harper brought her out to join the fun. The afternoon was spent decorating. In addition to the tree, there were snow scenes, a manger scene and a lot of fake greenery. Fat candles, shiny balls and lights had to be arranged on the mantel and on various tables and sideboards.

By late afternoon, Maya was content to lie on the floor. With her chew toy in one hand and Pebble cuddled close in the other, she stared up, wide-eyed, at all the lights and bright decorations.

Jayden was hyped. "Wait! We have to do the outside lights before it gets too dark."

"The handyman is going to put those up tomorrow," Linc said.

Jayden did not approve. "But the handyman isn't *family* and it is only *family* at the cottage."

Linc crouched down and gave Jayden's shoulder a squeeze. "We're making an exception in this case. The way we did for Harper."

Jayden was doubtful. "Is he a *nice* handyman?"

"Well, I haven't met him yet, but he has excellent references."

"What's 'references'?"

"References are when other people someone has worked for say he's a good worker and you can depend on him."

"Hmm." Jayden remained unconvinced. "What's his name?"

"Angus McTerly."

Harper knew she should probably stay out of it, but she stuck her nose in anyway. "I know Angus.

He lives nearby, two cottages south of my cottage. He is *genuinely nice*. And he has a friendly dog named Mitsy."

Jayden folded his arms across his little chest and pondered that information. "I like dogs. Will he *bring* the dog named Mitsy?"

Linc caught Harper's eye. She read his expression. It said, *Your move. Make it good.*

She smirked at him and then suggested to Jayden, "I'll call him and ask him to bring Mitsy along."

"Okay." Mitsy had tipped the scales for Jayden. "The handyman can put up the outside lights this year and bring Mitsy."

"Excellent." Linc rose.

"Uncle Linc?" Jayden stared up at his uncle hopefully. "I've been thinking. I *really* want a puppy for Christmas." Linc frowned. Jayden, as usual, just kept on talking. "And that 'minds me. I need to write my letter to Santa. You and Harper can help and then you can help me write one for Maya, too."

"One Christmas project at a time," Linc replied. "Today we did a lot. Let's save the letters for another day."

"Tomorrow? Please?"

"Sure. Tomorrow."

"And what about a puppy? Can I have a puppy?"

Linc kept his mouth shut and gazed down at his nephew patiently.

As for Jayden, he was a very bright boy who

knew when *not* to push his luck. "Maybe you could just think about the puppy, Uncle Linc?"

"I'll do that."

"O-*kay*!"

Linc paused. "You know what, Jayden?"

The boy wrinkled his button nose. "What?"

"*If* we do get you a puppy, it will be next year, after we're back home in Portland."

Jayden stuck out his lower lip. "No puppy for Christmas?"

"Sorry. No puppy for Christmas."

"But maybe sometime later?"

"We'll see."

Jayden seemed to realize that was as far as he was getting on the puppy question today. His "okay" wasn't quite as enthusiastic as before, but he gave a little nod with it that seemed to say he'd accepted Linc's decision.

On the floor nearby, Maya took her chew toy out of her mouth. "I hungwy," she announced to no one in particular.

Harper bent and scooped her up. "Let's head on into the kitchen and see what we can do about that…"

For the rest of the afternoon and evening, both kids were fussy, which was no surprise to Harper. All the excitement had exhausted them.

But when Harper mentioned bedtime, both of them objected.

Maya stuck her lip out. "No. No bed."

Jayden argued, "It's still early."

Harper and Linc tacitly decided not to fight them on it.

Five minutes later, for no discernable reason, Maya started crying and wouldn't stop. Jayden complained that she hurt his ears and couldn't they make her be quiet, please?

Then, in the middle of a long, sad wail, Maya dropped to her bottom on the floor, toppled to her side and went to sleep.

Harper bent down and felt her forehead, just in case. "No fever. I think she's just worn out."

Linc carried the little girl upstairs to get her ready for bed while Harper herded Jayden up there, as well. The boy spent a good half hour in the bathroom washing his face and brushing his teeth, after which he announced he would read to Harper—meaning he would choose a book he had pretty much memorized and "read" it by turning the pages and telling it from memory.

Harper cuddled up with him on his Star Wars quilt and Jayden began "reading" her the *Me and My Dragon* Christmas book.

Linc stuck his head in the door and mouthed, "Wine?"

She probably shouldn't. Wine was dangerous. Then again, last night they'd only had cocoa and look what had happened. Maybe their chemistry was just too powerful to ignore. She gave him a nod.

Why not? She deserved a nice glass of red and a hot guy to drink it with.

"Uncle Linc, come let me read you a story," Jayden commanded. "It's the one about the dragon and the Christmas spirit."

"Can't miss that." Linc joined them, circling around to Jayden's other side. It was kind of a tight fit, the three of them on the single bed, but Jayden looked pleased as he continued with the story of the little boy who taught his dragon all about what Christmas really means.

When he closed the book, Harper suggested that maybe he would like his uncle to tuck him in tonight. Jayden agreed that he would like that a lot, and Harper left them to it.

She was in the kitchen putting the last of the dishes in the dishwasher and tidying up when Linc joined her.

"How about champagne tonight?" he offered.

"Feeling festive?"

"Hey. We decorated the tree today. That's something to celebrate." His eyes got softer, more gold than brown. "And you came back."

"Linc." She dropped the sponge in the sink and moved a few steps in his direction. "I was only joking about quitting."

"Good."

She'd reached the marble-topped island, and he was near the fridge by then, almost close enough to touch. "I *was* annoyed with you."

"Yeah." He glanced down and then back up into her waiting eyes. "Got that." Energy seemed to vibrate in the air between them, an electric feeling, impossible to ignore.

She admitted, "I, um, felt a little guilty for being so hard on you. I know you were only trying to do the right thing."

He looked solemn suddenly. "I was, yes."

"I actually researched the harassment question last night, when I got home."

"You did?" Now he seemed cautious. "So then, you *do* think I was harassing you?"

She exerted great effort *not* to roll her eyes. "No. I was interested, so I looked it up online."

"Ah." He gave her a slow, wary nod.

"I learned that sexual harassment really is a particularly bad problem for housekeepers and nannies. It's different, working in the home where the employer lives. Domestic workers aren't formally covered by the same laws that protect most employees."

He watched her steadily now. "At Stryker Marine, the employee manual has a whole section on harassment. Anyone in a supervisory capacity is required to take an online course so we know they understand what is and is not harassment."

"And you're telling me that you took that course?"

"Yes, I did."

"But, Linc, you really weren't harassing me."

He put up both hands. "There's no need to go on and on about this."

"I'm not. I'm only trying to clear the air, you know? And what I'm getting at is that it's still about consent. *If* we ended up in bed together, it wouldn't be harassment because I can promise you, I would not go to bed with you unless I wanted to be there. Are we perfectly clear?"

"We are, yes. So very painfully clear." He looked more than a little uneasy. The muscles in his arm flexed beneath his snug sweater as he rubbed the back of his neck. "So what, exactly, is happening here?"

Was she giving him a headache?

Probably.

But she'd come this far. Might as well drill her point home. "We are coming to an understanding on the harassment question—meaning that there isn't any in our situation. And now that we've got that settled, we are tabling this discussion."

He seemed more confused than ever—and a little unsure as to whether he should allow himself to look directly at her. "Harper, I'm not completely clear as to what you're telling me. Are you still the nanny?"

"Do you *want* me to still be the nanny?"

"God, yes."

"And I need the money. So okay, then. I didn't really quit, and you don't want me to quit."

He shook his head and then he nodded. "Works for me."

"And I've made you uncomfortable, haven't I?"

"Yeah, kind of. But I'll get over it." He arched a sable eyebrow. "Champagne?"

She longed to say yes. But she'd made too big a deal about the harassment thing and now it was awkward between them. She needed to keep her feet on the ground here, to remember that, while she might feel sometimes that they were close and growing closer, they weren't.

They had a very temporary and practical arrangement. She needed to remember that she really didn't know him. He'd been engaged way too recently and acting on her attraction to him was a bad idea. When the holiday season was over, they would be headed in different directions.

"So, then." He was watching her, more wary than ever. "That's a no on the champagne?"

"Yeah, I think I'd better pass—and tomorrow's Saturday. I thought I would go with our original plan and take weekends off?"

"Of course." Did he look surprised? Upset?

Why wouldn't he be—on both counts? She'd handled this whole conversation with all the finesse of a toddler about to throw a tantrum. Probably by now he just wished she would shut up and leave. "I can get a lot done at the theater if I can work straight through a couple of days in a row."

"I understand. No problem."

"Well, okay then. See you Monday, around one?" She stared at him, waiting for… What?

There was nothing else to say.

With a plastered-on smile and a quick nod, she turned for the arch that led to the front door.

"I'm thinking these for the angels' robes…" Harper held up a stack of old white sheets. She and Hailey were downtown at the Pacific Bargain Mall, scouting props and costume materials for the Christmas show. "They're soft from years of washing, which means they'll be comfortable to wear and easy to handle. We'll just cut and fold and hem them at the neck hole. I've got a bunch of those gold graduation honor cords we can use as a tie at the waist. And gold foil on the wings and for the halos, I think. It's simpler and also showier from the stage than trying to do feathers…"

"Sounds good." Hailey paused. "Look at me."

Harper met her eyes. "What?"

"What's wrong?"

"Huh? Nothing."

"Liar." Hailey grabbed her arm. "Buy the sheets and let's go get a coffee."

Ten minutes later they had white chocolate peppermint mochas and a corner table at the Steamy Bean, which wasn't far from the Bargain Mall. John Legend crooned "By Christmas Eve" from a speaker above the espresso machine. Outside, the sky was gray and overcast, but evergreen wreaths hung from the streetlamps. Across the street, the Salvation Army bell ringer stood by her red kettle in front of the bookstore.

Hailey licked the whipped-cream mustache from her upper lip. "Is it the move? You're nervous about how it's going to work out?"

"Yeah. No. I don't know..."

"Well, that's specific." Hailey put her hand over Harper's. "I'll miss you so bad."

"And I'll miss you."

"But, Harp, it's the right decision for you. And I'll come with you when you go, stay with you in Seattle until we find you a good place and you're all settled in."

"You're the best." Harper turned her hand over and gave her sister's fingers a squeeze. "But it's not really the move."

"Hmm. Must be the guy, then."

"I have no idea what you're talking about."

Hailey scoffed. "Stop. It's not like I can't read your mind."

Harper covered her face with both hands and let out a groan. "I like him. I like him too much and I'm acting weird with him and... I don't know. It's like I'm thirteen again with a hopeless crush on Deacon Marsh."

Hailey grinned. "Wow. Deacon Marsh. Yeah, that didn't go well." Deacon was three years older than Harper. He'd played drums in a garage band and had zero interest in the skinny eighth grader with braces.

"I followed him everywhere." She put her face in her hands again. "He was always dismissing me, growling at me to get lost. It was so painful."

Hailey gave Harper's arm a comforting stroke. "I know. I remember." She sat back and had another sip of her peppermint mocha—a slow and contemplative one. "But you got over him."

"Yeah. One day, I woke up and…my heart no longer yearned for Deacon. I started going out with Brad Joiner."

"You notice how you always sound so blah about Brad?"

"Because I am blah about Brad—and I was blah at the time. I liked Brad. But he was no Deacon." She picked up her spoon and poked at the whipped cream on her coffee. "There was never that thrill just at the thought of him, never the burning need to see him, be near him, to get him to smile at me…" Glancing up, she met her sister's eyes.

"Enough about Brad. What happened with Linc?"

"Thanksgiving night…"

Hailey leaned in again. "I knew it. Things got cozy, didn't they?"

"We had hot chocolate by the fire after the kids were in bed. There was kissing. He stopped it and then apologized for taking advantage of me."

"*Was* he taking advantage of you?"

"No. But now it's awkward. *I'm* awkward. I'm thinking that I haven't felt this way since Deacon Marsh, that I've never had a boyfriend who thrills me, you know? I pick the blah boyfriends and I have the occasional fun, easygoing hookup. And my lack of experience in all the big, passionate emotions only makes me feel worse about the whole situation."

"So…you've got that thrill with Linc. You've got the burning need."

"Well, that just sounds ridiculous."

"No. It sounds like you *really* like Linc Stryker. And there is nothing wrong with that. I mean, come on. What's the worst that can happen?"

"He'll tell me it's gotten too weird and awkward. He'll tell me to get lost—in a kind and gentle way, and I'll lose several thousand bucks that I can put to good use in February."

"Meh."

"Seriously? You're meh-ing me?"

"Yes, I am. You weren't counting on that job before you got it. I know you've got savings and at least half of your inheritance left." The Bravos had all received some family money at the age of eighteen. "And then there's Valentine Logging." They all owned shares in the family business, which paid modest quarterly dividends. "And if all else fails, you can get money from Aunt Daffy or Uncle Percy or Daniel or Liam—and hey. There's also Roman. He's got plenty. I'm happy to hit him up for you if you need it."

Harper snort-laughed. "I do not need to go scrounging funds from the people I care about."

"My point exactly. You'll manage with or without this nanny job—though I do love the Hollister kids, and you're really good with them. That would be kind of sad, if they lost you. But then again, they're losing you at the first of the year, anyway."

"Okay, now you're just making *me* sad."

"You *want* to be sad. And conflicted. You need to stop with the whining and go after the hot CEO from Portland."

"But…"

Hailey waived a dismissing hand. "But what?"

"I have reasons."

"Of course, you do."

Harper glared at her sister. "*Good* reasons."

"Like what?"

"Well, he was engaged until a week ago yesterday."

"Is he engaged now?" Hailey immediately proceeded to answer her own question. "No, he is not. You need to enjoy your time with Jayden and Maya and let things happen with Linc if they're going to happen. Get out of your own way, Harp. Be open to…possibilities."

"Now you sound like Daniel," Harper muttered.

"What's Daniel got to do with this?"

"He took me aside at Thanksgiving. He likes Linc and he picked up on the attraction between us. He just wanted to encourage me to be open to whatever might happen with Linc."

Hailey reached across the table and tugged on Harper's single braid. "You are amazing and powerful and don't you forget it. And Daniel is right. Whatever happens in life, a woman should never miss the chance to get with the guy who has her burning and yearning."

"What if he breaks my heart?"

"What if he doesn't? What if he's as crazy about you as you are about him? What if this is the guy for you and you're too busy with all your thousand reasons why it can't work with him to relax and give him a chance? What if you lose him and then you meet another Brad or a second Kent and you settle?" Kent was her boyfriend at UO. "You're not a settler, Harp."

Hailey's voice had grown louder as she made her point. "If you settle for some guy who doesn't ring all your bells, you'll never find the happiness you deserve, and I think you know that. You've got to put yourself out there, open your heart, make yourself available for all the good things to be yours. Fortune favors the bold and she who hesitates is screwed and don't you forget it!" Hailey pounded the table for emphasis. Their mochas jumped.

They stared at each other, realizing simultaneously that it was suddenly way too quiet in the Steamy Bean.

And then the two baristas started clapping. The three women at the next table joined in. A guy by the window whistled and stomped his feet.

Ever the diva, Hailey got up and took a bow.

Chapter Five

When Harper let herself in the front door of the Stryker cottage Monday afternoon, silence greeted her. "Anybody home?"

Nobody answered.

But from the foyer, she could see that the tree was lit up in the living area. They all must be upstairs or maybe in the office. She swallowed down the nervousness that came from not quite knowing how Linc would greet her after the way they'd left things Friday night. Every time she thought about that, she cringed. She'd lectured him and turned down the wine she'd previously said yes to—and then raced out the door.

Really, she could hardly blame him if he found

ways to avoid too much contact with her now. And the more she thought about it, the more she worried he might be rethinking the wisdom of keeping her around at all.

Welp. No time like the present to find out.

She hung her coat on the rack by the door, dropped her tote on the hall table and went on into the living area, where the beautiful tree, ablaze with lights, stood in the window and the fire burned bright. She was about to detour to the kitchen when she spotted the trifold brochure on the coffee table.

Intrigued, she picked it up. The front had a company name, Acevedo Hybrid Homes, in a bold font, surrounded by color photos of modern-looking, boxy houses, with lots of windows and an interesting industrial feel.

She recognized those houses. They were increasingly popular all over the country. There was even a show about them on HGTV—*Container Homes*.

Made from retired shipping containers, the houses were sturdy and affordable. You could use them to create a tiny, eco-friendly, low-cost home with a modest footprint. You could also go big, find interesting ways to link them together, construct a shipping container mansion or even a whole apartment complex.

Was Linc considering building a container house? Or maybe investing in this company, Acevedo Hybrid Homes?

With a shrug, she dropped the brochure back on

the table where she'd found it and turned for the kitchen.

That was when she heard a tiny giggle, followed by Jayden whispering, "Shh. She'll hear us."

The sounds were coming from over by the tree. As she watched, the branches shook and ornaments clinked together.

She put a hand to her ear and asked, "What do I hear? It sounds like there might be elves behind the Christmas tree."

Another giggle, followed by more whispering—and then by both kids crawling out from behind the tree.

"Harper!" Jayden shouted, jumping up. "It's us!" He came running.

"Hawp!" It took Maya longer to get upright.

She managed it just as Jayden reached Harper. "We missed you!" he declared, gazing up at her with a giant smile of greeting. "You've been gone for two whole days."

"I missed you, too. But I'm back now." She dropped to a crouch to gather them both in just as Linc's tall, broad form unfolded from behind the recliner not far from the sofa.

"Surprise," he said a little sheepishly.

She hugged her two favorite "elves" and grinned like a long-gone fool at the handsome man by the fireplace.

"Hawp, Hawp!" Maya caught Harper's face between her little hands. "Hi!"

"Hi, sweetheart. It's so good to see you."

As usual, Jayden had questions. "Harper, are we going to go to practice for the Christmas show today?"

"Yes, we are."

"Are we going now?"

"Very soon. Did you have lunch?"

"Yes, we did!"

"Up!" Maya commanded. Harper gathered her close and stood.

Linc came toward them. He wore a steel blue thermal shirt that hugged his big arms and broad chest. His smile was so warm, like he'd been waiting forever for her to walk back in his door. All her apprehensions about seeing him again seemed kind of silly now that they stood face-to-face.

"Good weekend?" he asked.

She beamed up at him. "Very productive, yes. You?"

"Changed a lot of diapers, helped build a blanket fort and went camping right here in the living room in that bare spot in front of the tree."

"Sounds like fun."

Maya lifted her head from Harper's shoulder to announce, "Fun!"

"It was!" agreed Jayden.

Linc said, "And I haven't even mentioned that we wrote letters to Santa."

"Mine was really *long*," added Jayden, looking up at her eagerly.

Harper grinned down at him. "Did Angus and Mitsy come by?"

"Yes, they did!" Jayden replied. "I really like Mitsy and I *really* want a puppy, but I promised not to keep asking for one. And the lights outside look bee-u-tiful. Wait till it's dark. You'll see what I mean."

Linc nodded. "It's true about the lights. Angus did a fine job."

"And we made cookies," Jayden added. "They're sugar cookies, Harper. But they're kind of *hard*…"

"You're in for a treat," Linc said with a definite note of irony. "And I'm getting pretty tired of my own cooking. I was kind of hoping that you might be willing to stay late this evening?"

"To cook dinner, you mean?"

"Please." He put his hands together, prayer-fashion, and tapped the tips of his long fingers against that mouth she couldn't keep herself from hoping she might get to kiss again. "I am begging you." His voice was crushed velvet and that look in his eyes…

No doubt about it. If he'd been upset with her when she left Friday night, he'd gotten over it.

She gave him a slow, teasing smile. "Love that overtime."

"I was hoping you would say that."

She laughed. "I'll bet you have work to do."

"It's piling up, yeah. But my priority is right here in this living room." Why did she feel he meant her, in addition to his adorable nephew and niece? Oh, the guy was dangerous. In the best kind of way. "I mean it," he insisted. "Whatever you need my help with, I'm on it."

"Go," she said. "Work."

"You sure?"

Jayden's small fingers closed around her free hand. "Yeah, Uncle Linc. You can go. Harper's here. We have things we need to do."

That night, when she came down from tucking Jayden in, she found Linc in the kitchen.

They had a moment—her in the doorway, him by the counter, neither quite sure what to do or say next.

Harper remembered her sister's strong words. *Fortune favors the bold.* "It's been a long day. I'll take that champagne tonight—if the offer's still open."

He stepped away from the counter as she fully entered the room. They met by the island and then just stood there, grinning at each other. Her heart felt so light, like she might just float up to the gorgeous coffered cedar ceiling overhead.

"Champagne it is," he said.

"After all, it's Monday."

"You're right. There should always be bubbly on Monday."

She got down the glasses and he popped the cork. They went on into the living area to enjoy the tree and the fire.

Should she bring up the awkwardness last Friday night?

She was trying to decide whether to get into that when he said, "I have to tell you, I was kind of worried I'd blown it. Every time my phone rang over the weekend, I just knew it would be you, calling to say you weren't coming back."

She had a sip of fizzy wonderfulness. "I was afraid I had totally turned you off with my treatise on harassment."

He leaned a little closer. She could smell that wonderful cologne of his, woodsy and spicy and no doubt quite spendy. "Share your thoughts with me anytime." He tapped his glass to hers.

"You're sure about that?"

"Anything. I mean it. It might get awkward—"

"And weird?"

He chuckled, the sound low and manly, stirring a promise of desire. "Yeah, that, too. But I kind of like the way you think. I appreciate that you say what's on your mind."

"All right, then. Here's to speaking the truth." They touched flutes again. She sat back for a slow sip and her gaze fell on the brochure that was still on the coffee table. "So…considering building a container home?"

He looked flummoxed for a second, but then he followed her gaze. "You mean this?" He picked up the brochure. At her nod, he dropped it back on the table. "The Acevedos are a husband-and-wife team.

It's a small start-up. Mia designs the houses. Sam runs the builds. They've been after me for a while to give them regular access to our used containers at a price that's lower than we ordinarily get for them."

"Why would you do that—I mean, if you can sell them for more?"

"I like what I know of the Acevedos. Mia's a creative designer, and Sam's a good builder—brings it in on time and on budget. They've built a couple of large, beautiful container homes for people I know who love what they did for them. But they're not only in it to make it big. They're hooked up with Homes for the Homeless, too. They build a couple of houses a year for them." Like Habitat for Humanity, Homes for the Homeless built housing for people with limited incomes. "It's important—you know, to give back."

She wanted to grab him and hug him—but if she did, she probably wouldn't stop with just hugging. "Yes, it is."

"We've played a lot of phone tag so far, Sam and me. I never seem to get a moment to meet with them. He called again last Monday, as we were about to get in the car for the trip here. I felt guilty that I've kept putting him off, so I said if he and Mia were willing to come up to Valentine Bay, we could meet here, at the cottage. They're coming tomorrow afternoon. Between you and me, it's mostly a formality. I'm going to see that they get what they need from

Stryker Marine, but I like a nice face-to-face before I seal a deal."

"I would love to be an eavesdropper at that meeting."

"You want to hire someone to build you a container home?"

"I'm just interested. I minored in architecture at UO, and my senior project was hands-on with four classmates. We built a tiny container home right there on campus."

"Architecture? I thought you were all theater, all the time."

She realized she'd never explained her plans to him. "I'm thinking of changing things up career-wise, hoping maybe to get a paid intern job with an architectural firm—or an entry-level position in a company that designs the spaces people live in. I'm qualified right now to be a residential designer. And I'm planning on going back to school. I want a master's in architecture from a NAAB-accredited college. And you're helping me toward my new life goals, so thank you for that."

He looked confused, but interested, too. "Hey. Whatever I can do—which is what, exactly?"

"You pay me well and I'm socking every penny away to move to Seattle in February. U-Dub in Seattle offers an accredited master's degree. As for my next job, I've been applying for anything promising that comes up, but I think I'll have better luck if I'm already in town and don't have to relocate when the right job comes around."

"Whoa." He finished off his glass. "You're leaving Valentine Bay?"

"I am, yes."

"What about your sister, the director? You two are close, aren't you? And doesn't she count on you to run the technical side of things?"

"She does, yeah. But our lighting director can do my job. He'll step up to the tech director position when I go. As for Hailey and me, I'll miss her a lot. However, I just need to get out there and discover what I really want out of life. I love the theater. And yet I've always had this dream of helping to create the places people actually live and work. And Seattle's not *that* far away. I'll come home often."

He turned his body her way and brushed a hand against her shoulder. The simple touch shivered through her. "Why not try Portland? It's closer."

She loved that he would even suggest she might move to *his* town. But she shook her head. "Seattle's a bigger market. More opportunities."

"Yeah, but you know *me*, and I know a lot of people in Portland. Never hurts to use your connections. Networking is what it's all about."

He was right. Too bad she was so powerfully attracted to him. The attraction made using him to get her new start feel wrong, somehow. "I don't think so, Linc."

He held her gaze. Her lips kind of tingled with the memory of kissing him. She wanted to do that again.

But right now, kissing him again seemed as unwise as agreeing to move to Portland and using his connections to find a job.

She backed away a fraction.

He did the same. "If you change your mind, you only need to let me know."

"Thanks."

He picked up the half-empty bottle of champagne. She set her glass beside his and he refilled them both.

When he handed hers back, he said, "The Acevedos will be here at two tomorrow. You should meet them."

She started to turn down the offer, on principle.

But he did have a point. She'd pretty much decided to switch her career focus from theater to architecture. That meant she needed to make connections with people in the business of construction and design. Plus, container buildings fascinated her. "It's doable. I can take the kids to the theater at one. Hailey will make sure that Maya is taken care of…"

"It's settled then. Leave the kids at the theater for an hour or two and I can introduce you to Sam and Mia."

Sam Acevedo was a big guy with sandy hair and a ready smile. Harper liked him at lot.

She liked Mia even more.

A tiny woman with thick, wavy black hair and striking obsidian eyes, Mia was sharp and so creative. She loved that Harper had helped build a container home in college. The two of them talked design ideas. By the end of the meeting, they'd exchanged digits and promised to keep in touch.

In the meantime, Sam and Linc had made a deal. Acevedo Hybrid Homes would be acquiring shipping containers from Stryker Marine at a deeply discounted price.

When the couple drove off in their quad cab, Linc shut the door and turned to Harper. "Move to Portland. I'll bet you can get yourself a job with Mia and Sam."

She laughed. The guy was shameless, but in such an appealing way. "They're a start-up—you said it yourself. They've been in business for what—three years? They don't need a design intern at this point."

"They need to grow, and that means soon they'll have to hire someone to work with Mia on the design front. Why shouldn't that someone be you?"

She avoided answering that loaded question by observing, "Sometimes you remind me of Hailey."

He frowned. "That's good, right?"

"You're both so certain that you know what needs to happen next and how to make it happen."

"In this case, I do know what needs to happen— you, working with Mia and Sam."

"Yeah, but sometimes you have to let other people find their own way."

"Nah. I know better."

She gave him the side-eye. "What did I tell you? Just like my sister—and come to think of it, Roman's kind of that way, too. He and Hailey are always getting crossways with each other because *she* knows how it has to be, and so does *he*, and their ideas of how it has to be don't always match up."

Linc's frown had deepened. "But see, I know I'm right about this."

"Oh, of course you are. But I'm still doing it my way—and right now, I need to get back to the theater."

"Wait." He caught her arm.

Her stomach hollowed out, just from the warmth of his strong fingers pressing, imprinting themselves on her skin through the long-sleeved T-shirt she wore. "What?"

"I keep meaning to drop by over there, see what it's all about." His voice was low, half-teasing.

She answered in kind—softly. "Are you saying you want to come with?"

"Yeah." His eyes were on hers. She could stand here in the front hall forever, just the two of them, his warm hand still wrapped around her arm. "I think I will."

"That's good." She wanted to reach up, thread her fingers into the thick, coffee-brown hair at his temples, feel the texture of it against her fingertips. "I like Mia. A lot."

"I had a hunch you would."

"Thank you, for encouraging me to sit in on your meeting."

"You're welcome. Networking. It's what it's all about."

Reluctantly, she eased her arm free of his grip. "You coming or not?"

He grabbed the key from the bowl by the door. "Let's get out of here."

Linc was thoroughly enjoying himself. Things were good with him and Harper again, and he really liked just being with her.

It continually surprised him, how easy and right he felt around her. She kind of put a whole new light on everyday activities. Even a short drive to the old theater downtown became fun and interesting.

She pointed out the twisting driveway up to old Angus McTerly's house as they passed it. A few minutes later, when they entered the historic district, she showed him the art gallery that Daniel's wife, Keely, owned and ran.

He constantly found himself thinking that from now until New Year's wasn't going to be enough for him when it came to her. He needed more time to get to know everything about her, which was why he'd decided that he would keep after her until he convinced her that Portland was the place for her.

Lucky for him, he had five days a week for the next month—more if he could get her to work a few weekends, too. Surely in that amount of time he could make her see that she would find the right job for her in Rose City.

"Here we are," she said, and pointed at an empty parking space right there on the street twenty feet from the front entrance of the Valentine Bay Theatre. He pulled the SUV in at the curb.

The theater was one of those classic 1920s movie and vaudeville palaces. Outside, it had a lot of plaster moldings and Moorish-looking arches. Inside, it was white stucco walls, more arches and thick pillars holding up the lobby ceiling.

Harper led him into the auditorium where Hailey, with Maya on her hip, paced back and forth in front of the stage. Maya seemed content to chew on her blue teething toy and stare at Hailey with rapt fascination as Harper's sister directed a large group of kids through a song centered on a lost angel on Christmas morning—or something like that.

It was hard to tell what the song was about, exactly. The kids up on stage kept laughing and arguing as Hailey and a very calm, statuesque woman with dark copper skin and light brown hair coiled in thick locks tried to corral them and get them to focus.

"This is the finale," Harper whispered in his ear just as he spotted Jayden up there on the stage snickering at something the little girl standing next to him had said. "It's their first time through it."

No kidding, he thought.

The lights kept changing—flashing and blinking,

going very low and then suddenly flaring blindingly bright. Apparently, the guy up in the light booth was working something out in the middle of rehearsal.

The accompanist, on piano, patiently stopped and started as kids interrupted to ask questions, and Hailey called a halt every few minutes to give suggestions and then have them go over this or that section of the unrecognizable song yet again.

Beside him, Harper whispered, "What do you think?"

Looked like pure chaos to him. But he was having a good time watching the confusion unfold. The kids seemed happy and he was sitting next to Harper. He couldn't think of anywhere else he would rather be. "Great!" he replied with a lot more enthusiasm than the disaster up on the stage could possibly inspire.

Harper chuckled. The sound sent a ripple of pure pleasure rolling through him. How strange that just the sound of her laugh gratified him in a physical way. He thought of Alan Hollister, sitting in the kitchen at the West Hills house in Portland last Monday morning right before he and Jean left for the airport. The older man's face had lit up with pure happiness when he heard Jean laugh in delight at something Jayden had said.

Even when Linc was a boy and his parents were still making an effort to give him and Megan a real family life, he'd never seen his father react to his mother as if she captivated him completely the way Jean did Alan.

"I know what you see right now looks like a catastrophe in the making." Harper's warm breath teased his ear. "But wait till the opening performance. The children want to do their best and they will. It always turns out beautifully."

He gave up the pretense of admiring the so-called show and turned to gaze directly into those gorgeous gray-blue eyes. "If you say so…"

"Lincoln Stryker, when have I ever steered you wrong?"

He couldn't help slanting a quick glance at her supple mouth. That mouth had him remembering Thanksgiving night and the steaming-hot kisses they'd shared. He wanted to kiss her again. If he ever got that chance, he would have sense enough not to ruin a perfect moment with apologies.

Yeah, more than once over the weekend without her, he'd promised himself that if she would only come back to help him with the kids, he would keep it strictly business.

But that was then. Now, with her beside him, he knew he'd only been lying to himself. No way was he keeping his distance from Harper Bravo.

She was a revelation to him, so different from the women he'd been with before—sophisticated women, who harbored secret agendas, incurious women, completely uninterested in other people's children.

Yeah. A revelation. That was Harper Bravo.

And he wanted more of her. She'd already made

it excruciatingly clear that she didn't consider herself his employee, that she was a free agent and her own boss. Any intimacy they shared would be because they both wanted it. Didn't that clear the way for him to get to know her better?

Sure seemed like it to him.

From now on, he wouldn't miss any opportunity to get up close and personal with her.

Chapter Six

"So how about a movie or something?" he suggested that night when they met at the foot of the stairs after putting the kids to bed. His pulse thrummed in his ears as he waited for her answer. He just knew he would crash and burn. That she would look at him regretfully and say it wasn't a good idea.

But then she grinned. "Sure. First, though, I have to run over to my cottage and grab a few things I need to work on."

Yes! She said yes!

His pulse throbbed all the harder, with triumph. He could barely hear himself think and wondered vaguely if he might be a candidate for a sudden, early heart attack.

"What things?" he demanded. Not that it mattered in the least. She could bring a trailer full of woodworking equipment and set up shop in the living room, get a power saw going in there for all he cared.

She leaned a little closer. He caught a sweet whiff of vanilla and lemons and had to resist the urge to pull her into his arms. "Some of the costumes for the Christmas show need minor alterations and repairs," she explained. "I can do those while we watch."

"Fair enough. Popcorn?"

"Sounds pretty much perfect to me."

She left. By the time she came back ten minutes later, he had the popcorn ready. She took a Perrier and he had a beer. They sat on the sofa, with the tree blazing bright and the outdoor lights winking beyond the picture windows.

At her feet sat a basket full of stuff that needed mending.

He set the bowl of popcorn on the coffee table, plunked his ass nice and close to her and picked up the remote. "So, a romantic comedy?"

She slanted him a look. "I'm in the mood for horror. Something really gory would be fun."

He kind of got off on just looking at her. She seemed to glow from within and he loved her pointy little chin and prominent cheekbones. And those dimples...

He could write poetry about those dimples of hers.

Which was pretty damn spooky. Linc Stryker had never written a poem in his life.

She glanced up from mending a split seam on a set of plush antlers mounted on a fuzzy brown headband. "Not a fan of horror movies, huh?"

"Hmm?"

"Horror movies. You don't like them?"

He realized he'd been staring at her—ogling her, really—and felt more than a little embarrassed. "Oh. No—I mean, I've got no problem with horror movies. You just surprised me is all."

"Oh, right. Because I'm a woman, I should automatically want to watch a love story."

"Whoa. Did I say that? I don't remember saying that."

"Good—not that I don't love a good love story..."

"Uh. Great to know."

"It's just sometimes I want the blood and the gore."

"I understand." *Maybe. A little...*

She stuck her needle in the antler and neatly pulled the thread through. "All right, then. Let's have a look at our options."

He spoke into the remote and several choices came up on the big screen mounted above the fireplace.

She pointed at an image of a teenage blonde clutching a bloody knife standing in front of a Christmas tree. "That's the one. It's got Christmas and babysitting and home invasion, too."

He wanted to whip the plush antlers out of her hands and kiss that full mouth of hers. "You're a bloodthirsty thing, aren't you?"

And she laughed. "You'd better believe it." She instructed, "Keep the sound down low and turn on the subtitles."

"Why?"

"We don't want the kids waking up and hearing screams downstairs."

"Bloodthirsty, but thoughtful. It's an intriguing combination…"

"Give me that." She reached over and tried to whip the remote from his hand.

He yanked it away, up over his head, and faked a horrified expression. "What are you *doing*?"

She laughed again—a full-throated laugh this time. The sound echoed through him, leaving shimmers of happiness in its wake. "You're such a *man*," she accused. "Heaven forbid, you should lose control of the remote."

He lowered the device, pressed it close to his heart and solemnly intoned, "Never, ever try to come between a man and his remote."

She grabbed for it again. He let her get hold of it—that brought her in good and close. The scent of her taunted him.

And then he whipped the remote free of her grip, threw it over the back of the sofa and grabbed for her, smashing the plush antlers between their bodies, making her laugh all the harder.

She let out a yelp followed by more laughter and wriggled against him, trying to tickle him back as he tickled her.

Tickled her. When in his whole life had he ever tickled anyone—not including Megan, back when they were kids? When had he ever had fun with a woman, just being silly and playful, wrestling for the remote?

He realized at that moment that he'd never had a lot of silliness in his life and he needed more of it. More of *her*.

She squealed and shoved at him. He rolled, taking her with him. They fell to the rug between the sofa and coffee table, him on the bottom, her on top. She felt like heaven, so soft and curvy, round in all the right places, and she smelled so good. Her unbound hair fell all around them, a waterfall of wheat-colored silk.

A funny little sound escaped her—a hitch of breath on a tiny moan as she craned her upper body away to stare down at him through those enormous pale blue eyes. "We're crushing my antlers." She lifted up enough to pull the smashed headpiece from between their bodies. He stifled a groan as her movement rubbed him where it mattered.

"Here." He took the antlers from her. Reaching across her body, he slid them onto the coffee table next to the untouched bowl of popcorn.

"Thanks." She relaxed on top of him, lowering her head so their noses were only a few inches apart, bringing that mouth he couldn't wait to taste again so excitingly close. He was lost in those eyes of hers. They had a rim of darker blue around the iris. From inches away, he could see gold flecks fanning out from the midnight of her pupils.

She looked like an angel and she felt like everything he'd ever needed without even knowing it, all softness and the promise of some brighter, better future ahead, where there would be laughter and long talks about his day and her day—and in the morning, kids in the kitchen demanding blueberry pancakes.

He needed to kiss her. But first, he had to be sure that he wasn't overstepping or misreading the situation. He asked in a voice rough with desire, "Yes or no?"

The minute he asked the question, he felt ridiculous. *Yes or no?* The question made no sense—not even to him, and he was the one who had asked it.

But she understood. She understood exactly. Lifting a hand, she guided a heavy lock of hair behind her ear. It only fell down again and brushed against his cheek, smelling of lemons, satiny and warm. "I *want* to…"

She wants to! He resisted the urge to let out a shout of elation and instead asked quietly, "But?"

"Well, I mean, yes, if we're agreed it's just for now…nights, you know? When the kids are in bed?"

"A secret?" He didn't want to put boundaries on

anything he might share with her. But he didn't want to scare her off again, either.

"Not exactly. I mean, really, I don't care who knows. I like you. You like me. There's nothing to sneak around about—except for the kids. If they see us all over each other, they'll get ideas. They'll start to think we might end up together in a more permanent way, begin to expect that I will be around after New Year's."

So? he almost asked. After all, the way he saw it, keeping her around after New Year's was pretty much the goal.

And who was to say his niece and nephew didn't already think of Harper as part of their lives? Of course, they would miss her when he took them back home to Portland.

Unless she came with them.

She went on, "It would confuse them, Jayden especially. Maya's a little young to get what it might mean if she saw us kissing or whatever. But we would definitely have to be discreet around Jayden."

He stroked her velvety cheek and then guided that misbehaving lock of hair back over her shoulder. "I'll make that deal. For now. Subject to change, though, if we realize it could be more."

"But that's my point. It really can't be more."

"Wrong. You don't know what will—"

"Shh." She put two soft fingers against his mouth. He wanted to suck them inside, to scrape them with his teeth. "Now you're shushing me?" He said it gently, teasing her.

But she didn't smile. She gazed down at him, all seriousness. "You run your own company, Linc. You have two beautiful children to raise. Your life going forward is clear to you. *You* know who *you* are. I still have things to figure out. About myself. About my life. I'm not in a place to start building a lasting relationship. For me, right now, there really can't be *more*. It would have to end at New Year's when you and the kids go back to Portland."

He took her sweet face between his hands. "You don't know what will happen in a month. I'm just asking you not to close the door on the very real possibility that we both might want more."

She pushed away from him. He made himself let her go and stifled a pained groan when she rocked back off his groin. They both sat up and stared blankly at the big screen above the mantel. Finally, she said in a resigned little voice, "I'm still uncomfortable about your engagement."

Defensiveness tightened his gut. "What's to be uncomfortable about? I told you it's over. She broke it off and it was the right thing to do. It wasn't working, and we wouldn't have been happy together."

"But you were going to get *married*. When you love someone, you don't just stop. It's a...process, isn't it? It takes time to work through the loss and the unmet expectations and the changes in your life."

He pushed the coffee table away enough that he

could draw his legs up and wrap his arms loosely around his knees. The bald, ugly truth probably wouldn't help him much here. But it was all he had to give her. "I didn't love Imogen—her name is Imogen Whitman. I never loved her."

Harper's mouth formed a perfect O.

"Now I've shocked you."

She fiddled with her hair, rolling a curl around a finger, easing it back behind her ear. "Yeah. I mean, why would you ask someone to marry you if you didn't love them?"

"I was almost thirty." When she started to speak, he put up a hand. "Let me finish?"

She gave a slow nod. "Sorry. Of course."

He stared into the fire as he tried to figure out how to explain himself. "I was approaching the big three-O. I was doing well running Stryker Marine. I wasn't seeing anyone steadily, but I wanted to get married, to have a family. I saw it as the next step for me. Imogen and I had grown up together. We went to the same schools. Her mother and mine are life-long friends. Imogen and I knew the same people. I thought all that meant we had a lot in common, that we would make a good match. Eventually, I found out I was wrong."

Harper drew her own legs up and rested her cheek on her knees. Her gaze probed his. "What made you realize that?"

"Megan and Kevin died."

She seemed to be waiting for him to say more. When he didn't, she prompted, "Yeah, and...?"

He hung his head. "You really want the details?"

"What I want is to understand. And I don't. Not yet."

He tried again. "My sister and her husband died the week of my wedding."

"How awful."

"Yeah. It was a big deal, the wedding. Imogen had been planning it forever, a lavish destination event on St. Bart's, two hundred guests. We had to cancel."

She thought about that. "Well, really. What else could you do?"

He almost smiled. "See? You get it. Imogen didn't—I mean, yes, she knew there was no getting around it, with my sister dying the same week as our big day. But we could've just gotten married quietly."

"But you didn't want that?"

"At that point I did, yes. I suggested it, as a matter of fact. It wasn't what she wanted. She wanted a killer wedding."

"That's not unusual, Linc. Most women do."

He had to ask. "Do *you* want a killer wedding?"

"I don't really think about my wedding yet. Right now, I'm all about finding the right job, getting my life on track."

"You're just trying to be fair to my ex."

"I suppose I am. I can see how it would have been hard for her. She had you all to herself and then suddenly, her beautiful wedding was on hold and you had two children to bring up."

"True. And she was bitter about it. She didn't like that I moved Kevin's parents into my house, either. The kids, taking custody of them, having them in my life—they changed everything. For me. Not for Imogen. She felt cheated. She said so, and she kept after me to reschedule the wedding. I put her off. Then, she decided we needed a romantic getaway, over Christmas, just her and me. I told her I couldn't do that. I needed to bring the kids here, to the cottage, give them what I could of the Christmas they would have had if we hadn't lost Megan and Kevin. And I needed to send Jean and Alan on the cruise of their dreams as a thank-you for everything they'd done."

She was watching him so closely. "I'm guessing from your expression that your fiancée wasn't going for it?"

"You guessed right. Imogen hit the roof and delivered an ultimatum. I was to forget sending the grandparents on a cruise—Jean and Alan could easily do that sometime after New Year's, she said. For Christmas, the grandparents would stay home with the kids. I would go away with *her* for the holidays, just the two of us. If I said no to her plans, she and I were through."

"And you said no."

"Yes, I did. She broke our engagement. End of story." He should probably tell her about Imogen's call last week.

Then again, no. Really. He was done with Imogen. And hadn't he said enough about the whole depressing situation already?

Her expression thoughtful, Harper regarded him steadily. "You were relieved when she broke it off with you?"

"I was, yeah."

"You really *didn't* love her, did you?"

He felt like crap at the moment. "I just told you I didn't." He sounded pissed off to his own ears.

And maybe he was, a little.

She said, "I'm not getting on your case—I'm really not. I can see your position. But, well, I do sympathize with her."

"Terrific," he grumbled.

"You're defensive about this."

He bit back a harsh response. Because she was right. "Yeah, maybe. A little. Or a lot…"

"What I'm trying to say is, if you *had* loved her, I think you would have been more understanding of how she felt. You would have realized that you needed to put her first at least some of the time, to reassure her that she was a high priority for you."

It really annoyed him how right she was. What else could he do but admit it? "You do have a point. I should have been more understanding. I thought I was happy with her. I really did. It's embarrassing to me now, but I honestly didn't know any better. Until my sister died and left the kids with me, until Jean and Alan moved in to help me out and I saw what a happy marriage was—up till then, I had no idea of the path I was on."

"What path was that?" Her voice was gentle, her eyes warm. She really didn't seem to be passing judgment on him. And yet he felt like he was messing everything up, telling her all this.

He admitted, "I was on the road to being just like my father. A first wife who was everything everyone I knew expected me to marry. And then a trophy wife. And then a third wife half my age."

A wistful smile curved her lips. "I've been wondering about your parents."

"That they're nowhere in sight, you mean, at Christmas, when their grandchildren have been orphaned and families are supposed to be together?"

"No, more that I pictured them as loving and supportive. Apparently, I got that wrong?"

"Well, they tried, when Megan and I were kids. But they were never what you would call happy together. They were two people from 'good' families who did what was expected of them—until my dad decided life was passing him by and the way to fix that was to trade my mom in on a younger model."

"So…" She let the word trail off, her gaze locked on his.

Had he blown it completely? Was she about to leap up and run out the door again? "What?"

"We're both at a place of change in our lives. You aren't getting married, after all, and you've got two kids to take care of for the next twenty years or so.

As for me, I'm trying to figure out the whole career thing."

He wanted to touch her, to trail his fingers over her cheek, smooth her hair. Anything to make contact. To reassure himself and her that everything was right between them.

Because as soon as he'd started in about Imogen, everything started to feel all wrong.

He kept his hands to himself.

"Back to my original question…" She frowned.

He teased, "After that grim trip down memory lane, who can remember the original question?"

She giggled, and the knot of tension in his belly eased. "About you and me, till New Year's?"

"Right. I remember now. And I want that, Harper. I want to be with you till New Year's. Do you want to be with me?"

She faced him directly. "I do. Yes."

His heart bounced around in his chest again, doing fist pumps and cartwheels. "Whew. I really thought I'd blown it."

She bit her lip again and slowly shook her head. "I think you were honest. I appreciate that."

He did dare then, to reach out and touch her. Slowly, he traced a finger along the fine, pure line of her jaw. "And will you keep an open mind about the two of us, about what will happen after the holidays…?"

"Hmm." She chewed on her bottom lip.

He wrapped his arm around her and pulled her

close to him. She went willingly, even leaning her head on his shoulder with the sweetest little sigh. He pressed a kiss to the tender flesh at her temple. "Well?"

She snuggled even closer. "Okay. I will. I'll keep an open mind about the future." She looked up at him then. Her big eyes were so serious, so very determined. "As long as you know where I stand. I need to go to Seattle. First and foremost, I need to make my own life and feel good about it. If we take this any further, it should be just for fun, with the understanding that it ends when you return to Portland."

"An understanding that we can revisit before we say goodbye."

She gave a quick dip of her pretty chin. "Yes."

He knew he couldn't push for more. She wouldn't go there. But at least, she'd promised to reconsider a possible next step for them when the holidays were over. "All right."

She tucked her head under his chin, and he tightened his arm around her. "Now what?" she asked.

Easing his fingers beneath the fall of her hair, he cradled the back of her neck and waited for her to look up at him again.

When she did, he lowered his mouth to hers.

She accepted his kiss with an urgent little sound. He drank that sound into him and deepened the contact as she raised her arms and wrapped them around his neck.

Still kissing her, savoring the taste of her, he pushed the coffee table away enough to turn fully toward her and rise to his knees. She stretched her body up to him, chasing the kiss, her thick yellow hair tumbling down her back. He caught her face between his hands and then raked his fingers backward into the warm, satiny strands.

She let out a sweet, hot growl from low in her throat. He drank it down.

Satisfied that she seemed to want him as much as he wanted her, he guided her to her back again. It wasn't really a comfortable spot, between the table and the sofa. And now that he was on top, he worried that he might be crushing her.

But she was beautifully willing, wrapping her soft arms around his neck as her tongue played with his, bringing a rough, needful groan from him, one that echoed inside his head.

Had he ever felt like this? Full of urgency and longing, overexcited, burning for more?

As a kid, maybe? His first time?

Yeah—but then again, no.

There'd been nothing like this in his life, nothing like Harper, in his arms, saying yes to him with every hitch of breath, every tender sigh, every slide of her naughty tongue against his…

Her clever hands drifted down to press against his chest. She grabbed his shirt in her fists and yanked him even closer.

Closer was good. Closer was excellent. He was

achingly hard now, his straining fly pressed to the cove of her sex. Even with all the layers of their clothing between them, he could feel the welcoming heat of her, revel in the way she rocked her hips into him. She was so open to him, hungry for everything, her mouth and her clutching hands demanding all he could give her, eager to give in return.

He could not wait.

Time to get her upstairs, lock the door, become intimately familiar with every inch of her underneath her clothes…

But then, with a desperate moan, she flattened her hands at his chest again. Instead of pulling him closer, she pushed.

Oh, hell no.

She wouldn't.

She *couldn't*…

But apparently, she could and she would.

Carefully lifting away from her, he sucked in a slow breath and ordered his raging hard-on to chill.

She gazed up at him, flushed and so pretty, her hair a tangled halo around her angel's face. He gritted his teeth and waited for her to say they had to stop.

Almost shyly, she caught her tongue between her teeth. He would have sacrificed last quarter's profits at Stryker Marine to be the one biting that tongue of hers.

"I think," she said with a tender little smile, "we probably ought to take this upstairs."

Damn. She wasn't calling a halt, after all. He blinked in elated disbelief. "Yeah?"

Her smile trembled wider. "Yes, please."

"Excellent idea." With care, he eased one knee to the rug between her legs and the other on the outside of her left thigh. "Let me help you." He offered his hand and she took it. Rising, he pulled her up with him. "This way." Still holding her hand, he turned for the stairs.

She hung back. "We never ate our popcorn…"

He snatched up the bowl. "We'll take it with us, in case you want some later."

She laughed. "Where's the remote? We should turn off the TV." Over the mantel, the screen saver had activated. An ad for a streaming service bounced around in the blackness.

"I think I threw it behind the sofa." He tugged on her hand again, but she stayed where she was. Impatient, he faced her again. "Say it."

She only looked at him. God, she was so beautiful. Kind of…pure and somehow untouched. An angel in old jeans and a baggy sweater, with messy hair.

"Fine," he grumbled. "Hold the damn popcorn."

She took the bowl from his hand.

He circled the sofa, grabbed the remote and pointed it at the TV. The screen went completely dark. "Happy now?"

"Thank you." She stepped to the end of the sofa and then rounded it toward him.

He tossed the remote on the sofa cushions and reached for her, getting her by her free hand and guiding it around behind him so he could slide one arm under her knees and the other at her back.

She let out a silly squeal as he lifted her high against his chest. Popcorn went flying.

"Don't you even expect me to stop and pick those up," he grumbled.

She held the popcorn bowl in her lap now and reached out her free hand to touch his face. "Okay," she whispered, her eyes locked with his.

He kissed her, standing there behind the sofa, loving the feel of her, right here, in his arms.

When he let her mouth go, she taunted, "The fire's still on."

There was a remote for it, too. But there was also a switch next to the mantel. He carried her over there and she turned it off.

That left the lamps at either end of the sofa—and the tree and the outside lights. He shook his head before she could go there. "The lamps can stay on. The tree and the outdoor lights are on timers. They'll turn off at midnight."

"The baby monitor?" she asked. It sat on a side table by the wing chair a few feet from the sofa.

"Leave it. There's another one up in my room."

She kissed him again. "All right. Let's go up-stairs."

In the master bedroom, he set her down on the thick gray rug by the bed, took the popcorn from her and carried it to a table in the sitting area. He locked the door to the hallway.

When he returned to her, she lifted her arms and twined them around his neck. He needed to kiss her, so he did, taking her mouth gently, teasing her lips to open as she started unbuttoning his shirt.

"Clothes. Who needs them?" He kissed the words across her left cheek and then bit the tip of her chin—gently, of course.

She made a soft sound of agreement. And then she stepped back. He was about to beg her to touch him again when she grabbed the hem of her big sweater and whipped it off over her head. Ripping the zipper of her jeans wide, she shoved them down.

Captivated, he watched as she kicked off the short boots she wore and tore off her socks. When she stood before him, delectable in a yellow satin bra and little white panties, she demanded, "Why are you still fully dressed?"

He looked her up and down. Slowly. "It's too much fun just looking at you. I want to kiss every inch of you."

She tipped her head sideways with a thoughtful frown. "Hmm. I do like the way you say that."

But when he reached for her, she jumped back, shaking her head. "Come on, Linc. Everything off."

No problem. He went to work on the buttons of his shirt, picking up where she left off. When that took too long, he grabbed hold of it in either hand and pulled. She laughed as those last buttons went flying. He yanked on one sleeve and then the other and tossed the shirt away.

Her smile bloomed wide. "Now you're talkin'." She watched, nodding in approval, as he stripped off everything else. "Oh, my," she said on a sweet, breathy sigh when he stood in front of her naked. "Lincoln Stryker, you look even better minus your clothes." She stepped in close and put those nimble hands of hers on his chest, whispering, "I really like all these muscles." Her fingers strayed, wandering down over his belly, back up and outward to caress his shoulders. Shivers trickled down his spine with every touch. "My, my, my," she added softly when she tipped her head down and saw how glad he was to be here with her. But then she glanced up with a look of alarm. "Tell me you have condoms. I get the shot, but…"

"Don't explain. I do know the rules." It was their first time together, and even if he felt like he'd been waiting his whole life for her show up, they had only just met a week ago yesterday. They had a mutual obligation to be safe in every sense. Yanking open the bedside drawer, he grabbed a few Magnums and dropped them within easy reach. "Come here." He pulled her nice and tight against him. Claiming her mouth again, he unhooked her pretty bra.

She yanked it out from between their bodies, and he felt her naked breasts, soft and full, pressing into his chest, her nipples like pebbles, so hard and tight.

Was this really happening—him and Harper? At last…

So what if he'd known her for only a week and a day? It seemed he'd waited forever to be with her like this. He'd been hoping for this moment, longing for it, even going so far as to overnight the condoms from Amazon just in case.

Now that he had her in his arms, all he really wanted was never to have to let her go. She tasted so good and she felt exactly right, as though every smooth, soft inch of her had been fashioned just for him.

Scooping her high again, he set her on the bed. She pulled him down on top of her, hooking one silky, bare leg over his hip, sucking his tongue into her mouth.

He rolled them so they lay facing each other. That way he could touch her more easily. Palming the inward curve of her waist, he slid his hand upward to cup one fine, plump breast.

She moaned and then whimpered into his mouth as he flicked the tight nipple with his thumb. Nothing compared to her, to the sounds of desire she made, to the giving feel of her flesh under his hand.

He needed to touch all of her, to kiss every secret hollow and gorgeous curve. With some reluctance, he took his mouth from hers, but only to kiss his way down the side of her throat, nipping and licking as he went. The scent of her swam around him, sweet and tart and perfect, as he nuzzled the tight skin over the delicate ridge of her collarbone.

It wasn't far from there, just a scattering of quick

kisses downward, and he was sucking a nipple into his mouth.

She called out his name then, her fingers fisting in his hair as she lifted her body to him, offering him more.

He took it, sucking hard, swirling his eager tongue around the pebbled tip, letting his hand stray downward over the silky curve of her belly and under the waistband of those innocent white panties.

Another cry escaped her as his fingers found her. She was wet and so willing, raising her hips to him, offering him everything he couldn't wait to claim.

"Oh, Linc..." she whispered.

"Off," he commanded, hooking his thumbs in at the side of the panties, shoving them down.

She wiggled, chuckling a little, as he worked at pushing the panties below her knees and she kicked them off the rest of the way. He watched them drop off the tip of her toe, over the side of the bed.

"So pretty..." He admired the golden, neatly trimmed hair at the top of her mound, petting her and then dipping his fingers into the womanly heart of her again.

He needed to be closer. He needed to taste her.

So he kissed his way down her body, lifted one smooth thigh over his shoulder and settled between her spread legs. Now he had full access to all her secrets.

She clutched his head between her hands and

surged up, opening her legs even wider, letting him kiss her long and slow and thoroughly.

When she came, she cried out again. He stayed with her, stroking her with his fingers, feeling the flutter of her climax against his tongue.

The moment the tiny pulses stopped, she was grabbing his shoulders, pulling him up to her, until they were eye to eye again. She seemed dazed, almost delirious.

He completely understood. He felt wild, free—different. Looking into the silver-blue heat of her eyes, he thought, *This. Right here. This woman. This moment.*

This was how it should be, just the two of them. Every night, for all the nights.

But he was still connected enough to reality *not* to say that to her right now.

Right now, he kissed her.

For a long time, and deeply.

She reached down between their bodies and wrapped her cool, slim hand around him. He groaned into her mouth as she stroked him, driving him close to the brink way too quickly.

In the end, he had to pull his mouth from hers and groan, "Harper. Inside you…"

Those lush, swollen lips bloomed into a wide, happy smile. "Yes, please."

So he flung out an arm to the nightstand and groped around until he found one of the condoms he'd dropped there. He had it out of the wrapper and rolled down over his aching length in seconds flat.

"Come here," she ordered. "Now…"

He couldn't obey fast enough.

She pulled him to her, wrapping an arm around his neck, opening her legs for him. He settled carefully on top of her and she reached down between them to take him in hand and guide him home.

Heaven, easing into her, feeling her body give to him as she opened slowly around him. She was so hot and tight. He gritted his teeth and thought of logistics, back-haul rates and suboptimization—exerting superhuman effort to put his mind on anything and everything but how good she felt and how close he was to going off like a bottle rocket when he'd yet to fully fill her.

"Linc," she whispered, pulling him closer, her sweet breath warm across his cheek.

And then her lips were there, meeting his. He kissed her, tasting her deeply. Fisting his hands in the glorious mess of her lemon-scented hair, he deepened the contact by aching degrees.

And by some miracle, he lasted. She was all around him now, silky arms and strong, long legs holding him to her, pulling him closer.

And closer still.

Until she owned him.

Only then, at last, did he allow himself to move. Withdrawing slowly at first and then sinking carefully back into her, he drank her pleasured cries. She lifted eagerly to meet his every thrust.

A revelation, to be with her like this. To be happy and perfectly content in the center of this private storm that raged between them. He'd never known anything so tender, so sweet and somehow, at the same time, so wild and free.

What was it about her?

She could speak to him without using any words. Her pretty face and soft, curvy body excited him, but even more, he took a deep pleasure in her giving spirit, her wicked sense of humor and the way she called him on his crap.

He had it all when she was wrapped around him, holding him tight. With her, he knew that anything was possible as long as he held her close to his heart.

It was the best kind of torture, the kind a man never wants to end, even as he chases his completion, needing the sweet release at the finish, but craving *her* satisfaction even more.

She gave it to him, rocking up into him, scratching his back with her short nails, groaning, "Yes," and "Right there," and "Oh, yes, Linc!" as she came again.

By then, he couldn't hold on for one second longer.

Growling low in his throat, he buried his face against the fragrant, sweat-damp crook of her neck. Heat shot up his spine, arrowed back down and finally exploded in the hot pulse of release.

Chapter Seven

They never did eat the popcorn.

Not that Harper really minded.

Instead, Linc led her into the bathroom and filled up the gorgeous slipper tub. He climbed in first, settling against the high back of the tub as she used a brush she found in the cabinet drawer under one of the sinks to work the worst tangles out of her hair and twist it up into a knot on top of her head.

"Come here," he said and held out a hand. She took it and got in. The water felt wonderful, hot and soothing, as he guided her to sit in front of him, between his powerful thighs, with his broad chest to rest against.

"Feels so good." She closed her eyes and just

drifted for a little while, managing somehow not to think too hard about the wisdom of what had just happened between them. Instead, she indulged in the sheer pleasure of this beautiful man cradling her, with his big arms around her, his fingers idly stroking up and down her arm.

Her body felt all warm and limp and well used. Being with Linc this way was something of a revelation to her. She'd always enjoyed sex, but tonight was the first time she'd been swept away by it. She was used to seeing the compelling connection between her happily coupled-up siblings. Not so much for herself, though.

But she saw it now, felt it right down to the core of her. Finally, with Linc, she got what all the shouting was about. It was amazing, like an electrical current sizzling between them. She intended to fully enjoy herself, take a walk on the sexy side, until the first of the year.

Linc's stroking fingers grew bolder. They slipped under the water.

The excitement between them bloomed to life all over again. Those big, long fingers brought her to another searing orgasm.

When she finished begging him never to stop, she rolled over and kissed his impressive erection, which bobbed above the water. And she didn't stop with just kissing.

He raised his hard hips up to meet her, rocking his body up and down as she took him into her eager mouth and let him slide out again, the water shifting and sloshing around them. It was glorious. He groaned her name as he came.

A little later, he helped her out of the deep tub and dried her off with a huge, fluffy white towel, taking his time about it, pausing now and then so they could indulge in slow, sweet kisses.

Eventually, they returned to the bedroom.

They started kissing again and things got intense. She was going to be sore tomorrow, but she only smiled to herself at the thought of that.

Harper Bravo, insatiable temptress. It had a nice ring to it, she thought.

It was after eleven when she reminded herself that she really ought to put on her clothes and go home. But she felt so contented and lazy. And here, under the covers with Linc in his big bed, it was cozy and warm. With a happy sigh, she snuggled in nice and close…

Maya's voice jolted her awake. "Unc Wink, up!"

There was a tap on the bedroom door, and Jayden called, "Uncle Linc, can I please come in?"

Morning light filtered through the shut blinds. From the other pillow, Linc watched her, his thick brown hair a tangled thatch. "Morning, beautiful."

Jayden tapped on the door again. "Maya wants up!"

"Unc Wink, I so hungwy!" insisted the little girl

from the monitor on Linc's nightstand, next to the discarded condom wrappers.

Harper groaned. "Busted."

Linc eased a warm hand around her nape, pulled her close for a quick kiss and then rolled away and stood. Grabbing his pants, he shoved his bare feet in them. Swiftly, he zipped up. Padding over to a bureau, he got a long-sleeved T-shirt. Pulling it on over his head, he returned to the bed.

"I'll wrangle the kids." He kept his voice to a whisper, so Jayden wouldn't hear them. "Give me fifteen minutes and then come on down to the kitchen. We'll let 'em think you just came over from your place."

She sat up and forked her messy hair back off her forehead. "I can't stick around," she whispered back. "Not if we're still going to Portland tomorrow?"

"Please, yes. I've got two days of damn meetings and I really need you there."

"Then I have to meet Hailey and Doug for breakfast in an hour. Doug requires a rundown of his tech director responsibilities while I'm away."

Linc frowned. "I just realized that Jayden and Maya will have to miss two days of rehearsal."

"Not a problem. I've already worked it out with Hailey. She'll catch them up when we get back. It's all going to be fine." Jayden knocked again. Maya had stopped using her words and started to fuss.

"Kids," he muttered. "You can never just ignore them."

She couldn't help laughing—but softly, so Jayden wouldn't hear. "Better get moving," she warned. "Before those two stage an insurrection. I'm just going to sneak out once you're downstairs."

He leaned across the bed and planted a kiss between her eyes. "I'll miss you."

"Not for long. I'll see you at one—now go." She gave him a playful shove.

After sticking his feet in a pair of mocs, he headed for the door, opening it just wide enough to slip through.

She grinned as she heard Jayden complain, "I thought you were *never* going to get up…"

That night, after Jayden and Maya were in bed, Harper happily followed Linc up to his room.

This time, she took her phone up with her and put it beside the bed, next to the handful of condoms he pulled from the drawer.

Her phone alarm went off at ten.

Linc tried to get her to stay. "Just for another hour. Eleven's not all that late…"

Was she tempted?

Yes, she was. She couldn't get enough of his kisses, of his perfect, tender touch. "I'll be back at seven in the morning, me and my suitcase, all ready to go…"

He caught her hand and pulled her against him on the bed in the tangle of covers from two bouts of enthusiastic lovemaking. "It's just an hour."

She laughed and kissed him. When he relaxed his hold, she rolled out of his reach and off the far side of the bed. Landing with her feet on the rug, she grabbed for her scattered clothes.

He appeared to accept the inevitable. Bracing his head on his hand, he watched her get dressed. "I don't like it when you leave."

She bent down to him again, but only long enough to grant him a quick kiss. "You looked so much like Jayden just then—you know, when he's sulking." Linc stuck out his bottom lip, clearly playing along. She chuckled. "Yup. Like uncle, like nephew."

He seemed resigned to her leaving by then. Still, he pretended to grab for her as she backed away. "Get back here."

"No can do." She dropped to a chair to tug on her socks and her short boots. "Tomorrow. Seven o'clock." She blew him a kiss as she slipped out the bedroom door.

Linc's stunning modern house in the West Hills sat within Forest Park on ten acres of manicured grounds with the urban forest all around.

They drove up the wide, curving driveway, through the futuristic silver gates to the soaring stone, glass and aluminum facade.

It was 9:45 a.m. Linc had his first meeting at the Stryker Marine complex at eleven.

Promising to return by six that night, he dropped them off with the luggage, leaving them in the care of the very capable and friendly housekeeper, Oxana, and a burly guy named Gus who took charge of the bags.

The housekeeper led Harper and her charges straight to the ultramodern kitchen, where the friendly cook, Wendy, greeted both children with hugs and a promise of a snack. She shooed Harper off with Oxana for a quick tour of the house and grounds.

The house offered breathtaking mountain views from every room on all three levels, a true marvel, with a soaring, two-story open living/dining room, an elevator and a soundproof media room, a home gym and an indoor pool in the walk-out basement.

Outside, a gorgeous series of interconnecting slate patios gave way to a smooth, limitless expanse of grass. Dark, lush forest loomed all around, with the panorama of the city below and snow-covered Mount Hood looming proudly in the distance.

Harper admired the sheer elegance and grace of it.

Was she a little intimidated? Maybe—and that wasn't a bad thing. So far, she loved being with Linc and she fully intended to savor each moment she had with him. It didn't hurt, though, to be reminded that his everyday life was nothing like hers and this magical Christmastime they'd decided to share was only for right now.

The kids had rooms on the top floor, to either side of the room Oxana had given Harper. The master suite, Linc's home office and another large bedroom were on the second floor flanking the enormous kitchen and living area. Hailey took time to unpack her suitcase and stick her things in the drawers in her room, though she doubted she would be sleeping there.

Down in the kitchen, the kids had finished their snacks. Harper took them to the playroom off the gym on the bottom floor.

"I swim!" announced Maya at the sight of the pool.

Jayden agreed that a swim was a great idea.

"We forgot to bring our suits," Harper reminded him.

"There are lots of suits in the playroom." Jayden took her hand and led her to a cabinet full of swimsuits in various sizes. She found suits for Maya and Jayden and one for herself, too.

Maya's was a pullup seahorse-themed swimsuit diaper. Jayden chose a pair of trunks printed with dinosaurs. Harper shut the three of them in the playroom and asked Jayden to look after Maya so she could slip into the small bathroom there and put on the white tank suit she'd found in her size. She knotted her long hair up into a bun at the top of her head and rejoined the children.

"There's water toys in here." Jayden pulled open another tall cabinet. Harper found a Maya-sized life jacket with floaties attached and a swim tube and goggles for Jayden.

The kids loved it. They splashed around in the

shallow end. Harper hung out with them, guiding them back to their end whenever they strayed too close to deep water.

Maya spent most of their swim slapping her floaties, seeing how big a splash she could make. Jayden was more adventurous. He put on his goggles and dipped his head under the water, after which he puttered around in his swim tube. At one point, he even managed to steamboat from one side of the shallow end to the other.

An hour into the fun, both kids grew tired. Jayden sat on the pool steps and tried to convince Harper that, as long as they were here in the Portland house, they really ought to decorate the place for Christmas.

"Don't you think the house might be a little bit sad, Harper, not to get any Christmas decorations at all because we're not here to make it *festive* and pretty?"

"I pwetty!" cried Maya, and slapped at the water. She laughed as water flew in all directions.

"Yes, you are so pretty!" Harper enthusiastically agreed.

"Hawp, get me!" Maya launched herself toward Harper, who caught her, lifted her and swung her around as the little girl squealed in delight.

Harper complimented Jayden, "Good use of *festive*."

Jayden pinched up his little mouth. "But, Harper, can we *decorate*?"

"We're only here until Saturday morning, so my guess is no."

Jayden let his head fall back and groaned at the gleaming white quartz ceiling. "But, Harp-errr…"

She blew a raspberry against Maya's neck. Maya chortled at the way it tickled as Harper suggested to Jayden, "But tomorrow evening, we might talk your uncle into a visit with Santa and a drive across the river to see the Christmas lights on Peacock Lane." On the east side of the Willamette River, Peacock Lane was famous for its holiday displays.

Jayden considered her alternative suggestions and reluctantly decided they would have to do. "Well, if we can't decorate, seeing Santa and some Christmas lights would be really good."

Through the glass wall that partitioned off the pool area, Harper watched the elevator doors slide open. A man got off. He was dressed in gray wool slacks and a gorgeous white cashmere sweater. His shoes looked like the kind made in Italy by an artisan cobbler. He was middle-aged, but very well-preserved—handsome, really. He caught sight of her in the pool and smiled in greeting.

It was Linc's smile—just a little bit more reserved.

When he came through the glass door to the pool area, Jayden spotted him. "Grandpa Warren?" he asked almost hesitantly.

The man was Linc's dad, then. And judging by

Jayden's tone, the boy didn't know this grandfather as well as he knew Alan Hollister.

"Hello, Jayden. How are you?" Warren Stryker gave the little boy a crisp nod, one that managed to telegraph zero eagerness to have a wet child coming at him for a hug.

Jayden stayed where he was. "Hello, Grandpa," he replied, achingly polite. "I am fine. It's nice to see you."

Maya said nothing. She clutched Harper a little tighter around the neck and stared at the tall, good-looking older man.

"You must be Harper Bravo," Warren said. "Oxana explained that you'll be looking after the children while Lincoln has them at the cottage in Valentine Bay. I'm Warren Stryker, Lincoln's father."

"Yes, I'm Harper." She gave Linc's dad a polite smile. "Great to meet you. Did Oxana explain that Linc is at the office until six?"

"She did, yes. I was aware that Linc was coming back to town for meetings today. I thought I would stop by, see if I could catch him before he went to the complex."

"Sorry, he's already gone."

"Yes, I realize that." Warren stuck his hands in his pockets. The face of his designer watch caught the light, winking at her. She recognized the brand. Great-uncle Percy had one of those, an old one passed down from his father, Captain Xavier Valentine. The cost of it would have paid for her move to Seattle and covered all her expenses for the next year—with money to spare in case of emergencies. A secret smile curved the lips that were too much like Linc's. "I believe I knew your mother, actually. Marie Valentine?"

"Valentine was her maiden name, yes."

"You look like her—and I know it was a long time ago, but I did hear that she and your father died in Thailand. I'm so sorry for that—we met at Stanford, Marie and I. That was before she married your father, of course, and before Lincoln's mother and I began dating."

"Ah." Harper pasted on a smile and wondered why she felt so uncomfortable. Maybe it was that Linc's dad seemed to be…assessing her, somehow. Measuring her against some unknown standard. At least he didn't seem disapproving in his assessment. That was good. Right?

Honestly, she had no idea what was going on here. Maya had buried her head against Harper's neck and Jayden came off the pool steps and back in the water. He hovered close to Harper's side.

Warren said, "Well. I'll try Lincoln again after six."

Harper nodded. "Great to meet you." Okay, she sounded way too sweet and weirdly insincere. But Warren Stryker seemed to have a definite agenda, and she had no idea what that might be.

He was at the glass door that led out to the elevator before she realized she should have offered condolences on the loss of his only daughter. "Warren." He stopped and turned back. "I just wanted to say how much I liked and admired your daughter. I met Megan and Kevin last Christmas when they brought the kids to Valentine Bay. I'm so sorry for your loss."

His dark gaze slid away. "Yes, thank you. Megan was a ray of sunshine, always." With a final nod, he turned again and went through the door.

Linc texted at five thirty.

Sorry. This last meeting is running late. I should be there by seven.

By then, the staff had left. It was just Harper and the kids. She texted back:

No problem. I'll go ahead and feed Jayden and Maya.

Good idea. See you at seven.

She almost added that she missed him. But she caught herself. It would only sound clingy and what they had was a temporary thing. Plus, he was busy in his meeting and didn't need the distraction of unnecessary texts.

Right then, another text popped up. Miss you.

Grinning ear to ear, she texted back, Miss you, too.

* * *

When Linc finally got back to the house at quarter past seven, he was greeted by the welcome sight of Harper and the kids upstairs in the ensuite bathroom off Maya's room.

Jayden was already in his pajamas, but he enjoyed sitting by the tub and splashing with Maya, who was covered in bubbles and surrounded by floating rubber toys.

The kids greeted Linc gleefully and splashed with enthusiasm.

Harper, on a stool far enough back from the action that she wasn't soaked yet, gave him a big smile that made him feel rejuvenated after a long day of tiring encounters with colleagues and customers who expected him to have the answer to any and all of their questions and a satisfying solution to every problem.

"We went swimming, Uncle Linc," Jayden informed him. "Now we're washing the colleen off Maya."

Harper picked up a rubber bluebird that Maya had sent soaring and gently corrected, "Chlorine." She handed the toy to the toddler.

And Jayden nodded. "*Clore*-een."

"Perfect." She beamed at him and then asked Linc, "Hungry? Wendy did prime rib with these fluffy potatoes and glazed carrots. I had a foodgasm over it, I am not kidding you."

"What's a foodgasm?" Jayden demanded.

Harper answered sweetly, "It's when you really like your dinner."

"I had a foodgasm, too," said Jayden as he launched a rubber boat across the tub. "'Cept for the carrots. I don't really like cooked carrots."

Linc was careful to quell his grin. "Thanks, but we had something brought in when that last meeting went long." He and Harper shared a long look and all he could think of was later, the two of them, alone in his bed.

The com system chimed.

Harper asked, "A visitor?"

"Yeah. Someone at the front gate. I'll get it."

Out in the hallway, at one of the control panels, he engaged the *talk* function. "Yes?"

His father answered, "Hello, son. Just thought I would stop by, see how you're doing."

Warren Stryker rarely *just stopped by*. When he showed up, he always had an objective.

"Come on in." Linc punched the key that opened the gate and the one that unlocked the front door. "I'll be right down." Before he went, he stopped in the bathroom doorway to update Harper. "My father's here. Think you can handle the stories and the tucking in?"

"Of course—he dropped by this morning looking for you."

"Did he say what he wanted?"

She gave him a shrug. "Sorry, no."

He tapped his knuckles on the door frame. "I'll try to make it quick."

"No hurry."

He waved at the kids. "'Night, Jayden. Kisses, Maya."

Maya blew one of her lip-smacking kisses and Jayden sang out, "Good night, Uncle Linc!"

The sounds of their happy laughter followed him down the stairs.

His father had just come in the door. "Lincoln. Merry Christmas."

"Good to see you, Dad." Linc took his father's coat and hung it in the entry closet. "How about a drink?"

"Now you're talking."

They went to Linc's home office. He gestured at the teal blue tuxedo sofa and mid-century modern chairs over by the wall of windows. The view was of the city lights spread out below Forest Park and the broad shadow of Mount Hood looming off to the east in the night sky. His father took a seat on the sofa.

"What'll you have?" Linc asked.

"Brandy?"

"Works for me." He got out the snifters and poured the Courvoisier, passing one to his father and then taking a chair across the coffee table from him. "I thought you and Shelby were at home in Vail."

His father swirled the amber liquid in his glass. "Shelby's still there. I'll fly back tomorrow."

Linc had spent all day at the office and he didn't

want to dance around. He wanted to cuddle a little with his niece and nephew and then take Harper to bed. "What's going on, Dad?"

Warren pondered his drink. "Your mother called me from Italy."

Linc had a bad feeling. In the decade since Warren cheated on her and then dumped her for his secretary, Linc's mother had made it a point of pride not to give her ex-husband the time of day. At Megan's funeral, Alicia had snubbed him outright.

"I'm listening," Linc said.

"Your mother got a call from Sarah Whitman." Linc wasn't really surprised. After all, Imogen's mother and Alicia Buckley Stryker had been best friends since they were children. "Sarah cried on the phone, your mother said, and claimed that Imogen is inconsolable, that you won't take her calls and you've even blocked her number."

Linc had a sudden desire to fling his snifter of brandy at the window behind his father's head. "Look, Dad. First, if Mother's so upset over my breakup, why didn't she call *me*?"

"She said she knew you wouldn't listen to her. I quote, 'Your son is as stubborn, selfish and intractable as his father.' It's always annoyed me when she speaks of me in the third person."

"I will call her and explain my position."

"I'm sure that will go well," his father muttered into his snifter.

"Dad, Imogen and I are over. Completely over.

She broke it off and I'm happy with that. I think it was the best thing for both of us."

His father sipped his brandy. Slowly. "So then what you're telling me is that you will not be coaxed or bullied into working things out with her."

"That is exactly what I'm telling you."

Warren's next words surprised him. "Good for you." He chuckled. "Don't look so shocked."

"Okay, Dad. I'm confused."

"Roll with it. As you know, I was never thrilled with Megan's decision to marry Kevin. Kevin was a nice man from an ordinary family. I knew that your sister could do better."

What did Kevin and Megan have to do with this? What was his father getting at here? Whatever it was, Linc felt bound to defend his dead brother-in-law. "Dad. Do you have any idea how insulting you're being to the memory of your own daughter— let alone the man himself? Kevin was a great guy."

"Of course, he was," Warren said wearily. "And he loved his wife and children. He also loved that ridiculous Cracker Jack box of an airplane and killed my daughter in the goddamn thing."

Linc tried not to imagine wrapping his fingers around his father's neck and squeezing. Hard. "Will you get to the point? Please."

"Gladly. Imogen was an imminently suitable wife for you. But it wouldn't have lasted."

"Isn't that pretty much what I already said?"

"It is. I'm agreeing with you. But frankly, in my

humble opinion, who says a marriage is supposed to last, anyway?"

"Dad. *I* do."

His father sipped his brandy. "Just like your sister, so sentimental. And back to my main point. Now that you have custody of my grandson and granddaughter, Imogen becomes an impossible choice as a wife for you. She's nothing short of a disaster in the making."

"How many times do we have to agree that we agree?"

His father just kept talking. "It's a matter of degrees. Were Megan and wannabe flyboy Kevin still alive, Imogen would have been perfectly acceptable for you. You would have spent fifteen or twenty years with her, during which you would never actually have been happy. But she would have given you children, which is what really matters. However, everything's changed now."

"And I'm assuming you're going to explain how?"

"Simple. Sarah Whitman's precious only daughter is much too self-absorbed to appreciate your sister's children."

Linc's head was spinning. "Wait. Just tell me. Why are you here if you think I've made the right decision in refusing to get back with her?"

"To be painfully honest, I had planned to bite the bullet and take your mother's side."

After a bracing sip from his own snifter, Linc prompted, "Because…?"

"I would like to make peace with Alicia."

"Why? You never see her or talk to her. She came back to the States for the funeral last January. I believe that's the only time she's ever been in Oregon since you divorced her."

"True, but I'm not getting any younger. I would like to feel that there's no animosity between me and my exes—and taking Alicia's part in this, speaking to you for her, seemed a way to get on her good side. I thought I would try to talk you into reaching out to Imogen and somehow making it work. But I didn't *like* having to do that."

"Because, as you've already said, Imogen wouldn't be good for Maya and Jayden?"

"Exactly. I'm not an especially affectionate man, as you know. Children make me nervous with their grabby little fingers and needy little hearts. Shelby says I'm going to need to work on that." Warren had a strange, bemused expression on his face. Before Linc could decide to ask him what that was about, he went on, "Shelby's right, of course. She almost always is. And I want my daughter's children to grow up safe, well cared for and happy, if possible. Jayden and Maya were never going to be happy with Imogen at your side. I felt guilty about that."

"But you were going to plead Mother's case for her, anyway?"

"Yes. But then I met the Bravo girl."

"Wait. Harper?"

"Yes, Harper."

"Meeting Harper changed your mind about trying to convince me to get back with Imogen?"

"That's right—though, to be honest, I'd already been having second thoughts about taking your mother's side on this, mostly because of Shelby. When I explained the situation to her and said I thought I'd found a way to make a stab at getting straight with your mother, my wife was not impressed with my plan. In fact, she was livid. She said that you had a right to make your own decisions about whom to love and marry and your mother and I needed to butt the hell out. Shelby is a bit of a sentimentalist, too, if you must know."

Warren and Shelby had met in Paris—at the world-famous bookstore, Shakespeare and Company. A whirlwind romance ensued. They'd married in Vegas eighteen months ago. Linc had only met his father's much-younger third wife briefly, last January, at the funeral. He remembered her as softly pretty, with lustrous brown skin, a thick cloud of natural curls and a warm smile. "Well. Good for Shelby, then."

"Yes, she is special and I miss her." Was that a dreamy expression on his father's face? Until this moment, Linc had never seen Warren Stryker looking dreamy about anyone. He found the sight vaguely disorienting. "Shelby refused to come to Portland with me because she didn't like my meddling in your situation vis-à-vis Imogen. Frankly, I can't wait to get back to her."

Linc got up and poured them each another brandy. When he took his seat again, he confessed, "I'm still confused, Dad."

"I can't say that I blame you."

"If meeting Harper changed your mind somehow, why even come back to talk to me now?"

His father stared into his snifter some more. "Did Harper tell you that I met her mother at Stanford?"

This conversation was giving Linc whiplash. "No. I'd barely gotten in the door when you rang at the gate. Harper did mention that you dropped by this morning."

Warren settled back against the cushions. "I have a confession to make."

"Okay...?" he replied with a slow, wary nod.

"I was completely taken with Marie Valentine all those years ago, as in struck by lightning, love at first sight. That kind of taken. Unfortunately, Marie wouldn't give me the time of day. She called me a supercilious prig." He shook his head. "I was crushed—and then furious a few years later when I learned she'd married some guy named Bravo from Texas. The Valentines are an old and respected Oregon family. I felt Marie could have done so much better."

Linc didn't know what to say. His father had once believed himself in love with Harper's mother? No way had he seen that coming. And he had no idea why Warren would tell him this now.

His dad seemed to shake himself. "In any case,

Harper looks so much like her mother. And it's obvious she has that same spirit, as beautiful inside as out. The children clearly adore her. She stood in the pool downstairs with Maya in her arms and Jayden hovering close and I thought, someone like her, that's who Lincoln ought to marry. Someone like Harper Bravo is going to love my daughter's children as much as her own. That was when I decided that not only would I *not* speak for your mother on the Imogen situation, I would come back this evening to tell you outright that I disagree with your mother. I hope that when you do marry, you choose someone who makes you happy, someone who will love not only your own children, but Maya and Jayden, as well."

Chapter Eight

"Did everything work out all right with your dad?" Harper asked two hours later.

By then, the kids were in bed and Linc was feeling pretty damn good.

And why wouldn't he feel good? He'd already made love to his favorite nanny twice—once hard and fast and a second time with slow and satisfying attention to detail.

He braced an elbow on his pillow and stared down at her, naked in his bed with that gorgeous wheat-colored hair like a wild halo around her arresting face. "You look so good in my bed."

She chuckled, a sweet, happy sound. "Why, thank you."

He traced a finger slowly from the center of her smooth forehead, down between her eyes, along the bridge of her nose, over those lush pink lips to her pointy, pretty chin. "My dad said you're as beautiful inside as out."

"Wow. I'm flattered."

"He likes you—and that's saying something. As a rule he reserves judgment on anyone until he's known them for decades, at least."

"What about his wife?"

"Shelby, you mean?"

"Yeah, his current wife. He can't have known *her* that long."

"You're right. He hasn't. And he appears to be completely in love with Shelby. Like you, Shelby's an exception to his general disdain for anyone he didn't go to school with. The jury's still out on whether he even likes *me*."

She shoved playfully at his bare chest. "That can't be true." Sliding her slim hand upward, she eased her fingers around his nape and rubbed gently.

He tipped his head back a little, encouraging her touch. It felt right, when she touched him. Already, he had trouble imagining his world without her to come home to.

She gazed up at him, those big eyes so direct, free of guile. "Warren told me that he'd met my mother in college."

"He mentioned that to me, too."

"Small world, huh?"

"Yes, it is." He bent for a kiss. Her lips parted in welcome. He took his time kissing her. When he lifted his head, she asked, "So, he just dropped by to say hi, then?"

Linc tried to decide how much to tell her. She'd made it much too clear that this thing between them was just for the holidays, that they were both supposed to move on when he and the kids returned to Portland. Would hearing that his dad thought he ought to marry someone like her have her leaping out of bed and reaching for her clothes?

Probably better not to mention it. And as for the whole mess with Imogen, well, that was the last thing he wanted to talk about right now.

He told the truth, just not all of it. "My dad was in town and knew I would be here for meetings. So yeah, he came by to check in with me."

"You didn't get much time together. Want to invite him for dinner tomorrow?"

God, no. "That's a nice thought. But he's heading back to Colorado tomorrow."

"So then he lives in Colorado now?"

"In Vail, yes. Shelby, his wife, grew up there. She owns and runs a bookstore and her parents are there."

Harper tugged on his earlobe. "I guess I won't suggest that you invite your dad and Shelby to Valentine Bay."

"They won't come."

"You won't know if you don't ask them."

"Let it go."

"Gotcha." She whispered, "Come down here."

He lowered his head till they were nose to nose. "What?"

"I think you have issues with your dad."

Smiling, he kissed her again. "Figured that out, did you?"

"Mmm-hmm."

"He's not so bad, really. And I meant what I said about him and Shelby. He's different since he met her—gentler. Kinder. The man is in love with his wife."

"You're saying he wasn't in love with your mom?"

"If he was, he never showed it much—same thing with his second wife, for that matter. I always thought he had no heart. It's possible I was wrong."

"So he's making progress, as a husband and a human being."

"That's one way to look at it, I guess. They say that the third time's the charm." He rubbed his nose against hers and then nuzzled his way over her cheek to that perfect place behind her ear. From there, he carefully placed a line of kisses down the side of her silky neck.

She let out a soft, willing sigh.

And for the rest of the evening, Linc forgot all the troubling issues with his ex-fiancée. He gave no thought to his meddling mother or his suddenly rather likable father, who had once been in love—or at least deeply infatuated—with Harper's mother.

* * *

The next day, his meetings were shorter. He was able to get back to the house at a little after five. He and Harper took the kids out for pizza and then for a visit with Santa at Washington Square Mall.

Jayden was in his element. He perched happily on Santa's lap and talked the poor guy's ear off, posing for the photographer with a giant smile.

Maya was another story. She was fine at first, staring at Linc from Santa's knee, a little unsure of the concept, but willing to roll with it. The photographer snapped one shot of her, looking apprehensive.

And then she turned her head to glance up at the big guy in the red suit with the white beard.

"No!" she screeched and burst into frightened tears.

Linc scooped her back up again. She grabbed him around the neck, buried her face against his throat and wailed like it was the end of the world. He mouthed an apology at Santa and carried her back to where Harper waited.

"Hawp!" Maya cried, and reached for her, but without letting go of Linc. They ended up with both of them holding her, one of her little arms clutching each of them around the neck, the three of them all smashed together as she sobbed like the world was coming to an end, with Jayden standing close, staring up at them through worried eyes.

Slowly, Maya settled. Harper whipped out a tissue and wiped her tears away.

"I scawy," Maya whimpered, when the sobbing finally stopped.

Linc frowned at Harper, who translated, "Scary, I think—right, honey? You were scared?"

Maya sniffled and nodded.

"It's okay, Maya." Jayden tugged on her little pink shoe. "When you're scared of Santa, you can always try again next year."

Maya gave her brother a firm nod. "'Kay," she agreed.

Harper suggested, "I think right now what we all really need is ice cream."

Nobody disagreed with that. They went to Sub Zero, which made nitrogen-frozen ice cream to order. By the time they left the mall, Maya's fear of Santa had been forgotten, banished by a frozen concoction that included cookie dough, cake batter, chocolate syrup and sprinkles.

"Can we see the lights?" asked Jayden. "Please?"

It was a half-hour drive to Peacock Lane. They took the Marquam Bridge across the river to the Laurelhurst neighborhood in Southeast Portland.

Only a few of the pre-Depression-era houses on the four blocks that made up Peacock Lane had all their Christmas lights up this early in the season, but there were enough lavish displays to satisfy the kids. Linc drove slowly as the kids stared out the windows, happy and wide-eyed at the bright lights, the giant blow-up Santas, the prancing reindeer and waving snowmen.

The ride back to the house was a quiet one. Jayden and Maya dozed in the back seat. Linc played Christmas music on the Bluetooth, but down low. He and Harper didn't talk much, just shared a glance and a smile now and then.

He felt *connected* around her. Like everything made sense, all the random pieces of his life fitting together to make something good, something that felt so right.

So what if they'd only met a couple of weeks ago? Already he knew he needed to convince her to try Portland instead of Seattle when she made her move next year. Good thing he had the whole month to show her that she should be with him and he needed to be with her, and it shouldn't be that much harder for her to find satisfying work in his town.

That Sunday, he and the kids went with Harper up to Daniel Bravo's house for the regular Bravo family Sunday dinner. Jayden and Maya had a great time, trooping up and down the stairs after the older children, helping to set the tables when it was time to eat.

Linc enjoyed hanging out with Harper's family. They were a boisterous, fun crew. Being around them had him reflecting on how much he missed the sister he'd failed to spend enough time with while he'd still had the chance.

The Bravos also got him thinking about his dad, had him considering the possibility that maybe Warren Stryker wasn't such a poor excuse for a father, after all. He kept mentally revisiting Harper's suggestion that he invite his dad and Shelby to Valentine Bay sometime this month.

Tuesday at lunchtime, during a video chat with Alan and Jean, he mentioned that he'd seen his dad in Portland the week before.

Jean said, "I hope you got to spend some quality time with Warren. You don't see your dad enough."

He couldn't remember ever spending much time with his father—quality, or otherwise. "Well, he just stopped in for a drink Thursday evening, so we only had a little while together."

Alan said, "Megan used to reminisce on how your dad and your mother took you to Valentine Bay every Christmas, back when you and Megan were little."

"They did, yes."

"Why not invite him to the cottage?" Jean suggested. "You're in Valentine Bay for several weeks. He might find a time he can manage to fly out there."

It was so close to Harper's suggestion, he found himself replying, "I'll do that." And then instantly reconsidering. "Possibly…"

Jean smiled benignly. "Good, then. Think it over."

At which point, Maya held up Pebble and commanded, "Gamma, kiss-kiss." Jean blew a couple of big kisses, after which Jayden asked to see the ocean.

The giant ship was somewhere off the coast of

Guatemala at that point. Alan scooped up their laptop and carried it to a window of their penthouse stateroom so that Jayden could get a look at the view.

A few minutes later, as they were wrapping up the visit, Harper appeared.

Maya and Jayden greeted her with shouts of "Hawp!" and, "Harper! I drew more Christmas pictures!"

"Hi, Maya," Harper replied and then beamed at Jayden. "I can't wait to see those."

On the laptop screen, Alan and Jean shared a look. Jean asked, "Is that the nanny you hired?"

"It's Harper," Jayden corrected his grandmother.

Linc kind of loved that. Jayden saw Harper as a person, not a function. He signaled her over to sit with them on the sofa and made introductions as Maya crawled into Harper's lap and Jayden sprinted for the kitchen to grab the new pictures he'd stuck on the fridge.

Jean said, "It's such a pleasure to meet you at last."

Alan added, "We're glad you're there to help Linc look after the children."

"Me, too," replied Harper. "Your grandchildren are a lot of fun." She tipped her head to the side to make eye contact with the toddler in her lap. "Aren't you, Maya?"

"I fun!" cried Maya, and gave Pebble a hug.

Jayden came flying back in with his pictures.

Harper and the grands praised his work. "I think they're very festive," he proudly declared.

Jean said to Harper, "I hope we'll get to meet you in person one of these days. We won't be home from this trip until next summer. I don't know if Linc has told you that we live in the Sacramento area."

Harper nodded. "I think he mentioned that, yes."

"But they're thinking of moving to Portland," Linc couldn't resist putting in hopefully.

It pleased him no end when Alan backed him up. "Yes, we are," the older man said and added, for Harper's benefit, "Kevin was our only child..."

Jean sighed. "A beautiful, blessed, late-in-life baby." Her eyes were misty as she recalled her lost son. "And yes," she went on more briskly, "we're very seriously considering a move to Oregon, where we can be near the children and Linc."

"I'm holding you to that," Linc warned. Maybe he was pushing it, but he wanted them nearby. He'd grown attached to them in the past year. And it would be so good for the kids, to have their Grandma and PopPop dropping by often.

"Very seriously considering it," Jean repeated. "And lovely to get to chat with you a bit, Harper."

"Great to meet you, too."

Linc had to actively resist the need to hook an arm across Harper's shoulders, maybe steal a kiss— just on the cheek. A couple of simple, affectionate gestures that would let Alan and Jean know how important Harper had become to him.

But he had a feeling Harper wouldn't go for it. They were supposed to be keeping their relationship on the down-low around the kids. From Harper's point of view, his cuddling up to her in the biweekly video visit with the grandparents would be sending the wrong kind of signal.

They needed to talk about the future some more, him and Harper. And as soon as he found the right opening, they would.

After a flurry of kiss blowing and goodbyes, Jean and Alan signed off. Harper hustled the kids into their winter coats and drove them off to the theater for the afternoon rehearsal.

Linc went to his office, where for once there were no emergencies in Portland that needed to be dealt with immediately. He sat at his desk, trying to decide whether to check in with his assistant at Stryker Marine or start dealing with emails and messages, when his cell rang.

A glance at the screen had his stomach sinking.

It was his mother, whom he should have called days ago—ideally last Friday, after his talk with his dad on Thursday night. Or at least at some point over the weekend.

Yet here it was, the following Tuesday, and he was still putting off reaching out to her.

Well, not anymore.

He hit the talk button. "Hi, Mom. This is a surprise."

"Oh, I am sure that it is." Sarcasm dripped from every word.

He kept his tone light. "It's pretty late there, isn't it?"

"It's the middle of the night, Lincoln. The middle of the night and I can't sleep. That is very much due to you. Your father, who said he would talk to you, apparently gave you the wrong message altogether. After which, he got back to me and said *you* would be calling me. That was several days ago. Radio silence from you, thank you so much."

"Sorry, Mom." And he was. Sorry about a lot of things—including that he'd ever gotten involved with Imogen Whitman in the first place and that his mother was disappointed in her life and just generally unhappy. "I apologize for not calling. I did tell Dad I would get in touch with you. I should have done that days ago."

His mother let out a heavy sigh. "I just need to know when you are going to work things out with Imogen. Sarah is so upset and she says Imogen is miserable, longing to make it up with you. And yet you have refused to communicate with her. Lincoln, you *blocked* your own fiancée. I cannot believe you did that. I raised you better than that."

So much for keeping it light. "Look, Mom. There is no point in my communicating with Imogen. We broke up. I don't *want* to get back together with her."

"Lincoln, it's not all about you."

"It's 50 percent about me and *all* of me is through with Imogen."

There was more huffing from his mother. "I cannot believe you're doing this."

"Well, I am. And I'm sorry to be a disappointment to you, but your disappointment is not going to force me to marry a woman I don't love." At that, his mother gasped. He went on, calmly, "Marrying someone I don't love would be wrong and I think that you know it would."

"You made a promise."

"No, Mom. The promise happens when you stand up in front of the world and say, 'I do.' Imogen ended our engagement, thus saving both of us from making a promise we would only have broken eventually, anyway."

"She didn't *mean* to break up with you. She was upset and said things she regrets."

A headache had formed behind his eyes. Linc pinched the bridge of his nose between his thumb and forefinger and rubbed to ease the ache. He'd known this conversation was coming. But that didn't make having it any more bearable. "Look, Mom. This isn't about you. It isn't about Sarah. This is about Imogen and me and how it didn't work out. That's it. There's nothing more to say on the subject. You are not going to change my mind. So just give it up. Please?"

That seemed to silence her. But not for long. With

a hard huff of breath she demanded, "What am I going to say to Sarah?"

"I have no idea. The truth, maybe?"

"And what do you think is the truth? You have broken poor Imogen's heart."

"Mom, I think we've both said all we have to say on this subject. I don't want to talk about it anymore."

"Oh, that's just lovely. Stonewall me. You're just like your father."

He tried one more time to get through to her. "Let's talk about something else."

"No. This is important. We need to figure out a way for you and Imogen to—"

"Stop!" He didn't realize he'd practically shouted the word until he heard his mother gasp again. "I'm going to hang up now. Call me anytime, but not to talk about Imogen. I love you and I miss you. Goodbye."

"Don't you dare hang up on—" He disconnected the call, tossed the phone on his desk and dared it to ring again.

It didn't, but he flopped back in his chair and glared at it for several more seconds anyway, because when it came to his mother, he really had no idea how to get through.

Grabbing the phone again, he called his dad with the video-chat app.

Warren actually smiled at the sight of him. "Lincoln. What a surprise."

"Hey, Dad. I was just thinking about you, wondering if maybe you and Shelby might be able to make it out here to Valentine Bay for a Christmas visit this month? I would like to get to know Shelby a little. And Jayden and Maya should have a chance to know their grandpa on their mother's side."

Warren's brow beetled up. "I'll never be anyone's favorite grandfather."

"You don't have to be the favorite, Dad. But with grandkids, you really need to put in the time."

His father was quiet—until he said, "I'll check with Shelby."

"Excellent. We'll be here until January 2. Anytime between now and then works for me and the kids. Let me know."

At a little after five, Harper ushered Maya and Jayden in the front door. Jayden took off his hat and mittens and hung up his coat as he chattered away about how much he wanted it to snow.

Maya was exercising her independence. "*I* do. Me!" she insisted when Harper tried to help her out of her red puffer coat.

"Of course, you do," Harper replied. She planted a quick kiss on Maya's fat little cheek and stepped back to watch her take off her red-and-green beanie with the bouncing pom on top. Carefully, Maya set the beanie in the basket of hats and scarves by the door.

"How was rehearsal?"

Harper looked over to find Linc watching her from the open entrance to the living area. He had that look in those amber eyes, like he wanted to grab her and eat her right up. In three hours or so, he just might. A heated shiver skittered through her at the thought. "Never a dull moment," she replied.

"Ready for the big opening?" The Christmas show opening was four days away, on Saturday at two in the afternoon.

"Nope, we're not ready." She hung up her own coat. "But then, we never are."

"Hawp." Maya tugged on the hem of Harper's sweater. "Hewp."

"What do you say when you want help?"

The little girl's rosebud mouth curved in an angelic smile. "Pwease."

So Harper helped her out of her coat. Maya hung it up herself on the kid-height set of hooks above the basket of hats and scarves.

Three hours later, Harper let Linc lead her to his bed—by way of a long, lovely detour against the shut door of the master suite, where he knelt at her feet, hooked her left leg over his shoulder and then used his skilled fingers and clever mouth to send her to paradise.

Twice.

The man was amazing in so many ways.

Later, after another half hour of delicious love-making on the bed, Linc pulled the covers up.

CHRISTINE RIMMER

193

Wrapped in the warm cocoon of blankets, with his arms around her, she asked him about his day.

He reported that he'd called his father and invited him and his wife to the cottage whenever they might be able to make it this Christmas.

"Did he say yes?"

"He's going to talk to Shelby."

She kissed his slightly stubbly jaw. "That's great."

He gave a grumbly sort of chuckle. "Proud of me, huh?"

"You'd better believe it—and I have to ask, what made you rethink the idea of inviting him?"

The question seemed to make him uneasy. "Uh. Long story…"

Chapter Nine

Again, Linc found himself debating how much to tell her.

But she knew him too well. "What's going on, Linc?"

He could definitely scare her off if he reported what had gone down with his messed-up mom, not to mention sharing the story of the ex who refused to let go.

But the woman in his arms had taught him a lot—about the children he had a sacred duty to shepherd into successful adulthood, about how families worked and what bound people together. He wanted more with her.

When the New Year came, he wanted her with

him. And to have any hope of convincing her that they should keep being together, he needed to be honest with her.

Her soft lips brushed the side of his throat. "Not going to tell me, huh?"

He lifted up enough to gaze down at her. "Just wondering where to start..."

"It can't be that bad. Come on now, lay it on out there."

So he did.

He told her everything: that his father had once had a thing for her mother and Marie Valentine had shut Warren Stryker down, that *his* mother was trying to get him to go back to his ex. He shared all the details, everything he'd been keeping to himself, even that his dad thought that he, Linc, ought to marry someone like her.

When he finally fell silent, she asked in a hushed voice, "Is that all?"

"Are you kidding? Isn't it enough?"

"I am not kidding, no. However, you're right. It's a lot."

"I just need to know you won't run away screaming now you have a better idea of the hot mess that is my family." He bent close and kissed her, thinking how she made everything better. One way or another, he needed never to let her go.

Was he moving too fast? Maybe. But losing Megan and Kevin had taught him that life could be brutal, brief and completely unfair. When a man found something really good, he needed to hold on to it.

She captured his gaze. "All families have issues. And I'm still right here in this bed with you, no plans to take off running."

He realized he'd been holding his breath. "Whew. That's what I needed to hear."

She studied his face. "Your mom sounds so unhappy…"

"She is—and pretty much always has been. I used to feel sorry for her, for the way my dad cheated on her and traded her in on a trophy wife. I still hate that he did that to her, but she's had years to deal with it, to move on, to make a life that works for her. And yet here we are, a decade later, and she's still an emotional disaster, more concerned over making Sarah Whitman happy than she is about creating a loving relationship with the grandkids she hardly knows."

"Or supporting *your* happiness," Harper suggested softly.

"Right. That, either."

Her eyelashes fluttered down. She became very engaged in not quite looking at him.

He tipped her chin up with a finger. "What? Just say it."

"Okay…" She hesitated, but then forged on. "It sounds like you and Imogen aren't really through."

"That's not true. It's over between her and me. I'm done."

"But *she* isn't."

"You're going to think I'm callous, but Imogen is my ex. It's over. That means she's not my problem."

She stared at him for a long time. But then at last, she nodded. "Okay, I get that. And you did explain to me before that you didn't love her—which is just sad, by the way."

"Yeah, it really is."

She took his face between her hands. "I see what you're saying. She wasn't the right person for you and you're glad that it's over."

"*Yes*. And can we leave this subject behind now?"

"All right."

"Thank you." He rolled to his side, taking her with him, so they were facing each other, eye to eye. "Well, that went pretty well."

"You think?"

"Hey, I just dumped a bunch of not-so-great information on you concerning me and my family— and you took it in stride."

Those beautiful dimples appeared. "The truth is hard to share sometimes."

On the nightstand, her phone pinged with a text.

He curled a silky swatch of her hair around his index finger. "You need to check that?"

At her half shrug, he reached over, picked it up and handed it to her.

She smiled as she checked the message. "It's just Mia."

"Of Acevedo Hybrid Homes?"

She rolled to her back again and thumbed out a reply. "Yeah. She and I keep in touch. I like her. We kid around, sending each other design problems—fun stuff, specific challenges that crop up when you work with shipping containers."

"So it's a design problem she just sent you?"

"Mmm-hmm." Stretching out an arm, she slid the phone onto the nightstand again. "She already has a solution, but she likes choices. So tomorrow morning I'll look over what she's sent and give her a few other ways she might go."

He pulled her into his arms again and kissed the tip of her nose. "They're missing the boat not hiring you before you run off to Seattle."

Now she frowned. "We've already addressed and dismissed that pipe dream."

It was far from the response he'd been hoping for. "It's not a pipe dream if it comes true."

"You just want me to come to Portland so we can keep spending our nights crawling all over each other."

"You are so right. I like what we have, and I do not want it to end."

Her serious expression became downright severe. "We have an agreement, Linc."

"We do. And part of our agreement is that things can change."

"I think…" Her pretty mouth twisted as she pressed on his chest with both hands.

"What? Say it."

"I, um, I think that, yes, you and I really like each other, and the sex is amazing, and I adore Jayden and Maya. And maybe you see this—you and me, together—as a way to make a more solid family for the kids."

Okay, that hurt.

Yeah, he did see her as a very good thing for his nephew and niece. But that was not the main point, no way. "You really think I want you as a nanny with benefits?"

"That's not what I said."

"Good. Because that's not what this is about. Yes, I love that you love the kids and that they feel the same about you. But that's not the reason I want to keep seeing you when the holidays are over. Harper, this is about you and me and this thing we have that I've never had before. It's about finally getting a taste of what being with the right person could mean. It's about not letting something special slip away when all the obstacles are surmountable."

She pressed two fingers to his lips and whispered, "It sounds so good when you put it like that."

"It's only the truth."

She held his gaze. "I have more I need to say."

"I don't want to hear how it can't work out for us." But she just kept staring at him, reproach in those big eyes. "Fine. Go ahead."

"I need you to see the other side of it, the part where I'm still trying to figure out who I am in this world and where I fit in. The fact that a few weeks ago, you were engaged to someone else. You and me, well, what if we're just a rebound for you? And what if, for *me*, we're only a distraction, an interlude—a way for me to avoid figuring out what to do with my life?"

"We're not."

"We can't let ourselves get all swept away in some romantic ideal, we can't go all insta-love and happy-ever-after about this."

Insta-love and happy-ever-after sounded pretty damn good to him. But he got that she needed practical solutions. "I'm not asking you to move in with me tomorrow. I just want a chance for us. I swear, if it were the least bit doable, I would relocate to Seattle. Unfortunately, Stryker Marine isn't all that portable."

"Linc, honestly. I'm not asking you to move to Seattle."

"And I need you to know that I've thought about it, that I've considered the possibility from every angle, but it's not going to happen anytime in the near future. And if *you* won't move to Portland, fine. Do what you need to do. Go to Seattle. It's not the other side of the world. With effort and planning, we can still see each other. We can see how it goes…"

Her eyes shone with moisture. "You seem so sure."

"I am sure. And I don't need for *you* to be sure—not yet. Right now, all I need is for you to stop saying no, to be open to trying to work things out."

With a soft cry, she grabbed him by the shoulders and yanked him down for a hard, hot kiss.

When they came up for air, he demanded, "Please

tell me you'll think about it, about you and me and more than just till New Year's, about the two of us deciding to find ways to be together, to build on what we've started this Christmastime."

Her beautiful mouth only trembled a little as she smiled.

"Tell me that smile means yes," he said gruffly.

She nodded. "Yes, I will be open to the possibilities."

"And we'll find ways to see each other after the holidays are over," he prompted.

"Yes. All right. After the holidays, we'll keep seeing each other."

"Exclusively," he added.

She nodded again. "Exclusively. Yes." And then she grinned at him. "Happy now?"

"It's a start."

The next morning, Linc woke to Jayden pounding on his bedroom door. "Uncle Linc! Get up. It's snowing!"

Linc rolled over and opened his eyes. The other pillow was empty. Harper had gone back to her place. He looked forward to the time when he could wake up every morning and find her there beside him.

He wasn't going to rush her, though. Last night, they'd made progress. He'd revealed some unpleasant truths, and she'd agreed that what they shared didn't have to end with the holidays. It was far from a promise of forever. But he would be patient with her. He'd asked for a chance with her and she'd said yes.

"Uncle Linc, come see!"

"Unc Wink, up! Now!" Maya chimed in from the monitor.

He shoved back the covers, pulled on some sweats and opened the door to an impatient little boy with small fists braced on his hips. "Finally." His irrepressible nature got the better of him and he dropped the stern expression. "Snow! We got snow!"

Linc ruffled his hair. "Come on. Let's get your sister up, put on our coats and go have a look."

In her room, Maya stood in her crib. She bounced up and down. "I wet!" she announced gleefully.

Linc changed her diaper and put her in warm leggings and a fluffy pink velour top. "Want to see the snow?" he asked as he hoisted her off the changing table.

"Yes!"

So they put on their coats and went out on the porch—where the snow was half rain that melted completely when it hit the ground.

Jayden refused to be disappointed. He predicted, "I just know we will get some by Christmas."

Linc made them breakfast and then hung out with them all morning. They were eating lunch when Harper arrived.

She entered the kitchen with pink cheeks and a halo of moisture clinging to her hair from the rain still coming down outside. "Wet out there," she said, and brushed at the crown of her head.

"The rain looks good on you," he replied, because it did. She gave him one of those smiles—the intimate kind, just between the two of them. "Everything looks good on you," he added.

And one way or another, he was going to make her see that they could have a future together. They only needed to reach out and take it.

Christmas on Carmel Street had its opening performance that Saturday afternoon. Linc brought the kids early. Harper was already there. He texted their arrival and she met him in the lobby. Taking Maya in her arms, she ushered Jayden backstage to get ready for the show.

Linc stood around in the lobby for a while, waiting for someone to take his five-dollar admission fee. Once that was handled, he entered the nearly empty auditorium. He chose a seat in the first row, so he would be ready to help with Maya if the need arose.

A few minutes after he sat down, Liam and Daniel Bravo, both of whom had kids in the show, appeared with their wives. The men sat on either side of Linc as Keely and Karin lingered in the aisle to chat. The men talked about the Blazers, the Seahawks and the Christmas show the year before. Liam and Daniel agreed that the kids loved being part of it. A few minutes before showtime, Keely and Karin took seats beside their husbands.

By the time the curtain went up, there wasn't an empty seat in the house. The children were all on their best behavior, earnest and serious even when they missed an entrance or forgot a line. Prompters from the wings on either side of the stage kept things on track.

The audience of parents and grandparents and doting aunts and uncles seemed to love every minute of it. Linc certainly did. Maya played an angel in two of the biggest musical numbers. A girl of twelve or thirteen seemed to have been assigned to keep an eye on her. The girl held Maya's hand and whispered to her now and then. Maya never once froze up or fussed. Linc was so proud of her.

As for Jayden, he kept popping up in every other scene. He played an angel, too. He was also one of Santa's reindeer, a little drummer boy, a nutcracker and a singing, dancing squirrel.

As he pranced around in his squirrel costume, Daniel leaned in and whispered, "Kid's got talent."

Linc thought of Megan. His heart ached, missing her, wishing he could look over and see her, right there beside him, beaming in pride at her daughter and son.

After the standing ovation and extended curtain calls, Linc would have gone backstage to heap praise on his niece and nephew. But just about every other adult in the audience seemed to have the same idea.

He skipped the pandemonium back there and waited in the lobby. The place had pretty much cleared out by the time Harper emerged, holding Jayden's hand on one side and Maya's on the other.

The kids ran to him. He bent to gather them into a group hug. Jayden chattered away, excited at his success, with Maya interjecting, "I so good!" or "I happy!" every time her brother paused for a breath.

Linc told them how wonderful they were, glancing up now and then at Harper, who stood a few feet away wearing busted-out jeans and one of her big, floppy sweaters, that yellow puffer coat flung over one shoulder. She had her hair piled up in a sloppy bun, her face scrubbed clean of makeup. Never in his life had he seen a woman more beautiful.

"We should get ice cream to celebrate," he offered, when the pint-size thespians had settled down a little.

They all agreed that was a great idea. Holding hands, they walked up the street to a shop called Scoopy Do's. It was almost five when they got back in the car. Maya snoozed on and off during the ten-minute ride to the cottage. Jayden was still flying high, singing along to the Christmas tunes on the Bluetooth, reminiscing about his favorite moments in the show, announcing that he could hardly wait for their second performance next Saturday.

At the house, Linc and the kids helped Harper make dinner. After that, they hung out in the living area, enjoying the tree and the fire. It was a great night.

And it only got better. Once the kids were in bed,

he and Harper went to his room. She stayed until one in the morning. He tried to convince her to sleep over, but she insisted she really did have to go, so he put on some sweats and followed her downstairs for a kiss at the door.

"Text me when you get to your place."

She kissed him again, a quick one. "I know the drill."

"You really should just stay over. There's no need for you to go wandering around in the dark late at night."

She put a finger to her lips. "Good night, Linc." And she slipped out the door.

He stood there alone in the foyer, missing her already, though she'd just left. It wasn't long before his phone pinged with a text.

Home safe.

Come back.

I will. Tomorrow.

I'm so lonely without you.

He added a crying face emoji just to drive his point home.

Yes, he was a grown-ass man who'd always found emojis ridiculous. But then Harper Bravo entered his life, lighting him up with all the warm, fuzzy, gooey feelings he hadn't realized could be so satisfying.

In response to his emoji, she sent him a GIF of two teddy bears hugging in a rising cloud of pink and red hearts and a reply of:

Good night, Linc.

He still wished she'd stayed, but he went back upstairs smiling.

As for the week that followed, it was pretty close to perfect. Twice, he caught Harper texting with Mia Acevedo. Was he growing more and more certain that Mia would offer her a job?

You bet he was. He considered calling Mia, casually suggesting that Acevedo Hybrid Homes ought to hire Harper, maybe even discussing how he could help if the company needed an investor before they would be ready to take on a second designer.

He never made that call and probably never would, not without getting Harper's okay first. She'd made it painfully clear that she didn't want him butting in, that no way would she take a job he'd arranged for her. He didn't agree with her on that, but he respected her determination to do it on her own.

Saturday brought the second and final performance of *Christmas on Carmel Street*. There were more gaffes than last week, but the audience response was every bit as enthusiastic as before.

After the curtain calls, the Valentine Bay Community Club served coffee, punch and cookies in the lobby. They were trolling for donations to the arts council, which sponsored the events in the theater. Linc whipped out his black card and contributed.

Early Sunday, he put the kids in the Rover, picked up Harper at her cottage and they all four returned to the theater to help strike the Christmas show set. Linc and Harper took turns keeping Maya entertained and out of the way of the busy workers. In the afternoon, they drove up Rhinehart Hill to Daniel's for the family meal and ended up staying later than usual.

It was after five when they headed back home, with Jayden providing a running commentary about how fun the afternoon had been and Maya, as usual, dropping quickly off to sleep.

The twisting driveway to the cottage was lined with tall trees. Oregon grape and giant, close-growing ferns filled the gaps between the thick trunks. The house didn't come into view until they were almost upon it—which meant Linc didn't see the Lexus parked in the open space near the porch until the very last turn.

Jayden spotted the unfamiliar car about the same time Linc did. "We got company," the little boy said.

The driver's door opened and a good-looking middle-aged woman in wide-legged gray wool pants, high-heeled suede boots and a pale pink wool coat that flowed to midcalf got out. She carried a designer purse the size of a bowling bag and, though it was already dark out, she wore giant sunglasses pushed up on the top of her head.

She was the last person Linc had ever expected

to see at the cottage—or anywhere in Oregon, for that matter.

He glanced at Harper. She gave him a shrug. Apparently, she assumed that he was as much in the dark about their visitor as she was. "Don't ask me. I have no idea who that might be."

"It's my mother," he said.

Chapter Ten

"At last!" his mother exclaimed when he pushed open his door and got out of the Rover. "I've been waiting for hours." He met her midway between the two vehicles. She offered her cheek for a kiss, which he dutifully provided.

"This is a surprise." He pulled his phone from his pocket to check messages. She hadn't texted, called or emailed. "I had no idea you were here—or that you were coming."

"I confess." Swiftly, she peeled off her driving gloves and shoved them into a pocket of her coat. "I wanted to surprise you."

I'll bet. "Well, Mom. You did."

She put her hand against his cheek. Her smooth

fingers were cold. "So good to see you, darling." Her fond smile seemed strained. And why wouldn't it be? There was only one reason she would fly here from Italy without saying she was coming. She intended to confront him about Imogen face-to-face. "Merry Christmas."

"Merry Christmas, Mom."

Harper's door opened at the same time as Jayden's.

His mother ignored Harper and focused on Jayden as he climbed from the vehicle. "Jayden Michael, I swear you've grown a foot since last January. Come here this instant and give your grandmother Alicia a hug."

Jayden went right to her. "Hi, Grandma," he said politely, and submitted to the hug. Linc's chest constricted at the sight. Jayden recognized his mother's mother, but nothing more. She was a virtual stranger to him.

In the meantime, Harper had taken Maya from her car seat. The little girl yawned and rested her head on Harper's shoulder.

Alicia, her eyes narrowed now, finally looked at Harper—but only to issue a cold command. "Let me see Maya."

Harper carried the half-asleep toddler around the front of the Land Rover.

Alicia stared fixedly at Harper. "Hello." Her mouth tipped up at the corners—but barely.

Linc made the introductions. "Harper Bravo, my

mother, Alicia Buckley." His mother had taken her maiden name again after the divorce.

"It's a pleasure." Harper looked uncomfortable, but she managed to inject warmth into the words.

Apparently, Alicia had forgotten all about the little girl snoozing on Harper's shoulder. "You're a local?"

Harper smiled a gentle smile. "I am, yes."

"Ah. I wasn't aware that Linc had local—" she paused just long enough to make the final word of the sentence an insult "—friends."

Linc jumped in before his mother could embarrass him further. "I *do* have friends here in Valentine Bay. Harper has the next cottage over. She and her sister Hailey direct and produce the community Christmas show. Both Jayden and Maya performed in the show this year. You missed a treat, Mom. I wish you'd let me know that you were coming."

"I'm sure you do," Alicia replied sourly.

Maya lifted her head and squinted up at Harper. "Hawp. Hungwy." She rubbed at her sleepy eyes.

Alicia suddenly remembered that she'd been ignoring her only granddaughter. She loomed in close. "Hello, Maya Renee. Do you remember me?"

Still half-asleep, Maya frowned at the strange woman with the sunglasses on her head. Then she turned to Harper and asked again, "Hungwy?"

"It's been a while since we ate." Harper sent Linc a speaking look. He wasn't sure of the exact meaning, but he got the general drift. His mother was behaving badly and Harper didn't know what to do with that. "A snack wouldn't hurt." She held out her hand to Jayden. "Let's go in." The little boy darted right to her and slipped his fingers in hers. "Nice to meet you." She gave Alicia a much cooler smile than the previous one and turned for the steps.

Linc resisted the need to get right in his mother's face about her rudeness to Harper. Later for that, though. First things first. "Pop the trunk, Mom. I'll get your bags."

Alicia had the keyless remote in her hand, but she didn't use it. She waited until Harper and the kids went inside to demand, "What is she, the house-keeper?"

Linc answered flatly, "Her name is Harper, in case you weren't paying attention—Harper Bravo. And no, Harper is not the housekeeper. Pop the trunk."

Alicia punched a button on the remote and the trunk sailed up. "Is there something going on be-tween you and that girl?"

It was too much. "I had forgotten how rude you can be—and to answer your question, yes. There is. Harper is important to me. She matters. If you have any consideration for me at all, you will treat her with respect."

Alicia drew her shoulders back and spoke in a silky, even tone. "I'm your mother. I love you and want the best for you. I've come all the way out to the edge of the Pacific Ocean to get you to see what a horrible mistake you're making."

He considered suggesting she find a hotel. At least then he wouldn't have to deal with all her ugly shit. But he couldn't quite make himself kick his own mother to the curb. "What did I say the last time we spoke?"

"Is this a quiz?" she chirped aggressively.

"If you're coming in—"

"Of course, I'm coming in."

"Great. You will treat Harper with courtesy and kindness."

"Of course I will, Lincoln."

"And you will accept that Imogen and I are through."

"But I don't accept that."

"Then there's no point in your coming inside."

That set her back a fraction. "You don't mean that."

"Make up your mind, Mom."

She actually teared up. "I am so frustrated with you."

"Same. Make up your mind."

Alicia took off the sunglasses, put them back on and slid them up on top of her head again. "All right. I will say nothing more about you and poor Imogen."

He drew a slow, deep breath. "Good. How long are you staying?"

She put her hand to her mouth and then to her throat. "A few days?"

"Fair enough, then." He went around to the open

trunk and pulled out a pair of floral-themed Gucci suitcases. "It's good you're here. You can get to know your grandchildren a little."

Linc made certain to be standing in the hallway outside Jayden's door when Harper emerged after tucking him in.

She shut the door and turned to him. Her beautiful face had *I've got to get out of here* written all over it. "I think I should probably—"

"Stay."

She leaned in close and lowered her voice to a near whisper. "Your mother—"

"—is jet-lagged. She's gone to her room for the night. She won't be bothering us."

"Linc, come on. She doesn't like me. I just need a little space, that's all."

As far as he knew, Alicia had been civil, at least. But maybe she'd crossed the line at some point while his back was turned. If she had, he would get her a hotel room—tonight, if possible. "What did she say to you?"

That plump mouth twisted into a tight frown. "Look. It's not any particular thing that she said. It's just very clear to me that she doesn't want me here."

"She's messed up. She took a position as wronged and wounded when my father divorced her—and she *was*, on both counts. He was having an affair with his assistant at Stryker Marine while he and my mother were still married. Then he divorced my mother and married the woman he'd cheated on her with. She was deeply and understandably hurt by his betrayal, and also by the humiliation of being traded in on a younger model. But since then, she hasn't moved on. It's like she got stuck there, being the injured party."

"I just don't want to be in the middle of it."

"Harper, you have to see that my mother's issues are not your fault. Please don't let her chase you away."

"I'll be back tomorrow. But for tonight, I think it would be easier if I went home."

"What it would be is giving in. And giving in to my messed-up mother solves nothing."

She sagged against the wall by Jayden's bedroom door. "She came all this way to see you and the kids…"

He moved in closer, wanting to soothe her, needing to convince her to stay. "No, she didn't." The words were out before he stopped to think that they would require an explanation—and that explaining the real reason Alicia had shown up on his doorstep would not make Harper any more willing to stay.

"If she didn't come to see her son and her grandchildren, then why…?" The sentence met an untimely death as she put it together. "Omigod. Imogen. Is she here to talk you into getting back with your fiancée?"

"*Ex*-fiancée." And wait. Had he just admitted that Harper was right? He wanted to slap a strip of duct tape on his own damn mouth—but then again, she would have figured it out eventually, anyway. And she would not have been pleased that he'd put off telling her. He captured her hand before she could take off down the stairs. "Let's go to my room. We'll talk about this. Please."

She didn't look happy, but she did let him lead her along the hallway and into the master suite. Once he had her in his private space, he shut the door and turned the lock. She headed straight for the sitting area. Dropping to the sofa, she grabbed a throw pillow and hugged it to her chest as though to shield herself from whatever difficult truth he might be about to throw at her next.

At least she toed off her chukka boots and gathered her feet up to sit cross-legged on the cushions. "Okay. I'm here. What's going on?"

He made himself lay it out there. "I've ended my relationship with my mother's longtime best friend's daughter, and now my mother is determined I'm not going to do to Imogen what my father did to her."

"But the two situations are not the same."

"Exactly. But as I've said before, my mother is screwed up."

She gave him a long, unhappy look and then said, "What does your mother know about you and me?"

He didn't quite dare to sit next to her, so he took the club chair across the low table. "What do you mean, 'what does she know'?"

"Really, Linc? I have to ask all the individual

questions?" She tossed the pillow to the sofa—and then picked it right back up and hugged it again. "Will you please just explain to me what the heck is going on here?"

"I, erm, implied to my mother that we're together."

"You *implied*?"

"I didn't know how far to go. You've been pretty damn clear that we're not rushing into anything. I said that you mean a lot to me and she'd better treat you with respect."

A rush of color flooded up her neck and over her cheeks. "You *threatened* her—you threatened your *mother*?"

Adrenaline burned through him. Why was he the bad guy in this? "I said she couldn't stay here if she wasn't going to be civil to you and that I expected her to accept that Imogen and I are through. I said if she couldn't agree to those two conditions, I would find a hotel for her to stay in."

Slim shoulders slumped. "You threatened her. No wonder she hates me."

"She doesn't hate you."

"Oh, please. I've spent most of the evening in proximity to her. If her looks could kill, I would not be breathing."

"Harper…"

Her back snapped up straight again. "Does she know I'm the temporary Christmas nanny?"

"Harper—"

"Please answer the question."

"No, she doesn't know."

At that, Harper slapped the pillow against her face and groaned into it. He knew he was just about to lose her. But then she put the pillow down and groaned again—a softer groan this time. "Now I don't know *what* to do. I can't figure out which is worse, her thinking I'm the help—which is true, actually—or her thinking I'm some gold-digging local yokel chasing a rich potential sugar daddy, watching the kids and hanging around here all the time trying to worm my way into your good graces."

"Stop. You are much more than the help, and we both know it. And you know damn well you don't have to knock yourself out to get near me. The two of us can't get close enough, as far as I'm concerned. I mean it. You can't buy into her garbage."

Her cheeks puffed out with a hard breath. "She's your *mother*. I don't want her to hate me."

He got up and went to her. Sweet relief loosened the knots in his belly when she didn't pull away. Instead, she made room for him, shifting and tucking her legs to the side so that he could sit next to her. Better still, she didn't object when he pulled her into his arms. "Please don't get torn down about her."

"Oh, Linc…" She leaned against him and rested her head on his shoulder. "This is awful."

He pressed his cheek to the crown of her head and breathed in the lemony scent of her hair. "She's completely unreasonable. I don't know what to do with her. I think the best move is that tomorrow, I'll just tell her she can't stay here."

Harper tipped her head back to meet his eyes. "No. That would be wrong. I think we have to be gentle and direct with her."

He gave a pained chuckle. "Like we are with Maya and Jayden?"

"Yeah, pretty much. And we have to just tell her that we're a couple."

We're a couple.

Hallelujah! She'd actually said it.

Suddenly, in spite of everything, the world was a beautiful place. "Say that again." He couldn't keep the giant smile from stretching across his face.

"Well, I mean, we're not putting labels on what we have, but we *are* together." She looked so sweet and earnest. He wanted to kiss her. He wanted to make love to her. Most of all, he wanted to keep her. Forever, if possible.

Somehow, in less than four short weeks, he couldn't picture his life without her in it. Not anymore. Never again.

"Right?" she prompted.

He nodded for all he was worth. "Yes. No doubt. We are together."

"We have to say it, though. We have to tell your mother that we're together and that you're paying me to help you look after the kids until you go back to Portland. I think we need to just put it all out on the table, let her make whatever she wants to make of it. Hiding stuff from her is only going to come back to haunt us later."

"I love it when you say 'us.'" He closed his eyes and drew in a slow breath. "However, given the way she's been behaving, it just feels like anything we say about our relationship will only be handing her more ammunition, giving her more opportunities to wreak havoc."

Harper pulled away. "What's she going to do—tell Imogen?"

"Yes—or she'll tell her BFF, Sarah, who happens to be Imogen's mother, and then Sarah will tell Imogen."

"But, Linc, is there a reason we should care that Imogen knows about you and me?"

If Imogen scares you away? Absolutely, he thought. He said, "God, no. We should not care. *I* don't care."

"Well, okay then. Can we agree that we have a plan? That we'll treat your mother with kindness. We'll tell her exactly what we are to each other and refuse to be intimidated by her bad behavior because we are doing nothing wrong."

"Agreed." But he had to say it. "Though I'm afraid she's still going to do everything in her power to make you want to run away screaming."

"Yeah. That won't be fun. But family matters, Linc. It's important that you do your best to get along with her."

He wasn't so sure. "I understand why you believe

that. I've met *your* family. They're worth knocking yourself out for."

"All families are." Now those big eyes had turned pleading. "Linc. She's your *mother*. I couldn't stand to be the reason you aren't speaking to her."

"You are not and will never be the reason." He stroked a hand down the vibrant silk of her hair, wanting to soothe her, to get her to see that sometimes everything is *not* going to come out right. "She's impossible. I'll try to make it work with her, for your sake. But I'm only going to take so much of her bad behavior. Sometimes, even with family, a guy's got to draw the line."

As usual, Harper left around midnight.

The next morning, Alicia slept late.

Linc got up bright and early with Jayden and Maya. His mother had yet to emerge from the guest room upstairs when Linc's dad called.

"That invitation still open?" Warren asked. "Shelby and I were thinking of flying out there tomorrow. We'll charter a jet and fly into that little airport right outside town. We won't stay long, just overnight, arriving in the afternoon tomorrow and taking off around lunchtime Wednesday. I'm thinking I need to see Jayden and Maya, and I want to put something under the tree for each of them."

Linc hesitated. He couldn't help but be torn between how pleased he was that his father was making an effort—and how his mother would take being under the same roof with her cheating ex and his third wife.

"The silence on your end is deafening, son." Warren sounded vaguely amused.

"Sorry. I do want you to come. Full disclosure, though. Mom's here."

A beat, then starkly, "You're not serious."

"Yes, I am." Linc glanced across the living room, where Maya lay on the floor cuddling her stuffie, Pebble, and staring contentedly up at the Christmas tree. Jayden was up in his own room, where he couldn't overhear this conversation. Linc lowered his voice, anyway. "Mom's on the warpath over my breakup with Imogen."

Warren said something under his breath. "You also realize I'm not on her good side."

As if that was news. "I assumed as much."

"Are you sure you still want us to come?"

"I'm sure. Just as long as you know it probably won't be all that pleasant dealing with her."

"No it won't. And I have to update Shelby on this development before we confirm."

"I get that."

"Hang on?"

"I'll be here."

Two minutes later, Warren was back. "All right. You asked for it. We'll see you tomorrow."

"That's great, Dad." He realized he meant it. "I'm glad you're coming."

"Just one more thing you really should know…"

"Sure."

"You're going to have a baby sister. Shelby's pregnant. We're seven months along."

Alicia came out of her room at a little after eleven. She went straight to the coffee maker in the kitchen. Linc considered following her in there to give her a heads-up on Warren and Shelby's visit *and* to let her know that Harper was his girlfriend and the temporary nanny.

But then he thought better of that. Alicia was just too likely to behave badly when he laid the news on her. The kids didn't need to witness their grandmother in a meltdown.

He would have a talk with her this afternoon when Harper would be here to look after Maya and Jayden. Or maybe tonight, after the children were safely tucked in their beds.

Alicia fixed herself a late breakfast and returned to her room. When Harper arrived at one, Linc was sprawled on the sofa across from Jayden, who sat cross-legged on the floor, hard at work on another Christmas work of art, using the coffee table as his workspace.

"Look, Harper." He held up his creation for her approval as she entered the room. "It's Santa by the tree."

She went right to him. "I love it."

"I do, too," he agreed, and then put the paper

down on the coffee table again, grabbed a red crayon and bent to his work.

Maya toddled over to her from her favorite spot beside the tree. "Up, Hawp!"

Harper scooped his niece into her arms and turned to Linc with a smile that made everything better. She asked, "Where's your mother?"

"Upstairs in her room." She hadn't come down since she went up there after her late breakfast.

"Kiss," commanded Maya and stuck her stuffie in Harper's face.

Harper laughed, kissed Pebble and then asked, "Did you get a chance to talk to her?"

"I thought I would wait until you were here to keep an eye on the kids."

She nodded. "Good idea."

"There's more. My dad and his wife are coming tomorrow, just for overnight. Shelby's pregnant."

Harper grinned. "Go, Warren!"

And then both of them were laughing. It was all just too weird, like they were living in a soap opera.

Maya asked, "Funny?"

When both Harper and Linc nodded, she laughed, too.

Harper said, "I think I'll take the kids back to my cottage. We'll work on our homemade Christmas presents."

"Pwesents!" crowed Maya. She was a big fan of those.

Harper added the unfun part. "You can talk to her while we're gone."

Twenty minutes later, Harper and his niece and nephew set out for the Bravo cottage. Linc climbed the stairs in dread.

"Come in," his mother answered, so polite, cold as ice, when he tapped on her door.

He pushed it open and found her sitting in the corner chair, reading glasses perched on her nose and a book open in her lap. "Got a minute?" he asked.

"Certainly." She marked her place and set the book aside.

He crossed the threshold and closed the door behind him. "Just a few things I think you ought to know…"

She gave him a half-hearted smile that came off more as a grimace. "All right."

He had no clue of the right way to begin, so he just started talking. In five sentences, he got out everything he'd come upstairs to say to her. Lamely, he finished with, "So that's about it."

The look she gave him probably should have sliced him in half, but all it did was make him feel weary to the core. "All right, then. To recap. Your father is coming. His third wife, the child bride, is pregnant, and this Harper person, who is *not* your fiancée and whom you are paying to look after my daughter's children, just happens to be your girlfriend." Acid burned each word as it fell from her lips.

Get the hell out.

He wanted to say it so bad he could taste it.

But again he reminded himself that Harper wanted him to try to get along with her. "That's about the size of it," he said flatly.

"This is outrageous."

And that about did it for him. "I'm done with your crap, Mom. I'm sorry your life didn't pan out the way you wanted it to. But that's just not my fault— nor is it Harper's fault."

"That girl is—"

"Amazing and warm and wonderful and the best thing that ever happened to me—*and*, did I mention, my sister's children adore her? I'm going to do everything in my power to convince her to keep seeing me after Christmas is over. And I've got to tell you, Mom. You are not helping. You show up here without letting me know that you're coming and all you do is stir up trouble. I've had enough of your seething looks and your unacceptable attitude and your complete lack of interest in your dead daughter's wonderful children. I'm not putting up with any more of it. I want you to leave."

She rose. He waited for her to refuse to go and wondered what the hell he was going to do then.

But it didn't come to that. She merely shrugged. "Have it your way, Lincoln. I'll be out of here within the hour."

Chapter Eleven

"I notice the Lexus is no longer out front," Harper said mildly when she and the kids came back from the other cottage.

Linc stuck his hands in his pockets. "Yeah. We had a little talk. My mother decided it was time to go."

Jayden hooked his coat on a low peg by the door and turned to Linc, frowning. "Grandma Alicia left?"

"Yes," Linc replied. "She said to tell you goodbye and she hoped to see you soon." Alicia had said no such thing and he shouldn't be lying to his nephew. On the other hand, why the hell did an innocent five-year-old have to feel as bad as Linc did right now?

Answer: he didn't. And Linc had no qualms about doing whatever it took to make sure he wouldn't.

Jayden seemed puzzled. And why shouldn't he be? His grandmother had blown in and rushed out, and while she was here, the only attention she'd paid to him had lasted all of two seconds when she first arrived. Jayden suggested in a wary tone, "Maybe she can come for my birthday."

"Maybe," Linc agreed as noncommittally as possible.

"We'll talk later," Harper said to Linc.

"Yeah," Linc replied, feeling guilty that he'd driven his mother away—even though he would do it all over again in a heartbeat, given the same situation.

"I *do* it. Me!" Maya announced proudly. Linc glanced down at her. Totally oblivious to the disappearance of her maternal grandmother, Maya had taken her coat off all by herself and hooked it on a low peg beside Jayden's.

"Great job!" Harper dropped to a crouch, pulled the little girl close and blew a raspberry against the side of her neck.

Maya erupted in a fit of giggles and Linc felt better about everything.

That night, when the kids were in bed and he and Harper were alone in Linc's room, he explained what had happened with Alicia.

Harper took it well, he thought—and that was an-

230 A TEMPORARY CHRISTMAS ARRANGEMENT

other thing he loved about her. The way she rolled with the punches. She'd tried to get him to be patient with his mother. But once he'd had enough, she didn't jump his ass for asking Alicia to leave.

She also didn't say one bad word about his mother, though Alicia had treated her coldly, dismissed her as "the help," and disparaged the relationship he and Harper were creating together.

"Come here." He pulled her into his arms and kissed her.

She kissed him back as they undressed each other.

One kiss led to another—slow, intense, drugging kisses that went on forever and yet somehow were never quite long enough.

He guided her down to the bed and kissed his way along her soft, gorgeous body, settling in at the sweet spot between her sleek thighs. He could stay here forever, making love to her with his mouth and his stroking hands, as if they never had to get out of this bed for the rest of their lives.

Later, inside her, so deep and so right, he stared into her eyes and longed to just say it, *I love you, Harper Bravo.*

But now wasn't the time. He got that. He did. She had changes she needed to make, a new career to create. For her, it was too early to speak of love and sharing the rest of their lives.

And he could wait for as long as she needed him to wait. For as long as it took her to realize what he already knew—that she was smart and eager and focused and willing to put in the time. One way or another, she would find the kind of work that fulfilled her.

But she wouldn't believe him just because he said it. She needed to prove it for herself.

After the unpleasantness with Alicia, Harper wasn't sure what to expect of the visit from Linc's father and stepmother.

Warren and Shelby arrived in a rented red Escalade. Linc and Harper and the kids went out to greet the newcomers.

Warren was pretty much as Harper remembered him from that brief encounter at the indoor pool in Linc's Portland house a couple weeks before. Cool, distant and faintly amused at the sight of his grandchildren, Warren greeted Harper with an aloof smile and a surprisingly sincere sounding, "Lovely to see you again."

But when he wrapped his arm around his wife and introduced her to Harper, a whole other side of the man appeared. With his twenty-six-year-old pregnant bride, Warren Stryker was smiling and attentive and so clearly in love.

Seeing them together, Harper felt she understood Linc's dad at least a little bit better. He might have made a mess of things in a whole bunch of ways, but he'd finally found the right woman for him. Now, he was a happy man. And Harper could understand why.

Shelby, petite and very curvy with a giant baby bump, had a big, openhearted laugh and a smile that could put just about anyone at ease. Within ten minutes of entering the cottage, she had Maya in her arms and Jayden following her around, asking her a lot of questions and not waiting for the answers.

They all spent a couple of hours hanging around the cottage with the Christmas tunes playing. Shelby insisted the kids open one of the many presents she and Warren had brought. It was a simple board game called Little Garden. Players had to help Gardener Gabriel build the garden before Molly Mole ate all the fruits and vegetables. Even Maya could play. They all joined in, Warren, too, though a bit reluctantly.

They had dinner at the table in the dining room. Shelby raised her glass of sparkling cider in a toast to family and the holidays.

The kids were in bed by a little after eight and the adults sat in the living area for a while, the talk easy and casual.

Shelby explained that she'd taken over her family's bookstore right after she graduated from the University of Southern California with a business degree. "I planned to go on to study law. But my dad had some health problems. I went home to Colorado and started running the bookstore for him. What can I say? I loved it. My parents are my partners. We bought the shop next door, tore out the adjoining wall and now we have a bookstore café. Profits are up and we're opening a second store in Denver."

She said that she'd met Warren nearly two years before on her first trip to Europe.

"It was love at first sight," added her husband.

Shelby laughed her full-out, beautiful laugh. "Not exactly."

Warren conceded, "Fine. I was too old for you—meaning I was only a few years younger than your mother, and your mother did not want her brilliant only daughter marrying a twice-divorced, white senior citizen."

"You are fifty-seven," said Shelby. "Too young to qualify as a senior citizen—and we both know that my mama never said any such thing."

Warren didn't argue. "Whatever you say, my darling."

Shelby leaned his way and kissed his cheek. "Notice how he says he *was* too old for me. Past tense?"

Warren's smile was nothing short of smug. "It's a fact. Love makes a man young. And youth comes on swiftly. The younger I got, the more willing you became to accept that we were meant to be together. And then, after you realized I was the only man for you, I still had my work cut out for me convincing Louella."

"That's my mama," Shelby clarified.

"And she did come around," said Warren.

Shelby chuckled. "It didn't take that long."

"No, but it *felt* like forever until you were mine."
Warren took his wife's hand. "Finally, Shelby said yes."

Shelby turned a benign smile on Linc and Harper.
"It was two months from the day we met in Paris to
that Vegas wedding chapel with the minister who
looked way too much like Elvis."

Warren took her hand. "From the moment I met
you, every hour without you was pure torture." They
interwove their fingers and leaned in for a quick
kiss.

Harper glanced Linc's way and found him already looking at her. His mom might be a nightmare, but Harper really liked Warren and Shelby. It
seemed to her that Linc was thinking pretty much
the same thing.

She felt warm all over and couldn't help longing
to take a chance on what they had together, to go for
it with Linc, agree to move to Portland, follow her
heart instead of her need to get out there and prove
herself as a functioning adult.

A few minutes later, Warren brought up the ele-
phant in the room. "So then, Lincoln. Your mother
isn't here. What happened?"

Linc glanced away. "Yeah, she left early. I asked
her to go."

Warren frowned. "You have that look, son. The
one that says you don't want to talk about it."

"You're right. I don't."

"Then we won't. But if there's anything I can do—"

"I don't see what."

Warren gave a slow nod. "I understand. I'll let it go."

They sat in silence for a minute or two as Willie Nelson crooned "Pretty Paper" from the speaker on a nearby table. Harper sternly reminded herself that she had important goals to achieve and she couldn't afford to get too wrapped up in fantasies about her and Linc and happily-ever-after.

As the song ended, Warren announced, "Harper, I've been thinking that you should consider moving to Portland."

Harper barely stifled a gasp of surprise as she turned accusing eyes on Linc.

He put up both hands. "I swear. I didn't say a word."

Warren shrugged. "He didn't. Shelby and I aren't blind, though. It's obvious there's something special going on between you two. You should know that we thoroughly approve."

Harper wasn't sure what to say to that. Warren Stryker had no filter, apparently. He just came right out with whatever was on his mind. It was reassuring, though, to know Linc's dad saw her as a good match for his son—especially after the scathing disapproval she'd picked up from Linc's mom. "Well, thank you. And I am thinking of moving—but to Seattle, as a matter of fact."

To which Linc just had to add, "Don't worry, Dad. I'm not giving up. Somehow, I'll get her to change her plans…"

* * *

Shelby and Warren said good-night at a little after ten.

Harper intended to go on home then. But Linc whispered, "Stay. Just for a little while…"

She let him lead her upstairs.

"Your dad is so outspoken," she said an hour later, when they were cuddling in bed. "It's like, whatever he's thinking comes right out his mouth."

Linc traced slow circles on the bare skin of her shoulder. "Yeah. He's nothing like the father I grew up with. He used to be so preoccupied, so guarded and hard to talk to. He wasn't a good guy. But what can I say? I guess people really can change. I keep hoping my mom will get the memo on that."

She gazed up at him, meeting his eyes steadily. "She truly does not like me."

"She just has an agenda."

"Right. Getting you and Imogen back together…"

"That's never going to happen—and as for my mom, that she failed to get to know you is her loss." He tipped up her chin for a kiss.

She closed her eyes and thought how she really ought to get up and go home. But the bed was so comfy and Linc held her so tenderly. She turned on her side. He wrapped his body around her.

When she opened her eyes again, it was one in the morning. She popped to a sitting position and shoved her hair out of her eyes. "I gotta go."

But he pulled her back down. "Stay with me..." His voice coaxed and soothed her.

And she just didn't have the will to tell him no. His arms felt so good holding her close, and outside it was cold and drizzly and dark. He settled the covers back over them.

Nights like this, all wrapped up in his arms, she couldn't help thinking how fast the Christmas season was flying by. In a little more than a week, he and the kids would return to Portland.

It felt much too soon—to lose him. To lose *them*.

But she wouldn't be losing them, she reminded herself.

They'd agreed to keep seeing each other, to find ways to get together. He really did want to be with her.

And oh, she did love being with him.

When daylight came, Linc took the kids downstairs first, so that Harper could avoid having to answer Jayden's likely questions about why she'd been sleeping in Uncle Linc's room. She washed her face and combed her hair and put on yesterday's clothes.

When she entered the kitchen, everybody seemed happy to see her and no one asked where she'd spent the night. Really, it didn't feel awkward to her at all. She pitched right in helping Linc make breakfast for everyone.

Shelby and Warren stayed for lunch.

Finally, after hugs all around, good wishes for

the best Christmas ever and promises that they would get together again soon, Warren and his wife climbed into their rented Escalade and headed for Valentine Bay Executive Airport.

Back inside, Jayden went to his room to play with his train set and Maya fell asleep in her favorite spot on the floor by the tree. Harper stood over her, thinking that there was nothing so sweet as Maya, hugging her favorite stuffie, wearing a green velour top and matching leggings, a baby elf snoozing beneath the Christmas tree.

Strong arms came around her waist. Linc's warm breath brushed her cheek and his deep voice teased in her ear, "I like that you stayed with me last night."

She chuckled, but quietly, in order not to wake the sleeping elf at their feet. "You caught me at a weak moment."

"Good." He bit her earlobe. A shower of sparks danced across her skin. "I want you to go to your cottage and get your stuff."

"What stuff?"

"Clothes, fuzzy slippers, a toothbrush—whatever you need to sleep here with me from now on."

She loved that idea. Loved it too much. "You'll be gone back to Portland before you know it."

He nibbled on her neck. "All the more reason you should be in my bed every night while you can. I need my Harper fix. It's going to be hard enough going days on end without you if I can't convince you to change your mind and move to Portland—

but we're not there yet. I'm keeping a positive attitude about you and me and the amazing future we're going to build together. And the thing I want most—what you can give me for Christmas—is you in my bed every night, all night. At least until New Year's."

"I shouldn't…"

A low chuckle rumbled up. "That's a yes just waiting to be born. I know it is."

She turned in his arms and put her hands on his warm, broad chest. Beneath her palms, she could feel the steady beating of his heart. "All right, I'll bring a few things over. Now, let me go before Jayden wanders in and catches us canoodling."

Christmas Eve morning Jayden finally got his wish.

Linc was sound asleep when the boy bellowed, "We got snow!" from the other side of the master bedroom door.

The noise woke Maya, who let out a cry of surprise that echoed over the baby monitor by Linc's bed.

"What the…?" Linc startled awake as Harper's eyes popped open, too. They blinked at each other.

"Uncle Linc, you have to see!"

"Unc Winc! Up!" Maya chimed in.

Harper grinned sleepily at him. "You go. I'll be down in a minute." She looked so good, all rumpled and sleepy, her eyes low and lazy.

"I want to wake up next to you like this every morning."

"Uncle Linc, hurry up!"

She gave him a playful shove. "Go."

He rolled out of bed, put on some clothes and slipped out the door, where Jayden could barely contain his excitement.

"Let's go." The boy grabbed his hand.

"Whoa, hold on. We need to get your sister first."

"Hurry, then." Jayden turned for Maya's room, pulling Linc along behind him.

Linc got Maya up, changed her wet diaper and carried her downstairs, Jayden leading the way to the front door, which he unlocked and threw open.

"Snow!" With another shout of sheer joy, Jayden ran down the front steps in his slippers. Halfway along the front walk, he stopped and tipped his head up to the gray sky, opening his mouth wide, trying to catch snowflakes on his tongue.

"I got one!" he crowed. "It melts so fast!"

"Me, Unc Winc!" demanded Maya, bouncing up and down in his arms. "Me, too!"

So he carried her out beneath the sky. She tipped her head back and opened her mouth just like her brother was doing.

"We need to make a snowman," Jayden announced as they went back up the steps.

Linc herded him in through the door. "Let's have breakfast first and see if any of it sticks…"

In the kitchen, Harper was getting the coffee going. The kids didn't even blink at the sight of her. She'd become such a part of their lives in the past month, they never asked how she magically appeared in the kitchen when they came in from the cold.

Harper was having the best Christmas Eve ever.

Outside, the snow kept falling. By ten, there was enough to make a snowman, though a slightly malnourished-looking one. The snow was slowing by then, but the temperature stayed below freezing. Jayden's skinny snowman would no doubt last until Christmas Day.

At eleven, the kids and Linc Skyped with Jean and Alan, who were cruising the islands of French Polynesia. Linc called her over to join the conversation. Harper liked the grands a lot. They were good people.

For the rest of the day, they hung out, just the four of them. They played games, read stories and watched a couple of Disney movies.

Before the kids went to bed, they put out cookies and milk on the coffee table, in case Santa might want a snack.

It felt so right, just being here at the Stryker cottage with Linc and the kids. Like they really were building a family, the four of them. Together.

Was she getting a little carried away, spending too much time with them—with *him*? Losing sight of reality just a little bit?

So what? Why should she go home to her quiet, empty cottage when everything she wanted was right here? Yeah, reality mattered. But why shouldn't she let go and enjoy every moment of this perfect holiday season?

She understood the facts. The New Year would come. He would go back to Portland to live in a house that looked like something from *Architectural Digest* and run an international shipping company. She would head north on a wing and prayer.

And really, so what? It was still December. Her uncertain future remained out there, waiting for her. She didn't have to rush to meet it.

Why not lighten up a little, go with the flow? At the least, she would have a beautiful Christmas with a wonderful man.

And just maybe, it would all work out and they would end up together. Stranger things had happened.

Why shouldn't she *believe* that she was meant to be with Linc and the kids? It was the season of miracles, after all. And maybe this particular miracle— of her and this amazing guy and these two beautiful children—maybe it wasn't so crazy to reach out and claim what Linc offered her. Maybe he was tailor-made for her.

Why couldn't he be right about the two of them? Why shouldn't they be together?

Why not go ahead and make the move to Portland? The job prospects weren't quite as good for her there, but Portland State offered an accredited master's program in architecture, too. Jobwise, something was bound to come up.

Plus, it would be less expensive to get a place in Portland.

And most important, she wouldn't have to leave her love…

Love?

Wait. No.

She shouldn't let herself do that. It was too soon. She couldn't afford to go to the love place.

Slowly, she drew a deep breath and waited for the denials to rush in. Because she wasn't ready for love. Not now. Not for a few years yet, anyway. She needed to find her way as an adult first, get her own place in the right city and start creating a whole new career before she let herself get wrapped up in a man.

No. Uh-uh. Not ready for love.

Too bad love had found her, anyway.

She sat on the sofa by the fire in the living room, with the tree blazing bright and the outdoor lights winking merrily at her through the picture window. The kids were in bed. Linc had gone to the kitchen to open a bottle of Christmas Eve bubbly.

And here she sat on the sofa, unable to deny her true feelings anymore.

Love.

Love had happened to her.

She'd taken a temporary job to build up her bank account and ended up falling in love with the boss— only, no.

Not the boss.

She was her own boss, an independent contractor, as she'd made so painfully clear to Linc right from the beginning.

So, then. Boss or not, she loved him. Was *in* love with him.

Lincoln Stryker is my love.

It sounded so good inside her head.

But yeah, it was probably way too early to tell him how she felt. So she wouldn't. Not yet. They would discuss the future again at some point before he went back to Portland. And when they did, she would tell him that yes, she wanted to be near him and the kids. She would agree that yes, she would come to Portland in February and start looking for work.

"You look happy." Linc sat down beside her, an open bottle of champagne in one hand, two flutes in the other.

"I *am* happy. It's been a great day. The best kind of Christmas Eve, quiet and cozy with at least a token amount of snow."

He filled the two glasses, handed one to her and offered a toast. "To skinny snowmen and Disney movies."

"I will definitely drink to that." She tapped her glass to his, enjoyed a fizzy sip and wondered how she'd lived all her life up till now without him in it.

"I have something for you…" He set down his glass and went to the tree. Crouching, he pulled a mug-sized box from among the many brightly wrapped packages.

She grinned. She had a travel mug for him, too—and a pair of snowman socks. But she'd been assuming they would wait until Christmas morning to do the gift thing.

He took his place beside her again. "Merry Christmas."

"I should open it now?"

He nodded. "Please."

She untied the bow, tore open the pretty paper and took the lid off the box. Within, a smaller box, also brightly wrapped, sat in a cocoon of red tissue paper.

Something happened in her chest, something warm as a toasty fire, bubbly and bright as champagne.

Because that smaller box?

It was a ring-sized box.

She blinked at it in its cradle of bright tissue and that warm, fizzy feeling in her chest was expanding, taking over her whole body.

Really, she shouldn't be reacting like this—like he'd just handed her the moon all wrapped in Christmas paper. It was too early.

Too soon, and she knew it. They couldn't go rushing into something so huge as what could be waiting in this ring-sized box.

She put her hand to her chest where her heart pounded like it wanted to get out and bounce around the room for joy. This couldn't be right.

The words of love had yet to be spoken. They'd met barely a month ago.

No doubt about it. It was much too soon.

And yet, well, if it was too soon, why did it *feel* so right?

Breathless, yearning, ready to take the most impossible leap, she lifted the smaller box free of the tissue. Carefully, fingers moving slow and dreamlike, she set the other box on the coffee table and unwrapped the little one.

The box inside was black velvet. A ring box, no question about it.

Could this really be happening?

Stunned at her own reaction of sheer, unbounded happiness, she went with it. It was not what she'd planned, so far from anything she'd expected—of herself, or of him.

And yet...

She *was* in love with Linc. And it didn't matter that it had happened fast.

It was the real thing.

And damn it, she couldn't wait to say yes.

Because really? It was perfect—*they* were perfect, her and Linc, together.

They were right for each other and she loved the kids and she'd already decided she would move to Portland instead of Seattle. Who had she been kidding, telling herself that she didn't want more from him?

She *did* want more. She wanted everything, a forever, together, with Linc and the kids.

"Well? Are you going to open it?" He leaned closer, his voice low, kind of teasing.

As she raised the tiny hinged lid, her hands weren't shaking hardly at all.

Inside, a gorgeous pair of diamond earrings twinkled up at her.

She gaped down at them. Her lips felt numb and her heart had paused midbeat.

What had just happened?

What was the matter with her?

All her talk about not getting in too deep, taking it slow—and she'd just lost her mind assuming Linc suddenly wanted to marry her.

She needed to get a grip and get it fast.

Linc asked, sounding hopeful, "Do you like them?"

They were quite beautiful, two gorgeous round stones. And there was no way she could accept them.

She forced her head up and made herself meet his eyes.

Linc's brow furrowed in concern—because apparently, she had no control over her expression. "What is it? Harper, what's wrong?"

She pushed out appreciative words. "They're gorgeous."

The space between his eyebrows smoothed out. "Whew. For a minute there, I thought you hated them."

"Linc, I…"

Twin lines drew down between his eyebrows. "Okay, you'd better tell me what I did wrong."

Her silly heart had started in again—too fast and too hard. It was knocking away, a wrecking ball inside her chest. Her cheeks burned with heat. She wasn't ready yet, to love like this.

She had stuff to do, things to figure out. She couldn't go giving her heart over to a rich guy from Portland. "Linc, I got you an insulated travel mug and some snowman socks."

He sat back an inch. He had that look, the one a guy gets when he knows that whatever he says next will not be the right thing. "Great. I need a new mug and fun socks work for me."

Crap. No wonder she was in love with him. He might be hot and rich with the world at his feet, but he was also a good guy. "We've known each other for a month. It's too soon for diamonds, you know?"

"No, it's not. Not if you like them. It doesn't have to be a big deal. I bought them for you because I think they'll look great on you. Come on, I want you to have them."

"Well, thank you. But no. I really can't take them." She grabbed his hand, turned it over, set the velvet box in his palm and folded his fingers over it.

And right now, well, she just couldn't stay here. She needed to get back to her own place. She needed distance, to be away from him.

Her heart ached so bad. She felt like a fool— which was in no way his fault.

She didn't want to worry him. But really, she had to go home.

She said, "Linc, listen..."

He dropped the velvet box on the coffee table and took both her hands, his eyes probing, insistent. "Talk to me. Tell me. What's going on with you? What went wrong?"

"I just need to go home, okay?"

"No. It's not okay. I want to know what's going on."

"Please." She eased her fingers from his grip. He let go reluctantly. "I just need a little time to myself. I need to go home for the night. Really. Think about it. I've been spending every moment here."

"And I love that. I want you here with me—come on, just tell me what's wrong."

She stood. "I'm going to go. I'll be here tomorrow morning. I'll do breakfast—blueberry pancakes, just like we planned." She backed away as she spoke. "We'll open the presents, go up to Daniel's for Christmas dinner. It'll be great."

"Harper." His wonderful face—the face she loved, God help her—showed utter confusion. "Please."

She swallowed hard and shook her head, "I just need to go home. Everything's fine, really."

"No, it's not. Talk to me. Tell me what's wrong."

"I, um... What can I say? See you tomorrow." And then she whirled on her heel and got out of there.

Chapter Twelve

Linc longed to bolt to his feet and run after her. But she'd made it unnervingly clear she was leaving and nothing short of physical restraint would keep her there.

The sound of the front door closing behind her made him want to grab the champagne and throw it through the picture window—or maybe at the tree.

He lifted both hands and raked them back through his hair.

Really, what just happened? Yeah, he got that he'd screwed up somehow. But why couldn't she have just told him what he'd done wrong so he could fix it?

It wasn't like her to jump up and run away like that. She'd seemed so happy, that beautiful face all aglow—and then she saw the earrings—and shut down.

It had to be the earrings. Maybe she had a thing against diamonds.

But why?

Uh-uh.

It just made no damn sense.

He sat there in the living room for an hour or so, drinking the excellent champagne and hardly tasting it, resisting the urge to text her, to try to coax her into giving him just a hint of what had gone wrong with her.

But he didn't get out his phone. If she were willing to talk to him, she would have done it before she ran out.

Eventually, he got up and dealt with the cookies and milk the kids had left out for Santa. He turned out the lights and climbed the stairs to his bedroom alone. He still had no idea what had gone wrong with Harper.

He just knew that somehow, he needed to fix it.

At her cottage, Harper put on her oldest, softest flannel pajamas and then paced the floor.

She felt like such a loser. Poor Linc. She'd left him sitting there wondering what was the matter with her. He had no idea that he'd broken her heart—scratch that.

Linc had *not* broken her heart. It was not his fault that she'd gotten carried away with this thing between them, let her emotions take over when the plan was to keep it fun and no-pressure, to move their relationship along at a nice, reasonable pace.

That she'd come unglued was *her* fault. She needed to deal with that and then apologize to him for running out on him tonight.

And it would all work out, she reminded herself. She'd known going in that this thing with him was temporary. She'd had her eyes wide-open—and then, bam! Love had hit her like a safe dropped on her head.

But so what?

Nothing bad had happened, really—well, except for her bizarre behavior at the sight of those earrings. Linc had already made it clear he wanted to keep seeing her. Unless she'd scared him away with her disappearing act tonight, they would still end up talking about the future, about finding ways to spend more time together.

It was fine. Good. In the morning, she would downplay what had happened tonight. And later, Christmas night, when the kids were in bed and they were finally alone, she would apologize for her out-there behavior and say she hoped that they could let it go and move on.

The smell of coffee and breakfast scented the air as Linc brought the kids downstairs the next morning.

Harper was already there, looking a little tired,

maybe, but heart-stoppingly beautiful in a red sweater and white jeans that clung to every perfect curve, her waterfall of golden hair in loose waves down her back.

All morning, as they ate the breakfast she'd prepared and then opened the mountain of presents beneath the tree, she was sweet and bubbly, brimming with holiday cheer.

She really did seem okay—a little too cheerful, maybe. But overall, fine.

Which had him feeling more bewildered than ever.

Could he have read last night all wrong?

No.

She'd jumped to her feet out of nowhere and announced she had to go. And then she'd run away from him, out the door.

No matter how wide her brilliant smile this morning, she was not okay.

At eleven, they bundled up in coats, hats and winter gloves. Outside, it was raining, and Jayden's skinny snowman was no more. With four wonderful-smelling pies that Harper had baked and some presents for the Bravo kids, they piled into the Rover to head up to Daniel's.

Jayden and Maya were excited. Harper was all smiles.

As for Linc, he was no closer to figuring out what was going on with her than he'd been when she walked out on him the night before.

* * *

"What's going on?" demanded Hailey. She'd been lying in wait in the upstairs hall at Daniel's when Harper put a cranky Maya down for a nap in one of the empty bedrooms. "We need to talk."

Harper took her sister by the shoulders and looked her squarely in the eye. "There's nothing."

Hailey scowled at her. "You know I hate it when you lie to me. You've been weird all day. Too smiley. *Fake* smiley."

Harper groaned and pulled her sister close. "Can't talk about it now," she whispered.

Hailey hugged her. "When?"

"I'll call you. I promise. Just please, let's *not*. Not today. I'm not ready to go there." *And maybe I never will be.*

"When?" Hailey demanded in her usual take-charge way. "Did Linc—"

"Linc did nothing wrong."

"But he *is* the problem, right?"

Laughing a little, Harper pulled back. "Later. We'll talk. I promise."

Hailey wasn't happy, but at least she let it go for now. They went back downstairs with their arms around each other and joined Linc and Roman, who were talking real estate in the family room.

It was after eight when they got back in the Range Rover to return to the cottage. Yesterday's snow was long gone. A drizzly rain was falling. Exhausted from a day full of presents, good food and fun, both kids snoozed in the back seat. Even Jayden was too tired to talk.

"It was a great day," Linc said quietly, his face illuminated by the dashboard lights.

"Yeah." Harper sent him what she hoped was a genuine-looking smile. Inside, her every nerve hummed, and her stomach had managed to tie itself in a tight chain of knots. Once the kids were in bed, she would have to clear the air with him. Too bad she'd yet to figure out what she would say to him, how to apologize for her strange behavior without saying too much.

One month, she reminded herself. That's how long they'd known each other. Too soon for the big talk about love and forever, that much was certain.

Maybe she could just grab him and kiss him and let nature do the job for her. They would go upstairs to his big bed and she would exhaust him with sex. By the time she'd finished with him, he wouldn't remember his name—let alone her flaky behavior the night before.

It would be fine. She would keep it light. They would have a sexy Christmas night together. And she wouldn't have to admit that she'd fallen hopelessly in love with him and didn't know what to do with the strength of her own emotions.

They rode down the hill and across town to the cottage without saying much. But it didn't seem *too* tense to her.

At least, not until they rounded that last turn in the twisting driveway up to the cottage to find a silver Jaguar parked in front of the house and three women perched on the front step—his mother, a beautiful brunette who had to be Imogen. And another woman the same age as Alicia, who looked a lot like the glamorous brunette.

Linc could not believe what his eyes were seeing.

His mother and Sarah wore cool, determined expressions.

As for Imogen, she was dressed all in white, including her high-heeled boots and the fur collar of her big coat. Her lips were bright red and stretched in a defiant smile.

He pulled the Rover to a stop and she rose to her feet.

"Just give me a minute," he whispered to Harper, trying not to wake the children sleeping in the back seat.

"What's going on, Linc?"

"I have no idea."

He shoved open the driver's door and got out, taking care to shut it quietly behind him. By then, Sarah and his mother had risen to their feet. As for Imogen, she was already on him.

"Darling. Merry Christmas. It's so good to see you." She threw her arms around him and shoved her face up for a kiss.

He managed to pull back before her red lips

touched his. Taking her by the arms, he held her away and exerted superhuman effort not to go off on her right then and there. "What are you doing here?"

She tipped her head to the side and faked a wounded look. Her eyes told the truth, though. They glittered with reckless fire. "Oh, Linc. You know why I'm here. You wouldn't talk to me. I couldn't stand it anymore. I had to see you, *be* with you, find a way to make everything right between us."

It was a nightmare—his mother and Sarah, self-righteous and ramrod straight, glaring at him from the porch. Harper in the Rover, witnessing this awfulness. Imogen gazing up at him, uttering desperate words as her eyes threatened dire consequences if he failed to give her what she wanted.

Had she always been like this?

He knew the answer. She had, and he'd gone along with it, telling himself that they understood each other, that she was charming when she wanted to be, that he was ready to get married and the two of them were a good fit.

Fit.

As though a wife were a shirt or a new suit. She only had to be well-made, of quality material...

He gazed into those furiously glittering eyes and wondered. At himself. At her. At his mother's ongoing, vindictive bitterness. Was there any way to get through to either of them?

"I just need to talk to you," she pleaded. "I want some time with you, alone."

"And so you came on Christmas night and brought both our mothers?"

"Yes." She tossed her tumbling, dark curls. "I couldn't wait a moment longer. And our moms are here to provide the moral support I so desperately need."

"This is completely unacceptable. It really does have to stop."

In the Range Rover, Harper couldn't take it anymore. Clearly, Linc and the gorgeous brunette who gazed up at him so desperately had more to work out.

And Harper had no place here. Time to go home.

Quietly, hoping the kids would sleep through whatever was about to happen next, she pushed open her door, stepped out and shut it behind her. "Linc, I'm going to go."

All eyes swung her way.

"This must be the nanny?" said Imogen, nodding, her ferocious smile growing wider, perfect white teeth flashing with malice. "Yes, you are so right. It's time for you to go."

"Shut up, Imogen." Linc tossed the words over his shoulder, and then gentled his voice. "It's okay, Harper. Just get back in the Rover."

"No, Linc. I'm not going to do that."

From behind him on the porch, Alicia called, "Let her go, Linc. She has no business here. This is a family matter."

He turned to his mother. "Don't," he said low. "Just don't."

Meanwhile, Imogen lifted her left hand and waved Harper goodbye. A giant engagement diamond sparkled on her ring finger.

Somehow, the woman still had Linc's ring.

And it hurt. It hurt bad, that he'd given this woman his ring, that she'd been his fiancée a short time ago. Seeing that ring was a blow straight to the heart.

Because Harper loved him. She loved him so much. How could this have happened to her in a few too-short weeks? She was in so far over her head, drowning, going down for the final time, staring up at the sky far above, knowing she was done for.

She turned her gaze on Linc. "While you're carrying on out here, please don't forget that there are two little children asleep in that car."

"Of course not. Harper, don't go…" He looked at her as though she was everything to him.

Yet his gift to her had been earrings. The woman behind him, backed up by her mother and his mother, too—that woman got the ring.

"You have people you need to deal with here." And right now, Harper knew she was only in the way. "Good night, Linc." She started walking.

Silence followed her. She walked faster, never once looking back.

Chapter Thirteen

Linc watched her go, longing only to follow, to convince her to stop, to wait—to turn around.

But why *should* she be here? This wasn't her fight. It was his damn mess and he needed to clean it the hell up.

First things first.

He turned to address all three angry women, modulating his voice to a low, controlled rumble. "There are two innocent children in the back seat of my car. As long as they're nearby, I don't want one thoughtless or mean word from any of you. Is that clear?"

All three of them muttered, "Of course," simultaneously.

"Terrific. I'm going to get them both out of their car seats now and herd them inside. Just make yourselves comfortable. Help yourselves to a stiff drink, why don't you? Keep your thoughts to yourselves until I've safely tucked Jayden and Maya in bed."

"All right," said Imogen.

"We will," said his mother.

The kids really were worn out.

When he took Maya from her car seat, she wrapped her little arms around his neck and went right back to sleep. Jayden took his hand and walked along beside him, murmuring softly, "Hi, Grandma," as he went up the steps.

"Merry Christmas, Jayden," Alicia said softly.

Not trusting her in the least, Linc sent her a warning frown. She stared right back at him, but kept her mouth shut.

He left the door open for her and the Whitmans. Holding firmly to Jayden's hand, cradling Maya close, he headed straight for the stairs.

Twenty minutes later, he came back down. The women sat in the living room. His mother had opened a bottle of white wine. They each had a glass.

He stood by the tree and addressed all three of them. "What do you want?" It was probably a mistake to ask that question, but he really did need the answer. The sooner he could find out what they wanted, the sooner he could deal with them and they could go away.

Alicia said, "You owe it to your fiancée to hear what she has to say."

"She is not my fiancée and I owe her nothing." He went right on before anyone could argue. "But all right. Imogen and I will speak privately, after which all three of you will leave."

The women just sat there for several seconds as he wondered what they'd thought could possibly be gained by ambushing him at the cottage on Christmas night.

Finally, Imogen replied in a wounded tone, "Oh, Linc, yes. To talk to you, to get it all out and make myself finally clear to you. That's all I've ever wanted…".

"Great, then. This should be brief. Let's go into my office."

It was not brief.

For the next two hours, behind the shut door of his office, Imogen alternately cried and ranted, pleaded and accused. He sat in a club chair across from her and tried to listen without judgment or anger.

He didn't succeed, but he did manage to be outwardly gentle and firm, patient and kind—and not to say anything he would end up regretting. There really was nothing more for him to say to her, and he was just waiting for her to realize that she had nothing to say that mattered to him.

She cried all the harder. He handed her some tissues and waited some more.

"I'll never get through to you, will I?" She sniffled and dabbed at her eyes.

He answered in a mild tone. "I don't love you, Imogen. We're through. There's nothing more we need to say."

At that, she burst into tears again, tore off the engagement ring she shouldn't even be wearing and threw it at him.

He caught it in midflight, got up and locked it in a drawer of his desk. Was that an insulting thing to do? Maybe. But he didn't want her grabbing it back and waving it around as though it proved that they were still together.

"You have no heart!" she cried. "I suppose this is it, then. I'll go and you'll be calling the nanny to warm up your bed."

It was a bad moment. He almost lost it. He wanted to shout that he loved Harper Bravo, that she'd brought joy and laughter, tenderness and hope into his life and the lives of his niece and nephew.

But that wouldn't be right. He needed to say the words to Harper first, before he spoke them to anyone else. And the last thing he should ever do was to shout them in anger at his ex. "You don't know what you're talking about and I'll thank you to leave Harper out of this."

There were more accusations. He did his best to tune them out.

Finally, Imogen jumped to her feet. "That's it. That's all. I quit. I am finished with you, Lincoln Stryker."

"All right, then. We understand each other at last. Time for you to go."

Ten minutes later, he stood on the front step and watched the Jaguar drive away. His mother had gone with them. He didn't know what to do about her, and he kind of wondered if he ever would.

Inside, he poured out the last of the wine and put the empty bottle in the recycle bin. He loaded the glasses into the dishwasher, longing the whole time to call Harper, to make sure she was all right. But it was after eleven and he had a bad feeling she wouldn't welcome his call.

Upstairs in his room, he settled on sending her a text.

They're finally gone and not coming back. I miss you. When you get this, would you just let me know that you're okay?

He hit Send and then stared at the screen for a while, willing her to reply. She didn't.

So he got ready for bed, climbed between the covers alone and turned off the light.

He was lying on his back, staring blindly into the darkness, longing for the feel of her, the scent of her, there, close to him—when his phone lit up on the nightstand.

Grabbing it, he read:

I'm all right. And I've got some things I really need to do at the theater, stuff to catch up on. I haven't had a day off in a while. Tell the kids I'll be back soon.

"Not a chance," he growled at the dark room and the bright screen. "I need you here…"

But the dark room wasn't listening, and the bright screen had dimmed.

He ground his teeth together, hating that he had no choice but to give her the time she wanted.

Plus, she was right, damn it. Tonight had been a horror show. The least he could do was not argue if she needed some space.

Of course. When will I see you, then?

I would like two days off.

Hell, no. He needed to see her, to touch her, to find a way to reassure her that everything would work out.

All right. Get some rest. See you soon.

And by the way, I love you.

Good night, Linc.

Good night.

Two days, he thought as he set the phone aside. *In two days, she'll be back, and I'll make it up to her.* In two days, he would tell her that he loved her, that what he wanted more than anything was the chance to spend the rest of his life with her...

Harper had lied. There was nothing she just *had* to do at the theater. In fact, on the day after Christmas, she didn't leave the cottage. She dragged around in her pajamas, devouring a whole bag of Cheetos and half a carton of Tillamook Mudslide.

Being in love was awful, she decided. It was painful and messy, and she wanted nothing to do with it.

But she missed Linc so much. She had this enormous emptiness inside her, and the only thing that would fill it was his touch on her skin, his voice in her ear, his lips pressed to hers.

Three times that day, she almost threw a coat over her pj's and marched to the other cottage to declare her undying love.

Somehow, she stopped herself.

That evening, Hailey texted her.

I have a bad feeling. Are you all right?

She wrote back that she was fine.
Hailey replied:

Why am I not reassured? We need to talk.

Can't right now. Busy.

Doing what, exactly?

Things. Lots of things...

When, then?

Soon.

You can't put me off forever, Harp.

I love you, Lee-Lee. TTYS.

Early the next morning, on her second day off from dealing with Linc, Harper received a text from Mia Acevedo.

Got a minute? Can we talk?

Harper hit the phone icon. "Happy almost New Year. What's up?"

"Sam and I have been talking. Business is really taking off. We need another designer and we need it to be you."

Harper's pulse went haywire. She made herself draw a slow, deep breath. "Is this a job offer?"

"Yes, it is. Can you move to Portland? We would love it if you could start, say, January 15?"

Her heart ached as it soared. She had no idea how

things were going to work out with Linc. If they were over, she would rather be miles from him in Seattle—or better yet, Tanzania, or maybe Timbuktu.

But she wanted to work with Mia. The offer was a dream come true. And even if she and Linc weren't destined to be a couple, there was room enough in Rose City for both of them.

Mia quoted a salary that Harper could actually live on—frugally, in a studio apartment. Which sounded pretty much perfect to her.

Harper said yes and promised to drive down the week after New Year's. She would find herself a place to live, meet with Mia to fill out forms and discuss all the aspects of her new job with Acevedo Hybrid Homes.

When she hung up, she did a happy dance around the kitchen—after which she dropped into a chair at the table and burst into tears. She had the perfect starting job in her new career.

And she had no idea what was going to happen with Linc. She missed Maya and Jayden, yet here she sat in her pajamas for the second day, alone in the cottage that had seemed way too big and empty ever since Hailey had moved out.

She heard a car drive up outside and knew who it was without having to look. Sometimes it was like that between her and Hailey. One of them would think of the other.

And the other would appear.

Her sister came in through the short hall from the front door. "What's going on here?" Hailey shrugged out of her coat, draped it on a chair and went straight to Harper. "Why are you crying?" She grabbed Harper's hand and hauled her up into her arms.

Harper hugged her tight. "Now you've done it, got me sobbing again…"

"Again?"

"Shut up and hug me."

Hailey did hug her. She held Harper close and made soothing noises until the crying stopped. "Better?"

"Mmm-hmm, a little."

"All right, then." Hailey guided Harper back into her chair, handed her a box of tissues, poured them each a cup of coffee and demanded, "Tell me exactly what happened."

Harper let it all out—from her new job that would mean she would be living in Portland, to the awfulness of what had occurred Christmas night and even her self-defense strategy of avoiding Linc since then.

Hailey congratulated her on the new job—and then peered at her more closely. "You just said Linc texted you after the evil ex and the two mothers from hell finally left, that he asked you to come back. I don't get why you're crying. It's so obvious the man's in love with you."

Harper just sniffled, waved a dismissing hand and shook her head.

But Hailey was Hailey. She ran the show. And that meant she kept the pressure on until Harper told the rest of it—about the "ring" that had turned out to be earrings. "And then, well, his ex showed up wearing the giant diamond he'd bought her."

"But they *are* broken up, right?"

"Yes. They are."

"It's not his fault that his ex kept the ring and had the bad taste and terrible judgment to keep wearing it."

"I know that. Of course, I do. But, Lee-Lee, he gave *her* a ring. It just hurt, that's all. That *I* got the earrings and *she* got engaged to him."

Hailey scooted up close and enfolded Harper in another much-needed hug. "Honey, men mess up. The good ones finally get it right. Linc Stryker is one of the good ones. You need *not* to let that man get away."

She leaned her head on Hailey's shoulder. "Easy for you to say."

"Hey. Uh-uh." Hailey put a finger under Harper's chin. "Let me see those eyes."

"Fine." Harper glared at her.

"Don't you see what's going on here?"

"Um, nope. Not really…"

"Harp, this is *your* love story. You've got to own it. You've spent all your life behind the scenes, making the magic happen for the ones who take center stage. Now it's *your* turn. This is when you need to be the center of attention. You can't hide your light."

"Ugh. You and your theater metaphors. I can't even."

Tenderly, Hailey guided a straggling curl behind Harper's ear. "Sweetheart. Do you love him?"

She hard-swallowed and told the scary truth. "Yes. I do."

"Then you need to step up and tell him so."

Linc sat on the living room floor carefully combing the shiny brunette locks of Maya's new Carla Marie doll. "How's that?"

"O-*kay*!" Maya took the doll and began removing her dress. She was in love with Carla Marie's new clothes, the ones Harper had made and given Maya for Christmas. Maya was constantly changing the doll's outfits—meaning Linc had to do the buttoning and snapping that Maya's chubby fingers couldn't quite handle yet.

Harper…

Just thinking her name made him long to go find her. He hadn't seen her since Christmas night and she wasn't due back until tomorrow afternoon.

The waiting was killing him. He wondered constantly how she was doing, had to keep resisting the urge to call her—or better yet, march over to her cottage and beg her to talk to him, tell him everything that was bothering her, find a way to convince her that all he wanted was her. He kept going over what he needed to say to her, kept rehearsing how he might manage to tell her he loved her, *would* love her, forever, without scaring her away.

The doorbell rang. Maya's curly head shot up from trying to pull purple leggings onto Carla Marie's chunky bare legs. "Hawp?" She dropped the doll. Levering forward, hands flat on the floor, she stuck her butt in the air. From that position, she popped up-right. "Hawp!" And off she went, headed for the door.

Jayden came pounding down the stairs. "Who's at the door?"

Linc ordered his racing heart to settle down as he stood. "Let's go find out."

It wasn't Harper, but the kids were glad, anyway, because it was Hailey. They loved Hailey almost as much as they loved her sister.

"Lee-Lee!" crowed Maya and lifted her arms. "Up."

"Hailey," said Jayden. "Come in. I need to show you my train station."

"Hey, guys." Hailey swung Maya up in her arms.

Linc stepped back so Harper's sister could enter. "Good to see you."

Jayden tugged on the hem of her jacket. "Come on, Hailey. My train set is upstairs, and I got a second depot for Christmas."

She grinned down at him. "Hold on a minute, big guy." And she looked up at Linc. "I was just at the other cottage…"

His pulse rocketed into the stratosphere. "Is she all right?"

"As a matter of fact, it occurred to me that you could use a sitter for an hour or two. You can go check on her, maybe tell her all the things you probably should have said before she came face-to-face with your ex, who for some unknown reason was still wearing your ring…" He winced at the memory as Hailey continued, "And while we're on the subject of diamonds, I would also advise that you never give a woman you're serious about a small velvet jewelry box—that is, unless it contains an engagement ring."

It all came way too clear—Imogen wearing his ring, the earrings he'd tried to give Harper. "She thought I was proposing, that the earring box had a ring in it—and then she saw the ring I gave Imogen…"

Hailey regarded him patiently—and the kids stared, too. "How do you think that made my sister feel?"

"Okay, yeah. It all makes an awful kind of sense now…"

"I'm so pleased you get that."

"I need to talk to her."

"Yes, you do."

Linc grabbed his jacket off the hook by the door. "I'll, um, be back soon…"

"Take your time," Hailey advised. "We're fine, aren't we, guys?"

"Yes!" declared Jayden. "We got stuff to do."

"We fine!" Maya agreed.

Linc stared at Hailey, hardly daring to believe that Harper might just be waiting at home for him to come and get her.

"Why are you still here?" Hailey waved him off with an impatient flick of her free hand. *"Go."*

After Hailey left the cottage, Harper poured herself a third cup of coffee. She sat at the table, still in her red plaid flannel pajamas, thinking about washing her hair, putting her clothes on, working up the courage to go to Linc and tell him that she loved him.

Hailey said she needed to be the star of her own story. But she didn't *feel* like a star. She felt like an unprepared understudy with dirty hair.

And was that a theater metaphor?

Hailey would be so proud.

The doorbell chimed.

What now?

Reluctantly, she got up and went to the door, pulling it wide with no clue who would be waiting on the other side.

"Hey, beautiful," he said.

She blinked in disbelief that he was actually standing on her doorstep. "My hair's dirty and I'm still in my pajamas."

A smile quirked the corners of his wonderful mouth. "Like I said, you are absolutely beautiful. Can I come in?"

"Uh, yeah. Sure." She stepped back for him to enter and then closed the door behind him. "The kids?"

"Hailey's with them at the other cottage."

She groaned and felt the hot flush as it swept up her throat. "I should have known. How much did she tell you?"

He reached out, ran a slow, tender finger over the curve of her cheek. Her nerve endings sparked in sheer pleasure at the lingering touch. He said, "She just explained a few things I really needed to understand."

"Oh, God. She told you about Imogen's ring and the earrings, right?" She kind of wished the hardwood floor would just open up and swallow her whole.

But then he said, "I love you, Harper. You're my light in the darkness, my heart and my soul. I have no excuse for Imogen. I was a man without a clue. But I'm not that guy anymore. And I do want to marry you. Whenever you're ready—the sooner the better. I should have just made my move, but I really thought it was the right thing, not to push you too fast..."

She had no words. Center stage, in the spotlight. And she'd forgotten her lines. "Linc. Oh, Linc..." She reached for him.

"Harper. Damn it. At last." He grabbed her close and wrapped her up in those big, strong arms.

And then his mouth came down on hers. Heat and hope and love and longing pulsing through her, she jumped up and he caught her as she wrapped her legs around him, twined her whole body around him, like a vine.

"That way." She broke the kiss just long enough to point down the hall. He carried her where she pointed. When they reached her room, she grabbed the door frame before he could stride past it. "I love you, too. In here..."

He took her in there and laid her on her unmade bed. She pulled him down with her and started pushing on his jacket. "Get rid of this. Get rid of everything..."

They proceeded to tear frantically at each other's

clothes. It was awkward and ridiculous and absolutely smoking hot.

Finally, when both of them were stark naked, they rolled together on the bed, kissing endlessly, hands all over each other, unable to get close enough, unwilling to let go.

"Crap," he muttered. "No condoms…"

"No problem. Remember? I do get the shot—and I trust you, Linc. Completely." She hitched her legs around his lean waist, reached down between them and guided him home.

"I love you."

"I love you."

And then no more words were necessary. They were just Linc and Harper, joined in every way at last, making promises with their bodies, the most important promises, the kind two people in love are forever bound to keep.

Epilogue

Harper never leased that studio apartment. In the first week of January, she moved to the Forest Park house with Linc and the kids.

The new nanny, Elaine, started the first day Harper went to work for Mia and Sam. Elaine was kind and affectionate. Jayden and Maya adored her—but they came running when Harper got home.

It was during the third week in January that Linc took Harper shopping for the perfect ring. She chose a round, pale blue sapphire flanked by diamonds on a platinum band.

She and Linc got married in Valentine Bay on the last Saturday in March, a small celebration, mostly family. Maya was the flower girl and Jayden the ring bearer. Harper had Hailey for her maid of honor and Daniel to give her away. Linc's mother, now back in Italy, said she couldn't make it.

But Warren and Shelby came from Vail, with their beautiful new baby, Shaniece. And though Alan and Jean Hollister were still on their world cruise, they attended the ceremony via Skype.

When Harper threw the bouquet, she made sure that Hailey caught it. After all, Hailey and Roman were getting married at the end of May—and except for the long-lost Finn, Hailey would be the last of the Bravo siblings to say, "I do."

Up at Daniel's house after the wedding, Harper made a point to raise a glass of champagne to the parents they all missed to this day. "To Mom and Dad. We love you so much!"

Her words were picked up and echoed through the room.

Next, Harper saluted the brother they'd yet to find. "To Finn. Wherever you are, we *will* find you someday."

"To Finn," everyone answered in unison, each face solemn, the women with teary eyes, as they drank to the ongoing search for the brother they'd lost so long ago.

On the first Friday in May, Harper sat at her drafting table at Acevedo Hybrid Homes when her cell vibrated with a call from Hailey.

Harper picked up. "Hey. What's going on?"

"You will not believe this." Hailey spoke low—as if in awe or maybe shock.

"What? Tell me. You're freaking me out."

"It's official. We *didn't* find Finn."

"What are you talking about?"

"Finn has found *us*."

"Hailey, slow down. Finn *found* us?"

"That's right. A couple of hours ago, Finn—who lives in New York now and goes by Ian McNeill—walked into Valentine Logging and asked to speak with Daniel."

Harper's stomach hollowed out. If she hadn't already been sitting down, she just might have fallen flat on her ass. "You're messing with me."

"Never would I mess about Finn. He's coming up to Daniel's for dinner tonight. Can you get here?"

"Are you kidding me? I wouldn't miss it for the world. I'm calling Linc to see if he can come, too. But one way or another, you can count on me to be there."

When she hung up with Hailey, Harper just sat there for a minute, holding the phone, hardly daring to believe that their vanished brother had come home at last.

It felt so huge and impossible, the final closing of an open circle, her family reunited after so many years. She called Linc.

"How's my beautiful wife?"

"Stunned. Flabbergasted. Thunderstruck. And every other word that means shocked beyond belief. My brother Finn has come home. I need to go to Valentine Bay—now."

Her husband didn't hesitate. "I'll call Oxana to pack us a bag and tell Elaine to get the kids ready."

"Should I go get them?"

"No. You can leave your car there. I'll pick up the kids and swing by for you within the hour."

"Wait—what about Oscar?" Oscar was the rescue dog Jayden had chosen at the animal shelter two weeks before. They'd planned to adopt a puppy, but one look at the wiry-haired five-year-old mutt with the patch on one eye, and Jayden had changed his mind.

"How about we just bring him?" said Linc.

She laughed. "Sure. Bring Oscar. Why not? It's a family affair."

"Would you call the property manager to open up the cottage for us?"

"Will do."

"Sit tight, my love," he said softly. "We're on our way."

* * * * *

MILLS & BOON

Coming next month

TEMPTED BY THE TYCOON'S PROPOSAL
Rachael Stewart

'Come with us, Sophia—come with us to Iceland.'

Her eyes shot open and she gazed down at him, hardly daring to believe the question and knowing at the same time that she couldn't. The thought, the idea of being surrounded by her fear, by the past, by the snow... She shook her head and shifted beneath him to remind him of her body, of what she wanted in that moment. What he so wanted too.

'You can't ask me that, Jack. Don't ask me that.'

He raised himself up over her, his elbows planted either side of her body to bear his weight. 'Why not?'

'Because I can't. We can't.'

He kissed her until she was breathless, panting. 'Why?'

'We don't even know they'll be available for Lily's birthday yet.'

'That doesn't matter. They will be available at some point and I want you to come.'

She shook her head, the emotions clawing at her throat and her chest, making it hard to breathe. 'We both know this has to end and that the longer we spend together with Lily, the more likely it is that she will become attached too.'

His eyes were so serious now as they blazed into

hers. The 'too' spoke volumes; it told him that fear protected her own heart, but did it protect his as well?

'That's not the whole truth, is it?' he pressed, probing for more, probing for her to admit that she feared being faced with her past. All it took was one harmless-looking snowflake, the ice forming over her windshield, and the shivers would start.

'It's enough.'

He shook his head, one hand stroking her cheek and catching a tear she hadn't known was there. 'You need to stop living in fear of your past, Sophia.'

He kissed her to soften his words and she clamped her eyes shut over the rising swell of emotion within. 'You've taught me that; you've made me realise that avoiding a base, avoiding London, is running from it. And by doing it, Lily has suffered.'

She kept her eyes closed as the tears refused to stop. He was right. She'd been a hypocrite to tell him the same and not realise it was exactly how she'd been behaving all along.

'Come with us. Not because I ask you, not because it would make Lily happy to have you there... Come because you want to. Come because you are ready to move on from it.'

Continue reading
TEMPTED BY THE TYCOON'S PROPOSAL
Rachael Stewart

Available next month
www.millsandboon.co.uk

COMING SOON!

We really hope you enjoyed reading this book.
If you're looking for more romance, be sure to
head to the shops when new books are
available on

Thursday 10th December

LET'S TALK
Romance

For exclusive extracts, competitions
and special offers, find us online:

- facebook.com/millsandboon
- @MillsandBoon
- @MillsandBoonUK

Get in touch on 01413 063232

For all the latest titles coming soon, visit
millsandboon.co.uk/nextmonth

MILLS & BOON

THE HEART OF ROMANCE

A ROMANCE FOR EVERY KIND OF READER

ODERN

Prepare to be swept off your feet by sophisticated, sexy and seductive heroes, in some of the world's most glamourous and romantic locations, where power and passion collide.
8 stories per month.

STORICAL

Escape with historical heroes from time gone by. Whether your passion is for wicked Regency Rakes, muscled Vikings or rugged Highlanders, awaken the romance of the past.
6 stories per month.

EDICAL

Set your pulse racing with dedicated, delectable doctors in the high-pressure world of medicine, where emotions run high and passion, comfort and love are the best medicine.
6 stories per month.

rue Love

Celebrate true love with tender stories of heartfelt romance, from the rush of falling in love to the joy a new baby can bring, and a focus on the emotional heart of a relationship.
8 stories per month.

Desire

Indulge in secrets and scandal, intense drama and plenty of sizzling hot action with powerful and passionate heroes who have it all: wealth, status, good looks…everything but the right woman.
6 stories per month.

EROES

Experience all the excitement of a gripping thriller, with an intense romance at its heart. Resourceful, true-to-life women and strong, fearless men face danger and desire - a killer combination!
8 stories per month.

DARE

Sensual love stories featuring smart, sassy heroines you'd want as a best friend, and compelling intense heroes who are worthy of them.
4 stories per month.

To see which titles are coming soon, please visit

millsandboon.co.uk/nextmonth

JOIN US ON SOCIAL MEDIA!

Stay up to date with our latest releases, author news and gossip, special offers and discounts, and all the behind-the-scenes action from Mills & Boon...

 millsandboon

 millsandboonuk

 millsandboon

It might just be true love...

  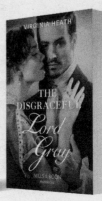

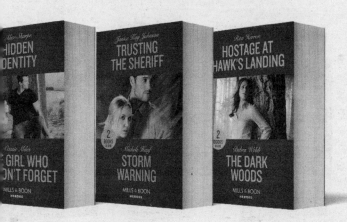

MILLS & BOON
MEDICAL
Pulse-Racing Passion

Set your pulse racing with dedicated, delectable doctors in the high-pressure world of medicine, where emotions run high and passion, comfort and love are the best medicine.